Desirable

Daughters

ALSO BY BHARATI MUKHERJEE

Darkness

The Tiger's Daughter

The Holder of the World

Leave It to Me

Jasmine

Wife

The Middleman and Other Stories

Days and Nights in Calcutta (with Clark Blaise)

The Sorrow and the Terror (with Clark Blaise)

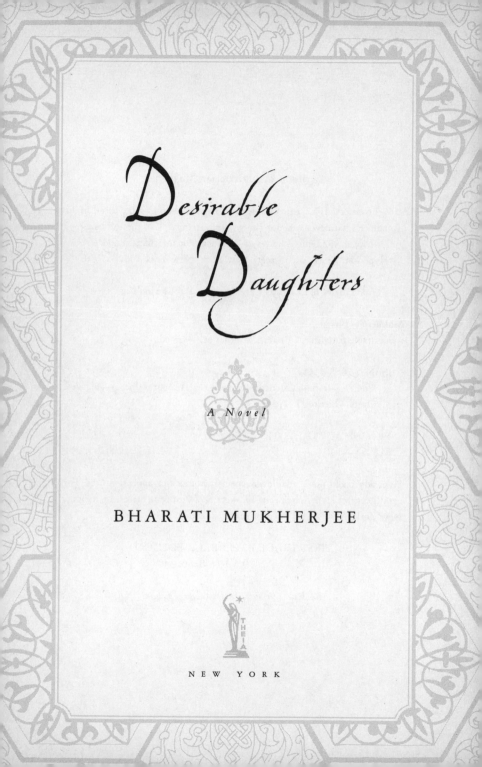

Desirable Daughters

A Novel

BHARATI MUKHERJEE

NEW YORK

Library of Congress Cataloging-in-Publication Data

Mukherjee, Bharati.
    Desirable daughters / Bharati Mukherjee.—1st ed.
        p. cm.
    ISBN 0-7868-8515-7
    1. Women—India—Calcutta—Fiction.   2. Calcutta (India)—Fiction.
    3. Sisters—Fiction. I. Title.

    PR9499.3.M77 D47 2002
    813'.54—dc21   2001053061

Hyperion books are available for special promotions and premiums. For
details contact Hyperion Special Markets, 77 West 66th Street, 11th Floor,
New York, New York 10023 or call 212-456-0133.

FIRST TRADE PAPERBACK EDITION
3   5   7   9   10   8   6   4

Book design by Caroline Cunningham

To Clark-*babu*

No one behind, no one ahead.

The path the ancients cleared has closed.

And the other path, everyone's path,

Easy and wide, goes nowhere.

I am alone and find my way.

—Sanskrit verse adapted by Octavio Paz and
translated by Eliot Weinberger

Part One

1

In the mind's eye, a one-way procession of flickering oil lamps sways along the muddy shanko between rice paddies and flooded ponds, and finally disappears into a distant wall of impenetrable jungle. Banks of fog rise from warmer waters, mingle with smoke from the cooking fires, and press in a dense sooty collar, a permeable gray wall that parts, then seals, igniting a winter chorus of retching coughs and loud spitting. Tuberculosis is everywhere. The air, the water, the soil are septic. Thirty-five years is a long life. Smog obscures the moon and dims the man-made light to faintness deeper than the stars'. In such darkness perspective disappears. It is a two-dimensional world impossible to penetrate. But for the intimacy of shared discomfort, it is difficult even to estimate the space separating each traveler.

The narrow, raised trail stretches ten miles from Mishtigunj town to the jungle's edge. In a palanquin borne by four servants sit a rich man's three daughters, the youngest dressed in her bridal sari, her little hands painted with red lac dye, her hair oiled and set. Her arms are heavy with dowry gold; bangles ring tiny arms from wrist to shoulder. Childish voices chant a song, hands clap, gold bracelets tinkle. I cannot imagine the loneliness of this child. A Bengali girl's happiest night is about to become her lifetime imprisonment. It seems all the sorrow of history, all that is unjust in society and cruel in religion has settled on her. Even constructing it from the merest scraps of family memory fills me with rage and bitterness.

The bride-to-be whispers the "Tush Tusli Brata," a hymn to the sacredness of marriage, a petition for a kind and generous husband:

What do I hope for in worshipping you?
That my father's wisdom be endless,
My mother's kindness bottomless.
May my husband be as powerful as a king of gods.
May my future son-in-law light up the royal court.
Bestow on me a brother who is learned and intellectual,
A son as handsome as the best-looking courtier,
And a daughter who is beauteous.
Let my hair-part glow red with vermilion powder, as a wife's should.
On my wrists and arms, let bangles glitter and jangle.
Load down my clothes-rack with the finest saris,
Fill my kitchen with scoured-shiny utensils,
Reward my wifely virtue with a rice-filled granary.
These are the boons that this young virgin begs of thee.

In a second, larger palki borne by four men sit the family priest and the father of the bride. Younger uncles and cousins follow in a vigilant file. Two more guards, sharp-bladed daos drawn, bring up the rear. Two servants walk ahead of the eight litter-bearers, holding naphtha lamps. No one has seen such brilliant European light, too strong to stare into, purer white than the moon. It is a town light, a rich man's light, a light that knows English invention. If bandits are crouching in the gullies they will know to strike this reckless Hindu who announces his wealth with light and by arming his servants. What treasures lie inside, how much gold and jewels, what target ripe for kidnapping? The nearest town, where such a wealthy man must have come from, lies behind him. Only the jungle lies ahead. Even the woodcutters desert it at night, relinquishing it to goondahs and marauders, snakes and tigers.

The bride is named Tara Lata, a name we almost share. The name of the father is Jai Krishna Gangooly. Tara Lata is five years old and headed deep into the forest to marry a tree.

I have had the time, the motivation, and even the passion to undertake this history. When my friends, my child, or my sisters ask me why, I say I am exploring the making of a consciousness. Your consciousness? they tease, and I tell them, No. Yours.

.   .   .

On this night, flesh-and-blood emerges from the unretrievable past. I have Jai Krishna's photo, I know the name of Jai Krishna's father, but they have always been ghosts. But Tara Lata is not, nor will her father be, after the events of this special day. And so my history begins with a family wedding on the coldest, darkest night in the Bengali month of Paush—December/January—in a district of the Bengal Presidency that lies east of Calcutta—now Kolkata—and south of Dacca—now Dhaka—as the English year of 1879 is about to shed its final two digits, although the Hindu year of 1285 still has four months to run and the Muslim year of 1297 has barely begun.

In those years, Bengal was the seat of British power, Calcutta its capital, its cultural and economic center. The city is endowed with the instruments of Western knowledge, the museums, the colleges, the newspapers, and the Asiatic Society. The old Bengal Presidency included all of today's Bangladesh, the current Indian state of West Bengal, and parts of Assam, Bihar, and Orissa. A reconstituted Bengal Presidency today would have over 330 million people and be the world's third most populous country. China, India, Bengal. There are more of me than there are of you, although I am both.

The eastern regions of Bengal, even before the flight of Hindus during the subcontinent's partition in 1947, and its reincarnation as Bangladesh in 1972, always contained a Muslim majority, though largely controlled by a sizeable and wealthy Hindu minority. The communities speak the same language—Muslims, if the truth be known, more tenaciously than Hindus. But for the outer signs of the faith—the beards and skullcaps of the Muslims, the different dietary restrictions, the caste observances, the vermilion powder on the hair-parting of married Hindu women—there is little, fundamentally, to distinguish them. The communities suffer, as Freud put it, the narcissism of small difference.

The Hindu Bengalis were the first Indians to master the English language and to learn their master's ways, the first to flatter him by emulation, and the first to earn his distrust by unbidden demonstrations of wit and industry. Because they were a minority in their desh, their homeland, dependent on mastering or manipulating British power and Muslim psychology, the Hindus of east Bengal felt themselves superior even to the Hindus of the capital city of Calcutta. Gentlemen like Jai Krishna Gangopadhaya, a pleader in the Dacca High Court, whose surname the colonial authorities lightened to Gangooly, and who, on this particular winter night squats with a priest in a palki that reminds him of wagons for transporting remanded prisoners, was situated to take full advantage of fast-changing and improving times. He spoke mellifluous English and one high court judge had even recommended him for a scholarship to Oxford. Had he played by the rules, he should have been a great success, a prince, and a power.

Jai Krishna's graduation portrait from the second class of India's first law school (Calcutta University, 1859) displays the expected Victorian gravitas and none of the eager confidence of his classmates. He is *a young man of twenty who looks forty; his thick, dark eyebrows form an unbroken bar, and his shadow of a mustache—an inversion of prevailing style that favored elaborately curled and wax-tipped mustaches—reveal a young man more eloquent with a disapproving frown than with his words.*

For ten years I kept the graduation photo of Bishwapriya Chatterjee, my husband—Indian Institute of Technology, Kharagpur—on our nightstand. Last icon before falling asleep, first worshipful image of the morning. The countries, the apartments, the houses all changed, but the portrait remained. He had that eagerness, and a confident smile that promised substantial earnings. It lured my father into marriage negotiations, and it earned my not unenthusiastic acceptance of him as husband. A very predictable, very successful marriage negotiation.

Had Jai Krishna been a native Calcuttan, or had he come from Dacca, Bengal's second city, he might never have suffered the anxiety of the small-town provincial elevated into urbanity. In my mother-language we call the powerful middle class "bhadra lok," the gentlefolk, the "civilized" folk, for whom the English fashioned the pejorative term "babu," with its hint of fawning insincerity and slavishly acquired Western attitudes. The rest of the population are "chhoto lok," literally, the little people. Jai Krishna Gangooly lacked the reflexive self-confidence of the bhadra lok. In his heart, he was a provincial from Mishtigunj, third son of a village doctor whose practice included the indigent and Muslims. He felt he'd been lifted from his provincial origins because of his father's contacts in the Calcutta Medical College. He was not comfortable in the lawyer's black robes and powdered wig.

And so, the story of the three great-granddaughters of Jai Krishna Gangooly starts on the day of a wedding, a few hours before the palki ride where fates have already been decided, in the decorated ancestral house of the Gangoolys on the river in Mishtigunj town. The decorations signify a biye-bari, a wedding house. Beggars have already camped in the alleys adjacent to the canopy under which giant copper vats of milk, stirred by professional cooks, have been boiling and thickening for sweetmeats, and where other vats, woks, and cauldrons receive the chunks of giant hilsa fish netted fresh from the river and hold the rice pilao, lamb curry, spiced lentils, and deep-fried and sauce-steeped vegetables, a feast for a thousand invited guests and the small city of self-invited men, women, and children camped outside the gates.

The astrologers have spoken; the horoscopes have been compared. The match between Jai Krishna's youngest daughter and a thirteen-year-old youth, another Kulin Brahmin from an upright and pious family from a nearby village, has been blessed. The prewedding religious rites have been meticulously performed, and the prewedding stree-achar, married women's rituals, boisterously observed. To protect the husband-to-be from poisonous snakebite, married women relatives and Brahmin women neighbors have propitiated Goddess Manasha with prescribed offerings. All of this has been undertaken at a moment in the evolution of Jai Krishna from student of Darwin and Bentham and Comte and practitioner of icy logic, to reader of the Upanishads and believer in Vedic wisdom. He had become a seeker of truth, not a synthesizer of cultures. He found himself starting arguments with pleaders and barristers, those who actually favored morning toast with marmalade, English suits, and leather shoes. Now nearing forty, he was in full flight from his younger self, joining a debate that was to split bhadra lok society between progressives and traditionalists for over a century.

A Dacca barrister, Keshub Mitter, teased him for behaving more like a once-rich Muslim nawab wedded to a fanciful past and visions of lost glory than an educated, middle-class Hindu lawyer. Everyone knew that the Indian past was a rubbish heap of shameful superstition. Keshub Mitter's insult would have been unforgivable if it hadn't been delivered deftly, with a smile and a Bengali lawyer's wit and charm. My dear Gangooly, English is but a stepping-stone to the deeper refinement of German and French. Where does our Bangla language lead you? A big frog in a small, stagnant pond. Let us leave the sweet euphony of Bangla to our poets, and the salvation-enhancement of Sanskrit to our priests. Packet boats delivered Berlin and Paris papers to the Dacca High Court, along with the venerated Times.

The cases Jai Krishna pleaded in court often cast him as the apostle of enlightenment and upholder of law against outmoded custom, or the adjudicator of outrages undefined and unimaginable under British law. The majesty of law was in conflict with Jai Krishna's search for an uncorrupted, un-British, un-Muslim, fully Hindu consciousness. He removed his wife and children from cosmopolitan Dacca and installed them in Mishtigunj. He sought a purer life for himself, English pleader by day, Sanskrit scholar by night. He regretted the lack of a rigorous Brahminical upbringing, the years spent in Calcutta learning the superior ways of arrogant Englishmen and English laws, ingesting English contempt for his background and ridicule for babus like him. He had grown up in a secularized home with frequent Muslim visitors and the occasional wayward Englishman. In consideration of non-Hindu guests, his father had made certain that his mother's brass deities and stone lingams stayed confined in the closed-off worship-room.

.   .   .

On the morning of Tara Lata's wedding, female relatives waited along the riverbank for the arrival of the groom and his all-male wedding party. The groom was Satindranath Lahiri, fifth son of Surendranath Lahiri, of the landowning Lahiri family; in his own right, a healthy youth, whose astrological signs pointed to continued wealth and many sons. Back in Dacca, Jai Krishna had defended the ancient Hindu practices, the caste consciousness, the star charts, the observance of auspicious days, the giving of a dowry, the intact integrity of his community's rituals. His colleague, Keshub Mitter, to be known two decades later as Sir Keshub, and his physician, Dr. Ashim Lal Roy, both prominent members of the most progressive, most Westernized segment of Bengali

*society, the Brahmo Samaj, had attempted to dissuade him. The two
men had cited example after example of astrologically arranged marriages, full of astral promise, turning disastrous. The only worthwhile
dowry, they'd proclaimed, is an educated bride. Child-marriage is barbarous. How could horoscopes influence lives, especially obscure lives, in
dusty villages like Mishtigunj? Jai Krishna knew these men to be eaters
of beef and drinkers of gin.*

*"I consider myself a student of modern science," Jai Krishna had ex-
plained, "and because I am a student of modern science, I cannot reject
any theory until I test it." And so far, the tests had all turned out
positive. His two older daughters, seven and nine, were successfully married and would soon be moving to their husbands' houses and living as
wives, then as mothers. They were placid and obedient daughters who
would make loving and obedient wives. Tara Lata, his favorite, would
be no exception.*

*In the wintry bright hour just before twilight blackens Mishtigunj, the
decorated bajra from the Lahiri family finally sailed into view. The bride's
female relatives stood at the stone bathing-steps leading from the steep bank
down to the river as servants prepared to help the groom's party of two hundred disembark. Women began the oo-loo ululation, the almost instrumen-
tal, pitched-voice welcome. Two of Jai Krishna's younger brothers
supervised the unrolling of mats on the swampy path that connected the
private dock and Jai Krishna's two-storied brick house.*

*The bajra anchored, but none on board rushed to the deck railings to
be ceremoniously greeted by the welcoming party of the bride's relatives.
The bridegroom's father and uncles had a servant deliver a cruel message
in an insulting tone to the bride's father. They would not disembark on
Jai Krishna's property for Jai Krishna and his entire clan were carriers
of a curse, and that curse, thanks to Jai Krishna's home-destroying,
misfortune-showering daughter, had been visited on their sinless son
instead of on Jai Krishna's flesh-and-blood. They demanded that Jai
Krishna meet them in the sheltered cabin of the bajra.*

Jai Krishna ordered the wedding musicians to stop their shenai play-

ing and dhol beating. His women relatives, shocked at the tone in which the servant repeated his master's message to Jai Krishna babu, the renowned Dacca lawyer, had given up their conch shell blowing and their ululating on their own. For several minutes, Jai Krishna stood still on the bathing-steps, trying to conceal at first his bewilderment, then his fury, that the man who was to have full patriarchal authority over his beloved daughter had called her names. Then he heard a bullying voice from inside the cabin yell instructions to the boatmen to pull up anchor.

"They're bargaining for more dowry," muttered one of Jai Krishna's brothers.

"No beggar is as greedy as that Lahiri bastard!" spat another brother.

Two boatmen played at reeling in ropes and readying the bajra to sail back.

"Wait!" Jai Krishna shouted. "Whatever the problem, I'm sure we can work it out!" He raced down the gangplank and boarded the bajra.

Members of the bridegroom's party, strangers to Jai Krishna, ringed him on deck. Their faces were twisted in hate or grief.

"Tell me, I beg of you," Jai Krishna pleaded, "please tell me what pain we have inadvertently inflicted." He stood, hands pressed together in a gesture of humility, among the hostile men entitled to his hospitality. "What discourtesy have we committed? How may I right whatever is currently wrong?"

Surendranath Lahiri stepped out of the cabin, as if on cue. Hammocked in his outstretched arms lay the limp body of a lifeless boy.

"What . . ." Startled, Jai Krishna took a step back. The bridegroom's relatives closed in on him, cutting him off from his own people, who remained, mute, aghast, on the riverbank.

"Your happiness-wrecking daughter is responsible." Surendranath affected the dazed calm of a man beyond grief and outrage. "May she die as horrible a death."

"Better a barren womb than a womb that produces such a luckless female!" someone shouted behind Jai Krishna. Others added their hostile

*counsel. "Hang a rope around her neck!" "May she have the good sense
to drown herself!"*

*"How did . . ." Jai Krishna couldn't finish his question. He could
guess the answer from the pain-stiffened expression on the corpse's young
face.*

"Snakebite," a man in the groom's party screamed at him.

*"When we were transferring from carriage to bajra," another,
kinder, man explained.*

*"You had no light? No lamps and torches?" Jai Krishna demanded,
the implications of that fatal snakebite for his daughter suddenly fore-
most in his mind. He imagined little Tara Lata, wrapped in a bridal
sari of scarlet silk embroidered with heavy gold thread, weighted down
with gold jewelry, sitting on display on a divan laden with dowry gifts
in a room in the women's quarters. She'd be nervous, dreading the immi-
nent inspection of the groom's party. The groom's folks were bound by
custom to be even more critical of her appearance and her dowry than
were the neighborhood women. They'd make loud remarks about her being too skinny, too dark, too fidgety. They'd complain about the dowry
furniture, speculating viciously that it was not built of best-quality
Burma teak. They'd scoff at the weight, quality, and size of the silver
dowry utensils that filled a deep, wooden chest. The poor child had no
idea that already she had been transformed from envied bride about to
be married to a suitable husband into the second-worst thing in her society. She was now not quite a widow, which for a Bengali Hindu
woman, would be the most cursed state, but a woman who brings her
family misfortune and death. She was a person to be avoided. In a community intolerant of unmarried women, his Tara Lata had become an
unmarriageable woman.*

*Around him elegantly dressed men were screaming. "There must have
been augurs and signs!" "You didn't disclose what you must have
known, Jai Krishna babu!" "You fancy city men, you have no respect
for Hindu traditions. Some rite must have been omitted!"*

He heard a reference to Manasha, the goddess who causes or prevents snakebites. "The goddess must not have been sufficiently appeased," someone accused. "You Westernized types think you are stronger than our Hindu deities!" Admonition swelled into vengeful judgment.

Jai Krishna assured them all rites had been faithfully observed.

"Why should we believe you when it is well known that all lawyers prevaricate?"

"You have my word," Jai Krishna said.

An elderly man in the groom's party came forward, pulling his embroidered shawl of fine wool tightly around his shoulders. "When the stree-achar rites were performed, some woman must have been unclean. You can deceive judges, but you cannot fool goddesses."

"The goddess exacts payment in mysterious ways." Others took this up as a refrain.

Jai Krishna Gangooly, the fiery-tongued pleader, had not thought of Manasha or any village goddess for that matter, not even Shitala, the goddess associated with smallpox, in decades. He'd defended Hindu tradition, with all its inflexibility and excess, against the scorn of progressive colleagues like Keshub Mitter as much out of his lawyerly love of debate as conviction or religious faith. Now he wondered about the lessons embedded in Hindu myths and folktales. The snake had not been charged to kill the thirteen-year-old bridegroom by a goddess enraged at having been defiled by a menstruating devotee. The snakebite had occurred to remind Jai Krishna and Surendranath how precarious social order and fatherly self-confidence are. He had thought himself smugly in command of the wedding night's arrangements.

Finally Surendranath Lahiri, still holding the body of his son in his arms, spoke. "You will arrange posthaste for the dowry cash and the dowry gifts to be brought on board, Jai Krishna babu. What you do with your wretched girl, the killer of my son, I make your business."

And that was the moment when Jai Krishna Gangooly felt his wounded consciousness begin to heal. The stars had been repositioned.

The pleader knew Surendranath's claim to the dowry was untenable, nakedly greedy. But the reborn Hindu knew the working of fate was more complicated than English law and cared nothing about life and death, even of innocent children. His daughter's true fate, the fate behind the horoscope, had now been revealed: a lifetime's virginity, a life without a husband to worship as god's proxy on earth, and thus, the despairing life of a woman doomed to be reincarnated.

"The marriage did not take place," he said, his voice lawyerly, loud, authoritative. "Therefore, there is no question of dowry giving."

"His son is dead! The boy has been murdered!"

Jai Krishna turned his back on the avaricious man who would have been Tara Lata's father-in-law if fate hadn't intervened. "I will see my daughter married to a crocodile, to a tree, *before you get a single pice! I give dowry only to one who does not demand it. There will be a wedding tonight, the auspicious hour will be honored."*

And with that, Jai Krishna Gangooly, who would soon reclaim the ancestral name of Gangopadhaya and embark on a second lifetime of wondrous adventure, walked down the gangway to the dock. The women on the riverbank, uncertain of what had happened on board the bajra, began their ululation once more. The shenai players led the procession back to the wedding house. When the procession reached the walled compound, Jai Krishna himself threw open the front gates and welcomed in the assembled beggars and gawkers. At nightfall, the naphtha lamps were lit, the bride and her sisters were gathered up and placed inside a palanquin, and the marriage party set out, on foot and in palanquins and sedan chairs, to find a suitable bridegroom.

. . .

Inside her palki, Tara Lata leans a cheek decorated with designs in sandalwood paste against the dank and warped wood of the palki's not-quite closed door, and fixes a kohl-rimmed, curious eye at the segmented outdoors. The most rakish of her bachelor uncles holds his fancy shoes

high above the jungle mud, where monsoon rains never seem to leave.
Then, a spluttery beat is clapped out on the drenched ends of a dhol and
a melancholy tune coaxed out of a shenai. One by one, the married sis-
ters, then the bride, are helped out of the palki. Somehow, in a protected
spot between the wide, stone-hard roots of a tree, in the succulent cold of
the jungle floor, the priest has managed to light a sacred fire. On the
way to the makeshift dais on which the marriage rites are to take place,
the bride suddenly begs to be carried. Her feet have gone to sleep. She's
cold. What if her fancy brocaded sari gets ruined? She needs to pee. She
struggles to unclasp the broad gold choker that rests like a noose around
her throat. All her ornaments feel too heavy. The thick, gold chains hurt
her neck and chest. Her many necklaces chafe the skin on her collarbones.
The weighty drop-earrings tear through the soft flesh of her tiny ear-
lobes. The thick, stiff prongs of her gold hair-ornaments and the sharp
points of her butterfly-shaped cloisonné lace-pin that anchors her face-
concealing bridal veil dig into her scalp. Why must the ceremony be held
in this dark, dangerous jungle and not in the lamp-lit, torch-brightened
wedding pavilion in the big house in Mishtigunj village?

Older aunts shush her. She is paying for the sins of a past life, they
explain. God is letting her off lightly. She is being saved from the fate
of a despised ghar-jalani, a woman-who-brings-misfortune-and-death-to-
her-family, by the quick thinking of their wise, god-fearing patriarch.
May she remain a wife, a wearer of vermilion powder in her hair-part,
and not a widow, well into the age of white hair. She heeds the counsel
of her elders. Veiled head bent low, she allows them to guide her to her
seat before the sacred fire. She concentrates on the lithe flash of scarlet lac
dye around the rims of her bare feet. She cannot shut out the sorrowful
whispers of the cursed girl, the unlucky child, *but she refuses to*
believe them. She smells flowers instead of rotting leaves and sour mud.

The Brahmin priest hustles Jai Krishna through gauri-daan, the
giving-of-virgin-bride-as-a-gift ritual, and speeds through Sanskrit
prayers. Four young uncles heft the veiled bride, seated cross-legged on

her wedding stool, and carry her seven times around the bridegroom in accordance with the ritual. Then, it's time for shubho-drishti, the rite of auspicious gaze when the bride gets her first glimpse of the face of the man she is marrying. This night's bride, the five-year-old Tara Lata, cannot disguise her curiosity as she waits, still held chest high by her solemn young uncles, to take her first peek at the husband she is to please and obey forever. Close to her bejeweled and aching ears, some aunts ululate, and one blows a conch shell. The bridal veil is lifted.

Tara Lata straightens her bowed head, and raises her gaze slowly, very slowly. Her bridegroom is brave and steadfast. He has waited for her all night in the perilous wilderness. He has waited for her alone, unflinching, though deadly snakes slither out of flooded holes at his feet, and leeches crawl across his toes, and crabs scuttle up his shins and predatory beasts gouge his solid stomach. The bridal gaze angles up his strong, slender torso as tall as a ship's mast, and scales up, up, to where the tip of his head disappears in the night-black of the winter skies. She feels his arms, as strong as tree branches, brush against her, enfold her, shield her from life's potential brutalities. The whispered lamentations were wrong. She is not a woman cursed by a goddess and shunned like an outcast by her community. She takes her greedy fill of the auspicious initial glimpse. And now she recognizes her bridegroom. He is the god of Shoondar Bon, the Beautiful Forest, come down to earth as a tree to save her from a lifetime of disgrace and misery.

. . .

All of my life, or at least ever since my mother told me the story of Tara Lata the Tree-Bride—and that I had been named for her—I have felt, for no discernible reason, a profound connection. She had two sisters, as do I. Perhaps we learned the same nursery rhyme: We are sisters three / as alike as three blossoms on one flowering tree. *But my sisters and I are Calcutta girls, a city that Tara Lata never saw. After the night of her marriage, Tara Lata returned to Mishtigunj and, at least by legend, never left her father's house. Unburdened by a time-consuming, emotion-draining marriage and children, never having to please a soul, she grew up and grew old in a single house in an impoverished village in the poorest place on earth, and in that house, the world came to her. She lived there seventy years and gradually changed the world.*

On the other hand, until last year when I finally yielded to that most American of impulses, or compulsions, a "roots search," I had never seen Tara Lata's house in Mishtigunj. I'd never even been to Bangladesh. The river still flows behind it, the bathing-ghat, though crumbled and discolored, is still in use for those foolish enough or desperate enough to wash in that fetid, constricted stream. The shell of the house is partitioned now among a dozen families. Its outer walls prop another dozen tin-roofed huts, uncountable children, and women of every age fanning chulas. Burning cow-dung patties, a street smell of my childhood, bring tears to my eyes, both defensive and nostalgic. Elderly gentlemen occupy the balconies, graybeards studying their Holy Qurans. I approached, wearing a plain cotton sari, no gold, little makeup, trying to pass at least as Bengali, if not Muslim. I wore no red shindur in the parting of my hair. Now I was just an unmarried Hindu lady, visiting a Muslim house. And even that frail disguise was useless—the children spotted me and called out, "America-memsaheb, America-memsaheb!"

And so I mentioned the name of Tara Lata the Tree-Bride and that I was on a mission of discovery. They knew her name and in the gracious way of country people, insisted on tea, and then on feeding me, and finally retelling the stories of Tara Lata that had been told to them. Tara Lata the virgin, the untouched, who opened the house to beggars, then to the sick, then to the young soldiers fighting the Raj. It's as though the crowd Jai Krishna invited inside the night of the wedding had never left. Tara Lata the saint, the freedom fighter. Whatever the bond between us, it is less than obvious. Until six years ago, I had been a married woman, though never with vermilion in my hair, living in a gated community in Atherton, California. I have given birth to a son. I have become, as befits an educated, thirty-six-year-old Californian, free and well traveled. I suspect I will grow old, but I know I will never change the world.

Toward the end of the evening, one canny old man asked the question that had been on everyone's mind. As another Tara Lata, did I ever talk to her? Did we speak in dreams? I answered enthusiastically, yes, yes, I often think of her. Good, they said. And did she ever tell you where the gold was buried? Because when she returned that night, she was just a plain little girl with one gold bangle and shindur in the parting of her hair, but the gold was gone. Did I know the location of the tree? The jungle is smaller now, the tigers are gone. The men of Mishtigunj, over the decades, have turned the soil under every tree tall enough to have been standing back then. In whatever dreamtime it happened, in Muslim, Hindu, or English years, the events of that night have entered the local language. A person from Mishtigunj is a dreamer, "to mishtigunj" is to dream of buried riches while your roof collapses on you, to pursue crackpot schemes of glory.

It would be comforting to think of Tara Lata, daughter of my great-grandfather, as my grandmother, but the family trees of nineteenth-century Bengali Brahmins, particularly those from the country and those espousing traditional values, are more tangled than anything found in "the Beautiful Forest." The Tree-Bride is stuck on a remote siding of the "Gangooly" family tree. The Gangopadhaya trunk line that leads directly to my mother, my sisters, and me runs through Jai Krishna's ninth wife and the birth of my grandfather in 1909, when Jai Krishna was seventy years old.

The display of raw greed by the dead groom's family at the very moment of its deepest grief could have brought Jai Krishna back to Dacca, back to the progressive ideas of Keshub Mitter and Dr. Roy, with an apology for having gone temporarily overboard on romanticized Hinduism. From now on, he might have said, I'll stick to the

*law (even the 1872 law against child-marriage). Having seen igno-
rance and superstition up close, I'll settle these horrendous injustices and
irrational lawsuits. A venomous snake, after all, is destined to discharge
its venom, whether Goddess Manasha is propitiated or not. To which
Keshub Mitter might have answered, "We must educate our snakes not
to bite."*

*But Jai Krishna did not go the logical route. Perhaps he'd had a
vision of the intractability of tradition, the futility of intervention, the
stubborn potency of myth in the face of overwhelming change. What
dwindling store of faith he had in Western reason deserted him—or
to put it less negatively, what kernel of comfort could be found in the
ancient faith was restored to him. The mother of Tara Lata and the
two older daughters continued to live in the Mishtigunj house, as did
Jai Krishna on his visits, but he did not return to Dacca. The role of
vakil, a native lawyer, took him on a circuit of the district and, in
outlying villages where girls outnumbered boys, he began picking up
wives in the settlement of bills, and since a woman could attain nirvana
only through worship of a husband and a Brahmin was permitted as
many wives as he could support, his excesses could be interpreted as a
form of noblesse oblige. The final number of wives, in fact, speak of re-
straint, a desperate search for an heir, in an era when some men boasted
fifty or more.*

*The son eluded him until the ninth wife, a girl in her mid-teens
whom he married at the age of sixty-eight. We are descended from that
son, whom my mother, of course—given the life expectancies—never saw.
I don't think of my mother as an old woman, but even she has witnessed
the fallout of polygamy. She doesn't have a birth certificate, but I know
how young she was when I was born, which would make her . . . well,
never mind. To calculate a parent's age is to hurry a meeting with
Yama, the God of Death. She remembers the shock she felt when she
discovered that her paternal grandmother, a woman of autocratic will
and sour temperament, wasn't her late grandfather's only wife. And*

during the Second World War, in the year that the Japanese invaded Burma, then captured Imphal, the easternmost city of India, a family of nine strangers suddenly showed up at the squat, solid house in Calcutta, demanding asylum because they were descended from one of the early wives of my mother's polygamous grandfather. The strangers stayed on for months.

When I said Tara Lata never left her house in Mishtigunj for the rest of her very long life, I realize I misspoke. She left her house, not of her own volition, on one occasion. There is a large signboard outside the old Gangooly property in Mishtigunj, a sign so large and gaudily painted, I first thought it was an advertisement or some sort of political poster.

Unless you knew Bengali, you would never guess its contents (I told you that Muslims were more faithful guardians of our language than we Hindus). In English it would read:

The Home of Tara Lata Gangooly (1874–1944?), known to the World as "Tara-Ma." Behind these Walls lived an Untrained Nurse, Spiritual Healer, and Inspiration to Generations of Peaceloving and Peace-seeking Individuals from Around the World. During the Bengal Famine of 1942 she fed the Town and the Outlying Villages. She rallied the Cause of an Independent India and United Bengal and protected Young Freedom Fighters from British arrest. She herself was Dragged from her Home on the Night of October 12, 1944, by Colonial authorities and Never Heard from Again. Her death was announced on October 18, 1944, and Attributed to a heart attack.

Erected by a Grateful Government in the Name of All its Citizens, whatever God They may Worship.

2

Sisters three are we . . . as like as blossoms on a tree. But we are not.

My oldest sister, Padma, was born eighty years after that marriage ceremony in the Shoondar Bon. My second sister, Parvati, was born on the same date, three years later, and I came along with the same birthday three years after that. Yes, we did our calculations and privately celebrated the same October night as our collective inception day. And just as our mother hoped in naming us after goddesses, we have survived, even prospered.

The city was Calcutta in the late fifties and early sixties. My American friends in California say *God, Tara, Calcutta!* as though to suggest I have returned to earth after a journey to one of the outer planets. It's one of those cities in the world with negative cachet, a city to escape, one of those hellholes made famous by Mother Teresa and mindless comparisons in the American press: Dirtier than Calcutta. Crueler than Calcutta. Poorer than Calcutta.

I grew up in a city that never pitied itself, a city that deflected all the abuse. Insults were the badge of our superiority, proof of others' ignorance. Someone in the family, deep in the gloom of East Bengal shortly after the First World War, long before independence and the Partition riots, had the courage or the despair to announce: *Baba, I am going to Calcutta.* Or some desperate father hopped the train to Howrah station, his wife and children trailing behind him. Blessed be his memory.

The city I knew was (and remains) the magnet of hope for the world's third-largest population, the target of all their ambition. To be a native-born Calcuttan was (and is) to be a Londoner, a Parisian, a New Yorker, at the zenith. To be a playwright, a moviemaker, a painter, is (or was) to aspire to have one's work on the North Calcutta stage, the Chowringhee screens, the South Calcutta galleries, and to be talked about by the only critics and audience in the world who matter. Businessmen aspired to join the Bengal Club. Matrons fought to be seen at the Turf Club during the racing season. To be Calcutta bhadra lok, as we Bhattacharjees were, was to share a tradition of leadership, of sensitivity, of achievement, refinement, and beauty that was the envy of the world. That is the legacy of the last generation of Calcutta high society, a world into which we three sisters were born, and from which we have made our separate exits.

It is true that we three sisters were as alike, at least to look at, as blossoms on a tree. (And if I may say so, we were blossoms.) Padma, the first, and six years my senior, was forced by our father to turn down movie offers. Parvati, three years older than me, took the annual "Miss Brains and Beauty" cover of *Eve's Weekly*. And in my turn, just about the time Communists were taking over the West Bengal state government and Calcutta city council, and my father and his friends were sensing the noose tightening, the future shortening, and bhadra lok bodies were being found on the golf courses, I was tapped for the same cover again: *Sisters Three: Can It Be?* Our world was dying, but we were the last to know. The narrow world of the house and city felt as secure to me as it must have to Tara Lata in Mishtigunj.

I was nineteen years old, holder of a B.A. Honours and M.A. First Class from the University of Calcutta, committed to gathering more honors and scholarships and to take up the graduate school offers that had already come from Paris, London, and New York, when my father said the magic words: "There is a boy and we have found him suitable. Here is his picture. The marriage will be in three weeks." My sisters were both married by then. Padma had already established herself in New York and Parvati's husband was waiting for his Green Card. The "boy" (they are always "boys" when fathers choose them for their daughters) who was selected to jumpstart my life, to be worshipped as a god according to scripture, was (and is) Bishwapriya Chatterjee, a first son from an outstanding family. Father, on the Calcutta High Court and decidedly not a Bolshevik. Mother, descended from Sir Biren Mukherjee. The groom's dak-nam, that is, his house-name, is Bishu. His American friends call him Bish, a not-quite-appropriate nickname, since it means "poison." I, of course, as a good Hindu wife-to-be, could not utter any of his names to his face. But we're progressive people; after crossing the dark waters to California I called him Bishu, then Bish, and he didn't flinch. We had (and have) one son, Rabin, short (of course) for Rabindranath, as in Tagore. His school friends call him Rob. We call him Rabi.

When the unthinkable occurred, Bish kept the large house behind the gates in Atherton, in one of the first developments to grow up with Silicon Valley. He was, and probably still is, wealthy beyond counting, or caring. So am I; money is no longer the point, if it ever was. With his friend Chester Yee, he developed a process for allowing computers to create their own time, recognizing signals intended only for them, for instantaneously routing information to the least congested lines. It sounds obvious only because I'm not doing it justice. Maybe, also, because I was in the room serving pakoras and freshening drinks when Bish and Chester, watching a Sunday football game on a new 52-inch screen suddenly had the inspiration. "Downfield blocking!" said Bish. "A West Coast offense!" chimed in Chet. "Short passes under the coverage, passes to running backs and wide receivers!" "Flood the secondary! A scrambling quarterback!" "It's about width, using the whole field, connecting in the flat, no interference, a billion short passes linked together!" They shouted out the magic word together: Bandwidth! Chet Yee demanded the legendary piece of paper that will someday go to the Smithsonian. My fingerprints are on immortality. Chester got the patent; Bish formed the company. They, or I should say, we, own fifty-one percent of the stock. The system is called "CHATTY" and without it, nothing in the modern world would work.

Now I live in a part of San Francisco called Upper Haight, or Cole Valley, with Rabi, and do volunteer work in a preschool two blocks away. It is a happy landscape, I like to think, reaching from the shallow depression of Golden Gate Park and climbing to the communication towers atop Twin Peaks. The area is given to summer fogs that make conventional gardening impossible, but that remind me, not unhappily, of mountain resorts in India. I almost expect the chattering of monkeys, corn and peanuts smoking on open braziers, the tinkling of women's bangles and Buddhist prayer wheels. From our back porch, I overlook the park and command a view of Berkeley, the Oakland hills, and the top spires of the Golden Gate Bridge. Cream-colored houses seem to have tumbled down the hillsides like children's blocks, or—on bright days under a cloudless sky—like cottages in an Etruscan landscape. Three-storied Victorians dominate our streets, particularly impressive in their coats of many colors, their fringes and gingerbread meticulously emphasized and proudly restored.

My house is a simpler affair. I've had to invest heavily in emergency retrofitting after the 1989 earthquake, which led to modernization and more preservation. The walls were cracked and buckling and covered a maze of old gas lines and water pipes. The windows rattled, the roof was a mess, and insulation did not exist. I had the last defrost-by-hand refrigerator in the area, and no way of replacing it short of removing the front windows and hiring a hoist. Generations of cats had bred in the basement, rats and squirrels in the walls, mice in the closets. After all the work, I felt for the first time in my life totally at home, unwilling to leave. I am one with the neighborhood, a young woman like so many others on the street: ethnically ambiguous, hanging out in the coffee shop, walking dogs, strolling with boyfriends, none of us with apparent sources of income. It's a work-at-home neighborhood where the older arts and newer technology seem to have come together. We're on a first-name basis with all the grocers, the restaurant owners, the clerks at the hardware store, the art framers, the wine merchants, the pharmacists, the hairstylists, the boys at the video rental. Their names inspire me: Ib, Selim, Moh, Safid, Ali . . . all the neighborhood services, except the laundries and the Japanese restaurant, are owned and staffed by crack-of-dawn rising, late-night closing Palestinians, whose shifting roster of uncles and cousins seems uniformly gifted in providing our needs and anticipating our desires.

I don't live exclusively with my son. There's Andy, my balding, red-bearded, former biker, former bad-boy, Hungarian Buddhist contractor/yoga instructor, the man Bish calls "Tara's mistri," my carpenter. That hasn't stopped Bish from hiring him for work on his Atherton house. He considers the fact that Andy sleeps with his ex-wife the best possible guarantee of quality work. It's one of those San Francisco things I can't begin to explain in India, just like I can't explain my Indian life to the women I know in California.

I have told my Calcutta stories many times, and Americans seem to find them endlessly amusing, and appalling. And yet, until last year, I'd never really understood what I was revealing or what I was suppressing. I was going for the effect, *Tara, No!*, the easy approval. *Oh, Tara, you're so brave!* I married a man I had never met, whose picture and biography and bloodlines I approved of, because my father told me it was time to get married and this was the best husband on the market. It *is* amusing, and appalling. My father might have guessed that Calcutta was dying, and his golfing partners were looking askance at any new caddy, and tennis was becoming a dangerous sport, but thank God, we were protected from such knowledge. My friends, even those who know him— even Andy—find Bish an intriguing and charming man, which he is (and was).

"Charming," in fact, doesn't do him justice. My teacher friends don't read the trade magazines or watch the financial networks where Bish Chatterjee is a frequent guest. He is the posterboy of Indian entrepreneurship, the reason why political parties sometimes reach consensus on loosening immigration laws, increasing the number of H-1B visas. ("We don't want to turn away the Bish Chatterjees of this world," they say.) They look at him—how can any woman *not* look at him, how could any nineteen-year-old girl whatever her looks and brains have been so lucky? And they look at me now, familiar old Tara, thirty-six-year-old divorced kindergarten teacher—and ask, how could any woman, even a nineteen-year-old, submit to someone else's choice, even a loving parent's? Obviously, a recipe for disaster. And we're thrown into the middle of a modern enigma. My enigma, and yours.

How can any girl with a certain amount of confidence and a

sense of style surrender them both to the whims of fate and the manipulations of the marital marketplace? It's a question worthy of some modern Jane Austen. Your parents, Tara, get a grip! What do they know of the needs of a modern woman? The simple answer could never satisfy them: I wasn't, perhaps I'll never be, a modern woman. These are the objections of modern American women who know me now, all of whom have passed through at least one un-arranged marriage and who are raising at least one child with or without the bottom line of child support. They have no idea of the wealth I came from—they hear only "Calcutta" and immediately feel sorry for me—and the money I now control. To them, I am a single mom, raising a boy and halfway teaching school. I am the supremely lucky one. Bish is generous and protective; he has more than enough to provide. Indian men, whatever their faults, are programmed to provide for their wives and children. If I had wanted only to be provided for, stupendously provided for inside the gated community, endlessly on display at dinners and openings, I would have stayed in Atherton.

"Love" is a slippery word when both partners bring their own definition. Love, to Bish, is the residue of providing for parents and family, contributing to good causes and community charities, earning professional respect, and being recognized for hard work and honesty. Love is indistinguishable from status and honors. I can't imagine my carpenter, Andy, bringing anything more com-plicated to it than, say, "fun." Love is having fun with someone, more fun with that person than with anyone else, over a longer haul.

He has refined the art of keeping things simple. It's a Buddhist thing, he says.

"Love" in my childhood and adolescence (although we didn't have an "adolescence" and we were never "teenagers") was indis-tinguishable from duty and obedience. Our bodies changed, but our behavior never did. Rebellion sounded like a lot of fun, but in Calcutta there was nothing to rebel against. Where would it get you? My life was one long childhood until I was thrown into marriage. The qualities we associated with our father and with god were not notably divergent from the respect we accorded the president of the country, the premier of the state (at least until the Communists came in), great names in history, science, and literature, older uncles, cricket players, movie stars, and—of course— the boys our fathers would eventually select for us to marry. Love was a spectrum upon which some men were old, like the Nehrus, Tagores, and Subhas Boses, and some were slightly ridiculous, like Mahatma Gandhi, and some were exciting and unavailable like Jack and Bobby Kennedy, but others demanded closer scrutiny; they lay within a narrow, caste-bound zone of contention. In the third-largest population of the world, even a narrow range is not a constricted choice.

For girls of our class, only a convent-school education would do. This meant that until we reached the age of marital consent, we could be certified (of course) as virgins, but also as never having occupied unchaperoned confined space of any kind with a boy of our own age who was not a close relative. For Hindu girls, entry to an exclusive Catholic convent school depended upon exhibiting flair without flash, class without pretension, a society name without notoriety. In return, convent education guaranteed poise, English proficiency, high-level contacts, French language skills, and confident survival in whatever future the gods or the Communists might dole out.

Calcutta's affluent minority communities, girls from the top Muslim and Indian-Christian families, the Chinese and Koreans, a few of the mixed-race Anglo-Indians, some Jews, Sikhs, Armenians, and Parsees, were admitted as matters of course, by a kind of Catholic affirmative action. By not being Hindu, they were de facto Christians, or at least open to suggestion. Their reserved slots made it all the more difficult for Hindu girls to gain admission, since, demographically, we constituted the vast majority of the potential enrollment. Even as proud members of the majority community, we were a blessed, elite minority, and we knew it.

. . .

I call Parvati "Parvati-di," older-sister-Parvati, but I call Padma simply "Didi," Big Sister. In the late sixties and early seventies, the six years between Padma and me seemed unbridgeable. She was born in 1958, and by the time I came along, she already knew the American songs beamed across the subcontinent from Radio Ceylon. When I was six, she was reading the movie magazines and knew the juicy scandals. When I was nine, she confided a career ambition to be, somehow, a performer, to act or to dance. She was beautiful enough, and perhaps even talented enough, although of course our father would never have permitted any form of exhibitionism. But most of all, to my wonderstruck eyes, she had stupendous breasts. My second sister, Parvati, at twelve, was heading in the same direction. At nine, I never felt greater fascination or deeper anxiety. Our father couldn't let either of my sisters out on the street. Our car was equipped with window shades. We had a driver, and the driver had a guard. The world didn't know it yet (it does now, with all the Bengali Miss Worlds and Miss Universes) but the sight of a fifteen-year-old cover girl like Padma Bhattacharjee could have destroyed the audience for any blondie-blondie bombshell like Brigitte Bardot.

Goddess Manasha, the cobra deity of East Bengal, will find a way to strike, no matter what precautions, what window shades, are put in place. She takes many forms in different places. In Mishtigunj she might even get away with no disguise at all, just do her snaky thing, slither, hide, and strike. A snake must strike, its venom must kill. Everyone knows the rules except, perhaps, eager little boys running off to get married. But expand the universe just a few degrees, remove it to Calcutta from a village in East Bengal, speed the calendar ahead a hundred years, and the same snake, to fulfill its destiny, must take a different form.

She's not even a snake. She was a perfectly sweet-natured, but rather dull-witted girl in Didi's class. Her name was Poppy Dey, tall, dark, and slender. Rather ordinary-looking for a Bengali girl in a convent school, so ordinary that my mother once said, "It's a good thing that Dey girl is a Christian," meaning Christians don't place as much store in good looks and full bosoms, and so her father would not be presented with an insurmountable challenge. There was sure to be a Christian boy out there in Calcutta or the wider Christian world who could love her for her meager charms and vast dowry. For Poppy, as a Christian, escape from India was not a romantic fantasy, as it was for us, but an article of faith. Her father, whom we called Nose-and-Throat Dey, was a well-regarded surgeon, FRCS, and thus permitted to cut into English flesh. The Deys and their many relatives and collateral families were crème de la crème of Calcutta high society, Christian or Hindu.

Poppy Dey and Didi, improbably, were inseparable. Spectacular beauties do not normally tolerate the constant attention of the notably unfavored. Young and innocent as I was, I saw something happening in that friendship, a "dynamic," as they like to say, that my parents could not.

Poppy had a brother, a brilliant and handsome boy named Ronald Dey. He was a Presidency College student, an all-rounder, debater and cricketeer, frequently in the papers. Say the name "Ron Dey" to a Bengali woman of my class and generation anywhere in the world today (and by now we are everywhere), and there'll be that flush of embarrassment as though awakened from a titillating daydream and a flurry of questions, "What ever happened to Ronald Dey? Wasn't he . . . ? Didn't he . . . ? He was so . . ." The most acceptable answer is, he became a surgeon like his father, but shunned the social spotlight. He left Calcutta in the middle of his college year, took a few years' training in England and the United States, then returned to India to establish a medical practice in Bombay, where his name carried less weight.

I have done something here for which I should apologize. I have structured a surprise event in such a way that it will seem to you obvious and inevitable. You will wonder how we missed it, and I might not be able to communicate the shock, the bolt of lightning that sent me to Bangladesh last year, that set me to writing this book, and started everything else in motion.

When the liaison between Ron and Didi began, I, of course, will never know. What she was thinking of, what future together they imagined, what plans they made, I can barely imagine. *Where* they even did it, under all those eyes, is unimaginable. Passion like Didi's is foreign to our family; recklessness unknown. She is our true American, our improviser, although I am the only one to hold the passport.

In the way of sisters who are socially and psychologically and in every definable Indian way (caste, desh, language, shared history) so very much alike, I always knew that something marked Didi as different—and at the same time I would have, of course, denied the possibility. I was only nine, but I could follow the bread crumbs, the genetic markers left by a young woman suddenly distracted, on a rocket ride. She loves someone, I thought, she's no longer a girl like us. Then I quickly figured out (how many possibilities were there?) the only person it could be. She spoke of Poppy's brother—Oh, what's his name? Don? Ron?—blushingly. He was such an attentive, charming brother, walking Poppy to our house and picking her up, despite his college duties.

But Ronald Dey was *not* possible. Daddy had not yet sanctioned someone for Didi to marry. And whenever that time did come, it would not be with a Christian, no matter what his social status and brilliant prospects. Therefore I must be wrong. Therefore, Ron Dey slipped under the most refined radar system in the world: Hindu Virgin Protection. So many eyes were watching, so many precautions were taken, and so much of value was at stake—the marriageability of Motilal Bhattacharjee's oldest daughter, which, unless properly managed, controlled the prospects of his second and third daughters as well—that any violation of the codes, any breath of scandal, was unthinkable.

Where, in Heaven's name, could anyone even be alone in Calcutta? What hanky-panky business, in my mother's words, could go on? Everyone knew the rules and the rules stated caste and community narrowed the range of intimate contact. The Deys, as their name proclaimed, were not only Christian today, but had sprung from a Hindu caste that was not even Brahmin. Friendship, yes; marriage, never. Even I, elfin, bright-eyed nine-year-old romantic, must have held the two truths briefly in balance, the evidence of my eyes and the suspicions of my heart, considered them, and laughed one of them—the wrong one—out of existence.

´   ´   ´

I have not yet spoken of our father, a trained engineer (B.E. Calcutta, M.E., Ph.D. Reading) who turned his skills and training to business, invested in a tea estate offered at a bargain rate by an Englishman anxious to get out before Independence, and ended up making a fortune in the tea trade in the 1950s and '60s. What began as a kind of gentleman's farm became (with his engineering mind) a model of efficiency. Tea was the refined centerpiece of Calcutta's prosperity, the respectable underwriter of Calcutta's standing on the world stage.

Our nineteenth-century Raj-style fortress of a home on Ballygunge Park Road was set behind a wall topped with glass shards, and the long yard with its landscaped garden was the scene of fabulous parties during the winter "social season." We sisters performed, old Britishers from the last days of the Raj returned in ever-dwindling numbers for the round of parties, and I have never been happier than the nights Parvati and I would dress in our specially tailored "English frocks" and carry hors d'oeuvre trays from drunken cluster to tipsy cluster, listening to their praise, "I say, Bhattacharjee, you've got a charming little girl there," or "I don't envy you, old man, keeping the boys away." The idea of Didi in a frock would have excited different fantasies. She managed to escape the parties with sleepovers at Poppy's.

Ballygunge Park Road was an outstanding address in those years, one that practically shouted "old money!" But we were not "old money" by any stretch. Both of my parents were born in Calcutta, but their parents still pined for the eternal greenery of East Bengal. My mother's family hailed from Dhaka, my father from a provincial town called Faridpur, both of which I had not seen until my impulsive visit a year ago. In the way of provincial gentry, my father's father was the bright boy with prospects, my grandmother the comely town girl from an established family. Her dowry enabled my grandfather to complete his education and move to Calcutta.

Bengali culture trains one to claim the father's birthplace, sight unseen, as his or her desh, her home. Although she has never seen it, my mother's desh is Dhaka, by way of Mishtigunj, the village even few East Bengalis have ever seen. When I speak of this to my American friends—the iron-clad identifiers of region, language, caste, and subcaste—they call me "overdetermined" and of course they are right. When I tell them they should be thankful for their identity crises and feelings of alienation, I of course am right. When everyone knows your business and every name declares your identity, where no landscape fails to contain a plethora of human figures, even a damaged consciousness, even loneliness, become privileged commodities.

✦ ✦ ✦

One late October afternoon last year, I returned home from teaching and found my son, Rabi—Rabindranath Chatterjee—and another young man sitting in the living room. Cigarette smoke lay heavy in the air, and I thought, always suspecting Rabi of having some sort of secret life, *Aha, now I've caught you!* But they were drinking Cokes, and it was the stranger who stubbed out his cigarette as soon as I entered the room.

He was a handsome young man recently arrived from India, not an Indo-American like my son. Don't ask me how I knew. The clothes, the mustache, the rather formal posture. He approached as though to embrace me. "How are you, Tara-*mashi?*"

I stepped back. "Who are you?"

"I've met Parvati-mashi already."

"Who are you?" I repeated.

The strange young man smiled at me. "That's what I'd like to know myself." He walked around the furniture in my cluttered room, touching things on shelves and tabletops, my things, little things, like silver pillboxes and sandalwood gods. His audacity scared me. "What is your name?"

Rabi answered for him. "It's Chris. Chris Day."

It meant nothing to me.

"Thanks, old sport," the stranger said. He lifted a silver pitcher off the coffee table and shifted it from hand to hand as if he were assessing its weight. That pitcher is the only real collectible I brought with me from Atherton. It's heavy, it's supposed to be three hundred years old, and it's rare because it's carved all over with camels instead of the usual flowers or elephants. "Mrs.

Banerji, I mean Parvati-mashi, is the one who gave me your address."

"Where does Mrs. Banerji live?" I wanted to catch him in his lie. He'd play safe and guess Calcutta for a Bengali family, any Bengali family.

"On Nepean Sea Road. We had a chat in Bombay just before I left for America. I told her I was looking for my mother. She said that since you were living in America, you could help me more than she could." He faked lobbing the silver pitcher to Rabi. "Nobody mentioned I had a cousin in San Francisco. Rabi, old sport, what do you make of that omission?"

"Put that damn thing back on the damn table!" I shouted.

Rabi looked shocked. "Ma?"

"I wasn't thinking of stealing it, Tara-mashi." With a benign grin, the intruder who called himself Chris put the pitcher down—on the floor, not in its usual spot on the coffee table.

"Ma?" Rabi whispered it this time.

But my mind was reeling: *Cousin? Parvati-mashi? Tara-mashi?* I wanted to cry out, how dare you call us your *mashi*, your maternal aunts, how dare you go to my sister or come to me, how dare you—an imposter in laughable clothes—demand anything of us. How dare you invade our homes with your sinister lies about being a part of our family! Rabi calls these sudden rages my Brahminical side, any time I'm about to say "How dare you?" to anyone he'll raise, and wave, a finger. *Don't be a Brahmin, Ma.* Maybe that's why I turned my rage on Rabi.

"What's wrong with you, Rabi? Parvati's sons are your only cousins. You know that, I know that. How could you've been dumb enough to fall for this man's stories? After all your father's lectures, how could you've been stupid enough or reckless enough to let a total stranger into the house?"

"It's okay, old sport. I'll do the explaining to your mother."

The intruder gestured to Rabi to relax. Then he turned to me. "It might help if I pronounced my surname instead of Rabi. It's Dey."

That minute vowel distinction, Day/Dey, established him as a Bengali. Dey is a common Bengali last name. Penelope "Poppy" Dey had been just one of seven Deys in my Commercial Geography class in Loreto House College. Rabi had introduced him as Chris, so I tried to intuit the Bengali version of his first name. "Krishna Dey?" I asked.

"Jeez, Ma. Give him a break." Rabi had taken the stranger's side. Predictable.

"No," the young man responded. "It's Christopher. Christopher Dey." And then he added, "Tara-auntie."

In India, every word relating to family carries a special meaning. My oldest sister, Padma, is my Didi, or Padma-didi, and my middle sister is Parvati-di. I'll always just be Tara. Children are taught to call every family friend "auntie" and "uncle," or, in our language, mashi and mesho for the mother's side, pishi and pishe-mashai or kaki and kaku for the father's side. It's how a family-based culture sees the world, outward from the protective weave of relatedness, suspicious of anything that can't be fitted inside it. Close friends, or the vaguely connected from the same desh, the same remote village, are enfolded as "cousin-brothers," much to the consternation of the Immigration and Naturalization Service. Important women in the community, unrelated to anyone by blood or marriage, become mashi-ma, "aunt-mother." But the word "auntie" directed at me and coming from a grown man whom I'd never met carried the opposite effect of intimacy. It landed on my ear somewhere between threat and conspiracy. Where was my Andy when I needed him?

"Ma," Rabi asks so innocently, "how come you never told me Padma-mashi had a son?" He smells scandal, and since most of the scandals in our family concern his father, apart from my liaison with Andy, anything juicy from the upright Indian Bhattacharjees comes to him as an unbidden blessing.

"Because, *duh*, she never had one." Then I turned to our visitor. "And now, Mr. Dey, what do you really want?"

"I think you should be sitting down, Tara-auntie."

Indians and most Europeans shudder at the breezy informality of American strangers, the dinner-hour *Hi, Tara* phone call from telemarketers. It's obnoxious, but easily retracted and never frightening. But "Tara-auntie," softly stated, intimate, familial, terrified me. It was an assault on me, not a libel of my sister. And I had not even begun to process the source of his presumption that he might actually be who he said he was. I started to shake.

If there's one thing Rabi has learned from our six overly close years together it's how an Indian woman responds to stress. "I'll put the kettle on," he said. "You sit, Ma."

          ,   ,   ,

A boy from India tracks you down in San Francisco, stating he is your nephew, son of your childless oldest sister whom you knew to be, like yourself, virginal until married, and, in her case, childless ever since. What would you feel? He sips his tea and retreats from his earlier aggressiveness. He has been granted an H-1B, of course, as a programmer. He is the child of Christian orphanages, subsidized by payments from his father, Dr. Dey of Bombay, whose identity was never kept secret. But now, he is planning to marry and he wants to meet his mother and secure her blessing. And as he speaks, I look for traces of my sister and whatever I could remember of Ron Dey. I see none, but then, Rabi bears few traces of me either. The Bhattacharjee girls flared, then burned out. "What is your auntie's name?"

"You are my auntie."

"I mean your pishi, not mashi."

"Please do not try to test me, Tara-mashi." He slips his left hand deep into his pants' pocket and pulls out a single cigarette.

The cigarette hasn't come out of a pack or a case, which is why it has the slightest hint of a break close to the filter. The cigarette and paan stall closest to our house in Calcutta sold singles out of cartons to the neighborhood's uppity servants who liked to smoke the same brand as their employers. I watch Chris Dey smoothing the bump out of the cigarette, before gripping it between thumb and forefinger. I'm in no hurry to respond.

"I mean it," Chris Dey says. "Don't test me."

I savor his misstep. No middle-class Bengali man would smoke in front of his elders. Even Parvati's husband in his chain-smoking days didn't dare light up in front of our parents.

"Poppy-pishi has four children and lives in Sydney."

"Please, no smoking in here."

"Her husband's name is Brian. Brian Dennis Kerrigan."

So, plain, gangly Poppy Dey is now Mrs. Brian Dennis Kerrigan, Australian housewife. Some day, if everything goes well, I might be Tara Karolyi.

Chris senses the testing is over. He drops the cigarette back into his pants' pocket. "Would you like me to recite the names of the four sons?"

Now he is taunting me.

"Tommy, Joe—"

"You've proved nothing."

He changes tactics. "I don't have to prove anything. I didn't come here to prove something. I came to *you*. Because you are a mother. Because you know how Rabi would feel if he were in my shoes. Every year in time for my birthday my father writes to my mother care of an ad in the personals of *The Times of India*. She never responds."

I want to deny his claim. I want to deny it on behalf of our family honor, but the evidence is mounting.

Questions have shifted in my mind from the boy to my sister. How can a mother deny her son? It's unnatural, especially a Bengali mother, whose possessiveness makes all Jewish and Italian mothers of books and movies as remote and bloodless as English mothers packing their children off to boarding school. And so, finally, I capitulate. "If what you say is true—and I warn you, I will verify every word—what do you want from me?"

He reaches into his Indian jacket's inner pocket. "Here is a letter to you, from my father." It is sealed; I do not open it. Rabi strains forward, reaching for it, and so I keep it on my lap. Something has happened that I don't want him to hear, but it is the same thing I was not permitted to hear, or to think, when I was his age. And in some cockeyed way, I feel that for the first time he is hearing something important about India. Not the India of doting grandparents, not the India of comfort and privilege, but the backyard of family, the compost heap. He comes over to stand behind me.

"You ask what I want? I want what everyone has. I want to belong. I want a mother, a family. Aunties. Cousins."

"Where were you born?" I asked.

He hung his head. "I don't know. The information was never given. I was turned over to the Sisters of Mercy and they told me there would always be money to raise me. There is no mother's name listed."

✓ ✓ ✓

When Chris Dey left, Rabi and I had a serious sit-down. He is fifteen, Didi's age when all of this began—if it began—but he is also American. He might inherit millions of dollars some day, but he's agitating for permission to flip burgers after school. He often

grows impatient with what he calls the secretiveness and hypocrisy—I see them as self-protective codes—that are built into
the Indian family drama. "Why not just call Padma-mashi?" he
asked. "He's a nice guy and she's been acting like a shit all her
life."

"Thank you, Mr. Compassion."

"Okay then, call Parvati-mashi and ask her why the hell she
put all this shit on you. Why do you guys hate each other so
much?"

"Hate?" I felt myself collapsing suddenly, like a balloon hitting
the ceiling and darting out of control all over the room. I love my
sisters. It's the purest love I've ever known. Hate is the last thing
I could feel for them; it's the only emotion that never entered our
little sisterhood. If I don't have them to talk to and believe in, I
have nothing. I look at Rabi and, for the first time in my life, I
want to slap him, scream at him and tell him to shut up, but
parents can't feel this way. No, that's not right, I've seen them in
parking lots and supermarkets. They get furious and make fools
of themselves and security guards have to be called and they get
in the papers for child abuse and end up in jail. Indian mothers
don't; we don't have violent feelings except against ourselves, and
never against our children, at least not against our sons. But he's
just sitting there smugly, smirking at me like I'm the child, and
I know he wants to say "So what do you think of your precious
India now, huh?" *Ma, get a grip!* How dare he?

The word just creeps out. "Shit!" I say, softly at first.

I don't know. I just don't know. "Shit!" I scream, and that gets
his attention. Is it a parent-child thing I never went through, a
teenager, single-mom scenario I never thought I'd have to live
through, or something every immigrant goes through, so much
we want to communicate, so much that they don't want to hear?
So much we can't let go of. Shit, shit, Shit!

Later that night, I read Ron Dey's letter. It was typed on Indian legal-size paper.

My Dear Mrs. Tara Chatterjee:

When last we met, you were a small child in your parents' home on Ballygunge Park Road. I pray that your parents are keeping good health and happiness, and of course I extend to you and your husband, Mr. Bishwapriya Chatterjee, of whom we hear so many inspiring stories, peace and continued prosperity in all your endeavours. I regret to inform that my father passed away five years ago, although my mother who is now in her eighties is keeping good health and living half the year in Bombay and half the year in Australia with my sister Penelope whom I do not imagine you remember.

The bearer of this letter is my son and your nephew, Mr. Christopher Dey. His mother is your sister, Padma. She and I had a love affair, for which I am totally responsible and have borne entire guilt and financial burden. This occurred when we were all very young in Calcutta in the summer of 1973. Christopher is the manifestation of that behaviour. I am proud to report that he has grown into a man of substance and sensitivity with a decent and forgiving spirit. He does not seek explanations or compensation in any shape or manner. I believe he wants to know more of himself than I have been able to provide. Over the years I have told him so much about your sister, and the life we all led in Calcutta in that beautiful time, that I have created and fed a psychological need that I cannot now satisfy. For that reason, I beg you to facilitate a meeting with his mother, whose married name and address I have not been able to find.

I cannot close without confessing that there have been heavy psychological, moral, and even religious consequences to my actions that have influenced my life nearly as profoundly as they have that of Christopher. After the events of that summer, I felt too ashamed to continue at Presidency College or to remain in Calcutta. I have tried to make amends, not only to him whenever and however I have been permitted, within the scope of basic discretion, but tangibly, in the form of medical charities and endowed foundations for the parentless population of Bombay and Calcutta. While this assuages somewhat my guilt, and addresses some questions of public duty, it does not begin to relieve me of guilt for the sorrow I have caused. I ask the understanding of the Bhattacharjee family, and pray that you will grant me the peace, and the hearing, that my son deserves. In the spirit of forgiveness and renewal,

Ron

(Dr.) R. (Ronald) Swarup Dey

3

read an article once about middle daughters, shortly after arriving in the United States as a newlywed. I was avid to learn, but not in school, and the women's magazines were my first great sources of forbidden knowledge. Middle daughters, Parvatis, are less assertive and more pliant than their older Padmas or younger Taras. They feel less certain of their father's love. Even if they are the more favored in beauty or intelligence, they are less confident. They seek ways to please rather than confront.

It seemed obvious enough to me that the Padma in a family enjoys extra, but perhaps more nervous and less expert attention, and that the Tara in any family commands (as I had) special, more relaxed indulgence. But when I tested its conclusions against my own experience, I found the article utterly unconvincing, relevant only to American families. In India, we didn't have outside influences like the media, or lax schooling, or cars and dating and drugs. We didn't know family breakdown. Our families existed inside an impenetrable bubble. Anyone entering or exiting was carefully monitored. We honored the proprieties. There was no rebellion, no seeking after individual identity. Why would there be? We three sisters were treated with absolute equality, and we responded in total unanimity.

Those were the conclusions of a twenty-year-old still making her way on the Stanford campus, working in the library, as her brilliant husband dazzled his professors and classmates. Americans agonized and complained, they worked too hard for too little recognition, they got extensions, they slept through classes, they doped themselves up for tests, but Indians just did their work on time and did it better and reaped the appropriate honors. Our training, not only in the old classrooms with second-rate equipment and uninspiring teachers, but also our training at home, duty and honor, obedience and respect, the whole dharma of studentship, spared us doubt and second thoughts. Bish became an electrical engineering student in India because his father told him he would be an engineer, and he excelled at it because that is what Chatterjees did. He received a scholarship to Stanford because that was the best place to go and everything Bish Chatterjee did was best. Best grades, best school, best wife. When he expressed a desire to get married, his father and mine cut the deal. Best boy, best girl. Why waste money or time and energy on dating or getting to know each other? Questions of trust and vulnerability and how far to go on what date? Such foolishness. Devastating breakups were distant entertainment, graduate school soap opera. We could always read about them, or hear about them secondhand. The Asian students plowed ahead. They handled duty very well.

We are Bengali Brahmins from Calcutta, and nothing can touch us.

Now, in one afternoon, that hoard of inherited confidence, the last treasure I'd smuggled out of India and kept untarnished for sixteen years in America, was about to be exposed and auctioned off. It's soap opera, it's too corny for soap opera, but it's happening to me! I'll have to call Parvati in Bombay. Depending on what she says, I'll have to call Didi in New Jersey. The monster is loose and he's coming for you, but he's a nice little monster. *You're* the monster. We'll be in shreds before this is over.

And when I thought about my sisters in light of this revelation, I realized I didn't know them at all. For the first time in my life, I couldn't confidently predict what they would say or how they would react. I had no insight into their feelings or their motives. Whose revelation was it anyway, theirs or mine? *Oh, you met Chris, did you? I told him to look you up if he got to California. How's he getting along?* Had they been keeping it from me, the baby, all these years? Mummy and Daddy had to know, why didn't they tell me? When did Parvati learn? She lives in Bombay, so does Dr. R. Swarup Dey. She had to know; she must have known for years. And if everyone but me knew about it and had kept it from me—why suddenly expose it now? If there's been a cover-up, who was its engineer, and who was being protected? I was looking at a blank sheet of paper and I didn't know where to start writing. I didn't know a single basic fact.

Andy, good old "boys-just-want-to-have-fun" Andras Karolyi, got back late from the job-site. He found me in bed with my box of personalized stationery, the good stuff I use for writing my parents and sisters, staring at the blank page under the greeting, "Dearest Parvati." I'd been staring at it for an hour. I was tempted to start a new page: *"Dear Mrs. Parvati Banerji: You do not know me, but it has recently come to my attention that we may have a nephew in common.*

When Andy listens, he really listens, he likes to close his eyes and sway a little. He learned it in a Japanese monastery, he says, and he has a big, round face that reminded me the first time I met him of the Buddha, eyes closed, absorbing chaos, radiating calm. He came into my life to build a deck, stayed to paint it, and never left. Retrofitting is his passion, a kind of mystical calling, making sure your house is the one that doesn't tumble in the next big quake. It's the perfect profession for a Zen devotee, to work like hell so something won't happen, to protect yourself against something you can't see and might never occur, to put all your energy and expertise into something, so that it will never change appearance.

He processed the story of the surprise visit, then read the letter. "It's perfectly understandable that your sister would behave that way," he said. He's never taken a deep interest in my Indian life, even though he's seen far more of India than I have, tramped through it barefoot from the Himalayas to the south, hit the holy places, stayed in hostels and flophouses, knows the religious practices, likes the food. He can handle the villages; it's upper-class Calcutta Brahmin life that he finds a little too exotic. "If this kid's on the up and up, and you think he is and his father says he is, then just call his mom and tell her he's here and he wants to see her. It's like an adoption case. Kid finds his birth mom and they fall in love, he forgives her, she welcomes him home. Or she refuses. Either way, end of story."

Brave words. I can't deliver bad news. I can't make ultimatums. I can only . . . What? Soothe. Oldest daughters ruffle feathers, cut loose, have adventures, middle and youngest make compromises, settle them down. I turned off the light, and we lay there quietly for several minutes. Andy works hard, sometimes he falls asleep when I think he's deep in thought. Sometimes, it's the opposite. He entered my life because the house insurance demanded that I retrofit, and I wondered at first why they were interested in my wardrobe. His panel truck advertises "The Zen-Master of Retro Fit," and he has a clientele that likes to engage him philosophically as he works. He charmed Rabi on the first day by alluding to "The Hound of the Baskervilles." *I make it so the house won't bark,* he said. *It's a matter of reading the fault lines. Especially the undiscovered ones.*

For once, according to my son, I'd found a man who was really cool. Andy found me tight and off-center, all wound up and nowhere to go. He got me with a back rub.

I was half-asleep when he started in again. "Of course she should acknowledge him, that's the decent thing, but there's no special reason she will. If she hasn't reached out in all these years, why should she start *now?*" A few minutes later he spoke again. "Of course, that's if you're sure the kid is who he says he is, and your sister did what he says she did, and the doc is really his father, and the letter is really from the doc, and it's not just a kid working some weird shit."

"That would be some very complicated shit to work," I said.

"It doesn't have to be that complicated. Of course, if you want to play it strictly by the rules you can check out his visa." I could sense him now turned to me, propped on an elbow, starting to get into it. "A couple of guys could have been working a scam on your sister in Bombay. So let's say she's already warned your sister in New Jersey, and just when they think it's all over and the cops are closing in, they find out there's a third sister in California, and they think, hey, maybe it's worth one more shot. Maybe you'll be too decent to call either sister, and you'll just try to smooth it over on your own and give him some money just to make him go away. It's your headache only if you're looking for a new headache to have."

I was thinking, *God,* another wrinkle. Youngest daughters are supposedly very trusting. Oldest daughters are innately suspicious. Middle daughters have a cynical optimism. I've always tried to follow Bish's last advice, delivered through his lawyer at our divorce, but I always remember it too late: *"People will find out you have money. They might see you as a helpless foreign woman and try to take advantage. Those people are very convincing. The more money involved, the more convincing they will be."* The only person I'd checked up on was Andy, and that was because Bish had bullied me into doing it. Bish, in fact, had offered to "take care"—his phrase—of the background check himself. We'd started the process of negotiation by e-mail with a terse, "I'm free to make a mess of my own life!" from me, then got stuck for a while on Bish's rejoinder, "You're not free to wreck our son's," and finally compromised with Bish allowing me to choose the private investigator at Bish's expense and without having to share the investigator's report with him.

As it turned out, I did get a report from a private investigator but Bish didn't have to pay for it. The teacher I got on best with at the preschool, and who, before she moved to Alaska, used to get me to try foods (like eels) and sports (kayaking and hang-gliding) without much success, was breaking up with a private investigator just about the time that I was considering promoting my mistri to live-in lover. The teacher's name was Hester Loo, her friend was Wesley Chang. Chang did the checking up on Andy as a favor to Hester. He turned up a POB in Hungary; a DOB: 01/18/54; two arrests for drug possession as a minor but no conviction in San Francisco; two marriages and divorces; no issue on record. That precisely squared with what he had told me; he'd been carried across the Austrian border as a two-year-old during the 1956 uprising. Wesley's report did not include the fact he, Andy, was the sole support for his sister's fatherless children.

If Hester and Wesley hadn't broken up, if Hester hadn't moved away, if I'd kept in touch with one or both of them, I might have been tempted to look for Wesley Chang in the yellow pages and retain him to check up on Chris Dey. The mysterious young man had certainly put on a convincing performance. But the letter had been carried, not mailed, and it wasn't on personalized stationery.

Surely no one but the real Ronald Dey would know that Poppy's name was Penelope. I clung to that; it was the only real estate that seeemed high, dry, and properly retrofitted. "I think what troubles me most is that I learned today the most shocking thing in my life—I still can't believe it—but it isn't the boy at all. It's the ignorance. It's what I don't know about me, and her, and . . ."

He must be asleep, I thought, the answer was so long in coming. "Zen's a bummer, babe," he said. "That's how it always is. The big facts are never learned. What you see is what's invisible."

4

Parvati now lives with her husband, Aurobindo Banerji and their teenage sons, Bhupesh and Dinesh, on the fifteenth floor of a spectacular high-rise that from the back three bedrooms overlooks the Arabian Sea and, from the glass walls of the living room, the sweep of Marine Drive, ending in the skyscrapers of Nariman Point. The rent is twenty-five thousand U.S. dollars a month paid into a Dubai account, and a million under the table for key money, plus half a million a year for lease-continuance. Aurobindo's company pays the bill. They consider themselves lucky to have found such a reasonable place before the prices shot up.

Although she married a Bengali Brahmin from a reasonably good Tollygunge family, his caste and regional origins were more a matter of coincidence than calculation. Parvati was in her second year at Mount Holyoke when her letter came: *Daddy, I have found a boy and we have fallen in love.* Parvati, the pliable middle daughter had done the unthinkable: she'd made a love match. They'd met in Boston, where he was working at a bank while finishing an M.B.A. at Tufts ("Wherever that is!" my father cried out). Harvard and MIT were the only schools we'd heard of in Boston. We saw Parvati's Aurobindo as a bank teller, like a South Indian clerk with a rubber thimble on his index finger, counting out stacks of money. More to the point, Aurobindo Banerji had not been selected by my father. He could have embodied every strain of Bengali beauty, wit, culture, athleticism, and intelligence, but if my father had not selected him, he would forever be seen as wanting and pathetic.

He was certainly not what brains-and-beauty Parvati Bhattacharjee could have commanded on the Calcutta marriage market. Small, dark, and nervous, he was frightened by my parents, and by the splendor of the marriage reception. His mother, who spoke no English, refused to come. His father worked on *The Statesman*, not as a writer, which would have been bad enough, but as something like a typesetter. A love-marriage was tragic enough, but even worse, Parvati was jumping the marriage queue. We had an older sister, and custom dictated that the first-born had to be the first married, even if she had not expressed an interest. Otherwise, we were sending a message to all the families in Calcutta with eligible sons that Dr. Bhattacharjee could not control his daughters. One of them, maybe two of them, had stepped out of line. What kind of husband would rise to such a challenge? She had to be pregnant, the rumors went. She wasn't.

In fairness to our father, Parvati had sent him no warnings, apart from her loneliness and longing to return home (which he considered a good sign that she wasn't partying and having fun) until the announcement itself. He had been resting, not interviewing potential families, not making shy inquiries of available sons, preferably boys with green cards or studying abroad on scholarship, not letting it be known in the clubs and boardrooms and at the parties that he was a father with three desirable daughters who would soon be sending signals. In fairness to Aurobindo, whatever success he achieved is, as my father likes to say, "sweat-of-brow" money.

I was sixteen and still living at home. Didi was twenty-two and living in New York and had found work "in the theater," although we knew from friends that she was selling tickets and handing out playbills off-Broadway. Her beauty, poise, and intelligence got her into parties. She now lives in Montclair, New Jersey, and is married to Harish Mehta, a non-Bengali businessman previously married, and with grown children. We chat once a month, and she always professes extreme happiness. And that, I realized on the morning that I was to call Parvati in Bombay, was all I knew of my oldest sister after she left Calcutta.

⋅ ⋅ ⋅

I'm bad at math, so I've settled on a simple formula for figuring out time differences between India and California. Parvati's dinner is my breakfast. When it's sunset on Rivoli Street, it's daybreak on Nepean Sea Road. Usually I call India. The rates don't seem as expensive when your income is in dollars rather than in rupees.

At least once a week I talk with Parvati in Bombay and about once a month with my parents in Rishikesh, a holy town on the banks of a holy river in Uttar Pradesh state, where they now live. As many times as I call them, I rarely have a clear agenda. I'm here, Rabi and I are safe and healthy, I say; so are we, they say. We recite what we've done and whom we've seen since the last call. We don't bring up what we're feeling or thinking, we especially don't divulge the three-o'clock-in-the-morning nightmares that startle us awake. Chronic depression runs in our family, passed on from mothers to daughters. To bring up the sudden sadnesses that shroud us is to play the blame game. The rules of our trans-continental relationships are intuited, never acknowledged. We accept that, given the international phone rates, our personal defeats are too banal to waste money on. The whole point of these phantom family reunions is to stop time to when we were the Bhattacharjee sisters of Ballygunge Park Road, three pretty virgins in pastel saris, three unfurling buds on a massive tropical tree. And so, until Chris Dey slithered into my San Francisco life, I'd readily conspired to string out our chatter for a half hour, keeping the confessions harmless, the voice cheery. We're all doing the usual things and seeing the same old people. Our sons are acing all their tests and quizzes. The gift you sent with so-and-so is exquisite. God's bounty has granted us health and peace.

My parents, devout Hindus with diseased bodies, have found serenity in their life of retirement in Rishikesh. We mention hypertension, diabetes, and arthritis only when I want to pass on a medical breakthrough or a drug recall I've learned of from CNN or MSNBC.

As for Parvati, if her life's boring or bleak, she spares me the details. I can't imagine her allowing herself chaotic emotions or running a disorderly household. In her Bombay flat each object has its rightful place. She doesn't waste time hunting in closets and drawers, as I seem to have to do, for basics such as needle and thread, spot remover, matches, scratch pads and postage stamps. No piled-up dirty dishes in her kitchen sink, even though she doesn't own a dishwasher, no wet towels on her bathroom floors, no beds left unmade, though she has three to four nuclear family members as houseguests almost every day of the year. The long-term houseguests are mostly Auro's relatives and family friends, modestly middle-class Bengalis from provincial towns. They are convinced, as is Auro, that they have earned the right to enjoy the sumptuous hospitality that God's grace, parents' sacrifice, neighbors' encouragement, and, of course, their "dear Auro's" diligence at universities in India and America and his masterful job performance in Bombay have finally produced. They come to Bombay to interview for jobs or to get Auro's advice on whether they should specialize in marketing or finance or human resources if they can get into an M.B.A. program. Or they come to Bombay to catch a flight overseas—to Frankfurt, London, New York, San Francisco—because, besides Bangladesh's Biman Air, how many international carriers deign to touch down in Calcutta? Forget flying out of smog-shrouded Delhi. Besides, Auro-da loves company and is a good, generous benefactor, a source of dollars and deutsche marks. Parvati jokes that she manages a hotel, not a home.

"They're taking advantage of you, Parvati-di," I once burst out on the phone. "Oh, I'm not complaining," was Parvati's snap response. "We have this great place that Auro's company pays for, so why not share it with my in-laws? How else are they going to ever see the inside of a Nepean Sea Road high-rise apartment? Anyway as long as Bholanath and Urmila-bai don't quit on me, I can avoid a physical breakdown!"

Bholanath is the live-in, Bengali cook that Auro enticed away from a Calcutta household, and Urmila-bai, the perky, thirtyish, live-in housekeeper. Urmila-bai isn't Bengali, but she was recommended to Auro by another Bengali tenant in the apartment building. Parvati also has a part-time cleaning man who doubles as dog walker for Rani and Raja, the two strays Parvati plucked off a public garbage dump and brought home ten years ago, and a full-time driver, Sunil, for her Fiat. Auro doesn't allow her to drive herself in Bombay's crazy traffic. If you cause a fatal accident in Bombay or Calcutta, you stand a good chance of getting lynched on the spot. The driver's salary is a necessary expense toward risk-containment.

That was the only time Parvati told me off, in her very indirect way. For all our Bhattacharjee family's snobby disapproval of Auro before the wedding, her marriage had proved to be more solid, her lifestyle more conspicuously luxurious than Didi's and mine. Tense, awkward Auro had managed to climb pretty close to the top of the corporate ladder and he'd done his climbing without neglecting his family.

,   ,   ,

For the angry call I had to make about her having given my address to a total stranger, I needed to catch Parvati at home, alone except for the domestic help, and undistracted by her homemaker duties. I aimed for her mid-morning so that Auro would have left for work and she'd have finished her bath and prayer rituals but not yet instructed the building's gate office over the intercom to page flat 15B's driver. The intercom is on the wall by the apartment's front door and the telephone—for the sake of privacy, I suppose—in the farthest back bedroom. I know from my twice-a-year stays with her that once she sends for the car to go on her daily shopping errands, she doesn't let a ringing phone hold her up. There was no way to calculate when she'd be back home. Auro's a picky eater, so Parvati makes her routine stops to her favorite Goan meat and poultry seller, Parsi baker, two or three freshwater fish vendors in the fish market, and half a dozen vegetable hawkers in the produce bazaar. Though she nags sweettooth Auro about his weight, she'd probably swing by the city's only store that flies in Bengali sweet-meats like mishti doi, raabri, rasamalai, and chom-chom from Calcutta. I'd also be wise to factor in the once-a-week run to the liquor store and the dry cleaners, maybe to the pharmacy and the tailor's shop, even the airport or the train station. Parvati's in-laws expect her to meet them when they arrive and to see them off when they leave.

I dialed Parvati's number, convinced—in fact, hoping—that

she wouldn't be home. Parvati answered on the first ring instead of the usual sixth. "Oh, it's you, Tara! You won't believe what's happening here! I thought it was the hospital! Or the police station!"

"Oh no, is Auro-da—"

"There was a robbery-murder in our building! Can you imagine that? I know it happens all the time in Delhi, but in our building? Just four floors down from us? Someone I see—I mean, saw—in the lift almost every day beaten to death with lead pipes? And poor Mrs. Sen is in surgery. She was stabbed in the chest and stomach!"

Parvati had introduced me to Mr. Sen, a Bengali, in the elevator a couple of years before, but all I could remember about him was that he had been wearing a showy coral and gold ring on his left thumb. Parvati had explained later that the ring had been given to Mr. Sen by a local saint who could make objects— fountain pens, gold chains, rings, watches—appear and disappear at will.

"The burglars ransacked the place. Cleaned out their Godrej safes. My housekeeper told me that the burglars made off with gold bars and stacks of cash as well as Mrs. Sen's gold jewelry."

"How does your housekeeper know about the ingots and the cash?"

"Because our housekeepers know everything about every household in this building. I call it the Support Staff Network. Besides, my Urmila-bai is a close friend of the Sens' housekeeper. They're cousins or something. I got Urmila-bai through Mrs. Sen."

"Didn't the Sens' housekeeper hear screams?"

"She slept through it all. She claims she didn't hear a thing. But my driver, who doesn't get on much with Urmila-bai, is sure the Sens' housekeeper was in on the job. *She* let the burglars in, he says. I don't know what or whom to believe. I don't know why such bad things are happening to decent people. I don't know anything anymore!"

When we were little, our maternal grandmother used to tell us the story of the village deity, Shitala, the goddess of smallpox and malaria. In a dream, Goddess Shitala visited a king named Virata, the brave, just, rich, honest, and benevolent ruler of a prosperous kingdom also named Virata. In King Virata's dream, the goddess demanded that he worship her and make offerings of goats and rams to her. In return, she would grant him a long life free of diseases. The king refused the goddess. So Shitala loosed an epidemic and destroyed the kingdom, turning it into one big cremation ground. Our grandmother had been a great believer in gods and goddesses talking to mortals through dreams, cautioning them not to get too uppity. She grew up before vaccination against smallpox became routine. That's why she could comfort herself with myth.

Parvati, hysterical, went on to the gruesome details of the break-in. Mrs. Sen had apparently thrown herself at the burglars' feet. She'd begged them to spare her husband's life but they had spat in her face. They'd chopped off Mr. Sen's right thumb for his coral ring. Then they'd forced Mrs. Sen to serve them a round of Johnny Walker Blue Label. They stabbed and slashed Mrs. Sen after they'd emptied the two Godrej safes.

I didn't try to comfort Parvati with the Shitala story from the old days on Ballygunge Park Road. I didn't bring up Chris Dey either.

* * *

We're sitting on the deck off the kitchen, Andy and I—Rabi's in Amsterdam for the weekend, with his father—eating a dinner of takeout Thai. The deck's not really a deck; it's more an unlawful extension of the landing of the wooden fire escape. It's a sturdy

deck. It will still be standing, Andy says, when the Big One hits.
The man I bought my condo from was a building contractor, not
an entirely honest one, I discovered, when I applied to the city for
permission to renovate my kitchen and was given a hard time
about raised ceilings, additional bathrooms, and two decks that
jut out too far. I paid for the former owner's misdemeanors.

"It's too cold out here," I grumble.

Andy looks up from the skewered shrimp he's been chewing
on. "You're kidding! It's October. That's summer out here."

"I'm going by body temp," I say. "I'm cold. I don't know why
anyone built a deck up here. It's always windy."

Andy moves on to the carton that has the squid salad. He's a
good eater.

"Or it's too foggy. To think I bought this place because of the
view!" The realtor had shown me the Rivoli Street wreck—"It's
beyond TLC," he had warned as we were going in—only so I
would prefer the fixer-upper high on Clarendon Avenue that was
next on his list and that he'd been talking up as the real bargain.
It had been a cold, gray afternoon, but I'd been in a brave, romantic
mood, determined to be a happy woman, and in that mood I'd
found the fog on the lopped-off tops of tall trees in the neighbors'
gardens enticing.

Andy sticks his chopsticks into a carton, fishes out a sliver of
chicken, and offers it to me. He avoids most meat, though the first
time I cooked for him, before I'd any idea I'd let him move in, he
ate my goat vindaloo and asked for seconds. "Open your mouth,"
he says, softly. He means to feed me the morsel. It's a lover's
gesture.

"Thanks, but I'm not hungry."

"Sweetie, you did the ordering." He drops the chicken piece
back in the carton and licks off the lemongrass sauce dripping
down his chopsticks.

There are four opened cartons and one still unopened on the plastic white table between us. "I guess I thought I was hungrier than I am."

"We need a log fire," he says. "A log fire to keep you warm."

"We don't have a fireplace."

"I'm going to build you a fireplace."

"I don't want to live through another renovation. Not even a small one, Andy."

He pushes his chair back. "What do you want from me?"

"I'll tell you when I know." I gather up the leftovers and am about to carry them into the kitchen when he stops me with a shout. "Hell, Tara, whatever it is, take care of it! Now. Don't make it my problem. I have enough shit of my own."

That's what I did, right then, leaving Andy on the deck to meditate in the deepening darkness. I called Parvati from the wall phone in the kitchen.

"Tara?" Parvati sounded concerned as soon as she heard my voice. "It hasn't been a week, has it? I've lost track of dates. You can't believe the tamasha that's going on in our building. We're moving crisis to crisis. Crazy business! Our Urmila-bai—"

I cut her off. "Parvati-di, how dare you give my address to Chris Dey? How dare you not warn me at least?"

"What're you talking about?"

"Don't act innocent. I grilled him."

"I have no idea what you're talking about, Tara. Are you okay? Is Rabi there with you? Can I talk to Rabi?"

"This man knew where you live, where Auro-da works, the boys' names, everything. He wasn't guessing."

"This man? Which man? Who, Tara? You sound bonkers, you really do!"

"Are you telling me you don't know anyone by the name of Christopher Dey?"

"A Christian Dey? Frankly, the only Dey who was Christian was that girl, Poppy, who was Padma-di's best friend in school. What did we used to call her behind her back? Beanstalk Poppy? No, I think it was Floppy Poppy. That's it, Floppy Poppy. Padma-di used to get so mad with us, remember?"

"Floppy Poppy had a brother—"

"Heartthrob Ron? Gosh, the man's aged, Tara. Remember how all us Loreto girls used to swoon over him? Even you, and you couldn't have been older than twelve!"

"So you admit that you've seen Ron Dey since the Calcutta days?"

"Tara, what is this? A cross-examination?"

"How would you know that Ron Dey has aged if you haven't seen him recently?"

"I've run into him at a couple of fund-raisers. Old Heartthrob's now a cancer doctor in Bombay. Minting money, I believe. He's tight with the NGOs, people say. That's where the real funds are these days. Foreign governments are behind all the nongovernmental organizations. Those NGOs are pouring money into their pet projects."

"This Chris Dey is Dr. Swarup Dey's son."

"Was that his name? Swarup? I didn't think he'd have an Indian first name. The sister didn't. Poppy was just Penelope."

"Chris carried a letter from his father. The letter was addressed to me."

"No, don't tell me what it said, Tara, let me guess. It said, Dear Mrs. Deep Pockets, my son has been admitted to medical school in San Francisco and I'm beseeching you, on the strength of our two families' enduring friendship, to make him feel he has a home away from home in your city, etcetera, etcetera. He's not asking you to put the son up, is he? No, Christians probably don't make those kinds of demands. That's more the style of our relatives."

"He wants me to help Chris find his mother."

"What!" She began to laugh. "This is too, too good. Tara, the amateur sleuth. Remember how we used to love Enid Blyton's the Five Find-Outers series. This is your big chance, little sister."

"Chris wants me to give him Didi's address."

"What! He wants to drop in on Padma-di so he can harass her too?" This time it was outrage. "The gall of the chap, whoever he is! How dare anyone have the audacity to insinuate that a Bhattacharjee daughter . . . I'd have set the dogs on him if he'd pulled that on me. I hope you called the police, Tara. The bloody cheek!"

"I served him tea."

"What does that mean?"

"He said you gave him my address."

"He's lying. I've never heard of this chap!"

"He said you told him that I would give him Didi's address."

"The man's a criminal, Tara. Or he's a loony. You must have figured that for yourself. No stranger strolls into your home and says, I'm the bastard child your family threw in the dustbin, and now I've come to claim my share of the patrimony, I mean, my matrimony."

"How did he find my San Francisco address if you didn't give it to him? People in India don't know about my divorce."

"That's what you think! We do our best to field questions, but everybody here knows everything. Except poor Mummy and Daddy. They don't ask; we don't bring it up."

I suddenly found myself weeping on the phone. It had to do with the quaintness of our calling Ma and Baba "Mummy" and "Daddy." Rabi thinks we sisters are pathetically clueless about colonial absurdities. He never calls me Mom, always Ma. He is a bright student in a private school known for its radical educational philosophy, alert to the politics of our everyday vocabulary. How can I explain to Rabi what I *feel* each time I say "Mummy" or "Daddy"? Chris Dey evaporates. I am back on Ballygunge Park Road, in a garden purple with jacaranda and scarlet with flame-of-the-forest trees, playing badminton, but not hard enough to get sweaty, while Mummy shoos away flies from a pyramid of wafer-thin green-chutney sandwiches and Daddy dozes over an open Agatha Christie.

Parvati's crying too. She's crying because she is hurt that I should have believed her capable of endangering me. Why, Tara?

Because I hate you guys? I still couldn't answer Rabi's questions.

"Finding an address on the Web is child's play. You know that, Tara. Even our Bombay bandits use computers to come up with names, addresses, financial info, you name it. They are so organized, it's scary. The cops know their M.O. They bribe a servant, get inside the flat, clean you out, and kill you if you get in the way. That's what happened in the poor Sens' case. The big gangs keep some policemen in their pay. The papers have hinted at it. The gang members are all from the minority community. Nobody can catch them because they slip across the border, then fly off to Dubai. The important thing is that you don't talk to this criminal fellow again. I'll have Auro e-mail you about what you must do next to protect Rabi and yourself. Auro's taught me not to trust anyone in Bombay. Rabi's probably their target. You should lay down the law to him. I don't care how American he is, he should never bring strangers into your flat without getting your okay. Promise?"

I promised. The conversation immediately turned pleasant, full of giggles, our jokes at everyone's expense. We caught up on children, on relatives. We ended with agreeing that it was the first serious talk we'd had as adults, that we hadn't avoided saying what we felt about each other. It seemed a sad and extraordinary admission. When I talked about it to Andy later that night, along with the new fears that Parvati had managed to awaken, I realized again how odd our family dynamics must appear, the fluctuating current of innocence and paranoia. Just when I thought I had lost all my old self-protectiveness and was looking out on the world with trust. Just when I thought I was adjusting so well to being a California Girl.

⸱ ⸱ ⸱

Rabi came back from his weekend in Amsterdam, happy. "He's a sport," he said of his father. From hints Rabi let drop, I assumed that Bish had caught him smoking pot and not made a fuss about it. Or Rabi had caught Bish in the red light district. The Bish I had been married to would have hit the roof. He used to rant to me about Chet Yee doing recreational drugs. "Chet's messing with his brain, the bloody idiot!"

Rabi's cheeriness was catching. We had a whole week of hot, dry weather, hot enough for Andy to barbecue on the deck and for me to need to cool off in shorts and a halter top. My raggedy backyard got more of my attention than it had in months. The desolate lawn turned bristly green, and flowering creepers speckled the weathered-dark wide planks of the garden fence with mauves and pinks. Andy bought us a secondhand piano, which he had to hoist up to my second-floor condo on pulleys and into the dining room through French doors because the front door's too narrow and the staircase too winding, and he threatened to compose a love song to me. I tamped down my natural paranoia and made a self-conscious effort to be happy.

Then, out of the blue one afternoon, while Andy was away on a job building wall-to-wall library shelves of cherry wood in Pacific Heights and Rabi was at tennis camp, I had the bad luck to catch a made-for-TV movie about a middle-aged woman giving up her job, selling her house, emptying her savings account, buying a pickup truck, and taking to the highway in search of the daughter she had given up for adoption within days of childbirth when she had been an unwed mother of sixteen. The TV mother was a Texan, the flashbacks to her love affair were set in the early forties. The TV father went off to war, not knowing about the pregnancy, and was killed in action off screen. The mother, young, poor, naïve, and rural, did what the doctor told her was best for her bastard infant, and hitched a ride to the nearest city. There were no parallels between the characters in the movie and my family. Why then did I suddenly remember the summer of 1974 when Daddy announced that that very week he was taking Didi to Switzerland to enroll her in a "finishing school." How Parvati and I had envied her the trip. Two other girls, a year ahead of her at Loreto House, had gone through a diploma course at some Swiss establishment and come back to Calcutta, speaking fluent French and smelling of unfamiliar perfumes. But Didi had acted resentful. She had refused to pack a bag for the trip, and Mummy, red-eyed from crying behind closed doors, had had to decide what saris Didi should take abroad with her.

*　*　*

When Rabi and I had visited Parvati in Bombay five years earlier, just after my divorce, we sat in the sea-facing bedroom we shared and looked down on the low surf and watched the tide rise and fall over the flat, black rocks, no sand, that passed for a beach. Fishermen had erected a city of reed-woven huts on the rocks. Children and dogs ran free. Women spread their washed saris on the rocks every morning and gathered them up in midafternoon before the tides rolled in. High tide reached to the opening of every hut. At night Parvati and I sat enjoying our our gin-and-limes by the wall-length window—Auro retired to his favorite chair with his business magazines and his single malt—while Rabi chortled through reruns of familiar shows like "Frasier" and "Seinfeld," and each of us was conscious that immediately below us hundreds of people lived on tide-time, in a tidal village, never looking up at the walls of glass that curled in an unbroken arc around the bay. Rabi wanted to go down to the rocks. The kids and dogs looked like they were having fun, he said, more fun than he was, anyway. I felt guilty about Rabi. I had failed Bish, and now I was failing Rabi. He didn't have his cousins to play with, because they were across the country in Calcutta for a month, visiting both sets of grandparents during their vacation from boarding school. I couldn't bear for Rabi to join his cousins in Calcutta—I needed Rabi, it was that selfishly simple—but I might have let him explore the rocks and the tidal pools.

"That's an outrageous idea!" Auro exploded when he got wind of Rabi's pleas. "Doesn't the boy understand he's not in San Francisco?" The housekeeper, Urmila-bai, added vivid warnings of what happened to high-rise residents of Nepean Sea Road wandering too close to the huts. The tide-people were smugglers and murderers, she said. They wouldn't think twice about cutting Rabi's throat. She had heard stories of hacked limbs washing up on the rocky beach at high tide. That was why the tide-people's dogs were fatter than the stray dogs on Nepean Sea Road. Even the police, she said, were afraid to patrol that part of the beach. Parvati scolded her housekeeper for wasting time making up silly stories about corpses and flesh-eating dogs. Then she scolded Rabi for being bored. "Why don't you play solitaire or something. If you look in Bhupesh's and Dinesh's cupboards, you'll find a bunch of board games. Do you like chess, Rabi? I could take Bhupesh's electronic chess set out of the Godrej cabinet for you."

Parvati wasn't scolding Rabi as much as she was criticizing me.

Hers were good Bengali boys, good Bombay boys, good students at elite English-language schools. To Auro and her, ten-year-old Rabi must have seemed a savage, a trust-fund American savage.

As sisters we were close, certainly closer than either of us was to Didi, but we didn't have a language for divorce and depression, which meant we couldn't fit in concepts like powerlessness and disappointment. We couldn't talk about why a young woman with everything she could ever want would decide to leave her protector and provider. I was, as always, debating a return to India—that was something we could discuss. I feared for Rabi, who would never fit in. A year before, he'd been living in the big Atherton house, behind the iron gates, attending a stiff little academy with other high-achieving, first-generation Silicon Valley kids. He had never seen me cry; he had never heard our fights. Now he was living with his mother in a nice condo in San Francisco, going to a freewheeling private school that seemed more like an extended playgroup than a learning environment, and he saw me crying all the time. "Stay as long as you like," Parvati and Auro both said, which probably meant, "Come back to India, our parents are getting old and weak and your child isn't American or Indian and if you stay there any longer, you won't be either." They thought my "American adventure" was over. I wondered if it was just beginning.

Parvati had had her one bold "adventure" five or six years before my postdivorce recuperative stay with her in Bombay. She had snatched Raja and Rani, mangy pups the size of a fist, from a nursing pariah-dog on the street outside their building and brought them inside to raise as house pets without asking Auro's permission. Auro had been furious. How dare she not have checked with him first? How could she, foolish woman, not realize that ticks and worms and God-only-knew what other parasites would crawl from the pups to Bhupesh and Dinesh? She had fought hard to keep the dogs. They would be good companions for the boys. With soaring crime rates, dog adoptions from the street had become quite common. Others in the building had done the same. When he, Auro, walked down the hallway to the elevator, didn't he hear snarls and loud crashes of neighbors' monster dogs, grown to muscular full height on owners' table scraps, throw themselves against the heavy, padlocked front doors of apartments? Auro had given in. In fact, he had come to care for the rescued puppies deeply, and for nearly a year he had walked them himself twice a day—before and after work—in the parking lot of the apartment building. The other tenants sent their dogs to the overcrowded street below with servants. Auro had persuaded the building's head gardener's out-of-work son, who came in once a day to water indoor plants, to take on the evening dog-walking chore only when he began to travel two to three days a week for his company. The housekeeper, who had at least one friend on each floor, volunteered for the dogs' morning round. In Bombay, there is no scooper law.

Raja and Rani bloomed like an irrigated desert on good food (cooked for them with mild spices by Bholanath the Bengali cook) and attention. They were pure white and longhaired, quite unusual for pariahs, and affectionate within the family, although never trainable. Raja means king, Rani queen. On the street they might have survived a year or two, at half their height and a quarter their weight, before traffic and disease bore them off.

They took to Rabi from the time they were puppies, but it wasn't until the trip to Bombay just after my divorce that they began sleeping at the foot of Rabi's bed. They must have sensed his loneliness. Rabi had bribed the housekeeper, Urmila-bai, with a couple of lipsticks stolen from me and with the promise of lessons in American English, into letting him walk the dogs in the morning. I didn't learn of the bribe until months later. At the time, watching Rabi lavish love on Raja and Rani, and watching the dogs reciprocate—by now sleek and strong as wolves—eased my guilt a little. For the dogs, the new arrangement meant racing in the park next door, exploring new neighborhoods. For Rabi, it was getting away from an overprotective Indian household. He looked forward to mornings. For the first time in his Indian travel experience, he said, the dogs made him feel like someone who belonged. India mightn't be so bad, with cable, a dog, and a cook who made prawn-mustard curries and spicy fish chops half as good as Bholanath's. People who passed him on the street saw just another boy walking his dogs. They said things to him in Hindi or Marathi that he didn't understand, but politely acknowledged nonetheless. No one could guess he was an English-only American on a visit to his Indian relatives. ("Oh, yes, they can," Parvati whispered in Bengali, another language he doesn't know.)

One evening at dinner as we lingered over tea, Rabi rose from the table and carried his plates back to the darkened kitchen. We weren't watching; he must have strayed close to the corner where Raja and Rani cached their separate hoards of table food. Suddenly, we heard a scream and the crash of plates and by the time we got to the kitchen the dogs were all over him, tearing at his arm, and his screams had turned convulsive. At the hospital that night after his arm had been treated and stitched, Aurobindo had to pay a bribe to the clerk who wrote the report, to keep the dogs from automatic destruction. Parvati stayed back with the dogs to soothe their nerves, fearing for their serenity after such excitement.

"We never enter the kitchen in the dark!" Parvati explained, and showed me a stitched-up gash on her leg where they had once attacked. Their massive heads lay on my sister's lap, big brown eyes full of submissive tenderness. She fed them bits of toast by hand. It was as though my son had attacked her dogs, and the dogs cried as long and loud as he did. The lesson was simple enough. It is the nature of pariahs to attack any movement in the dark; it is their nature to guard their food and the people who provide it, no more regrettable, but for this exception, than a snake or a tiger fulfilling its own destiny. My instinct would have been to destroy the beasts, the hellhounds; they had become anomalies, more dangerous than their slinking relatives on the street. The dogs effectively settled the issue of our permanent return to India.

Images from that disconcerting visit—Raja and Rani curled up, sleeping at Rabi's feet; self-protective street dogs sinking their fangs into Rabi's arm; the tide-people scavenging and scrambling on the stony, black beach—battered me when Parvati called in early November. Her words were rushed, her voice panicky.

"I want to apologize for any mean words I might have said to you, ever, ever in my life, Tara. You don't realize what's important, how precious your family is, how fast disaster can strike until you survive a phanra." She switched to Bengali in her agitation. Only God can snatch you out of death's grasp. She hoped with all her heart that just because I lived in America I hadn't stopped praying to Adya-Ma.

Adya-Ma had saved Auro and Parvati from being murdered in their beds. That's what would have happened if Adya-Ma, in Her all-knowingness, had not caused the water pipes to get suddenly, inexplicably rusty—rusty in a newish building, would you believe—and the water supply, therefore, to be temporarily shut off without the management's usual notice and apology to residents.

The day before, soon after Auro had left for the office around eight-thirty, Parvati had turned on the shower and discovered what the management had done. In a rage, she had lifted her bedroom phone to chew out the building supervisor, but found herself in the middle of an odd conversation in Marathi. "Bengalis don't resist," a woman was saying, "they are too soft and slack for that. It's thanks to the mounds of rice and fish they eat every day. Lunch and dinner, rice and fish, rice and fish. It's Sikhs and Marathis who give trouble. Bengalis are easy." The listener at the other end, judged by his snorts and laughs, had to be a male.

At first Parvati had assumed she was a victim of crossed lines somewhere in the building. That enraged her even more. Couldn't the management fix anything? Then she realized that she was eavesdropping on her own housekeeper. Urmila-bai was using the extension in Bhupesh's and Dinesh's room to flirt with some man. That was what upset Parvati. Was the housekeeper bringing lovers into the apartment, having sex on the bed in which she and Auro slept—or worse, in the boys' room . . . ?

"Thursday," the listener said.

"Madam leaves for Calcutta on Tuesday, saheb on Wednesday. Whole week, so no problem when. Wednesday, Thursday, Friday, all equally good."

"The cook?"

"A fish-and-rice eater. No problem."

"You'll poison the mongrels?"

She heard her housekeeper laugh. "Gladly," she said. "Glass or arsenic."

Parvati hadn't waited for more. She'd left the phone off the hook, grabbed Raja and Rani by their collars, and rushed out the front door in her bathrobe. She'd taken the servants' elevator, which was already at her floor, and run screaming into the manager's office on the ground floor. By the time the manager—Parvati described him as "a gutless dimwit"—sent a couple of security guards up to flat 15B, the housekeeper had disappeared. The fugitive had had just enough time to scoop up the watch, gold ring, and gold chain that Parvati had taken off and dumped on the dresser top in preparation for her shower.

Parvati's faith in God had been strengthened by the near-disaster, her wariness of human capacity for evil enlarged. The housekeeper was a thief, a murderer's accomplice.

I have lost my Indian radar. My mother used to enter in her little laundry book every shirt, sari, and pair of underwear sent out with the dhobi, and then check them off when the dhobi returned with the clothes, whacked clean, sun-dried, starched, ironed, folded, and stacked high inside a cloth bundle. The elaborate counting and checking was the final act in a quotidian drama, ending in payment. Nobody spoke of distrust when I was growing up. It was a given. My father used to stand at the counter of any shop, loudly re-adding every bill. He rechecked the waiters' calculations in restaurants, even fancy ones. He looked for mistakes when the driver filled up at the petrol pump. We lived in a culture of vigilance, not distrust.

In our first months in Palo Alto, Bish was the same. At least until he was told by a mean-mouthed cashier at a supermarket to back off and asked by a waiter at a Pizza Hut to take his business elsewhere. Bish never found a cheater, but I don't think he has given up his checking and rechecking. In America, he merely does it in his head. I'm afraid to question any bill that's presented to me.

I have no clear take on the vanished housekeeper. Was she a poor and desperate widow, a survivalist willing to cut moral corners? Or a woman besotted with love for a burglar? Or was she just another greedy, impatient consumer in the fast-changing India? Urmila-bai merges with the tide-people in my imagination. A titanium watch on her wrist, a thick, gold chain at her throat, and a sassy dash of color on her lips, she prowls the halls of seafacing high-rises in Bombay; she slips into nightmares.

Last February when I stopped overnight in Bombay on my way to find what remains of our ancestral village of Mishtigunj, Aurobindo and Parvati were mourning the death of one dog and the slowing down of the other. The vet ascribed the dogs' poor health to their malnourishment as pups. Rani was cremated. Her photo has been installed on a ledge in the vestibule to the prayer alcove. A fresh flower is placed in front of the framed photo every morning and an incense stick lit at dusk. Raja was lethargic. He slept most of the day, morose head resting on arthritic front paws, on a quilt outside the prayer alcove. Bombay was slower and more congested. The tidal village had spread on the black rocks, the huts of braided reeds made sturdier with bamboo poles, tin sheets, and waterproof canvas.

5

*A*ndy's Hungarian connections keep popping up in the strangest places. Usually he avoids them, often he shudders at the memories, but at other times, as though prompted by an inner voice, he practically embraces them. I know the feeling, I once told him. Anyone from his parents' village who got out in 1956 is called uncle, aunt, or cousin. (I know that, too.) It was Andy's father, a man usually described to me as lost, bitter, and withdrawn, who had organized the entire village's escape route and kept it secret from the authorities. Twenty families, grandparents down to babes-in-arms like Andy, poured into refugee buses parked inside the Austrian border. Happenstance brought the Karolyis to the United States, just as it took others to Australia and Canada.

It also brought various branches of the Petocz family, who actually had distant relatives in San Francisco. And so Andy's family followed the Petoczes to California. For a few years, Andy's father basked in the collective gratitude of the former villagers, and that, apparently, was enough. He remained a school janitor, while the others started branching out, especially old man Petocz.

The rumor was, on his last morning in Hungary old man Petocz had taken clippings from the vines he cultivated. He kept them alive, and he planted them in Napa soil when it was still possible for a few family members to pool their money and buy some land, back when Tokay grapes did not sit too heavily on the refined California palate. The old man lived to see his family established, his vines flourishing, and even to build a small winery. It was his son, the impeccably renamed Jason Peters, who was Andy's life-long friend.

Some weekends, Jason calls Andy for retrofit "consulting," shorthand for satisfying the tax man and celebrating an obscure anniversary in their collective pasts. The old language, the private wines, the comfort foods of home, the hot tub, the whole California good life. I understand all that.

That is why, one warm Saturday morning in November, Biker Girl Tara found herself on Andy's Suzuki and clinging to his soft leather jacket, heading to Yountville for a luxury weekend. Rabi had an Atherton father-visit, which would either be a reunion with some of his old schoolmates—boys he found now too programmed, too blazered, too tennisy, too Stanford-fixated (lord knows what they found him)—or Bish would turn it into a business/pleasure jaunt. These days, he's learned to take his family with him, or what remains of his family.

⁕ ⁕ ⁕

The Peters' winery-turned-country-inn rides like a cream-colored yacht high on a rolling green sea. Jason Peters lived up to his invented name: tanned, lean, elegantly graying—every inch the perfect Napa host, the Janos Petocz of his childhood nearly anagrammed away. ("I am what he was," Andy had said on the way up.) His wife was a blond Californian with no discernible ethnic roots. I can't help but think that if Bish declared himself, starting today, Bill Chatham, computer-geek California boy, people would still ask him, *But who are you, really?* They still do the same of me.

We were met with a light "morning wine" and a plate of heavier sweets. Horses were in the barn, the paths were well laid out, the groom on call. The tennis courts were open all day. What is there to fear, in such a life? If this was Andy's way of lifting the gloom, the cobwebs, the dithering of the past few days, I loved him for it.

This is the life I could afford; it's even the life I once expected. I could imagine any number of Atherton families, Bish's friends, coming here for the weekend, flooding the courts and riding paths, steaming away the hours in a hot tub, loving every precious minute and being loved in return by such a gracious host, but I could not imagine Bish enjoying it. I know I shouldn't be thinking of him, who only wanted me to look like a princess and live like a queen, not on a perfect day arranged by a man who's had to come so far to achieve these pleasures. Lavish spending in India, conspicuous luxury, we never thought twice about, but the same thing here makes me guilty. Maybe it's nothing more than seeing Andy in an unfamiliar setting, hearing him talk and laugh, and my not understanding a word. I'm feeling just a little alien and uncomfortable, a tinge of not-belonging, in the midst of such welcoming comfort and I think it must be the way Bish feels.

After a perfect day, the rides, the lunch, no tennis, but a nap, we even splashed around in the hot tub. Through the steam, Andy's big round face actually looks Asian; the Magyars really do come from the steppes. Through the bubbles, his words seemed less ominous. We were into the heavier afternoon wines. "Baby," he said, "I don't like what this thing is doing to you. You've got to step away from it, else you'll fall into it. You keep tugging at it, pretty soon you'll have nothing left."

I hung my head, a kind of submission, a kind of promise.

"When I say nothing, that includes us. The past is nice, this place is nice. It's nice to visit the past every now and then. Just don't live there."

Suppers came late at the Peters B&B. It was understood that the hours sandwiching the long and perfect sunsets were devoted to some kind of lost art of lovemaking. For what other reason do B&Bs exist? Country light and air are love; the bike ride, the wine and food are love; the horseback rides, the hot tubs—especially the hot tubs—are love; the various wines changing colors like mood rings, the king-size bed without creaking springs, the fluffy duvets, the long mirrors, the utter absence of clocks and radios and, in our case, even a television set, they are New World equivalents of a courtesan's chamber.

"See the grapes, they're so sweet from gathering the last of the summer sun that now they're ready to burst," Jason Peters had said that morning, plucking one for me, one for himself as we walked between the vines down to the riding stable. He invited me to crush it gently with my tongue, press it tenderly against my palate. It did burst, and I thought, sex is like that, the sudden flooding explosion, and I could see in a flash, in the little smile, that the very proper Jason Peters had read my mind. All too silly of me, of course, but it was a small private image I clung to during my ride, through lunch, and in the late afternoon hours, drowsy from wine and hot-tubbing.

Andy carried me to bed ("While I still can," he laughed, as weak and rubbery as Andy ever gets), and there we made love worthy of the setting. First, we had to recover from so much relaxation. Our bodies were still water-bound, still of the perfect twilight, we were too much in harmony with nature to feel much of anything for each other. That of course changed, we shivered, we again needed each other.

The two long-term lovers in my life are such opposites there are no points of comparison. Whatever one is, the other isn't. Andy isn't rushed, he isn't methodical, but sometimes his presence is a kind of absence. Sometimes I feel I should call him back. I never had to do that with Bish. Thousands of years of arranged marriages had somehow habituated us even before laying eyes on each other; there would be nothing in our sexuality that was, finally, exotic.

When intimacy first struck me as inevitable between Andy and me (long before it occurred to him, he said), I was intrigued, and just a little anxious about his size. This would be a selfish act, no hundreds of generations looking on in approval. We were exotics to each other, no familiar moves or rituals to fall back on. He interpreted my fear as shyness. He was not my first American lover, but he was twice the mass of any man I'd ever known, a bear-man, red-bearded, woolly armed, hairy-chested, gently spoken but, I was sure, given to violence. Something in me (and it's not hard to figure out where) responded to those incongruities. The Buddhism, the placidity, the meditative streak, and the brute force. With Andy, violence is a given: He was bred on it, he's yielded to it, and it nearly killed him. His search has been for softer ways, kinder speech, gentler company, and (he says) I am in possession of the best Andy ever, the final version in a series in reinventions. He hasn't raised his voice in anger or used his fists, or even his menacing bulk, in more than ten years.

In the early days he would show up for work on his big Suzuki, which he eventually stored in my garage (and which we rode to Napa), so I knew he'd been a biker, with all that implies. He still knew some of the central valley and Oakland Hell's Angels (not the Harley Club stockbrokers on weekend outings). When we're out together I've seen them, or him, flash a little thumbs-up signal, and frankly, it thrills me still.

　　　　　　　　　　　✓　　✓　　✓

There was a message waiting for me at school on Monday morning. Books I'd special-ordered for the first grade—I handle the "multicultural" acquisitions as a school volunteer—were being held for me at the bookstore down on the Haight.

I can't teach, lacking a certificate, but I donate time and money. The little kids are ninety percent Asian, Latino, and African-American, the teachers, at least during the two years that I have volunteered here, all European-Americans. The rhetoric of modern San Francisco makes me invisible. I am not "Asian," which is reserved for what in outdated textbooks used to be called "Oriental." I am all things. When the little kids climb on my lap to be read to, or just listened to, I don't think they see me as anything different from their parents, the school nurse, or their teachers.

I thrive on this invisibility. It frees me to make myself over, by the hour. In the last municipal election, it empowered me to canvass enthusiastically for a gay Chicano candidate running on his work in homeless shelters, needle exchanges, and AIDS screening. There is no explaining this collusion with the Other anywhere in my background. Yet I'm still too timid to feed my Ballygunge Park Road identity into the kitchen Garburetor. That dusty identity is as fixed as any specimen in a lepidopterist's glass case, confidently labeled by father's religion (Hindu), caste (Brahmin), subcaste (Kulin), mother-tongue (Bengali), place of birth (Calcutta), formative region of ancestral origin (Mishtigunj, East Bengal), education (postgraduate and professional), and social attitudes (conservative). Playing with the preschool children who teach me nursery rhymes in languages I don't speak or inside the bookstore on Haight Street where I immerse myself in heavy tomes on history of science or cosmology, I feel not just invisible but *heroically* invisible, a border-crashing claimant of all people's legacies.

✦   ✦   ✦

The moment I step outside the bookstore on to crowded Haight Street, I lose the heady kinship with the world that I feel through my reading. Nobody pays attention to me other than to ask for spare change or press a handbill into my closed fist. I am not the only blue-jeaned woman with a Pashmina shawl around my shoulders and broken-down running shoes on my feet. I am not the only Indian on the block. All the same, I stand out, I'm convinced. I don't belong here, despite my political leanings; worse, I don't want to belong.

Tourist buses, mostly German and Japanese, still stop at Haight-Ashbury to take pictures of the street sign and of hippies. The free spirits, the revolutionaries, the flower-children dropouts, have grown up, grown old, maybe grown bitter. The tourists snap away all the same. The street people pose, often profanely, and scrounge for money. Andy, who keeps shocking me with little disclosures of his pre-Buddhist youth, spent "sweet times," he says, on the Haight thirty years ago. "More a digger than a hippie," he says, a distinction I'm unlikely to be able to clarify. To me, they are a small army of America's untouchables, a mockery of everything immigrant behavior stands for. For every Bish Chatterjee and Chet Yee there's a cluster of green-haired waifs with pit bulls outside the new kiddy Gap and Starbuck's, begging for cigarettes and drug money. I feel guilt and sorrow when I walk past them, but a few blocks later, rage takes over. Their marginality is rooted in a deep and profound ownership that I will never know. The families in Atherton who worked their way to the big houses behind iron gates and posted guards could lose it all in a minute.

That Monday morning I came out of the bookstore, head high,

feeling an unfamiliar solidarity with the Atherton community I had abandoned. There were the usual squatters, passed-out drunks, cart-pushers, shopkeepers on smoke break, window-shoppers, camera-loaded gawkers, when I registered an Indian man in a Giants baseball cap and a dirty down vest across the street, chatting up three young girls in net stockings and vintage dresses. They were standing outside a restaurant. I knew the man was Indian not long out of India from the cut and cloth of his slacks, and from the way he was holding his cigarette, pinched between the thumb and index finger of his right hand. But he didn't have the watchful posture of food handlers or sales assistants without visas and work permits. The girls cadged cigarettes from him. He showed them, one by one, how to hold the cigarette his way, and in doing so, he managed to get in long, crude strokes and squeezes. I watched those molesting hands, shocked, fascinated. In Calcutta, a man brushing up against a woman in a rush-hour bus or tram might cause a riot.

Then I saw Rabi, heavy school bag on one shoulder, amble out of the restaurant with a cardboard tray of takeout coffees and join the group. The Indian man reached, grinning, for a coffee cup. Rabi swapped the baseball cap for the coffees. That's when shock made me dart back inside the bookstore. Chris Dey. If Andy had asked me to describe Chris Dey's features last weekend in Napa, I don't think I could have. Seeing Rabi at ease with the man, I was sure it was Chris Dey. Come to think of it, wasn't that down vest Rabi's? How often had Rabi met this man in secret? Hell is doubting your children. Shock, shame, rage: I didn't know what I felt, what I *should* have felt. I rushed out of the bookstore to confront Rabi. By the time I crossed the Haight, waiting for the tourist buses to pass, two of the three girls were still there, but not Rabi or the lecher. The girls were sitting on the curb, baby-faced panhandlers with smudged mascara, holding out their empty coffee cups.

"Hey, lady, how about a dollar for a beer?"

I turned away. If I'd had a daughter instead of a son, maybe we could have sat down and cried together about my naïveté and my neuroses, my failures and my recklessness, and we might have concluded that her father had tried to be the best husband and father he knew to be.

"Kiss my ass, lady," someone shouted.

I spent the afternoon at home, dreading Rabi's return, and angry that he hadn't yet. I envied Parvati's clarity and confidence. She would have known how to tackle a truant son. But then I couldn't imagine either Bhupesh or Dinesh hanging out in an unseemly neighborhood of Bombay. Should I risk a messy confrontation? Should I make it easier on both of us by pretending I hadn't spied on him on Haight Street? Confide in Bish and let him handle the problem? Did I dare tell Bish that our one and only child was playing hooky?

This was Andy's world, but it was Bish I would rather have called.

·   ·   ·

When Bish and I first arrived at Stanford as a young married couple, he wanted me to work in the library, then join him (though, like most Bengali women, I didn't drink liquor, beer, or wine) at the student pub. I sat at a long table with other Asian engineering students, sometimes with their girlfriends and wives, none of them Indian, and their sheer brilliance inflamed me. This is the life I've been waiting for, I thought, the liberating promise of marriage and travel and the wider world. Bless Daddy and Mummy, they found me the only man in the world who could transport me from the enchanted garden of Ballygunge to Stanford University in the early 1980s, which has to count as one of the intellectual wonders of the modern world. I was just a teenager trained to be adoring, sitting in a California bar with the most brilliant boys in the world, listening to ideas that would shape the twenty-first century. That's all.

(I've since learned from some of those young men, since my divorce, and in some cases—but not all—before theirs, that it was my presence that had inflamed them.)

When I left Bish (let us be clear on this) after a decade of marriage, it was because the promise of life as an American wife was not being fulfilled. I wanted to drive, but where would I go? I wanted to work, but would people think that Bish Chatterjee couldn't support his wife? In his Atherton years, as he became better known on the American scene—a player, an adviser, a pundit—he also became, at home, more of a traditional Indian. He was spending fifteen hours a day in the office, sometimes longer.

He was in demand as a speaker, in Boston, New York, Tokyo, Taiwan, Malaysia, Manila, but I couldn't travel with an infant. My world was Atherton, and the two weeks we spent each winter in Calcutta visiting his parents—with a few side visits to mine—and the arrival-and-departure nights in Bombay with Parvati. In India, he was even more the Indian husband, showing off for his mother, perhaps, how well-trained this upper-class Ballygunge girl had become, what a good cook, what an attentive wife and daughter-in-law. What a bright and obedient boy she was raising. I wanted to take courses in the local community college, but we had a child at home.

There was a group of young Indian wives with children in playschool, one of whom, Meena Melwani, a Sindhi from Bombay, had a car and no domestic resistance to using it. It's true, one of our children could have choked on a toy or fallen from the jungle gym and no one would have been home to receive the body, but we took the chance. Those were delicious little sabbaticals from conscience, driving out to the beach or to the open fields south of San Jose, into the mountains, or simply walking through the Galerias and eating burritos in the Mexican food courts.

Meena read the American magazines, and she would quiz us as we ate: *Does your husband know how to satisfy you?* ("First time I have heard 'husband' and 'satisfy' in the same sentence," giggled one of us.) *Are you his breakfast, his snack, the main course—or the dessert?* ("Definitely his Alka-Seltzer!" we giggled again. These American magazines and American marriages were not geared to the lives we led.) *Do women marry the best lovers they ever had?* ("I think, unfortunately, we can all say yes.")

Those magazines encouraged women to talk over their problems, to share their disappointments, to experiment with hair color, sexual positions, and pointedly meaningless one-night stands. We read them with the same guilty pleasure as we'd read movie magazines, in our bedrooms, under the fans, back in India. In America, it seemed to us, every woman was expected to create her own scandal, be the center of her own tangled love nest.

We studied the breezy advice given in those columns, but how could we apply it to our experiences and situations? The magazines weren't writing about us or for us. What did they care about us?

Soon after Bish and I got married, his mother had taken me, still in my Benarasi sari and marriage gold, so that I could pay my respects to a bedridden uncle-in-law. I never learned his name. He was an emaciated figure in a fetal position. I was expected to touch the feet in the gesture of obeisance we call pronam, "taking the dust off an elder's feet," which I did. I could have been touching wood. His wife, an exhausted-looking woman in her early fifties, explained that he had Parkinson's. She said, "He has become a statue. His mind is trapped in a body made of stone." My mother-in-law said, "You are providing all of us married women a shining example of wifely service." Turning to me, she added, "She holds the bedpan under him. She cleans him with her own hands. And she has a master's degree from the Delhi School of Economics. How many modern girls are prepared to do that?"

I might have enjoyed talking to someone. Someone like Meena

Melwani. All that mad giggling wasn't just amusement at American absurdity, all that selfishness and self-involvement we'd been warned against—but over our innocence. I will take with me to the grave my first married-woman question to Bish, the night of consummation. The evidence of my virginity was soaking in the bathtub. "Where did you put the stick?" I asked him, "I'll wash it at the same time." "What stick?" he asked. "The broomstick, the stick you used to, you know . . ." and when he finally understood my confusion he pulled this smooth, pale, tapered little thing out of his pajama bottoms and for the first time, I saw it. It was not the hot, cable-like thing I'd felt during the night tearing away and finally breaking through. This little thing was not capable of causing all that burning and all that blood. "Keep watching it," and I did, as he peeled off my sari. I thought he was the most extraordinary magician, surely no man in the world could perform such a transformation. I must be the luckiest woman alive. All I had to do was touch it, any time I wanted, or just look at him in a certain way whenever he was certain we were alone, and he would turn from the carefully dressed, oiled-haired, well-behaved engineer into something controlled from down below.

How could I have been put in charge of a man like that? How can I admit that I knew so little, that Ballygunge Park Road had left me so unprepared?

Poor Rabi. I am not worthy to raise a son.

In my Atherton life, the mall was where I was at my boldest. I felt pretty and predatory; I sensed come-ons in casual stares. I wasn't Bish's wife; I was a mall siren. One time Meena Melwani and I were perched on bar stools at a coffee shop, sipping cappuccinos and entertaining each other with caricatured sketches of bridegroom candidates whom, on our behalf but without consulting us, our parents had rejected when an American woman—a very stylish woman in all black, and I mean, jet black hair, black tee, black suit, blackish-purple lipstick—broke into our conversation with a "Those eyes, ladies! Those cheek bones! You've got great faces. Both of you." She introduced herself as a casting director and reeled off names of film directors she had worked with. They must have been famous in the film business. Bish wasn't a film buff, which meant I rarely went to the movies. I could tell from Meena's put-on smile that she hadn't recognized any name either. But she had lit up at the compliment. I was relieved, too. The woman had been staring at us from her table for quite a while.

"I couldn't help noticing how you two just fill up the space here," the woman went on. "I mean that in a good way, you command attention." She took her business card out of her pocketbook. Would we consider auditioning for the part of a featured extra the next morning? The film called for an Indian motel owner in the Tenderloin. We wouldn't have to learn lines. There'd be some money. Seventy-five dollars was the figure that was mentioned.

"You have charisma," the woman said to both of us, but handed her card to me. She told us where and when to show up if we were interested.

"My husband would kill me," Meena said, smiling.

I clutched the card. "Do you think I could act?"

"You won't know unless you try out, will you? Many are called, few are chosen. Ciao, ladies!"

After the woman left, Meena said, "She was trying to pick us up. That's what this was all about, I bet." As it turned out, Meena Melwani was the only woman in our little subcommunity of South Asian Wives of Silicon Valley to walk out on her husband and son for another woman; in her case, her Guatemalan cleaning woman.

I didn't show up for the audition, but I kept that card for years, sometimes feeling that the casting director with the dyed black hair held the only key that could possibly fit my complicated lock.

Eventually it and my address book with all my early addresses were lost in a purse snatching.

'   '   '

Rabi goes to a private school. On the walk back to Rivoli Street, I called the school, pretending I had an urgent message to deliver. I would have to get him on his cell phone, the principal's assistant advised. His class had gone to SFMOMA for an exhibition of Impressionist paintings. The curator himself had given a lecture. The students had then gone to Yerba Buena Gardens after the tour and lecture and painted in the Impressionist manner.

If the school official was right, he could not have been on the Haight in the middle of the day. But I *had* spotted Rabi outside a grungy coffee shop. Rabi with Chris Dey. I was sure it was Rabi. Doubles only exist in made-for-TV dramas.

When I got home, the answering machine had four stored messages for me to deal with. I hate listening to messages, maybe because I didn't grow up with answering machines. The blinking red light stirs up panic. I expect bad news to come in phone calls. E-mail is different. I love e-mail. Thanks to Bish, I've got to thinking of e-mail as the most natural way to communicate. It's a lot easier than talking. I wished I could confront Rabi by e-mail instead of in person. I pressed MESSAGES halfheartedly. There was a slight chance Rabi had called in.

Message 1: "Hi, this is Mandy. Hope you're free for dinner three weeks from today. Kevin's giving me a to-die-for birthday present. That's Kevin Drummond, *the* Kevin of Kevin's Kitchen on Mission. He's going to close the place early, so I can cook a genuine restaurant dinner for fourteen with him as my kitchen slave. Oh, and is Andy still in the picture? I'm thinking place-settings, not nasty heartache. Ciao!"

Mandy Dubin's three-year-old boy and four-year-old girl attended the preschool where I help out two mornings a week. They're in private school now. Mandy likes anything and anyone connected with India. Her India, the backpacker's India, feels as remote, as alien, as Mars.

Message 2: "Your prescription refill is ready, your prescription refill is ready." . . . That was Walgreen's, talking Fioricet.

Message 3: "Hi Babe! Just sending shanti vibes your way." Andy, of course.

Message 4: "Tara? This is Beth Young from the school. I have a favor to ask. It's about Nafisa's mother. I happened to be in the front hall when the woman dropped Nafisa off this morning. I'm not sure I know what I'm asking you to do. The thing is that the woman had a very nasty bruise on her face. Smells like domestic abuse to me. I wonder if . . . she might talk to you, you know, open up to you. We can direct her to the right agencies. Do you speak the same dialect? Anyway, it's just a thought. Until Tuesday."

Nafisa's mother and I don't speak the same dialect. We don't even speak the same language. I am tired of explaining India to Americans. I am sick of feeling an alien. Worse, I hate myself for being irritated with Beth. With dear, concerned-about-other-women's welfare Beth. The kids at the preschool adore her. She's the youngest teacher there, and the only one who brings her dogs to school. Two big, drooling, goofy Lab mixes.

No word from Rabi.

Didn't I have a mother's right to be reassured? So I let myself into his room. Nothing seemed ominous. No pot paraphernalia that I recognized, no weapons, no dirty magazines. There were posters on one wall; rock stars, I assumed. The top CD on a stack by the expensive music system that Bish had given him for his thirteenth birthday was of some girl band called the Go-Go's. The only surprise was a picture of Julia Child thumbtacked to his cork bulletin board. He must have torn the picture out of one of the four food and wine magazines I subscribe to but never finish reading. Bish would be more ashamed of a son who knew his way around the family kitchen than one who stashed pornographic magazines under the bed.

Rabi came home around four-thirty. He carried a poster tube and a small sack from the SFMOMA gift shop as well as his book bag. While waiting for him I had decided not to bring up having spied on him on Haight Street, but I heard myself say, "Don't you ever dare talk to Chris Dey again!"

Rabi rolled his eyes and took a deep breath.

"You heard me, Rabi. That man's dangerous!"

He extracted a Kandinsky coffee mug from the gift shop sack and presented it to me with a flourish. "Love it?" Then he pulled an Impressionist rendering of the Metreon Center out of the tube. "It sort of speaks to me," he said.

I felt foolish. Had paranoia made me hallucinate? I blamed Parvati for my putting harmless sights in an alarmist context. "Darling," I said, "we have to talk."

Rabi dropped himself heavily on an ottoman across the coffee table from me, stretched his legs straight out. It is Rabi's personal posture of defiance, and he was adopting it even before I could ask a question.

"Look, Rabi, I know you're going through a rough time."

"What rough time?"

I wanted to say, son, help me compute the effect on you of our not-quite belonging. If only we were one of thousands, grazing placidly in the middle of a vast herd, protected by our markings. I've strayed to the edge of the herd where the grass is tall and the predators are hidden. "I'm not saying I'm not to blame, Rabi."

"What's your point, Ma?"

"I had to pick up some books at The Booksmith today. When I came out of the store, I saw you. Around lunchtime. You were having coffee."

Rabi cupped his forehead in his hands. "Bad timing," he groaned, without looking at me.

"You were having coffee with . . . friends."

"I'm not allowed to have friends?"

"That man you were with is dangerous. I don't want that man in this house. I don't want you meeting him behind my back. I'm dead serious, Rabi."

"Isn't family a big Indian thing?"

"That man isn't family!" I exploded.

"Are you sure?" Rabi smirked. "Have you talked to Padma-mashi in New Jersey?"

"I spoke to Parvati-mashi last night. That man's a crook!"

"Oh, everyone's a liar and a crook except the perfect Bhatta-charjee sisters."

The smirk again. *He hates us,* I realized. *I am not exempt from his hate.*

"Do you want my opinion?" Rabi continued. "What you should be doing instead of grilling me and calling Chris a liar is phoning the biggest liar of them all, and that's Chris's mother."

"I don't know who that man's mother is, and I don't want to know!" I snapped. "What I do want to know is why you skipped school today."

He shook his head. "Why are you playing this charade? Why don't you phone Padma-mashi. It's not that late in New Jersey."

I picked up the coffee mug he had brought me, "When did you buy this thing? Not today, I bet."

Rabi grabbed the mug out of my hand. "I went on the school

trip, then I left early. I lied to the teacher, okay? I told him I was feeling real sick and wanted to get home. The schmuck let me. Satisfied?" Then he hurled the mug against the far wall and began a rant. "I can't believe you're treating *Chris* like a liar and a criminal. You've decided he is the liar because you called all the way over to Bombay to talk to your lying bitch of a sister—don't shush me, Ma, I'll call her that as long as I live. I'm getting to know you real well, Ma. You'll believe anything *she* says, and you'll play along with the big bitch's cover-up and she won't lift a finger to help him. Who's going to give Chris the benefit of the doubt? He's the wrong religion for you guys and he's the wrong fucking caste for the great Bhattacharjee family, and now you want to get him deported—he knows you won't stop till you've destroyed him. Parking him in an orphanage isn't enough, is it? You'd like to flush him down the toilet like some piece of shit that stuck to your shoe, wouldn't you, but he's not going away."

He stormed out of the room, took the steep, creaky stairs two at a time, and left the house, slamming the front door so hard behind him that he probably didn't hear my plaintive, "Rabi, wear something warmer. Please don't do this to me." Either he hadn't heard or he was through with my flawed mothering. It's the dog bite. He won't forgive her.

I swept up the broken china, and punched Andy's pager number.

Rabi wasn't gone that long, I suppose, but while he was, I became the one slouched in the chair with my legs stretched out. I was howling in a way I had not since childhood. I didn't hide my pain; I couldn't have, even if I had wanted to. During the last couple of years of my marriage I had learned to cry silently, in rooms where no one would follow me.

I let Rabi pull me up from the chair and guide me to the bedroom.

Andy came home at eight o'clock. Of course, I had forgotten his Meditations, one afternoon and one evening a week. He could read the signs: the dark bedroom, the early hour, and the shuddering breath. I was still dressed. I cry too easily and once I start, I can't stop. Everything is collapsing, there's no one to stop it, and no one to save me, no one cares.

Andy laid his hand on my forehead; either I was hot, or he was freezing. "First thing we're going to do is cool down," he whispered.

"I'm scared," I said. I didn't open my eyes. In a few seconds, I felt a soggy washcloth over my forehead and eyelids. Andy was trying to help, and I was grateful that he was trying. From the sounds in the bedroom, I could tell Andy was unlacing the leather thongs of his work boots, then peeling off his thick knit socks. Water from the washcloth dripped uncomfortably down the sides of my throat on to the pillow.

Andy joined me in bed. His weight on the mattress pitched me against his side. I smelled incense mixed with sweat. The brave smells of my "American adventure"; that was Parvati's wry term for whatever Andy and I had going. Bish would have smelled of . . . what else, besides sandalwood soap and Listerine?

"Let it go," Andy said.

"You mean, not discipline Rabi?"

"No, the toxicity. It's in your body. It has to be expelled."

"I should call his father. Bish would know how to handle him."

Andy snorted. "He needs to be left alone." I felt his knuckles press deep into the small of my back. "And you need a deep tissue massage."

He talked about himself as he worked my whole back. He had been fifteen, Rabi's age, when he left home. Home had been a rented place in South San Francisco. No reason why he had run away from home. He had made straight for the Haight, where else? It hadn't been that tough on the street. He had scored, done drugs, heard great music, man, the best.

I didn't mention the check I'd had Wesley Chang run on him at Bish's urging. Why spoil Andy's nostalgia with reminders of arrest sheets?

He worked his toxicity-expulsion magic on my shoulder blades, then he turned me gently over to face him. "If Rabi had any guts, he would run away," he said, playing with my breasts.

I snatched the wet rag of a washcloth off my eyes. "What're you talking about?" I gasped before I could stop myself. "We're not that kind of a family! Boys from good Indian families don't run away!"

Andy was in a zone, talking to himself. "He's on the edge, babe. All this fighting is just piffle and puffle. That's what thirty years working construction has taught me: It's piffle and puffle. I fix the piffles and I look for the puffles. "A PIFL is a Previously Identified Fault Line." Someone calls me to retrofit his house, I bring all the slide studies and everything I've added to them, and say, 'You're sitting on a piffle, my friend. Here's how we correct it, here's what it will cost you, and here's what I can guarantee.' " A PUFL, a Previously Unidentified Fault Line, is a killer. "I walk around the place, I walk up and down the street, I go inside, I study cracks in the sidewalk, I do some ultrasound on his foundation, I run a soil analysis, and I have to tell him, 'You're not safe, but I can't tell you where it's going to come from or how strong it's going to be, or how I should try to protect you. I just know it's out there.' "

He sat up suddenly, staring down at me. "The scar that Rabi has on his arm. That scar's a piffle. It's gone and it can't come back. He should wear it proudly, which is what he's trying to do. Tara, sweetie, put all that Calcutta shit to rest. Your marriage is over. Growing up like a princess is over. They're cold faults, understand? You've got to separate what's over and gone from what's still out there."

"That's what I'm trying to do," I said.

Calling the East Coast is always a nuisance. By the time I get home and make supper, it's already too late. To reach New York early in the morning requires getting up at four o'clock. It's easier to call India than New York, and I have more to say to Parvati even when she's got family members hanging from her like caterpillars on a tree, than I do to Didi, who lives in the same country. My middle sister suffers an excess of engagement with her world and mine, but Didi has beat a wondrous retreat from everything around her.

The logical time to call her is Sunday afternoon. Even then, she is rarely at home, which forces me to make small-talk with Harish, which is to say, empty blather spread over ritual inanity. Our sister act sets off Rabi's anger like nothing else. He promises me some day to write a play about two Indian sisters on the telephone. While they promise to support each other through the bad times and to share the good, to visit and to travel, they deny any problems in their own lives but point out the flaws in everyone else's. Their children are brilliant and loving and well behaved but everyone else's are selfish little monsters. Their husbands are faithful and successful while everyone else's scandalize the community. His play will show the Indian family as a turgid Ganges of hypocrisy. Sooner or later, everything empties into it. It carries the swill and stench of repression, it pollutes everything it touches, and still, people plunge into it for purification. Where he sees evil incarnate, I see—on my good days—high comedy.

I have never visited Didi in New Jersey, nor has she come to me in California, even when I was mistress of the gated home, and Bish would have gladly driven us to his favorite Napa vineyards. We sometimes meet in a restaurant or my hotel when I'm in New York. The idea that I should have a sister within a hundred miles of the city and be forced to stay in a hotel is unimaginable in our culture, but somehow I've never found it bizarre.

She lives in Upper Montclair, New Jersey, in a nice part of a nice town with many Indians in the neighborhood. She and Harish socialize almost exclusively with Indians. In the nearly twenty-five years that she has been in the United States, she has become more Indian than when she left Calcutta. She is a "multicultural performance artist" for local schools and community centers, staging Indian mythological evenings, with readings, slide shows, recitations, and musical accompaniment.

The gap between youngest daughter and oldest, the disparity of our marriages and the paths our immigration have taken, have made us strangers. Her reaction to my divorce (that I had brought shame to the Bhattacharjee family had been her refrain) had hurt. We don't call or write each other often. Occasionally she sends me reviews from suburban newspapers of an "exotic evening with Padma Mehta." People confuse her with Zubin Mehta and all the other famous Mehtas in New York. She gets credit for writing books and directing films but even greater credit for graciously disclaiming her accomplishments. It's a nuisance, she admitted to me, but no one can pronounce Bhattacharjee. She's on the invitation list when Indian dignitaries arrive for UN functions, or Hindi film stars give a New York concert, and I've sometimes spotted her among the glitterati on the Indo-American television channels that play in California on Saturday morning. Harish never seems to accompany her.

And so, I dither. Only Didi knows the truth, but I don't know how to ask her for it or if I can trust her answer, or even, after so many years of denial, if she knows it herself. "Go ahead, call," Andy urges, and Rabi picks it up, "Yeah, Ma, call," even though it is past midnight in Upper Montclair. And so I call, wait the four rings, and hear Didi's cheery voice, "I'm *really* sorry I cannot come to the phone. Please don't think me rude for relying on a machine, but Harish and Padma Mehta are not available to take your call. Please consult your local papers for the next performance of *Gitanjali* in words and music."

Didi, I have an urgent question for you. I know it's late, but please pick up if you are home. Or call me in the morning—I'm three hours behind you—or tomorrow evening after eight o'clock your time. Everyone is well; there are no health emergencies.

She did not call in the morning, and no messages were left during the day. A courier packet had been left, however, from Mrs. Parvati Banerji, in Bombay.

6

Dearest Tara,

I always thought that you and I were so close that we could guess each other's thoughts. Remember how we would answer questions out loud that we hadn't actually asked? And how mad Didi would get because she assumed we were ganging up on her? But after your phone call yesterday, I feel an estrangement has settled around us. I cannot fathom what is going on in your life to force you to make such a bizarre request. Do you have any idea how mad you sound? Maybe you have lost touch with the way things work here, in which case I think you need a good long Indian vacation away from all those crazy soap operas that keep putting bad ideas into susceptible minds. With everything that's going on in your country I have no doubt that strange behaviour rubs off even on very sane and decent people. There is no question, absolutely no question at all, about following up on you know what.

Did you really think I could be so direct as to approach the person you mentioned and ask him the question you're so desperate to find out? Have you become so American that you don't realize how absurd your request is? We don't even mention your divorce to friends and relatives here. I don't mean that we lie, or that we are ashamed of anything, but we don't let the wrong questions come up. When Auntie Bandana asks about your husband, we tell the truth about how well he is doing and how well you are doing and what a sweet brilliant boy Rabi is, but we don't let on that Bishwa-da and you are leading parallel happy lives.

·I don't feel comfortable writing about this matter. How do we know that an unscrupulous person, I'm thinking of that orphanage-raised chap who showed up out of the blue at your door (the nerve!), won't get hold of our letters somehow and misuse them? (This courier service is supposed to be very reliable.)

Evasion isn't the same as lying—I think we learned that in convent school. If we didn't learn it from the nuns, we were forced to learn it as the Golden Rule of Family Life. Remember Uncle Import-Export, and the sacks of peppercorns he kept on the balcony of his second-floor flat for twenty years all because some Englishman told him he might have a use for spices? No one ever asked Uncle when he intended to move the smelly sacks or sell them at a loss or just plain get rid of them by dumping them in the Hughli River. Taj Mahal Exports (Calcutta) Ltd.! Remember that? Daddy had to buy a brass signpost for Uncle to hang from his balcony railing and then Mummy had to bribe Uncle's servant's son to polish it every morning?

I prefer that we talk on the phone. It's too expensive for me to call you from here, so you'll have to call me. I don't even have space enough to write. Right now we have Auntie Bandana's daughter, Ruby, whom I'm sure you remember from vacations in Darjeeling, and Subodh, her husband, and their baby son. They had some worries about him since he was born prematurely, but he seems lusty enough now. They're off to America next week, where Subodh is starting work in Chicago. When you call, remember that the time difference is about thirteen and a half hours—I don't know about your daylight savings stuff. I love our new heart-to-heart talks. We all have our worries, but at least I have a houseful of relatives to share them with. I worry about you all alone in San Francisco. Especially with that criminal fellow bothering you. I never met that man. Please get that straight. What I don't understand is what's prompting you to dig into other people's pasts. Let sleeping dogs lie, etc. You don't want to end up hurting anyone, however accidentally.

(next day)

If Didi ever fell for Poppy's brother, it was probably all in her head. I'm sure you remember how we used to tease her for falling in and out of love constantly with guys she had seen at school dances but never spoken to? There was a song they used to play on Radio Ceylon called "Love Potion Number Nine" and I would hum it under my breath at dinner and she'd get so mad she'd throw her serviette on the floor and Mummy would make her drink her milk without Bournevita. But secretly, I think we used to envy her for being such a romantic. She didn't get those top marks, remember, because she was always "wool-gathering," the nuns said, which used to make me laugh. (Can you imagine Mother John Michael gathering wool? She could barely bend over to gather the eraser.) Didi was going to be some great and glorious this or that, while we just stuck our noses to the grindstone and behaved like insufferable little goody two-shoes. (Well, I speak for myself.)

The puzzle you should be solving is how a romantic like her ended up with such a nonentity as Harish. He's at least twenty years older, and he was no bargain even in his prime, if he ever had one. Okay, that's cruel. The fact is, you're the only one of us who got the full Bengali marital treatment, and look what happened. I'm not questioning what any of us did, I'm just saying it's all so complicated no one will ever get to the bottom of it and no one should ever try.

I don't want to know anything about Ronald and Didi. Beware what you might discover. It's not our business. *More importantly, it's not a stranger's business.*

Got to end for now. Raja needs to be walked and the new maidservant is afraid of all dogs, even cockers and poodles, so I have to walk Raja myself. The poor fellow's becoming arthritic. Hard to believe that he's as old as he is. I know I could never convince you and Rabi, but he's an old sweetheart. I can still remember Mummy opening her heart to him and holding him, ugly little street dog that he was, the lowest thing on the street.

Mummy and Daddy are in as good health as can be expected. I get a weekly letter from them. They ask after you and Rabi. I wish you would write them at least once a month. Mummy may not have mentioned it to you, but she has been diagnosed with onset of Parkinson's disease. It seems as though there's an epidemic of Parkinson's disease going around among our relatives. Our doctor says it isn't hereditary, but I have my doubts. Mummy can't really take the mountain walks that had meant so much to her, but she is still able to garden. Daddy continues in good health and his blood pressure is lower than Auro's!

You know how they long to hear from you and Didi. In fact, Didi is more considerate than you are in this respect. She even remembers their wedding anniversary each year. They keep all the letters and greeting cards, including the Mother's Day, Father's Day, and Valentine cards, in shoeboxes in a trunk. Didi's pile is five times bigger than yours. I hope that makes you feel guilty, Tara. In any case, why don't you redirect your energy writing them—better still, visiting them, and us—instead of digging into whatever did or did not happen when Didi was seventeen.

Affly, Parvati-di

P.S. I wish I'd been able to mail this letter earlier, but Auro is out of town on business and my driver has been a no-show for three days. The driver is supposed to show up at nine a.m. every morning and hang around till five-thirty or six whether I have errands to run or not. You remember Sunil, my driver, don't you? He used to be so reliable. He must be ill, but he has no way of reaching me because he lives way out near the airport and doesn't have a phone or a neighbour with a phone. So I have no way of getting to the post office to mail this. The new house-keeper (sent to me from Calcutta by Aunt Bandana) is more afraid of crossing streets than I am, and who can blame her, given the craziness of Bombay traffic? The simplest tasks become problematic here. Maybe it's because daily life is too easy in San Francisco that you have so much time on your hands for narcis-sistic projects like the one you are currently engaged in.

Anyway, as a result of your call about the weird young man the other night, I'm suffering from insomnia. Bits and pieces are coming back to me though I don't want them to. Come to think of it, the "fling" with Poppy's brother does seem now to have lasted longer than all of Didi's other infatuations. What I remember now is that while Mummy and even Daddy found her romantic nature charming and feminine, they were uneasy about her spending so much time in Poppy's house. Of course at the time I thought it had been just the fact that Poppy's family was Christian, and therefore, not like us and (further therefore) not a good place for us to absorb influences. They were more Westernized in their relationships and more permissive about who could talk to whom. Maybe Poppy was allowed to date by her parents. Remember how much trouble I got into that one time I went to Khorshed Modi's birthday party and her bachelor uncle said I was pretty and I was so flattered or so dumb that I mentioned him to Mummy and Daddy when I came home, and they threw an absolute fit that men had been invited to the party and I couldn't get them to understand that Parsi families didn't seem to mind mixed parties, and they kept yelling, "But we're not Parsis!"

Well, one thing—I'm not sure it qualifies as a bona-fide memory—keeps sneaking back from the past. It's about the time that Didi went to that "finishing school" in Switzerland. Daddy went with her to drop her off, remember? We begged him to bring back some cheese and chocolates and he said he forgot. I think I heard the three of them, Mummy, Daddy, and Didi, discuss the pros and cons about marrying an unsuitable boy. I wasn't in the room. The door was closed. (Okay, I was eavesdropping. That means I must have been really intrigued by their secretiveness.) I seem to remember Mummy telling Didi something like, if you want to marry this man, you better know what you're getting into, because you don't just marry a boy, you marry his family, his religion, his biases, his politics, and if all those things are totally different from yours as they are bound to be, then you can prepare yourself for a lifetime of being lonely.

Divorce was not in our family vocabulary in the sixties. And I'd expected Didi to fight back with how love levels differences, etc., or some feistiness like that. Instead, and this is where I can't be sure I actually heard this, I think it was Daddy and not

Didi who answered Mummy. He said something like, "The boy knows it and he's not prepared to be lonely. I swallowed my pride for her sake. I humbled myself before this Christian boy and his parents. I told them that for the sake of my daughter's happiness, I was willing to make the necessary mental adjustments and withdraw whatever objections I may have earlier expressed, and this boy from a minority community and a low caste and with little prospect of high salary had the cheek to say to me that he was grateful for my offer but that he didn't wish to take me up on it because he could never satisfy a rich girl, and one as beautiful as this one, and that he was not interested in trying, nor in taking unnecessary risks."

I don't think I have imagined this, Tara. In fact, the overheard scraps keep getting stronger. I don't just hear the hysterics, but I see them, which can't be since I wasn't in the room. The point I want to make is that I don't blame Mummy and Daddy for whatever may have happened. I don't blame Didi either. It was Daddy who did the final begging. He lost interest in the tea gardens soon after, didn't he? And he started getting into gurus and chants and ashram hunting after that. He was in such a hurry to get you married off.

I never told you, but he sent me names of suitable boys as well when I was in Mount Holyoke, and they frankly disgusted me. If that was the choice, I thought I would never get married. Then one day I was given my scholarship check and instead of just depositing it in the local bank, I took it to Boston to the bank where it was drawn, and that's where I met Aurobindo. I swear it was a matter of fate, just as though a pundit had drawn it up. I was given a number, and I saw a number of men sitting at a number of desks in the lobby, all of them looking very important, and I found myself praying that he would be the one to take my cheque. He was so flustered when I came to him.

He tried not to pay any attention to me, as if I were any other American. He called me "Miss Bhattacharjee," as though he had never seen such a complicated name or an Indian girl in the bank before. I saw the nameplate "Banerji" on his desk and for some reason I decided to speak to him in Bengali and at first he blushed and then he asked me where in Calcutta I was from, and we sat there looking at those deposit forms, which really could have been taken care of at one of the front windows, but he started asking me if I had gone to Loreto House, and if I knew so and so and so and so (I think he is the cousin of Somini Chakladar, who was in Didi's class, although I didn't remember her.) I told him how silly I felt coming all the way in to Boston to deposit the cheque (although it was really because there was a Bengali Students Association meeting in Cambridge that some girls at Smith and Mount Holyoke were going to) when I could very easily have done it in Northhampton, and he said he was very glad I had. He had been waiting for his parents to find him a wife, and he'd rejected every candidate they'd sent him. He said to me, "I am Aurobindo Banerji and I am twenty-nine years old and will soon have a master's in business administration from Tufts University." He gave me his parents' names in Tolly-gunge and said that they were respectable middle-class people although not rich or powerful, but that he was certain they would agree to a marriage.

I am convinced that this computer programmer chap on the H-1B visa is scamming you. But I'm also convinced that Poppy's family damaged ours in a way more serious than the two of us realized before now. I do run into "R" alias "S" at occasional fund-raisers. He is on the asking side for suspiciously Christian-sounding charities, and Auro's company is on the giving side. We've exchanged the usual small talk about how are your parents, your sisters, etc. He has not shown any particular interest in the answers. It could be a cover-up. It could be indifference to past indiscretions. Don't open the door to con artists.

Affly, Parvati-di

(next day)

Dearest Tara,

I've been sending out telepathic messages to you to call me, but I guess they haven't worked. Mail is so slow that by the time I get your answer to a question I must have asked I've already forgotten that I'd asked. I suppose I could send you a fax through Auro's secretary, Mr. Malhotra, but Auro doesn't like to use the office staff or equipment for any personal business, not even a one-line fax, because of (1) potential labour union protests, and (2) fear that his boss, a nasty brute who should have retired by now, will accuse him of misusing office funds. Poor Auro is caught between old-style management that trusts only distrust, and new crude, cocky labour leaders who are quick to wave their red flags. He has worked himself up into such a state that I am afraid he is going to have a stroke or a heart attack.

Of course, it's not his style to ask me for any kind of help. It's not his style to do anything but yell at me if the dhobi hasn't done his white shirts just right (as though I'm the one doing the ironing and starching and not the dhobi) and scream at the boys that they're going to end up as paan and biri sellers because their grades aren't as high as his were when he was their age. My idea is that he should talk to a headhunter—there are lots of them in Bombay—but who am I that he'll take my advice? I just don't want to end up a widow because Auro has an evil boss. Don't suggest he get on Prozac. We Indians don't run to psychiatrists for every problem. Come to think of it, I don't know a single psychiatrist.

All the doctors in our social circle are regular doctors, like cardiologists and orthopedic surgeons, and do you remember the girl we used to call Fatty Fatima who was a hanger-on in Didi's circle? Well, Fatty Fatima's oldest daughter has just come back from the U.K. as a cosmetic surgeon. Not just noses, though she says Indians have slightly bumpy noses and so there's enough money to be made from just nose jobs. But this woman does total body work, whatever that means. I hope you aren't doing bad things to yourself like taking Prozac and having cosmetic surgery. Please, please, don't become that Americanised.

I'm having no success trying to drag Auro to old Dr. Contractor—what would we do in Bombay without our Parsi doctors?—for something as simple as heartburn, which has become so chronic that I'm afraid the acids are eating through his stomach linings. Auro is convinced that I'm adding to his heartburn by wanting to get a part-time job. Bombay is such a horribly expensive city. The four of us going out to dinner is prohibitive—and I don't mean eating at the Taj or at one of those restaurants at the Oberoi. It's no wonder that only you nonresidents on hard currency salaries can hang out in those places. I'm just talking of a decent place with great food for desi connoisseurs. Weren't the Crabs Goa a Go-Go fabulous that time we all ate there and Bish and Auro got into competitive crab eating?

Don't jump to the conclusion that we're hard up and need a second job in the family. In fact, Auro is so dead set against my getting a job that he keeps reminding me that he'll have to spend more on petrol, driver, and car maintenance than any paltry salary I might bring in. And of course, it's true. Where does our kind of convent-school education get us? I'm not putting down Loreto House and Loreto College or Mount Holyoke, but I didn't learn any skill I can now put to use to earn money.

Please don't think that I'm criticising Daddy's ideas of education for us. He didn't expect us to ever want to work, let alone to have to work for money. Only middle-class women went to coeducational classrooms and studied useful things like law or medicine or engineering. Mummy even thought having to make a budget was demeaning. If you have to worry about money, you're already poor, wasn't that one of her sayings? Maybe that's why they withdrew to that ashram in Rishikesh. India changed on them. We were changing on them without even knowing it.

The only way you are ever going to find the answer to your question for certain is by asking Didi, and by going to Daddy, and I don't think either one is capable of giving a straight answer. Didi has always had a great capacity for starting over, for wiping her slate very clean. Daddy is becoming more and more detached from the world, which I suppose is a good thing, at least it is something we are supposed to aspire to, but in his case I feel Daddy is fleeing this world, rather than seeking the next. I can't imagine a way in which you could begin to frame such an embarrassing question to him.

I didn't mean to get off on a track, but I did hope that you would call even before you received my last letter in which I said something to the effect that we all have our own troubles. I feel I'm heading for the kind of depression that hit me out of nowhere at Mount Holyoke during my first semester. I just wanted to hear your voice.

In answer to your request about you know what, there is a possibility that I'll run into "R" alias "S" at a fund-raiser next week. I'll do my best to get him beyond the usual small talk, but I'm not confident I'll get anywhere. I'm not too keen on getting into a serious conversation with anyone at one of these fund-raisers. There's an etiquette of superficiality that no one except the ill-bred violates. I hope I don't lose my nerve and end up totally avoiding him at the party.

Now here's a favour you can do for us. Not for Auro and me, but for Aunt Bandana's number-four son. I haven't met him, but he is coming to stay with us in Bombay because he has just joined the sales department of a paint company. It's a small outfit called Krishna Paints. They don't offer housing allowances to recruits at his level, so I expect he'll be staying with us for a year or so, until he gets a better job or gets married. This is where you come in. Aunt Bandana has asked that you please find him a suitable Bengali girl from a good family settled in California. Here are Aunt B's two main requirements: that the girl be an American citizen or green card holder who can legally sponsor her husband's immigration to the United States, and that she be a Brahmin. Aunt B. is of the old school, I'm afraid, so there is no point in us getting on our high horses. I've tried and got absolutely nowhere. Her stock answer, and I think it comes from the Laws of Manu, is if you sow the wrong kind of seed in the wrong kind of soil, you are bound to end up with an unhealthy sapling. That means no intercaste alliances.

I've met this boy just once, at a family wedding, and don't really recall what he looks like, but if he looks anything like Aunt Bandana he is probably pleasant enough to look at. He is related to us, in however roundabout a way, so I am willing to vouch for his character. Remember how fair Aunt B. is, with cheeks that actually turn pink in the winter just like an English-woman's? I'll let you know more details, once the boy moves in. I am surmising that he is around twenty-six, twenty-seven. His dak-nam is Montu, but I'll let you know his formal name as soon as I find out, so you can initiate matchmaking in California. And just in case you've forgotten everything about your poor suffering relatives in India, their family name is like mine though spelled differently—Banerjee. Auntie says please look only at Mukherjees or Chatterjees, but if the girl is exceptionally pretty and well-situated, in a pinch (even) Bhattacharjees, Lahiris, and Gangulys will do. *Remember sometimes Chakravorty is just a title, like a Chowdhury, and not a caste name. Do not be fooled, because sometimes people don't even know their own family origins.* (Aunt B. wrote this in a P.S. so she must think I'm a real ninny.) I don't know where they come up with such strict observance in this day and age, but I suspect it has something to do with living in Calcutta and never having left. A few weeks in Bombay and believe me, you lose all sense of who you are and where you came from. We're getting to be as mongrelised as you Americans. Thank goodness, this company flat has enough bedrooms so I don't have to dislodge either of the boys to accommodate a long-term houseguest.

Don't worry, I haven't let out a beep about your flirting with that Polish or Hungarian mistri to anyone, not even to Auro, and he's more broadminded than our blood relatives. If you come, however, the boys go back to the old bunk bed. I'll keep you posted about my "chance" encounter with "R" aka "S."

Affly, Parvati-di

7

*P*adma did not call back. My messages on her machine went unanswered. It had been only a day since Parvati's rambling letter arrived, but I felt I had to talk to her right away. Courier services, no matter how reliable, were too slow. I needed a friend to talk to. I didn't have a single close friend in San Francisco. Meena Melwani and her Guatemalan partner had drifted off my radar. The Atherton wives treated me as a pariah. I didn't belong in India or in the Silicon Valley Smug Indian Wives' group anymore. Parvati was more than a sister; she was my only confidante.

It was early evening in Bombay when I dialed her number, knowing I was selfish and pathetically needy. Parvati picked it up on the second ring instead of the usual sixth.

"Hello, Tara, I can always tell when it's international," she said, even before I spoke. Her boys were doing their assignments, Aurobindo was not yet home. The new houseguest, our cousin,

Montu, was flipping through the cable television channels. I could hear Raja's high-pitched whining and imagined his drooling jaw lying across Parvati's lap. "First of all, Andras is Hungarian, not Polish, and he is a live-in lover, not a 'flirtation,' " I said.

"So, it's even worse than I thought." Parvati didn't sound troubled.

"I didn't call to straighten out my love-life. I had to know if you talked to . . . you know . . . him."

"Really, Tara, there's no mystery. You make it sound like it's me that's having an affair. *Him?* Dr. Dey and his wife were at the fund-raiser for spastics last night, and we exchanged a very few words. I didn't think they were what you wanted to hear, and so I didn't call you."

"First of all, are you absolutely sure he's Ronald, Poppy's brother? Ron Dey and R. Swarup Dey, they're not cousins or anything? He was tall and lean and good at games, remember?"

"Well, all the minority communities do breed like rabbits, but I can assure you he's a filled-out version of the boy I remember. He's got a little potbelly from all the laddoos and mishti. And no exercise! I tell you, even Auro thinks he's an Olympic athlete if he squeezes in nine holes of golf once a month. If he has to walk half a block, he grumbles at the driver the whole day! Anyway, you and Didi would probably still recognize him, but he's no heartthrob anymore."

"You said he has a wife. Did he go for a replica of Didi?"

"Eeesh! She is so fat!" and then she started giggling. "Dr. Mrs. Dey is *mountainous!* She's so fat that she had to sit and have their son bring heaping plates of pakoras to her. She's actually a very nice lady with a British medical degree, but to look at her you'd think she didn't know the first thing about nutrition."

"You said a son?"

"Tall and skinny, about Bhupesh's age."

"Could the boy you saw be adopted?"

"Christians do that sort of thing. Who knows? Oh! You're still thinking of that orphanage boy, that Chris. Tara, you should come over here and we'll sit down and write a book about a conspiracy of Christian orphans. In fact, I have a great idea. What if that boy is my old housekeeper's son or brother? What if Urmila-bai decided to take revenge on us, on all the Bhattacharjee sisters, for sending her to prison? They caught her, you know. I heard it from my driver. He was gloating. The police must have thrashed the truth out of her, he said. My housekeeper, the one you wanted to take with you to America, was part of a big gang that operated out of all sorts of fancy buildings. What if the boy was just a lookout or something, but now he's been promoted by the big bosses? How do you even know he's Christian? I can't tell the minorities apart anymore—I'll bet he's Muslim! Maybe Urmila-bai is behind it all! A feminist gangster, a sort of cut-rate Phoolan Devi!"

I remembered our years in Calcutta reading Enid Blyton's Famous Five mysteries from the lending library, even our attempts to write one. "And maybe she went to Calcutta and conducted research and maybe she interviewed Mummy and Daddy to find out what really happened that summer, then she tracked down Poppy in Australia . . . Really, what exactly did you say to him?"

"I said, 'My sister ran into your son this week.' He looked very surprised and said, 'Oh, is she in Bombay? I'd love to see her!' He sounded very sincere and not at all flummoxed."

"Maybe he's a very practiced liar."

"So I said, 'No, she's in San Francisco. He had her address and came straightway to her door.' "

"Did that shake him up?"

"Not at all! He said very coolly, 'Mrs. Banerji, are you sure you are talking to the right Dr. Dey? That boy over there with his mother is named George, and he is my only son.' He said the boy was going to St. Xavier's school and the only traveling he has ever done has been to Goa. Then he excused himself."

"Did you say to him that boy has my address and he says he gave it to him? Did you mention his letter?"

"Oh, yes, Tara, I went chasing him across the room and caught up with him just as he reached his big, fat wife and said, 'My younger sister demands to know the story of the bastard son you had with my older sister.' Thank God I'm a Bhattacharjee girl with a convent education so I can carry off little moments like that in polite society that might bring ruin to lesser breeds. Are you totally mad? I already got the distinct impression that he will avoid me at the next party. He'll think I'm as bonkers as my sisters! But I can tell you this: Dr. Dey is totally innocent. And I know more than ever that that boy who claims to be his and Didi's son is an absolute fraud. Lock your doors and call the police. Make sure your Polish carpenter is always with you."

I promised Parvati I would drop the subject.

"Thank God, you've come to your senses," Parvati said. "Oh, that's Auro coming through the front door. I have to ring off."

Rabi taught me how to find addresses the world over on the Net. He thought he was preparing his Luddite ma for the twenty-first century. The offices of the Drs. Dey, along with their clinic and a small receiving hospital, were in Worli. Not the poshest address, I noted, but the Drs. Dey seemed to be managing quite comfortably.

* * *

Daddy believed in Hollywood. Hollywood values were Bhattacharjee family values, as opposed to the standards of Europe and, especially, those of Bombay. He told us tales of Metro Cinema in its golden years, after he'd returned from England, and the English language still pounded in his veins. Metro Cinema had a seven-foot usher, the tallest man in West Bengal. Every week it unveiled a new Hollywood wonder, a musical or a drama. The rajahs of the silver screen were Cary Grant and Gregory Peck, the presiding genius was Alfred Hitchcock, and the most beautiful woman in the world was Grace Kelly. No woman, however, quite competed for his favors like Doris Day, whose very name pulsated with the promise of sunshine and optimism. Essentially, Daddy approved of any Technicolor movie in English featuring familiar stars in glamorous settings. Their names engendered security.

Daddy felt that movies from Hollywood were safe, even though by the time I began going, in the late sixties, the Hollywood formula had begun to fall apart. Sundays were still Metro Cinema days, with the three daughters dressing to be seen: Padma in a sari, Parvati and I still in white dresses. We never saw the seven-foot Bengali giant usher Mummy still talked about. There were no musicals, no Doris Day over whom Daddy claimed to have swooned, no Greg and Cary. Grace Kelly was someone we read about as a princess, not a movie star. But we Loreto House school-girls loved Thursday matinees at the Metro Cinema all the same. We convent girls had the theater more or less all to ourselves on Thursdays. Students in non-Catholic schools didn't get Thursdays off as we did. We reveled in plots that turned on outrageous mis-taken identities or coincidences. We shuddered as the innocent and the virtuous were falsely locked up in jail. But we knew that eventually, love and truth would triumph. Order and harmony would be restored. Not just for those screen innocents, but for us as well.

Calcutta girls of our social set who attended convent schools and aspired to successful marriages with foreign residence were never taken to desi Hindi movies. We read film magazines about the Bombay stars' outrageous sex lives and criminal activities.

Their biographies were far more interesting than their performances. Bombay plots were both implausible and repetitive, the
acting mere camera mugging, and the music and dance sequences
were aimed at the level of scooter drivers and paan dealers. Even
today, I have never been to a "Bollywood" spectacular, despite their
recent popularity in the West.

Now, I was regretting my sanitized upbringing. The plot and
the participants in my San Francisco drama belonged more to
Bombay than to Calcutta, and the India that had stayed on, not
the one I had left. I had a state-of-the-art alarm system, but not
an armed chowkidar outside my door, no half-wild dogs inside.

I remembered other Hollywood movies that Daddy would not
have liked. Black-and-white *Rebecca* with its paranoid vision: wives
being driven crazy by their husbands. The wife's doubts are dismissed with a chuckle, clues are cleaned away by sinister maids,
and family members are enlisted against her. Innocence taken out
of context, turned against you. I didn't have a husband, and Andy
was remote. I feared my son and his friend. My sisters wouldn't
take me seriously. In those movies, everyone had a double-nature.
Loving husbands would make tea and serve it in bed; they would
engage the finest doctors and take their wives on expensive vacations. And there would be moments, driving along the coast highway, when the car would nearly swerve over a cliff, or when the
tea tasted strange, or the doctor suggested a discreet institution-
alizing from which she would never return. Which movie was
playing around me in San Francisco? The person who might have
solved it all, my oldest sister—assuming I could even raise the
question—wouldn't call back and couldn't be reached.

"Rabi!" I shouted out when I heard him come in, "tell that
Chris Dey to come back here. I want to talk to him again!"

"I'm not my cousin's keeper."

I told him I had compelling evidence from Bombay, from Dr.

Dey himself via Parvati-mashi, that Christopher was not his son. It was hard to gauge Rabi's reaction; at least he chose not to dispute it. I sent a message to Andy's pager: come home the minute I punch in "Dey." And then I couriered Dr. R. Swarup Dey, at the Worli address.

Dear Dr. Dey:

I am taking the liberty of assuming you are the same person as Ronald Dey, brother of Poppy (Penelope), and friend of the Bhattacharjee family of Ballygunge Park Road, in the early to mid-1970s. You might remember me as the nine-year-old sister of Padma and Parvati Bhattacharjee. Padma was sixteen years old in the summer of 1974, and attending Loreto College with Poppy. My recollection is that Poppy and Padma were the best of friends, and I seem to recall times when you walked Poppy to our house, and picked her up. If indeed you are the same gentleman, I am writing now from California, requesting your help in clarifying a delicate personal matter.

I have just spoken with my sister, Mrs. Aurobindo Banerji, in Bombay, who reported on a brief conversation she'd had with you last evening at the benefit dinner for spastic children. I believe she informed you that I had met a young man last week here in San Francisco who claims to be your son. You stated that you have no such son. I am relieved by this statement, which closes one path of speculation, but it means, unfortunately, that there is no "innocent" explanation for this young man's sudden appearance and bizarre behavior. I fear this matter is destined for legal, if not criminal, conclusion.

Dr. Dey, this same young man presented me with a letter, allegedly signed by you and addressed by you to me. This letter describes its deliverer as your natural son, raised in a Catholic orphanage. The young man told me that he has only very recently learned—from you—the identity of his mother. He also told me that you were the person who furnished him with my sister's name and address in Bombay, and that Mrs. Banerji had encouraged him to get in touch with me. I have verified from Mrs. Banerji, my sister, that no meeting took place between her and this young man.

This "letter of introduction" was delivered to me in person. Since it was hand-carried, it bears no Indian postmark or return address. The sheet of paper on which the letter was typed carries no identifier, either personal or professional, and of course the authenticity of the signature is open to question. Clearly, the possibility of an extortion plot or blackmail scheme exists, although in many ways it can be termed a crude attempt. Adding to the complication, the young man has thus far made no threats and has stated no objective apart from gaining access to the woman he considers to be his natural mother. The threats, I believe, are at this moment implicit, and I take them seriously.

I find it impossible to believe that a family friend and gentleman such as yourself could have played any direct part in this unfortunate affair—yet I find it equally difficult to believe that your connection could be entirely coincidental. The names are not randomly selected. Connections between our families do exist. If you can shed any light, or if you possess any knowledge that might help us solve this disturbing matter, I beg you to communicate it to me.

May I request that you respond at the earliest possible date concerning any knowledge you may have of this person, or the events he describes. I need to know: 1) if you have had any contact with this young man; 2) if he bears the relationship to you that he claims; and 3) if you repudiate or endorse his activities. Events are moving rather quickly here, so I ask for these answers at your earliest convenience.

I of course feel terrible for my role, however accidental it might be, in this intrusion on your privacy. I remember those Calcutta days with special fondness, and your parents, especially, as kind and generous hosts and community leaders. Please accept my best wishes for your continued health and prosperity, for you and your family.

Sincerely,

Tara (Bhattacharjee) Chatterjee

And now, all my irons were in the fire. I actually hoped that Didi would not call back, at least not until I had had a response from Ronald Dey. I implored Rabi that if he saw the boy—his friend— again, on the street or not, to have him drop by so that we could talk. Certainly, it seemed, the odds of Chris Dey's being a member of the family were lengthening, and I wanted Rabi and Chris to understand that.

The next day I was coming out of our neighborhood market on Stanyan, carrying two bags, when a voice called out from the little parking lot behind the store, "Would you like help, Tara-mashi? They look very heavy."

Chris Dey emerged from between a row of cars, with his arms extended. In the week since I'd first met him, he had filled my days and nights with such malignancy and dread that seeing him in daylight actually surprised me. When I'd first seen him that night in my living room, he'd been sitting and I had retreated when he'd stood and advanced. Now I saw that he was short and slight, barely taller than me. I managed to ask him how he had been. "I believe I saw you the other day," I said, attempting to sound casual, "down on Haight. With Rabi."

He shrugged, one of those ambiguous I-get-around Indian gestures of partial agreement. He fell into step beside me. I handed him one of the bags, if only to keep one hand free, over the pager.

How could he have known I would walk past this open space, that my hands would be occupied, that I would be alone? I told myself, in case I must identify him or pick him out of a lineup, remember his face. Look for identifying features. He had a slight mustache, a chipped front tooth, no visible scars, ears that lay close to his scalp. I dared not look more closely. I would not call him Bengali, looking at him, but what do I know? I've lost the Indian radar. I can't tell anymore, and this boy, according to his own account, grew up among nuns in Delhi. Five foot six and a half, a hundred and thirty-five pounds.

"I've been hoping to see you again, Christopher," I said. "I want you to know that you cannot hope to get away with this."

"Auntie? What is the problem? Did I frighten you that first night? Perhaps I should have written first."

"You know very well what the problem is, and please do not call me by familiar names. I don't know who you are, but I know you are not the son of Ronald Dey."

"I can show you proof."

"You have already shown me enough." The bags of groceries were so heavy that I had to set them down for a second to flex my hands. "And I know you have not spoken with my sister."

Chris snatched the bags, spilling red and yellow beets on the sidewalk. "You've talked with my mother? No, you are right."

"Don't waste time on these lies." The pager was in my hand, my thumb was on the beeper.

"But you believe me, Tara-mashi. And Rabi believes me. And when you talk to my father, you will see he believes me."

"Yes, tell me about your father. Is he married?"

"Of course."

"Describe his wife. What is her name? What does she do? Do they have children? Where do they live?"

"Tara-mashi, please. I will answer everything. Of course he is married. Her name is Camilla Bhatt, she is from Ahmedabad. She is a doctor; they met in England at medical college. They have a boy, I believe. They live behind their surgery in Worli. She is stout."

"I don't believe you," I said. "This little game of yours has gone far enough. You offer no evidence of your claim, and your father denies your existence. Excuse me, I have a message." I took the pager out of my jeans pocket, and punched in "Dey." If we coordinated our movements, Andy would arrive at just about the moment Chris and I reached the house.

It was a three-block walk, up the hill past my school and the public tennis courts, then down the side of the hill toward the valley of Cole Street and my house. As I walked, I wondered: Was this my final neighborhood excursion? Was this what it was like to be marched in the company of the man who would kill me? All those articles in the paper, the irate husband or boyfriend with a court order against him, suddenly showing up. *I just want to talk, honey. Just let me in for chrissakes. What's the harm in that?*

He asked, innocently, "Have you spoken to my mother?"

"And who might she be?"

He responded with a nasty laugh.

We started down the hill, above the tennis courts. My house was two blocks away, and I did not see Andy's "Zen-Master" panel truck parked outside. "You could have a lawsuit on your hands. Libel. Defamation. Emotional damage."

He grinned. He knew we wouldn't risk publicity. "Forgive me, Tara-mashi, but I am curious to know my mother's reaction to the news of my arrival."

"The woman you call your mother doesn't have the foggiest notion of your existence, and I'm going to keep it that way. I'd be the last person in the world to tell her," I said.

He switched suddenly to Bengali. He spoke in the rapid, street-smart Bengali I associated with the children who hustle shoppers for small favors in the densely packed area of lanes around New Market. A few years older, less ingratiating, they cluster on stoops or low retaining walls, keeping up a steady, lewd, rhyming patter, sometimes witty, often crude, always irritating, directed at everyone passing before them. *Rockey-bosha chokra*, they're called, verandah-sitting boys, wiseasses, insult comics, low-rent rappers, we'd say. In their world it was always open season on pretty girls, on fat women, on rich men, on foreigners or minorities. Rows of boys would sit on their haunches outside Loreto House, passing cheap cigarettes and improvising little songs about each of us, Hindi movie tunes with twisted Bengali lyrics, as we got out of our cars and ran to safety behind the gates. Some of the songs hit home, and even Loreto House girls could on occasion be seen blushing and hiding a wide grin behind a modest hand.

I'd never thought of the verandah-lounging wits as particularly dangerous. Every Bengali fancies himself a poet. I'd always assumed, in those innocent days and in my naïve way, that they eventually grew tired of street life, got married, and turned respectable.

"Tara-mashi, it is not my intention to cause my mother grief. But listen to me now—" and then Chris Dey grabbed my arm, holding me tight by the wrist. We stopped walking. I will remember this scene for the rest of my life: the greenery behind us with houses spilled on the hillsides like children's blocks, the sky a deep Mediterranean blue, like that at the edge of some Greek or Etruscan village. "I have waited twenty-five years for this moment, and nothing you or anyone else can do will stop me. You have denied me two times. You shall not deny me a third." Perhaps I was imagining the change in his voice, but I certainly felt the pain shooting up my arm, and a sense that the reality of Chris Dey was suddenly exposed. Denial three times? He thought he was Christ.

The battered truck turned in from Cole Street.

We could start walking again; I would be safe. I felt my life was back on hold. "Remove your hand immediately," I said. "Never presume to touch me again." He let go of my wrist and smiled and we continued walking downhill, he with one sack of groceries, I with the other. We had come to Shrader, the final corner before my block, and whatever Christopher Dey intended for me, it would not happen there. I decided to confront him.

"I know what's happening here. You've decided to destroy my family, and Dr. Dey's family, any way you can. I don't know who you think you are or what you think gives you the power, but I will fight you—"

"Mashi," he begged, "I want only to belong to your family, not to destroy it. It would mean nothing to me if your family disappeared. I wish only that it were as powerful today as it had been." The conversation was continuing in Bengali, clearly his mother tongue.

"Then you know," I continued in our language, "that in our family there is even less of a place for a liar than for a bastard."

"This is your answer, Tara-mashi? I ask you for help, I ask for your hand, and you pull it away? I ask you to open the door for me, and you bar it instead?"

"I've done nothing of the sort," I said. "This 'hand' of yours is a claw. Your demands are threats that I reject, and you've made claims that no one has verified. The 'evidence' you've presented is clearly manufactured."

We were nearly at my house. Andy was leaning against the side of his truck and had never looked broader or more quietly menacing. And my timed outburst took us to Andy, who took my sack of groceries and set it down by the front door, then came back to take the bag Chris had been carrying, which he passed on to me.

"Let me guess—you're the young man I've been hearing about," he said, and took Chris's hand before he had a chance to extend it. "The long-lost what's-it, cousin or is it nephew?" My arm still ached from the pressure point he had pressed, and now he and Andy were locked in a grim test of a handshake that Andy appeared to be winning.

"What do you say I walk Cousin Chris around a bit, show him the neighborhood. Let's go, buddy." As they ducked in front of the truck, Andy called back. "You'll be okay? You might want to catch up on those phone calls."

There had been no messages during the day. Didi wasn't expecting a call from me on a weeknight, so she answered on the first ring. I'd never heard such a wary and subdued tone from her, like a truant answering the principal's call or the debtor's cringe. The moment I identified myself the old Didi was back in command. "Where have you been, Tara? I've been calling and calling!"

Liar, I thought. "That's what I want to talk about," I said. But before I could start, she was off on her travels about the state, a performance coming up at the Asia Society in New York, the promise of a major show at the Indian Embassy in Washington. Everyone so loved and admired her and her new show, students were in tears, and parents wanted to visit India. Harish was looking into chartering a plane and putting Didi on as the tour guide. She could ride free, stay free, even take a stipend. Harish was lining up the luxury hotels, the internal travel, the meals, giving fifty families the luxury tour of exotic India. She would do her shows, new and old, in Delhi and Bombay and the south. Calcutta might be too daunting for New Jersey tastes. "That's a gross of a quarter-million and a bottom-line of maybe twenty-five thousand for us, plus infinite amounts of goodwill for the future. Not that a quarter-million sounds like much to you."

"Didi, I hate to bring you down off cloud nine, but—" and

then I asked the easiest question. "Do you remember a boy in Presidency when you were in college? I think he was the brother of a Christian friend of yours."

"Poppy! Oh, she's a wonderful girl! If she's coming to New York I'm positively dying to see her again! The last I heard she'd left for Australia and married some white bloke—those were her words—in Sydney. She couldn't get out of India fast enough, poor thing. She thought Christians didn't have a future in India, and there we were, thinking they ran the whole show because of the nuns and all."

"It's not Poppy I'm thinking about. It's her brother. What was his name? Randall, Robert, something like that?"

"I think you're right, it was an 'R' name. Frankly, back then all those Christian names sounded the same to me. Remember Joyce Chu and her brother Bertie? And there were so many Rosies! Like Rosie Merdichian, remember her? Christians were very big on flower names for their girls. Pansies and Poppys and Camillas, and don't forget all the Normas and Belindas, like the Gupta twins. *Ronald!* That was his name. Tara, I'm so glad we're having this conversation, I can't tell you how happy it makes me just remembering those names! You were so young, I'm amazed you have any memory of it at all. Next time you come to New York we should sit down and have a long sisterly chat."

"Dey, wasn't it? Ronald Dey. What ever became of him?"

"Oh, why talk about him? He went to England, I think."

"Did he come back to India?"

"Not if he knew what was good for him. No, no, I mean, if he was a Christian doctor already established in England, why would he want to come back to a place that didn't want him? He could never rise to the top in India."

Maybe *because* he's a Christian, I started to say. Guilt? Some Christian sense of duty? Or because he had a son? But all I said was, "I thought his father was a very famous doctor." I remembered a phrase that had stuck with me for years, a caption that had appeared under his father's photo in *The Statesman*: "Removing Polyps from the Chief Minister."

"Old Nose-and-Throat Dey? He got his big start in the British days. He was *such* a snob, Tara, I can't begin to tell you. A real brown sahib of the worst sort, and he absolutely hated India and Indians, by which I guess he meant people like us. People like the Deys never see how people are laughing at them—Ronald and his family were practically black! You remember Poppy—the nuns called her Black Poppy behind her back." Didi's voice grew conspiratorial, as though she were spreading a story that had not yet surfaced. "And let me tell you, old Dr. Dey was sinking fast. He drank a lot, I remember. He was drinking all the time. They used to serve wine at dinner—can you imagine how much it cost to bring wine to India? They went through cases of the stuff! He'd drink imported Scotch all day long and French brandy at night. They were really a very degenerate family, although Poppy was sweet enough and her brother managed to keep himself a little above it. The father's been dead a long time."

"And is the son married?"

"Tara, dear, really! How would I know? I live here. Are you interested in Ronald Dey? Well, he wasn't a total blackie like his sister. You should ask Parvati, she's the one who keeps track of everybody."

"Let me ask you something very personal, Didi. Were you ever interested in Ronald Dey?"

"Whatever are you asking? You know me, I was a terrible flirt, but so were you, and so was Parvati, that's what we were trained for. He was Christian, so how serious could it get? If you remember me smiling at him or laughing at his jokes, it's just the thing we girls did whenever we had an audience. What I remember is waiting for a sign from above, or from some boy, or from Daddy that my life could start. I waited six years, dressing up every night, smiling, laughing, collecting gold and saris and thinking I was getting old and no one would marry me. Even Poppy was getting offers! I started begging Daddy to find someone because I was already sixteen and I hated school and the nuns and I knew I wasn't cut out to be the wife of some bigshot businessman, and Daddy kept saying no, no, I had to finish school, and no boy was good enough for me. But let me tell you, I was about ready to scoop up . . . I don't know. Anyone."

By the time she finished, she was breathing hard. I hadn't heard that much sincerity from her in twenty years, and I wished I could let it go at that. "I'm not talking about flirting, Didi. There's a situation here, right now, not five minutes ago in San Francisco that is very, very disturbing. There's a young man prowling my neighborhood who calls himself Christopher Dey. He just suddenly showed up one night and demanded that I give him your name and address. And he did it again this afternoon."

"Well, he's obviously confused. Why would a stranger want my address?" And that's when I began to lose my confidence. Whenever I confront Rabi in a lie, he first throws my question back at me. But he's young and not yet a practiced liar, not a performer.

"That's what I want to know. I know what he says, but what do you say?"

"Well, what does he say?"

"I think you can guess. He says you are his mother, and Ronald Dey is his father."

"How dare you!" she cried. Then she was silent for a few moments, before suddenly erupting into a gale of chirpiness. "Harish! Oh, Tara. Harish just came through the door carrying the biggest bouquet of flowers I've ever seen! He's such a romantic! I'll have to get back to you. Love you! Bye-bye!"

I started shaking. It wasn't just my sister, whose guilt—if that was a word that could be applied—whose involvement was now clear to me; it was my own blind vanity. Ten minutes earlier, I had been in control. So cool, so eloquent, so ineffably Bengali Brahmin. If an attack was coming from this boy, I wanted to be armored against it.

Andy and Christopher Dey had had their little chat about bad manners and barging in on a person's life and demanding restitution for something that person had never done. Christopher said he was deeply apologetic. He agreed that he had not handled it well and that I'd been right to resist him, even to deny him. He hoped I would not jeopardize his visa by contacting the authorities.

But it's not just "barging in," I wanted to say, it's more than an attack from some outraged stranger, it's more than being forced to pay for an old sin or even someone else's sin. It felt like a car jacking. One minute you're backing out of your driveway or stopped at a light and the next second you're being dragged to your death. Three or four years ago I had read in the papers about a young Bengali mother killed during a car jacking in Washington, D.C. She had been on her way to the baby-sitter's house to drop off her infant before going to work. The car jackers had tossed the baby, still strapped into her baby seat, out of the car. The mother had tried to leap out of the driver's door to protect her baby from oncoming rush-hour traffic, but the lower part of her body had become entangled in the seat belt. You do everything right, be a caring, careful mother, a law-abiding driver, and it's your seat belt strap and the mother bond that kills you. It's the last thing you expect, you aren't braced for it.

Really, Tara, don't be melodramatic. And so I finally said, "It's like an earthquake, isn't it? One minute everything is steady, and the next, without warning, it's all fallen down. Unless, of course, you've got your personal retrofitter."

Andy had taken his accustomed half-a-sofa and propped his

naked feet on the coffee table. Eyes closed, swaying slightly, his head a perfect egg rimmed in a flaring red beard and thinning hair, he looked every inch the aging biker. With his belly and sleeping eyes he can look threatening and Buddha-like at the same time.

"Sweetie, that's not what an earthquake is all about." His hands were propped in front of him, elbows on his belly, index fingers steepling the flat, wide roof of his hands. "Earthquakes aren't all jolt and damage. They're *silent*, they're nonevents. People forget that. For decades, for centuries, plates rub up against each other where no one can see and no one can measure it. Everything's stable so long as the pressures are equal . . . but every few years, one side gets the upper hand, if we're lucky we start getting signals, and . . . *bang*." He suddenly, almost violently, slipped one hand over the other. "So, which part is the earthquake, the violent last two seconds or the very quiet two hundred years?"

"You think he's telling the truth, don't you?"

"I don't deal in truths. You want truth, get a scientist. If you want DNA truth, take a swab of your saliva and compare it with one of his. I think there is a Christopher Dey out there somewhere. Maybe it's him. And I think your sister is his mother. And my advice is, drop it. Christopher won't let it go and you guys can't admit it so the harder you deny, the harder he pushes back. You guys are like those plates pushing against each other."

"When he confronted me today, I was so sure of myself that if there'd been a policeman around I would have flagged him down. If I'd just gotten through to Didi before he grabbed me, it might all be different. Now that I've talked to her, I think he might be who he says he is."

"And Padma? What does *she* say?"

"Who knows? I'm not even sure she listened to what I had to say. She's never been much of a listener."

"I guess that's progress of sorts. You believe the punk kid who

threatened you today more than you do your own sister. Correct?"
He whistled.

I wasn't so sure anymore. "So, who do you believe?"

"I believe him and I believe you. When you told him he was
lying, he knew you might believe him. When I told him that
letter from his father was a piece of total bullshit, he knew *I* might
believe him. I said, Your whole claim rests on a forged piece of
paper with a forged signature and there's not a court in the world
that would honor it, and his eyes lit up—now the whole world
believes him."

I moved next to him on the sofa, his arm closed around me. I
laid my bare feet over his.

"I should be hearing from Dr. Dey very soon. That could settle
things."

"Things are already settled."

Yes, yes, I heard myself agreeing. *Things are already settled, we
just don't know how they'll turn out.* It was too late for a truce. The
self-righteous letter I had fired off to Ronald Dey, back when I
believed I was defending the Bhattacharjee family's innocence,
threatening the arrest and deportation of a common criminal pos-
ing as his and Didi's son—that was all the imbalance those plates
could stand.

8

Dear Madam:

Needless to say, your missive arrived here as something of a shock. I surmise that the frankness of its phrasing is a consequence of your long residence in the United States, that land of frank expression. It permits me an equally frank response.

The encounter between Mrs. Aurobindo Banerji and myself at the spastic children's benefit to which you referred did indeed unfold as Mrs. Banerji reported it. Needless to say, her mention to me of my son having encountered you in San Francisco struck me with a suddenness that was momentarily disorienting.

Let me turn to the substantive core of your letter, and what light I might be able to shed upon the concerns therein. The concerns can be reduced to three simple questions: Do I know a young man named Christopher Dey? If so, what is my relationship to him? And finally, did I send you a letter per his hand?

I acknowledge, if not publicly, that I have a son whom persons other than myself christened Christopher in his infancy. My wife has been made aware of the boy's existence. She has no wish to meet the boy in person or to be apprised of the circumstances of his origin. Neither my wife nor the boy have had disclosed to them the identity of the other involved party. The decision re disclosure of that party's identity will have to be made exclusively by that party. I have had no contact with that party in over two decades. I know for certain that that party has never tried to locate Christopher.

Mrs. Banerji's inquiry was disorienting, because over these many years I have made a concerted effort to suppress the memory of the short-lived misalliance that led to Christopher's existence. I have done so in the hope of occluding my own guilt at having allowed inappropriate passions to develop and my pain at not having resisted the communal and religious prejudices that enforced a quick and complete breakup of the misalliance. In the name of "propriety," and in the cause of "maintenance of social appearance," our elders disposed of the "debris" from that misalliance. In pragmatic terms, I believe in all earnestness, the damage to the birth-mother's reputation has been nil.

So far as I know, knowledge of the birth-mother's identity is limited to the birth-mother herself and her parents. I pray that unnecessary knowledge not be disseminated.

As to vouching for the character of the youth, I can do so without hesitation. He grew up in a Christian orphanage and has been successfully instructed in the orphan's virtues of cleanliness, humility, diligence, and self-reliance. He knows me only as a benefactor who takes a special interest in his welfare. My contact with him to date has consisted of sending a money order (for a very modest amount so as not to excite envy among the genuine orphans) the first of each month until he turned eighteen. During his residence at the orphanage, I visited him every

Christmas morning. Since his leaving the orphanage, our communications have been infrequent. I was aware that he had departed for California in the month of June or July in order to commence studies toward a diploma in computer science. Through the good offices of their order, the nuns at his old orphanage helped him obtain a scholarship. I am glad to have his safe arrival in California confirmed by you. It is my fervent hope that he will do better for himself than I have for him. He is a man of superior intelligence and equanimous temperament. He is, in short, the child "of which mothers preen and fathers crow."

As for the letter you claim to have had hand-delivered by him, I am at a loss to explain its origin. This is not to imply that I disbelieve your claim that you are in possession of a letter that purports to have been penned by me. If such a letter exists, I am not its author. Though this is a new and barbarous age, I am dismayed that you should, for a single moment, have thought me capable of such barbaric manners as to inflict untoward confidences on you. By my accounting, the last time I saw you—it must have been to pick up my sister Penelope from having spent the day with your family—you were nine or ten at most.

However puzzling the instrument of the encounter, it pleases me very much that you have met Christopher. I like to think that you must have recognized his lineage the moment you saw him. Surely you must have remarked on the fact that he is taller than nearly any Bengali since Satyajit Ray himself. Where I fault myself is that I shut him out of Bengali culture and language. Alas, the orphanage I placed him in from infancy was in remote Madhya Pradesh. I selected it for its very remoteness. I do hope you will forgive him, and especially me, for his lack of even rudimentary Bengali.

I pray for the safety of you and your family. I do not mean

to alarm you but unscrupulous forces in this country and abroad would seek to destroy the incautious and the innocent. Tennyson's monstrous Kraken roars awake "far, far beneath the abysmal sea," readying itself to rise to the surface. I beg you to indulge me by looking up the poem. It is titled simply, "The Kraken." As a schoolboy in shabbily gracious Calcutta, I was attracted to the poem for nothing more than a phrase like "enormous polypi." These days the poem delivers gloomy auguries.

Forgive my lapse into sentimentality. Hearing from you brought back memories of coming to your house to pick up Penelope and staying on for tea and the Bhattacharjee sisters' company. Those were gentler times.

> Yours truly,
> Ronald Dey

Christopher Dey must have acted on his own. What puzzled me, though, was that his father had described him as tall. As very tall. Almost as tall as the filmmaker, Satyajit Ray, the tallest Bengali I'd ever seen. Satyajit Ray's height had to have been over six feet four inches. Christopher was no taller than I, no more than five feet six inches.

Fortunately, in this world that Bish helped create, the scholarly itch can be scratched by a minute or two on the Internet. Victorian poetry/Tennyson/Kraken yielded the text, the sort of thing that Loreto House nuns who were otherwise enamored of Tennyson would have kept from impressionable girls lest it disturb their sleep, but which, as Ron Dey might say, "portends" the present day:

> *Below the thunders of the upper deep;*
> *Far, far beneath in the abysmal sea,*
> *His ancient, dreamless, uninvaded sleep*

The Kraken sleepeth: faintest sunlights flee
About his shadowy sides: above him swell
Huge sponges of millennial growth and height;
And far away into the sickly light,
From many a wondrous grot and secret cell
Unnumber'd and enormous polypi
Winnow with giant arms the slumbering green.
There hath he lain for ages and will lie
Battening upon huge seaworms in his sleep,
Until the latter fire shall heat the deep;
Then once by man and angels to be seen,
In roaring he shall rise and on the surface die.

That night, I lay in bed grieving for Didi. Our happy house on Ballygunge Park Road, the protective parents and loving daughters, the Brahmins' pride, the Bengali arrogance, the Calcutta sophistication—seemed now the darkest cave, and we, blind stumbling creatures. How could we have allowed the instinct bred within us over the centuries to draw lines and never cross them, an infinity of lines, ever-smaller lines, ever-sharper distinctions? I grieved for Didi's generation of "girls of good family," who put caste duty and family reputation before self-indulgence.

What might I have done, in Didi's place? I could imagine myself meeting a boy (although I didn't) and falling in love with the same instinct for mayhem as had Didi, maybe even with the same consequence, but I couldn't picture my nineteen-year-old self giving in to social pressure. Maybe I was more stubborn than her. Or maybe I was just lucky that I had been born when fathers had become weaker, society was already in shambles, the nuns in retreat. The fault line ran directly through my family, separating sister from sister, the forward-looking from the traditional and the adaptable from the brittle.

I understood better why Didi had condemned me for going through with my divorce. According to her, I had become "American," meaning self-engrossed. She had chosen to echo our mother and our aunts—things are never perfect in marriage, a woman must be prepared to accept less than perfection in this lifetime— and to model herself on Sita, Savitri, and Behula, the virtuous wives of Hindu myths. I had dismissed her as a hypocrite and schemer, because all the while that she had criticized me for acting too "American," Harish Mehta, her beloved husband, reveled in his "family connection" to the famous entrepreneur-inventor, Bish Chatterjee. Bish still receives funding proposals, real estate brochures, and business cards from New Jersey "friends" begging an audience.

In the years of our estrangement, I had never thought of her as bold, defiant, or pathbreaking. Her clinging to a version of India and to Indian ways and Indian friends, Indian clothes and food and a "charming" accent had seemed to me a cowardly way of coping with a new country. Change is corruption; she seemed to be saying. Take what America can give, but don't let it tarnish you in any way.

How could she deal with admitting a flaw, let alone with a son showing up in Montclair? I couldn't imagine her coping. I could not square Ronald's love, even his admiration, for the boy I found lacking in charm, and sinister to boot. Bengali mothers are famous for overestimating the brilliance of their sons, but never the fathers. Fathers are hypercritical of their sons, predicting failure, withholding praise. A father's duty is to harangue, bluster, push, and prod. Bish had been that way with Rabi, constantly finding fault, accusing him of wasting time drawing cartoons and memorizing old comic routines from used record albums. "You're very lucky someone in this family studied hard and made a success, because you're headed straight to hell!" he'd rant, when the boy was nine years old. Maybe Christians were more forgiving.

"Andy?" I whispered. He stopped snoring. "I've made a huge mistake."

He groaned. I could read his mind: *Again?* "About what?"

"Everything. Didi's not a monster. She really is a romantic."

"Okay, she's great. Is that it?"

"Didi's the only one of us who followed her heart. Her mistake made everything possible."

"Bully for her." His breathing deepened.

I awoke from a dream, nearly screaming. I was up on Stanyan by the tennis courts, walking again with Chris. It was a restaging of our Bengali encounter of that afternoon, only more eloquent in dream than in life. He was more than holding his own in Bengali. I turned to him and said, just as I woke, "But you don't speak Bengali!"

"What?" said Andy. "I don't what?"

Chris doesn't speak Bengali. His father had confessed it in the letter, and no Bengali father would admit to such a defect unless he was aiming for absolute honesty. But the Chris I knew spoke Bengali far better than English. And didn't Ronald describe him as tall and handsome? The Chris I knew had nothing of what I remembered of the tall, athletic Ronald Dey.

"Listen. We were speaking Bengali."

"Sweetie," he said, "it's okay."

"*He* was speaking Bengali." I thought I'd lost him back to sleep, but he finally responded. "In a dream?"

"We were speaking Bengali on the walk. Chris speaks better Bengali than English." This time, I didn't wait.

"Remember Ronald's letter?"

"Not every syllable."

"He said Chris doesn't speak Bengali."

"Sweetie, that's not against the law."

"And he's not tall."

"Ahh," he mumbled. I was losing him. "Round up all the short Bengalis."

I rolled his shoulder, pulling him to me. If his eyes had been closed, I would have slapped him awake. But he was watching me, and his arms were reaching out for me and I said, "I know for sure, he's an imposter. He's not Chris Dey." That's what Ronald Dey's letter was all about, the Kraken, the stiff formalities, the elaborate hints about height and Bengaliness. As though some cheap Bombay film were unrolling on our walls, I could see him, writing a letter with a gun to his head, using all the resources of our inherited English to send a message across class and religion and a quarter century.

9

I promised Andy in the morning to give it a rest, do absolutely nothing with sisters, nephews, or distant family friends. He was determined to extract a promise from me: *Drop it*. Rabi pressed me for another promise, to show up at his school that evening to see his work and meet his teachers. Just like any other responsible parent. Of course, I said, to both.

By morning light, alone in my house, the fantasies of the dark kept returning. Ron Dey was trying to tell me something. Short of coming out and accusing the boy named Chris, he was saying there might be an imposter out there. There are evil forces out there. He was begging for help, just as Andy was pleading with me to give it up.

My suspicions were based on ancient prejudices. He doesn't look Bengali! He doesn't look artistic and refined, meaning, I guess, he doesn't look like a half-Bhattacharjee. Andy's prescription was reasonable, very New World, very democratic: It's none of my business.

I was wearing Andy down with mood swings. He worried I would only hurt myself, trying to lift every rock and throw open every door. It's good to rediscover my roots, but not if they rise up and strangle me. I wanted to be persuaded by cool logic. My sister couldn't be both a child-denying monster and an angel; Chris couldn't be a victim and a villain; my father our protector and destroyer.

There were rational, boring explanations for everything—there had to be. Of course Didi was upset when I called with the news of her "son"—who wouldn't be? That didn't mean she couldn't cope with acknowledging him, eventually. She might be stronger than I gave her credit for. And why should I be surprised that Chris's father exaggerated his son's accomplishments? Fathers are often critical at home, boastful away. And it's hardly strange that Chris doesn't know how to behave around me. He's brand new to the country. He's spent his life in an orphanage—of course his manners are less than polished.

Hoping to catch Rabi in a communicative mood, I'd asked him that morning what he honestly thought of Chris Dey, but he answered only, "Why?"

"Well, you want to think of him as family, right? Didn't you introduce him to me as your only cousin here?"

"I don't have an obligation to get friendly with every Indian cousin, do I? God, think about Poopesh and Dimmest, sorry, Bhupesh and Dinesh? Chris is a lot more interesting than they are, believe me."

"Interesting how?"

"The places he's gone. All the things he knows about."

"And how does he live? Where's he working?"

"Ma, you make a lousy investigator. You'll have to trust me on this. We just don't spend a lot of time talking about his place of employment." End of communication.

I've often walked past the police station at the base of Stanyan by Golden Gate Park, watching the dope dealers and drunks being pulled in, thankful that the inside view of the police station is one American experience I'll never have. And now, as Bish had once cautioned in the months after our divorce, as we were making our way through the courts and lawyers' offices, sooner or later, we'll all know humiliation. This country exempts no one.

The desk sergeant, a Chinese or Korean man a few years older than me, offered a cheery good morning, and a fully attentive, "How can I direct your inquiry?"

"I don't know," I said.

"Is it a question of law, or language, broadly defined?"

"Not exactly language, but definitely cultural."

"You want an ethnic officer? Find your group here, and just give me the number." He handed me a worn sheet of thick paper. Bengali was listed, along with all the other languages of India.

"My language is Bengali, but I'm fairly certain I'd be assigned to a Bangladeshi." In fact, I could see the name provided, Farookh Ahmad. "I'm really sorry, but I don't think a Muslim would understand."

The sergeant kept peering down the list.

"We're terrible, aren't we?"

"I'd just say special. Indians are . . . very special."

"Perhaps just someone with an Indian background."

"Male or female? Is it . . . personal?"

"It's more like a missing person, but a male officer might be better."

And so I was assigned to Sgt. Jasbir "Jack" Singh Sidhu, a tall Sikh with a trimmed beard and a thoroughly American manner and accent. But for the powder-blue turban, he looked more like a college student than an officer of the SFPD. Under the glass of

his desktop he'd pressed photos of a wife and children and a painting of a Sikh saint. He uncapped a fountain pen, and took out a
yellow legal pad. "Okay, Mrs. Chatterjee, let's rock and roll." I
never thought I would be discussing intimate family matters with
a Sikh.

"I don't even know if I have a complaint. I just feel that I've
maybe done a lot of damage, and I might have put myself in a
great deal of danger."

"Well, I'd call that a good beginning. Let's start with your
fears. Who do you think is putting you in danger?"

"There is a young man who calls himself Christopher Dey." He
wrote and I spelled the name, knowing he'd get it wrong.

"Ah, *Dey*. I should have known." A flicker of a smile, as he
crossed out the *a* and added an *e*. "I should tell you from the get-go
that if this is a domestic complaint, I should get a female officer
in here right away." I shook my head. "Okay. Then forgive my
nosiness, but there's something with the name. Is this guy an
American, a half-American, something like that?"

"He's an Indian Christian. He's supposed to be my nephew."

He carefully set his pen down, capped it, and stared. "Supposed?"

"We're not Christian" (*God*, I could hear three thousand years
of relatives). Then I explained the basic situation, as I understood it. I left out nothing. He managed to fill three long yellow
legal pages. When I was finished, he kept staring down at his
notes.

"You say your sister's kept this bottled up for twenty-six years.
That's pretty good, even for Indians. If you're concerned about
protecting your sister's reputation or proving her innocence, let
me tell you up front, SFPD isn't family therapy, okay? If you
suspect he's a false claimant to family money, that's probably a
civil matter. If you've got a narrow criminal concern, let's hear it."

"You'll have to tell me. I'm worried that the boy who calls

himself Christopher Dey might not be the real Christopher Dey."

He picked up his pen. "So what's your proof?"

I could only hope Sergeant Sidhu was as much a Jasbir as a Jack. I could feel myself blushing. "Christopher Dey is supposed to be tall, well-educated, accomplished, and totally non-Bengali speaking. The young man I've met is short, uneducated, rather crude, and Bengali speaking. I know how racist this sounds, believe me."

"A crude Bengali, eh? This *is* news." He had a sly smile. "You're aware that a person's height and language and educational level are not the concerns of the SFPD?"

"I said I know how it must sound."

He spread his hands. "So what exactly is it you want us to do?"

"Listen?"

He leaned back in his chair. We were raised to flirt, to put men at their ease. I glanced at his wife's photo under the glass, and smiled. Your wife? Your children? Very attractive. "For instance, if this boy is not Christopher Dey, can you find out who he really is? Or if anything happened to the real Christopher?"

"You mean, do we have any unidentified male Indian bodies floating in the bay? Not that I am aware of. Are you asking if we have known criminal activity by Indian nationals in the Bay Area? You better believe it. But violent crime isn't part of the pattern, except maybe domestic violence. Statistically, if you're going to be hurt by an Indian, you're more likely to be gouged by an accountant than some killer on the street."

An amusing thought, getting whacked by an accountant. Bish's money man, Mr. Venkatesan, a mild and pious south Indian, used to show up for work fresh from his morning puja with an orange paisley mark of drying yogurt on his forehead. Instead of squashing flies and ants, he would cup his hands around them and carry them back outdoors.

I showed Sergeant Sidhu the original letter from Ronald Dey.

"He sounds like a nice man," he said, after reading it. "But there's still nothing there for us."

"He's a lovely man. That's one reason I want to make sure nothing is wrong." Then I showed him the second letter.

"You doubt the authenticity of the first letter, is that it, Mrs. Chatterjee?"

"Please call me Tara."

"Very well . . . Tara. Let me give you a hardheaded answer. Everything you've told me so far still adds up to a domestic misunderstanding. Off the record, I could say that you and I, as Indians, might put our heads together and agree there are cultural anomalies here, but under California law, I'm sure you agree, they don't rise to criminality. A guilty father thinks his son is tall and handsome, but he turns out to be short and crude—show me a father, Mrs. Chatterjee. A teenage mother panics and covers up the fact she ever gave birth? A judge would say at least she didn't throw him in a Dumpster. Maybe you've got a circumstantial case here for attempted extortion—I don't know, I'm not a lawyer—but it looks to me more like a matter for the courts than the police."

"I must have sounded very foolish. I'm sorry to waste your time." I meant it, but I also felt tears beginning to rise. I'd wanted to be the good San Franciscan, tolerant, accepting, open to possibility, not judgmental, not quick to condemn.

Then Jack made a startling statement. "I'll make you a deal. You come clean with me, and I'll do something for you. First, I demand total honesty."

"What do you mean, 'come clean'? You're the second person outside the family who even knows."

"Mrs. Chatterjee, you'd be surprised what I know."

"What do you know, Sergeant Sidhu?"

"There's nothing strange in the fact that this boy you suspect of not being your real nephew should know your name and where to find you. I know who you are, and I even know your address. If you're trying to hide your identity, let me tell you it won't work. It's admirable in a way, and I appreciate your situation, but it's not always realistic. You can't be anonymous."

"What in the world are you talking about? My 'situation'?"

"Look at my badge. What does it say? 'Ethnic Squad.' This conversation is off the record. SFPD expects me to keep tabs on the Indian community. Bishwapriya Chatterjee *is* the Indian community."

"We've been divorced for over five years."

"I know that. The State of California knows that, but that doesn't matter. *'In the eye of Brahma . . .'* isn't that what Hindus say? Under California law five years is a long time, people move on with their lives. But in the eyes of Indians you'll always be linked. If Mrs. Bishwapriya Chatterjee comes to me with a problem, I have to ask myself, whose problem is it, really?"

"Mine, obviously."

He shook his head, not exactly disagreeing, an Indian gesture. "I wish."

How hopelessly sexist! I wanted to shout. I come to you with a concern and you can only see it as my ex-husband's problem? I stopped smiling, stopped thinking of dear old Venkatesan and the gentle Ronald Dey, stopped thinking of myself as an Indian-lady school assistant trying to raise her son as a single mom. The ancient, tattered thread that connected me to Bish made him the surrogate target, not Chris, not my sister. Bish, and me, and Rabi.

In Jack Sidhu's mind, the fact that I would always be attached to Bish Chatterjee seemed to change the significance of a great many minor crimes committed by Indians just about anywhere on this continent. Visa fraud and marriage rackets and prostitution and sleazy temple managers; pickpockets and burglars, they had nothing—nothing overtly—to do with legitimate businessmen like Bish. But look what happened to the Russians, he said, or the

Chinese, the Vietnamese, and the Italians, of course. The successful members of any community are the special prey of petty criminals who make their way under the radar, who live generally hidden lives, who are all roughly organized either here or in a distant homeland. There were lots of Indian millionaires who weren't too choosy about where they put their sudden money. Scratch an Indian millionaire, said Jack Sidhu, and you don't know what you'll find. Did I know any of them? Probably I did. Did Bish ever talk of threats against himself or his property? He wouldn't have told me even if there had been.

He had worked himself into a righteous anger, a young man with a patriarch's rage. Even his books, the special files he kept on every Indian criminal, the clippings, the exchanges with fellow officers in Toronto and Vancouver, L.A. and New York, were sometimes defiled. Indians (and I thought I heard an unmistakable echo, *you Hindus*) often came to him with legitimate-sounding complaints and asked him to open the books, asking him as a special favor, sometimes with a little money on the side, as "one of their own" in a position of power and sensitivity, to help them screen potential business contacts, marriage candidates, or employees. To Jack, the books were sacred, like the Sikhs' Holy Granth, or the Muslim's Quran. How dare they demand he defile them for personal profit?

And what did the books display? I'd expected something neat, rows of pictures like a college yearbook. It was an immense scrapbook with the bulk of a medieval Bible, bulging like an upholsterer's sampler. Face after unremarkable face flashed by, none leaping out, all vaguely familiar. Furtive black eyes, mustaches, full heads of longish black hair. Most could easily pass unnoticed on the streets of Bombay or Delhi. My Indian radar had let me down again. Contrary to Jack's assurances of their general nonviolence, many were wanted for murder.

"Mostly, it's from drugs and alcohol. 'Poor anger-management skills' or 'bad conflict-resolution models,' we like to say. Most of these guys are from villages, they come to Bombay and Delhi and fall in with a bad crowd. So let's check the Bangladesh book."

"He speaks the Calcutta dialect," I said. Jack rolled his eyes. "He's not Bangladeshi." My family spoke both.

"That would be very helpful in India, but to the SFPD all Bengalis are brothers in crime."

"Why should I waste my time looking at pictures from India?"

"Because all these guys are now here, Mrs. Chatterjee. They get smuggled in, they owe money to the smuggler so they work it off by committing crimes. Usually petty stuff, usually within the community. Sikhs were smuggling guys in to start a war against India. Most of these guys are expendable. If they get caught, they get deported. Most of them aren't caught."

"I thought better of us before I came in here."

"I'm glad you came anyway," he said, and left it there. Glad for my sake, or his? Glad meaning it was good that my innocence had suffered?

"Can I ask you a personal question?"

"I was born in Punjab, assuming that was your question." It was.

"You seem so American, but you've got an obsession with India, a very strange aspect of India."

"I am interested in the fact that an essentially peaceful culture like India's can periodically erupt with such violence, does that answer your other question? I did a thesis on it. Then I started looking at individual behavior. I did another thesis on that. When I was two years old, in 1976, we moved to Vancouver. My father had been a policeman in India, so the Sikh fundamentalists marked him down as a traitor. They killed him. I've been here since 1984.

I got a lacrosse scholarship to Stanford. B.A., M.A., Ph.D. Doctor Jack."

I must have been smiling. "You find something amusing?"

"This boy we're looking for is your age exactly. I got married in 1984 and came here the same year you did. I was thinking about the tides of history washing all of us up on the same beaches at the same time, that's all." Dr./Sergeant Sidhu would probably call that a soap opera version of history, but Jasbir seemed to ponder it. "Did you ever see *The Talented Mr. Ripley?*"

"Now you're frightening me," I said.

"You said you have a son."

"He's fifteen. And he's met this . . . Ripley. I think they see each other." I mentioned the time on Haight.

"Please be careful, Mrs. Chatterjee. I don't mean to alarm you, but off the record, I happen to take your inquiry very seriously. I can imagine this boy you're worried about, the one you call the 'real' Christopher, meeting someone, maybe one of these faces in the book. Maybe they meet in one of those cheap downtown potels"—he used our community's shorthand for motels owned by Patels—"with the fancy names that advertise in India. They start talking, Indian to Indian, and even Bengali to Bengali. Some of these guys," he pointed to the books, "they hang out in the lobbies of the cheapest hotels where they know Third World tourists are booked and will be too shy to cancel once they see their rooms. Let's say your nephew, who's new to the country, is very trusting. He might be afraid of American men, but not an Indian. He's assuredly carrying cash—you say his father is rich. So this other young man strikes up a conversation. 'What brings you to San Francisco?' Perhaps he answers 'My mashi'—that's the Bengali word, isn't it?—'lives here. Perhaps you've heard of Bishwapriya Chatterjee? She is married to him.' He doesn't know you have divorced, that wouldn't be the Indian way, would it? 'Oh,' he says, 'of course I know her! Everyone knows the Chatterjees!' Perhaps your nephew asks 'Do you know where Rivoli Street is?' 'Let me show you,' says his new young friend."

"That's very convincing. Very frightening. Do you think that first letter was written here?"

"It could have been. If we had a real case to go on, we might run a test on the paper and the envelope. May I ask another thing? Are you and your son living alone? Do you have someone else in your house?"

"The Zen Master of the Retrofit," I said.

"I've seen the truck. You're instantly connected, pager, cell phone, something like that?" All that, I assured him. "Take my card, and let me get your phone number. I'll check up on a few things."

"What kind of few things?" I remembered my friend, poor Meena Trivedi, back in my Atherton days. *My doctor said everything was fine, he just had to check up on a few things.*

"If you can explain what the 'Zen of Retrofitting' means, I might tell you."

I'd asked Andy the same question. "It means protecting yourself against something you can't see that might never come. But if it does, you'll be glad you did."

"Sounds like my job. Here's what I'll do. I'll fire up the CHATTY network, thanks to Mr. Chatterjee, and we'll try to get the official Christopher Dey visa photo from INS. That'll settle things with one call."

I must have looked skeptical.

"All I want to know is if I'm being totally hysterical or very clever. Last week, if anyone had suggested to me that my sister had had a child out of wedlock, I would have laughed in his face. Coming this far is a big thing, but now I don't know if I've gone too far too fast and made a total idiot of myself."

He sat on the edge of the table where the books had been.

"Probably," he said, "but I'm still glad we talked. You've raised some doubts in my mind at least. Now you've got to turn it over to the professionals."

"My sisters think I'm crazy. I've broken the bond between us."

"If this guy's crooked, he might give it one good shot and just disappear. If he starts hinting at blackmail or something, we can be on him in two minutes. And don't forget, the photo might come back positive, he might turn out to be the real Chris, and you'll just have to deal with it."

"I keep thinking you're holding something back."

"I can't hold back what I don't know, Mrs. Chatterjee. Officially, this conversation ended half an hour ago. Unofficially, I'm taking it a step further. Until I know more, all I can say is that old line from 'Hill Street Blues.' "

Be careful out there.

        ✓   ✓   ✓

Andy also has a giant holy book, but he keeps it in his head. Buddhist stories, haiku, and koan, appropriate for all occasions. They bring him peace, and it's that peace that attracted me to him.

For Hindus, the world is constructed of calamities. The stories are wondrous, lurid, and beautiful, full of shape-changing, gender-bending, grand-scale slaughter, polymorphous sexuality. Miss a ritual and a snake will invade your wedding. The gods destroy and remake the world every four billion years. When the stories are rendered as paintings, they inspire great flights of fancy and color. My mother told me hundreds of stories from the puranas and the Mahabharata—even girls from the upper classes going to English-language Catholic schools got the classic exposure. In school, we listened politely at what passed for miracles in the Old and New

Testaments, but in a village setting they would hardly have raised an eyebrow.

In Andy's telling, the stories are plain and every day. "Traveler Po came across a fork in the road. . . . Farmer Jiang had three beautiful daughters. . . . Pears from farmer Wu's fields were considered the sweetest in all China. Japanese and Chinese paintings came to life. They were not the hot, phosphorescent colors of India, but the cool, black-and-white stick drawings of winter trees against the winter clouds, white geese flying across a gray mountain range in the snow.

I would bring great problems to him and he'd listen patiently and then reduce them to parables by spinning a story about the tailor with inferior silk who gets an imperial commission, a singer in the opera who comes down with a sore throat. Or a fish in a net, a bird whose song is so impossibly beautiful she must be caged, or the fisherman's cormorant with the ring around its throat. We are like that cormorant, he would say, diving because it is in our nature, capturing fish, also because it is in our nature, unable to swallow, because something is in conflict with our nature. Always starving in the midst of plenty. All the lures of the world—beauty, wealth, ambition, desire—are not tests to be overcome, like the Hindu sadhus, or urges to be suppressed, like the Christian saints. They are simply aspects of creation to be ignored.

I was still a little ashamed of myself for having broken my word and gone to the police, and worse, depressed from what I'd found. I'd raised the stakes, exerted new pressure on that invisible tectonic plate, perhaps causing "Christopher" to do the same. I'd deal with that much later, after coming back from Rabi's school. Something worthy of serious talk over spiced tea should always be left at the close of day. Rabi and I left Andy greasing the track of the automatic garage door.

When you are armed with Hindu stories, every earthly tragedy is a shadow of something greater, from a previous time. Consolation comes from comparison. Andy called it "Suck-It-Up Hinduism." Modern calamities, losses, and disappointments that seem inconsolable are minor indeed compared to the suffering of giants on battlefields in the immemorial past. We took our comfort, or moral instruction, from the glory and folly of the gods. Had a hard day at the office? Bad test scores? Well, at least you didn't get decapitated and have to go through life with an elephant's head replacement. For the Buddhists, suffering is not the echo of some far greater terror, but a continuation of something no different. Something no greater than the tides, the wilting of flowers, the dying of leaves. Consolation follows from continuity. The death of your love is no larger than the problem of Grandmother Shui-Ying, who lost the proper thread to sew her husband's button. While she looked and looked for the right color and just the right strength of silk, her husband died of the cold.

10

I didn't know it would ever become a big thing between us, but I'd been a convent girl and I hated it, and Bish had been a St. Xavier's boy before going to Presidency, then to the Institute of Technology, and finally to Stanford, and he credited St. Xavier's for everything in life he'd ever accomplished. He'd loved the ties and blazers, the white shirts, the polished shoes, the little striped beanies for cricket, and the modified diet of British food. "Comfort food" for Bish Chatterjee (should any woman be looking for the most direct entry to a divorced billionaire's stomach, or heart) is trifle and just about any other pudding of unimaginable composition. I remember thinking of "pudding" the first time I heard it from our Christian cook as "put in" and that's the way it's remained for me.

And so, when we were blessed with a son in Atherton, California, Bish looked for a school like the ones we'd known in Calcutta, and not finding one, created it. There were by then sufficient numbers of Third Worlders in Silicon Valley from Hong Kong, Singapore, India, and Pakistan, suffering from the same nostalgia and anxiety over their children's future, to endow a school and to lure the proper kind of regimental schoolmasters from their retirement cottages on islands off Vancouver, or sheep stations in New Zealand, or even hill stations in India. Their time, obviously, had long passed in England, but for them, no matter the country or the clientele, the food, dress, curriculum, and discipline would remain uncompromisingly English.

Rabi spent his first six years of education in an Atherton school, a California school, that prided itself on the English model, with a "Commons" for lunch, prayers in the morning, Greek and Latin, and hard-fought sports whose rules, vocabularies, and passions were unreplicated anywhere on this continent, and perhaps any time in this century. Indian millionaires were the new monarchs of snob, and the old schoolmasters took note, spiking their vocabularies with Indo-Anglicisms of the 1920s ("Let's take a dekko, shall we?") and their lunches with "curries," that conveyed their sympathies with excessive turmeric that stained our children's shirts with bright yellow that no amount of bleach could wash out.

When we divorced, "The Academy at Atherton" was the first thing to go. Rabi was an artistic child. His earliest talent was for drawing. At the beginning, he was like an idiot savant, copying anything from books and the papers without any knowledge of, or interest in, the figures he was copying. But his special gift was for cartooning, which is hard to justify to a very serious-minded father who'd arrived in America as a scholarship student and within ten years was employing five thousand workers and had a net worth of $700 million. Going against reality with some personal exaggerated corruption of reality was an invitation to poverty.

Since Bish had been recognized as a genius from his earliest school days, anything less than perfection from his son had to be a veiled attack on the standards he'd set for himself and for us. They were coming from "the Bhattacharjees," by which he meant the effete side of the family, a gaggle of women who exemplified the worst in the Bengali tradition, its self-centered, egotistical, fantastical devotion to poetry and the arts.

I cannot remember a night at home when Bish did not complain of Rabi's careless appearance, his sloppy penmanship, his slouching posture, his shuffling walk, his talk, his manners, and his limp handshake. "Remember, people are judging you by what they see. They can't look into your heart, into your soul, into your brain. Is your shirt tucked in? Are your shoes polished?" *I know*, he'd say with a certain glee. *Let them judge, what do I care about people like that?* To Bish, Rabi was too dependent, except when he was too adventurous. He was too fanciful, but not sufficiently bold. Life was all a matter of shaping up and hitting one's mark, satisfying expectation, achieving a quota. Repudiations of reality were destined to die a dishonorable death.

And so, I found him a school in San Francisco that was slanted to the arts, that never missed a theater or gallery opening, that staged its own students' work with student directors, actors, set designers, and wardrobe managers. They visited restaurants and reproduced the recipes. They dished soup at shelters. They interviewed the homeless. Initially, Rabi was terrified of so much freedom. Everything he had achieved in Atherton had been sweetened by resistance. (And not just resistance, I now think, but a certain fury.) Overnight, he was going to school with the children of San Francisco's bohemian elite, kids who'd never harbored an illiberal thought, nor suspected the existence of repressive social codes and norms of behavior.

Such schools are not easy for Bengali mothers either. I cannot describe it to Parvati, mother of topflight students in a topflight school, for whom entry to anything less than the Ivy League would be unacceptable. According to Bish, Rabi will be lucky to catch on as a dishwasher in one of the restaurants he's visited. He'll also be lucky if his father doesn't rescind details of his trust fund.

Bish could not tolerate a son who was not a perfect replica of himself; hardworking, respectful, brilliant. Soberly sociable. Effortlessly athletic. All the other fathers we knew, Indian or not, seemed to have succeeded in that most delicate and demanding of endeavors, steering an America-born son or daughter through the pitfalls and temptations of an American life. Existence was too easy in Atherton, they agreed, America made children soft in the brain as well as the body; it weakened the moral fiber. They grew up without respect for family and tradition. At the same time, they were protective men who did not want to expose their children to the grade-dampening distractions of after-school jobs, or to the possible heartbreak of dating, particularly of dating American boys or girls. Noncontact sports were acceptable. Classical Indian music was safe. Computer camps and AP science classes were de rigueur. For boys, art was out. None of those fathers, in their carefully orchestrated teenage years in various countries, had worked after school or in the summer, none had run free with a pack of school friends, and none of them had ever had a date before marriage.

The challenge was to create degrees of difficulty for their children that would emulate the stress and simple deprivation most of them had known in the tropical cities of their childhood. Most children were sent back to Asia every summer, to soak up the culture and language from their cousins and grandparents. We tried it with Rabi, and he rebelled. So here he was, Bish Chatterjee, the most prominent Indian of all, the man everyone looked up to, and he suspected he was being laughed at behind his back. Rabi hated all sports, and therefore played none unless his father was watching, in which case he would deliberately stumble on to the field and proceed to muck it up. He refused to play with other boys, he'd spend hours in his room, drawing and listening to old albums scrounged from yard sales.

It is with a certain dread that I attend each semester's open house for parents, to meet with his teachers and review the portfolios of his work. My Zen Master doesn't "do" schools, since he dropped out at fifteen and disapproves of all teaching, or any kind of "knowledge" that a truly educated person will have to discard before real learning can take place. Rabi and I head down to Mission on the Muni, I, bracing myself for the semiannual confrontation with the consequences of my difficult love for this country. I would not have survived in an unstructured environment; how dare I subject my son to it? Out of structure, Bish created greater order. Out of order, I created chaos. Out of chaos, one hopes, Rabi will create something resembling a new American consciousness.

With a boy like Rabi, every report card and conference is an adventure. What a pleasure it must have been for my parents, or Bish's, to know that top marks could merely be reassigned to us semester by semester, year by year. Rabi, with all the artistic talent in the world, could bring home B's and C's simply by deciding not to show his work. On the bus ride he told me things were going moderately well. His science teachers had capitulated. They were letting him illustrate a panel of Galapagos finches and iguanas, a biodiversity and food-chain chart for San Francisco Bay, even Andy's favorite, the known fault lines of the Bay Area. Still to come: human reproduction! Twenty-four hours in the life of a cancer cell! It was good to see him excited.

"Have you seen Christopher recently?" I managed to interject, as casually as possible. We were passing through an area of cheap hotels, "potels," with pretty names (the Casa Prieta comes to mind).

Surprisingly, he answered me. "I don't think he is who he says he is."

My blood ran cold. "And when did you come to that conclusion?"

"A while back."

"And why didn't you tell me?"

"Ma, I treat you on a strictly need-to-know basis. Believe me, it works out better for both of us."

"Well, anything about Christopher is something I need to know."

He went into one of his retreats, rather like Andy, but without the closed eyes and rocking motion. More like, *Who is this annoying woman?* "He was asking too many questions, if you must know."

"Like what?"

"Like you're doing now. They were the kind of questions that wouldn't be strange in a normal conversation but he was asking them like from a prepared list. It didn't sound natural."

"What . . . kind . . . of . . . questions was he asking that sounded so unnatural?"

"If I told you they'd sound even weirder. Like, what's your mother's social security number? I thought that was a little strange."

That's enough.

"Don't worry. I made up a bunch of numbers."

"What worries me is you didn't tell me sooner."

Then I told him of my afternoon at the police station, the suspicions of Jack Sidhu, even the minor investigation he'd launched into the visa. And he surprised me yet again.

"Sounds smart," he said.

"Who do you think he is?"

"I've seen him hustle money and drugs down on the Haight.

He told me he learned how to do it in the orphanage, and I believed him. Let's say he probably learned it in a public institution of some sort."

"Do you think he's dangerous?"

"Ma, life's dangerous."

The Kraken is breaking through the ocean's surface: Hadn't that been Dr. Ronald Dey's warning? "I meant, dangerous to you and to us. To the other Chris Dey."

"You think he's dangerous. The police think he is. You seem to think I think he is." He cracked his knuckles, first the right hand, then the left. I hadn't seen him do that before. It was something Bish did when he was thinking through problems. "I don't know a single bad thing he's done, and I don't even know for sure he isn't who he says he is."

At the school, I was on my own with a list of teachers and rooms to visit. Rabi had some actors to rehearse for a directing class. We'd meet in a couple of hours.

. , .

"I want you to notice how much freer Rob's brush strokes are," she said, as we riffled through his portfolio. I was astonished not just by his freer brush strokes, which were, as always, a wonder to me, but by his art teacher. Her nametag said Indy Verma, which stood for Indira, I imagined, and Verma denoted her caste and region and native language as plainly to me as mine did to her, if she cared, or knew. She couldn't be more than twenty-five, wore a linen jacket over faded jeans and a T-shirt, and talked like a Valley girl with "likes" and "totallys" in every sentence and "he goes" and "I'm like" instead of "he said" and "I said." She had gone to UC–Santa Cruz. How do our children learn the language, I wondered, thinking back to our elocution lessons in Calcutta, the prime directive for convent education being Cambridge-standard English, and the memory still fresh in the minds of the older nuns of Language Inspectors coming out from London every year to grade Loreto girls' degree of acceptable Englishness. Like Rabi, she was probably born here, a flawless American with American ways and "issues," as they like to say. He'd never mentioned an "Indian" teacher, not that he ever would, and as we talked, she didn't ask sly or leading questions about India or acknowledge our joint ancestry. We've become so numerous and sophisticated a community that we're like Italians or Jews; it would be gauche to run over to another Indian face thinking, *Mon semblable, mon frère*, and asking, "Where are you from? Would you like to come over for tea? Do you have children?" I wonder if she'd noticed an Indian content in his painting and cartooning. Duh, Tara. These second-generation kids are a wonder to me. Is it only my vanity that insists I'm as great a mystery to her as she is to me, that she yearns to find a way to draw me aside and pour her heart out? "Auntie, Auntie, my parents want me to marry a boy from Bhopal and I'm suicidal about it." Or is she dealing drugs out of one of these cheap Mission apartments nearby?

"He's still this totally great cartoonist, but I've told him, Rob, you've got this awesome lyrical style and you've got this hard-edge R. Crumb thing going, too, y'know? I told him to send off a portfolio of his stuff to the 'zines. His captions are awesome, too. I told him he should be applying to art schools right now, but he said that he was bored of doodling and wanted to try something completely different."

"But art has always been his passion," I said. Imagining any kind of future for Rabi was difficult, but ever since I'd left Bish, I'd clung to the notion that whatever else I had done that damaged my son, I at least had saved him from a life of ridicule and maladjustment. He was an artist, he was my artist, and I didn't care that he'd turned his back on all the career options that had been presented to him at the Academy of Atherton.

"Well, you see in some of these sketches that he did in the last couple of weeks, he's got a kind of dream-landscape going. Pretty scary stuff, actually. And here, he's sketching some scenes for a play."

"Did he tell you what's 'more interesting' than art?"

"I've seen him hanging with the film department. These sketches here, they look like film studies, you know, what they call a storyboard? A shot planner, like. That's the Haight, isn't it?" She flipped the pages. Hippies, tourists, outdoor cafes, beggars. "Some interiors here, the free clinic, the AIDS clinic, needle exchange—the school went down there a couple of weeks ago and passed out needles—that's probably where he got the idea. He hasn't told me, but it looks like he's planning to make a documentary. He'll probably do very well. I'm just sorry to lose him. You don't get many like him."

Two doors down, in the room marked "Drama Department" a middle-aged white man with a tight beard and close-cropped graying hair leaped from his desk and pointed a conspiratorial finger at me, grinning broadly. His name was Joe Corrigan. "I know you! You've got to be Rob's mama. And a very proud woman you must be!" Rob's play about two Indian sisters on the telephone, it turned out, was not just a future project; it was finished and would be performed in the spring semester. "It's deliciously wicked," said Mr. Corrigan, "as you doubtless know."

"He hasn't shared it with me." I tried to sound amused and unconcerned. "How wicked?"

"Well, let's just say we're not in 'Our Town' anymore. Rob's got this Indian thing going, but it's India the way *Streetcar* is New Orleans if you get my meaning. It's Ravi Shankar meets Albee, or Beckett meets Ivory and Merchant. You've got this bright little boy and parents who are absolutely, I mean totally clueless about what's going on in his life. The mother and the aunties are always on the phone boasting about their kids' lives and what successes they are—it's *hilarious*, if you haven't heard it. The boy's listening in, so the audience gets to hear both sides."

"Sounds like I should speak with him." I tried to sound amused.

"I'm sure Rob's just holding back for the right moment to spring it. I wouldn't be worried about any autobiographical elements. In fact, I was really worried how this meeting would go. I pictured you as sort of a traditional East Indian, and a whole lot older. You're obviously not like the mother in the play. If you were," and here he allowed himself a little giggle, "you'd be all decked out in a fancy sari and positively dripping with gold." I assumed this was a compliment, gay man to Indian woman. There's so much in this life for a little Calcutta girl to assimilate.

"Mostly, I just want to thank you for Rob," he said. "If he wanted to act, he could act and maybe even become a great actor. If he wanted to direct, he could do that. I mean, the boy's what, fifteen years old, and I already think of him as a"—he scratched the air in front of him, indicating quotation marks—"man of the theater. By the way, have you seen Mike yet? I've got a note here. 'Please tell Mrs. Chatterjee to see Mike.' Last office on the left, end of the hall."

The name on the door was Dr. Miguel Salvidar, and under it, "Counselor." It had been a winning night so far, the best reports on Rabi I'd ever got. Two teachers, two raves; I was ready for the counselor. From his name, and the neighborhood, I'd expected a short and heavyset Chicano, but Dr. Salvidar was tall and fair with sandy blond hair turning to gray. "I have a message to see you," I said. "I'm Tara Chatterjee, Rabi's mother." We must have registered a brief, mutual surprise.

He gestured to a leather chair. "We seem to be in the middle of a Rob Festival. He's got paintings in the hall, cartoons in the yearbook, and a play in the spring. I'm even more impressed by his photos, and we don't have them up yet. You should be very proud."

"Oh, yes."

He shuffled some pages in a folder, then looked up. "He's not easy, is he?"

"Why would you say that?"

I must have sounded defensive, because Dr. Salvidar shot me an amused glance.

"All right, let's try that one again." He closed the folder and put it away in a desk drawer. "How would you describe him, Mrs. Chatterjee?"

"Not exactly as 'not easy.' "

He was immediately apologetic. "I wasn't implying any neglect on your part. I should have said that there will always be an imbalance between what we can do for him and what he'll do for himself. In fact, I should have said from the beginning that he's always very complimentary toward you. It's in his files."

I must have looked confused. "What kind of files are you talking about?"

"We ask all the students here to write self-evaluations, then we can upgrade them if we spot an anomaly. If we think it's something serious, we ask the student's permission to discuss it with a parent. They're children, after all, so there's a guardian's legal right to know what we're talking about."

Suddenly, I didn't want to know. "And what are you talking about with Rabi?"

"Don't worry, Mrs. Chatterjee, I have his permission. In fact, he was quite insistent that I talk with you. He said he'd rather that I talked about it than him."

"What is this 'it'?"

I know, I wanted to say. It had to be something more about Christopher. I just hoped the police weren't involved. From his youngest years, I'd sensed that Rabi had not just an inner, artistic life to hide from Bish, but an even more secret life that he guarded against me. At least he occasionally showed me his cartoons and paintings. *When have I ever interfered with your life? When have I ever behaved like a Bengali mother, sucking the life out of you?* I've always been open about Andy. He likes Andy. He didn't know about the others, and they were over quickly. Andy's been a better father than Bish. They joke around; Rabi's interested in koans and haikus. But he's always held himself aloof from me.

"Yes," I agreed. "He can be difficult."

Dr. Salvidar reached into the thick folder on his desk and pulled out a single sheet. I thought of Jack Sidhu's book of Bengali felons. "Rabi says here, earlier this year: *I am like a camera, faster than the brain or the eye. I take in everything, but I don't always know what I've seen until I develop the film. If I don't continually dump it out there, I'll blow up.* I think he means all his self-expression. I've got his play here, and a few odds and ends. He can be very funny. I think the word is 'wickedly' funny."

"He doesn't always show it," I admitted.

"Comics are famous for their unhappiness. How we see things and how we show them can be very different. He sees how you love him, and he's trying to show you . . . greater love."

What kind of school is this? How could Dr. Mike know the insults, the contempt that passed so easily from Rabi's lips? I wanted some sympathy, I wanted my own counselor. "The last five years haven't been easy for him," I said. *For me. For me.* "His father and I divorced, which is rare enough among Indians." *I was brave. I stood up for myself and my son.* "If we're unhappy, we're expected to suck it up for the kids' sake or our reputations. We worry what our parents will think, even when they're halfway around the world and we're middle-aged adults." *It's never for ourselves.* "He's had to make some big adjustments." *And recently, he's been hanging out with murderers in drug clinics and lying about it.* "Sometimes, I feel like I don't know him at all."

"That's what I want to talk about. You may be on to something. Rabi does have something very important on his mind, a lot more important than all his plays and paintings and even his photos." *I know. We're worried about a murder. He knows a lot more about it.* "There's no way this is going to be easy, Mrs. Chatterjee. I can promise you that you and Rabi are going to leave here tonight with a very different relationship than the one you came in with. I wouldn't be doing this if I didn't think it will be a better and much healthier relationship. I'm going to ask you to listen to what he has written, and please not react in any way until I've finished." *A poem!* I thought. *What a perfect Bengali, after all.* "I think by the end you'll be very proud of Rob in ways you can't even imagine now." *What could it be—an epic? Your grandfather will be so proud!* "Here's the statement he wanted me to read."

Ma: I am sorry to burden you at a time when you are worried about Christopher. This is not about him, either the real one or the fake. It is about me, another kind of fake, who is very tired of playing games. I know I have been a bad son to you and I haven't been supportive of your needs, and sometimes I act and sound disrespectful, and more times than I'd like to admit, I've acted like an asshole. I don't think that's the kind of person I really am, and I'm going to make an effort to change.

Ever since I've been a little boy, at least since I was five or six years old, I have been aware that I will only grow up to disappoint my father, which is something I can deal with, but that I might also cause you great pain, which is something unbearable to me. What is it I realized when I was so young? I understood that the games people played and the shows on television and the books I read and every conversation I had in school were lies, meaning that everyone and everything was lying to me. No one else even seemed to notice it, or to care, and I never heard anyone say it was all a pack of lies. That's not entirely true—there are always a few people, like in the comic strips and comedy records I used to listen to who spoke directly over the heads of other kids, and teachers and adults, and so I listened exclusively to them.

I naturally assumed there was something deeply flawed in me that kept me from getting the point of so much good advice from Dad, and sometimes from you and always from the teachers. I just couldn't believe that intelligent people actually cared about 99 percent of the stuff they did or actually believed the stuff they were saying. *I just couldn't get it*. Either I was too stupid to go on living, or too smart to survive in such a world, and either way it didn't point to an interesting future. More times than I want to admit here, I thought of ending my pain, Dad's disappointment, and your unhappiness. I'm glad I didn't, of course, and I think those years are behind me.

Now: here's the one thing I knew back then that might come as a big surprise to you now. I knew that I had a different "sexual orientation" long before there was an ugly name like that for it (just bring your compass, and everything straightens out). Ma, I am gay (that's the name of my play, incidentally). It's another first for the family, another distinction we're going to have to work on. I've always known it, and I've tested it. Don't worry, I'm too Bengali to be reckless.

I remember one of Andy's haikus, about a fish or a bird or a herd of caribou, some vast horde that acts as a single body. They move on impulse like they're all wired to the same computer, but—and here's the haiku—there's always going to be one of them who's first and another one who's last. Some are going to be in the middle and some are going to be at the edges.

You can tell Andy I've drawn a lot of strength from that. I don't know if I took away the right message, but to me it meant some individuals in society are just fated to be on the outside and some are slower, and some just never get that whole wildebeest thing down.

Mike's a cool guy, we call him the Gay Gaucho since he's from Argentina (but has probably never ridden a horse), and he volunteers as the Gay Students' adviser. He's helped me a lot. I thought I had probably gone as far as I could go in disappointing Dad, but this will definitely push him over the edge. I'm not going to hide anything from anybody, but don't worry, I won't rub his face in it. When he gets a ticket to my play, he might actually figure it out for himself. Eventually it might sink in that he's not going to get grandchildren, at least not from me.

I think my first words were "You're Argentine?" which sent him into gales of laughter that renewed itself every time he looked up at me, sitting bland and composed in the leather chair. I had meant to say "thank you very much" or "how exactly have you been helping my son?" or "how many students are you helping in this way?" because the gay population had suddenly exploded in my life, and there was a clear possibility that everyone I had ever known could be gay, or gay without knowing it. It was like the onset of a power outage in Calcutta, a sudden chill or darkness that cut the fans and the lights and brought all the sounds of the school and of busy streets indoors. The ambient noises were so loud I couldn't hear myself, or Mike Salvidar, talking. I only remember him looking directly at me, still grinning after all the laughter and begging me to stop in anytime to talk about Rabi, and pronouncing me the coolest mama in San Francisco. Are you Argentine? Fabulous!

I looked at his rows of books, some in Spanish, many others

familiar from the counselor's office in my school. No strange titles leaped out, and I know I thought, *But you don't look gay*, the way Mr. Corrigan had, and I thought, *From now on, I'm going to have to stop thinking this way*. It would do me good to have something other than Christopher Dey to focus on. In fact, I didn't care at that moment if Christopher Dey were alive or dead, if he was a Bhattacharjee or not, if he posed a danger to us or not. I wondered if Andy already knew about Rabi, or had guessed. What would he think, did he have a story for it? *When it came time for his marriage, Farmer Zhang's son declared himself repulsed by every woman in the village* . . . All the dangers in the world seemed manageable at that moment, they'd shrunk against the magnitude of this revelation. How to understand it; how to explain it to others; how to behave with the nearest, closest male in my life? I suddenly remembered driving Meena Trivedi to the doctor's. She came out with a diagnosis of inoperable ovarian cancer and said, Let's go shopping. Let's run up a bill! Let's put it on credit! She said, *Finally* I have perspective. She was the first of my age to die.

I tracked Rabi down in the theater and stood a few moments at the back entrance, watching my son. He was seated in the middle with his long legs slouched over the rows in front. I hadn't realized how tall he'd become. He was shouting out instructions to two girls and a boy on stage. No, no! You're overacting! One of the girls was playing me, I realized. The boy was him. One of the girls was Chinese, the boy seemed an Indo-American mixture, the other girl was white.

Outside, the hookers had reclaimed the streets. We picked up a taxi that had just dropped off a john, as they say. I called Andy, but there was no answer.

"I liked your Doctor Mike," I said. "And I liked the letter you wrote."

He seemed not to hear me. He was staring at the double-parked cars just outside his school. "I should have brought my camera. Look at all that shit going down."

Our Sikh taxi driver seemed sinister, staring at me through his rearview mirror and dropping his eyes each time I looked up. The street was an open drug market. Provocatively made-up girls in tight, colorful dresses weren't even girls. Yesterday, practiced daughter of Calcutta that I was, comfortable within a filtered gaze, I might not have noticed any of it. One door had closed, another opened. I could hear a pretentious television voice playing in my head: *And this is how it will be from now on.* We know, but we do not talk, silent conspirators in a slightly altered world. Something more for Bish to hold against me: effete Bhattacharjeeness or my excessive Americanness.

The route home took us up Seventeenth Street through the Castro. I know divorced women who've recently bought houses in the Castro and revel in its services and safety, but I'd never felt a connection. For yesterday's Tara, it felt freaky. When Parvati visited me from Bombay just after the divorce, I drove her down the Castro. We had coffee in a sidewalk cafe. Notice anything different? I asked. A lot of good-looking men, she said, but hardly any Indians. Finally, she said, a place in America without a bunch of fat women showing off their varicose veins. No, she didn't notice, and when I told her to look again, and what she was looking at, she refused to believe. She didn't linger over the coffee.

A gay city the next valley over from our house, its sidewalks teeming with young men in T-shirts and jeans and leather jackets. Short hair, beards, nineteenth-century mustaches, and military postures. At a light on the crowded corner of Market Street, a middle-aged man in full white tie, tails-and-tux held a bouquet of long-stemmed roses.

"I tell you, Ma, always carry a camera."

"It's such an interesting area," I said. *Please*, I wanted to add, *am I getting it right?*

"It's okay, Ma. I think they're silly. In fact, I think gays see the whole world as just slightly ridiculous."

I thought, I'd like to see it that way, too.

Andy likes to talk about "the shift," the moment when Zen finally picked him up, moved him slightly, and then set him down again, like a phonograph needle. Same record, different groove, and he never got back to the place he'd started. He was always a few beats behind everyone else and that was the way he liked it.

I picked up my phone messages. "Mrs. Chatterjee, this is Jack Sidhu, SFPD. I have some new information on the matter we discussed. Please give me a call at my home number this evening." Jack Sidhu was a name from yesterday. It seemed like weeks since I'd gone through his photos.

✎   ✎   ✎

The dark side of Buddhism. I never learned the haikus to illustrate anger. When we arrived, Andy was standing by his truck, the garage door still open, the garage light still on. He was loading his truck with boxes. I was still a little numb from Rabi's letter and looking forward to a long, spiced-tea discussion.

He greeted me instead, "Good-bye, Tara. Have a happy life."

I must have said, "Okay, okay, what's this about?" and maybe even reached out to touch him, and then he asked, "Who is this Jack Sidhu?"

"Oh, for God's sake, you're not jealous, are you? He's just an officer I met," I said.

"You either have a very high opinion of yourself or a very low one of me. This isn't about jealousy. You went to the police today, didn't you?"

"I couldn't just wait around."

"You went to the police when waiting around was exactly the right thing to do. We agreed not to escalate it. You went to the police even though we decided not to. And now the police are calling back. Now they've found something. They always find something, that's what they are, professional complicators. They're like surgeons, they find something, they've got to start cutting."

"Andy, it's no big deal." *Let me tell you what's a big deal.* Rabi was already inside.

"No, it is a big deal. You broke your word. You broke our trust. And you've started something you don't have a prayer of being able to stop. Go ahead, call your Jack Sidhu."

"He can wait. I've got something more important—"

"No, call him now. You just don't get it, but believe me, you're going to. I know the cops, they take over your life. When you went to him, you put everything else on hold. You had a chance to hold back and get your head straight, but you wouldn't take it. So call him. He's yours, you're his. The woman I knew is gone."

Jack Sidhu was on my speed-dial. A woman with a thick accent answered: mother? wife? Yesterday's Tara would have asked.

"Jasbir, please," I said.

While Andy loaded the last of his boxes, Jack Sidhu told me Christopher Dey's visa listed him at six feet three inches. "On the basis of that, Mrs. Chatterjee, I've issued a bulletin to pick up him, or anyone in possession of his documents. That means we've started a sweep of the hotels and shelters. I'll be in touch."

"All right, it's over. I'm going to be down at my sister's in case things come in for me. I'm really sorry it had to end like this. We had fun, but these last couple of weeks—no way."

I wasn't taking it in. I need you. I need you more tonight than I've ever needed you. I held out my arms and started toward him, and I give him credit for at least holding me while I cried. I was begging him, "Don't do this," and "We have to talk about Rabi," and if I understood his response it was, Let this thing blow over. Take a long Thanksgiving break. Send Rabi down to Atherton for a couple of weeks. And you, Tara, get out of town.

And then he was gone; he left me. My Zen Master just disappeared from my life as cleanly as he'd entered it. He even returned the key.

Part Two

11

Three nights later, I landed in Newark, ready for the "sisterly chat," ready to find out, once and for all, the story of Ron Dey. I arrived in plenty of time, and waited, as instructed, next to the baggage carousel. Harish Mehta, my brother-in-law, was a man I'd never met. Didi had never sent me his picture, although they've been married twenty years. I never thought it a problem, just one of those family oddities, until I landed in Newark Airport expecting a friendly Indian face to greet me and was reduced to asking every Indian man—and in Newark, there are a great many—excuse me, are you Harish Mehta? A few, I could tell, wanted to play, a good thing to know in my present condition. After three hours, I took a taxi to Upper Montclair.

Car breakdown, Harish apologized. Cell-phone mix-up, he added. I doubted he had either. For a Punjabi, which to the Bengali imagination conjures an image of Jack Sidhu–like athletic good looks, Harish was short, dark, and rather stout. Age had left him a gray fringe of hair around a shining pate. He was wearing a traditional white cotton kurta-pajama. "Mrs. Chatterjee," he said, bowing slightly and extending his arms toward the darkened interior, "welcome to our humble home. My wife is not yet returned from her work in the city. Allow me to make some tea."

I was already growing nostalgic for those brief hotel visits, a quick trip from JFK, midtown Manhattan, and a bottle of wine. It was eight o'clock—what kind of job did Didi have? After making the obligatory pot of tea, Harish mixed himself a little drink and returned to the basement, world headquarters of his mysterious consulting company.

I sat in the dark for another hour, sipping cold tea. There was no evidence that anyone actually used the living room; no television, no books, no papers or magazines strewn on the tables. The house was kept cold and dark, uncluttered as a crypt, with halls sealed off and the curtains drawn. Nothing out of place, but nothing to get misplaced, either. I could not imagine their home ever having been used for parties or dinners.

Didi got home at nine o'clock. She was not in a good mood. She gave a hug, a greeting, and a preemptive strike: "I'd rather fly cross-country than go cross-town on public transport." (I suppressed a naïve response: *When have you ever flown cross-country, Didi?*) "The filth of Port Authority! The human scum and riffraff! That poky little bus, and the 7 train and then getting shoved around on the shuttle, I don't know how I make it through the day." All of which translated as, *Why do I put up with this? We were not raised for this!*

Didi is forty-two years old, but doesn't look it. We have genes to die for, natural emollients, soft, black hair, and white teeth that have never known cavities or the need for straightening. In her fur-trimmed coat, the lustrous black collar sparkly with flakes of melting snow, she looked young as a schoolgirl, a dark-haired Lara from *Dr. Zhivago.* For both of us, the rewards of good genetic fortune were not looking so bright.

Her arrival was the signal for Harish to reappear and offer compliments on her beauty and stamina. In English, their only common language, they managed to sound both overwrought and insincere. He poured orange juice into Dixie cups for us, and we retired to the living room, while he started the dinner.

Didi had started working for a major tycoon in Queens with big plans for starting a TV show. He already had a community channel. It would be a vernacular soap opera for North American thirtysomething Bengalis, full of the vicissitudes of American life from an Indian perspective. And what were they, these vicissitudes, I wanted to know, wondering if murderous stalkers, gay sons, and breakups with Buddhist carpenters had any kind of communal resonance.

"Oh, dealing with the old in-laws," she said. "Wives working outside the home. Stopping the daughters from wanting to date. Maintaining a healthy home life and respect for culture and tradition."

"What about infidelities," I asked, and she professed shock. "Really, Tara! None of your X-rated American stuff here!" Divorce, wife-beating? "I'm sure that happens," she sniffed. "Just because bad things happen doesn't mean we have to show them on television. People watch television to escape their miserable lives. It's hard enough to keep up hope, why ruin it for people?" And what about the shady stock deals, the corrupt accountants, the land scams in India, the anorexic girls, and the endless intrigue of the arranged-marriage market?

"Maybe some of that, little bits here and there," she said. "Marriage negotiation is unavoidable."

"And are you acting in it, or writing it, or advising? You always wanted to act, Didi, this is your big chance!"

The answer came out of nowhere, harshly, in English. "And what does my little sister know about my big chance?" Almost immediately she slipped back to her lilting Bengali. "Well . . . there is a Joan Collins–like character we're talking about. She's unattached—divorced or something—very glamorous, very mysterious, and all the husbands are madly in love with her. She could break up marriages with a snap of her fingers. But really, of course, she's a very moral woman with a strong sense of virtue."

"Of course." I saw my sister as the vamp, just the right age, the perfect degree of worldly beauty, the style, the voice, the manner, and Lord knows the provocation.

"I was thinking of you when I suggested it," but she wrinkled her nose and I knew this time she was joking. It was wonderful returning to my native language, rediscovering that mocking tone just shy of aggression. I liked the person I became when I spoke it. I could detect an adolescent squeal in my voice, something close to delight.

"Doesn't this continual orange juice and tea and 'No thank you, just water for me, please,' get you down, Tara? I used to drink, I remember the pleasures."

"A little wine wouldn't hurt," I said.

"He doesn't like wine. Only snobs drink wine, he says."

"Thirty years ago, maybe."

"That's probably when he learned it."

When I was just a little girl in that safe, protected Calcutta of long ago—I was to learn that night—Didi had already been plotting her escape. "You probably didn't know I already had my big chance to be in movies." And then, I heard Didi's story. I waited for the name of Ron Dey to appear, but it never did.

In the early 1970s, the towering genius of our city, Satyajit

Ray, was looking for his "new girl." Towering in height, towering in authority, towering in vision. I was eight or nine years old, and of course I had never seen a Ray movie. I am reporting now on my adult feelings, from scattered viewings in San Francisco during my Andy years. My father might have loved Hollywood films, but he was suspicious of anything carrying a local label.

When Ray was working on a film down in his shabby Tolly-gunge studios, all of artistic Calcutta was at work as well. The actors, the stagehands, the caterers, the reporters, the Electric Supply Company (guaranteeing there would be no power cuts during the hours of shooting), the idlers, the hangers-on, the hopefuls, the carpenters, the cabbies. The knowledge that every college boy and would-be intellectual displayed concerning Ray's current and upcoming projects, even those he'd not yet written, was the Calcuttan's mark of sophistication.

Ray's recurrent actor, his alterego, was Soumitra Chatterjee, a permissible heartthrob for girls slightly older than me and my sisters. He starred in practically all of Ray's major works, including my personal favorites, the nineteenth-century Tagore tales like *Charulata* and *Post Office*. The actresses were great as well, Madhabi Mukherjee, Sharmila Tagore, and Aparna Sen. But Madhabi had retired, Sharmila married a cricket star and moved to Bombay to start a Hindi career, and Aparna, the daughter of a director, wanted to make her own movies. In the seventies Ray was turning, for him, to politics. He wanted to film Bibhuti Bhusan's "Asani Sanket" (Distant Thunder) in color. It concerned the 1943 market-manipulated famine in East Bengal in which millions had died. Those were the times of the war against the Japanese, the uprisings against the British, the hoarding and manipulating by grain merchants and the indifference of the colonial authorities. That was the famine that caused our distant relative, the Tree-Bride, to feed her vil-

lage and take up arms against the British and had sent distant
relatives to Calcutta to live with my mother when she was a little
girl. Soumitra Chatterjee would play the virtuous village school-
teacher, a Brahmin, who finally discovers the levels of perfidy un-
derlying the apparent "natural" disaster. Starvation in lush shades
of green.

Who would play the Brahmin's wife? What actress was fresh
and unknown, sixteen or younger, capable of speaking the East
Bengal dialect and behaving like a village Brahmin girl, but then
turn around and star in a cluster of contemporary, middle-class,
business-oriented Calcutta films? Who was beautiful enough,
English-speaking enough, Bengali enough, Brahmin enough,
worldly enough, and sophisticated enough, and still unknown?

All Calcutta rebelled when Ray announced his choice for *Distant Thunder*. Her name was Babita, a Bangladeshi actress. Pretty
enough in an urban sort of way, but not young enough, too ac-
tressy, and, most unforgivably, a Muslim. What would a Muslim
girl, no offense, know about serving a Brahmin's food, cooking,
how to sit, how to speak, to keep her eyes a certain way, to wear
her sari with pride but not arrogance?

Ray was Brahmo-Samaj, part of that progressive wing of
nineteenth-century Bengali culture—we were not. Our family's
"Westernization" was superficial, confined to convent school,
Metro Cinema, and movie magazines, which overlaid a profound
and orthodox Hinduism. Brahmos were scary to us; their knowledge of Western classics was thorough, their Bengali proud and
chaste, their Hinduism ruthlessly reformist. Ray's arrogance,
Daddy must have felt, was typical of a Brahmo. Who (but a
Brahmo) would expect educated people to pay for a black-and-
white movie about a poor East Bengal village boy in the nineteenth
century, trying to get to Calcutta? Who but a Brahmo would make
an Indian film in an Indian language without singing and dancing

and concentrate on ugly images instead? Who but a Brahmo would turn his back on his country's opinion and build his reputation on foreign acclaim?

How like a Brahmo, my parents and their friends complained, trampling on Hindu tradition like that! Really, I heard them saying, I left the movie halfway. I'll never go back to another Ray film. He's lost contact. That girl ruined it for me. Can you tell me there's no Hindu girl in all of Calcutta worthy enough to play in the great man's movies?

There was, of course. I never knew it, not until I found myself having that "sisterly chat," sipping orange juice from a Dixie cup in the darkened living room of Didi's house in Montclair, New Jersey. My sister had been the "new girl," and our father had destroyed the opportunity. And she remembered every bitter moment for the next twenty-seven years.

"So," she concluded, "the happy news you can report to Daddy is that he saved me from a life of corruption, and twenty-seven years afterward I have a recurrent slot on 'Namaskar, Probasi' and a voice-over for a Jackson Heights tandoori mahal."

*   *   *

I remembered all the rumors. Daddy had prevented it. But I had never known that the overtures were serious. We were told about the rejection with nothing more than amused dismissiveness. We'd heard from Daddy one night at dinner, "Didi has a little announcement," and Didi blushed and finally admitted that she'd received a letter asking if she was available for a movie role. What impertinence! we must have said. It meant that someone unknown to us had been watching, or that someone we trusted had reported on us, and someone who presumably respected us had assumed Didi's interest and availability. The "film crowd" was something we enjoyed reading about in magazines and gossiping over, though it was not anything that self-respecting people welcomed into their lives.

But now I learned that the offer had not come from the "film crowd" or a vague group of lecherous Marwari businessmen or some other nouveau-riche, alien money caste from the western deserts of India that specialized in the debasement of Bengali culture and along with it, Bengali girls. Didi's invitation had come from Satyajit Ray himself. She could have been his "new girl."

"Can you imagine, Tara! He couldn't find anyone for *Asani Sanket* or *Jana Aranya* so he was asking all the boys in the Presidency film club, 'keep your eyes open. Who is the prettiest and smartest Bengali-speaking girl in Calcutta?' *Satyajit Ray*, can you imagine! And he wrote this perfectly charming letter to Daddy, filled with those beautiful story-boards to show there would be absolutely nothing scandalous about it, and Daddy laughed it off. So Ray had to use old ladies like Aparna Sen. Then he had to use a Bangladeshi—eesh!—for *Asani Sanket*—how totally Brahmo, using a Muslim to play a Brahmin's wife. I could have done all that. She couldn't even serve his food properly!"

This bit of knowledge, the name of Didi's would-be discoverer, had always been suppressed in the family. Despite Bish's assertions to the contrary, we Bhattacharjees of Ballygunge Park Road disparaged history, art, and intellect. We were not effete and artistic—we were traditional Hindus, very orthodox Bengali Brahmins, despite Daddy's occasional peg of Scotch in the evenings and the MGM musicals. We were afraid of Brahmos, fearing contamination from our own side, our own best side in many ways, more than from true aliens like Catholic nuns. He was trying to construct a traditional life for his family in a city and a time when the props had all but disappeared.

For some reason, perhaps the six years' difference in our ages and the invisible fault line that ran between us, I loved my family and culture but had walked away from the struggle to preserve them. In San Francisco, I barely knew any Indians. But Didi, whose every utterance was couched in hatred for those times and for the family and for the city, was trying to lead a traditional Bengali life in New Jersey.

Harish stepped out of the darkened hallway, where he must have been listening. He was holding a highball glass of brown liquid, with a single tinkling ice cube. Although I had never warmed to Scotch, the universal elixir of the Indian business elite, I could have wrenched the glass from his hand and downed the contents in a single gulp.

"I'm very hungry, my love, my dove. Is the feast nearly ready?"

"When coriander leaves are chopped. Two minutes."

Harish Mehta, it turned out, was the Bhattacharjee family's greatest fan. He feasted on our nostalgia. His family, part of the great Punjabi uprooting of 1947, never reestablished itself successfully in India. He was one of "midnight's children," though he might not have recognized the literary reference, born in a family that dreamed of landscapes and a city in Pakistan they could never revisit. He was a man rooted in nostalgia, with no place to put it. And so, as we worked our way through a regal repast of lamb vindaloo, cauliflower and potato curry, and puffed potatoes, Didi and I repaid our debt to the cook with the happiest, gossipiest stories of Calcutta that we could imagine, stripped of the slightest complication. Stories of rascally servants and clueless nuns and of course the endless comedy of Loreto House girls and what finally became of them. Poppy Dey's name did not come up.

Didi apologized for absence of fish and rice, but she'd do better by me over the weekend. Thanksgiving, I wanted to say, but I knew the term would have no traction. She'd have fixed me a genuine East Bengal dinner with fish in mustard sauce, shrimps in coconut milk, fish-fry, fish chops, the works, if she weren't going bonkers at her new job. The only problem was the commute. "You can get everything in the Indian groceries in Edison, you don't have to go into Queens anymore." Harish was lucky, she said, to be working out of the home. Harish was so lucky, she repeated, louder than before. "How many Indian families do you know, Tara, where the wife goes out to work and the husband stays at home?"

"That's why Bengalis are so flabby and gabby," Harish snapped from the kitchen, "too much fish-fry in ghee and rice." He was pulling Tupperware containers out of the fridge and stacking them near the microwave. "Armchair politicos and hot-air intellectuals."

"What's wrong with being intellectual?" Didi retorted. We were in the eating nook of the kitchen, and we were clearing the table. "You non-Bengalis are jealous that we have so much to be proud of. Even Daddy wrote love poems before he went off to engineering school."

"Daddy?" It was unimaginable. Those six unbridgeable years again; such are the privileges of the oldest daughter.

"Yes, Daddy. Mummy once showed me one of his old exercise books with three poems stuck in the middle of math problems."

"Were they any good?" I couldn't imagine Bish taking time off to write poems to me.

"Put the dessert into the new blue serving dishes. Please! They're so pretty, they make any course look edible." To me she said, "It's the thought that counts, isn't it? Flowers, moons, nothing profound." She went back to describe her new job. Her boss was an Indian businessman, Danny Jagtiani—I'd meet him tomorrow. A genius, she called him. The name revealed his community; a money-grubbing Sindhi, a dubious Hindu from Pakistan, our Calcutta training would say.

Keeping it simple, keeping it light, without bitterness, wasn't easy. Didi had spent two hours excoriating Daddy for ruining her life. And the life he'd destroyed was not, as I had imagined, a passionate, progressive, and ecumenical love-marriage to Ronald Dey and the joys of motherhood; it was the possibility of becoming the savior of Bengali cinema.

For Harish's sake, over tea and rice pudding, we talked about the good old days in Calcutta, the lawn-parties, the collapse of great families and their fortunes, the parts we'd played in Loreto House performances of Gilbert and Sullivan. We'd taken the same parts in the same plays six years apart, and we still remembered all our lines. We avoided all mention of Ray and Tagore, or any other touchstone of defiant Bengaliness except for Ravi Shankar, who had twice appeared on Didi's show, "Namaskar, Probasi," and declared himself enchanted by Padma Mehta.

Harish lived in Didi's shadow, and he lived in the moment, and in this particular place and time, Didi was a television star. Her radiance helped him wipe out his past, her past, India, his former marriage, his children in Texas and California, and his multiple failures to establish himself as entrepreneur, consultant, money manager, and venture capitalist. Didi's appearances on Saturday-morning Bengali telecasts were more consequential than anything a Calcutta filmmaker that no proper non-Bengali had ever heard of might have cranked out thirty years ago.

And I, who prided herself on a vigilant but enthusiastic adjustment to American life in all its perverse temptations, felt that night that I'd been bested. Harish Mehta was the American. He'd tied his future to a star, and the star was growing brighter by the day. Like my sister, he'd blotted out all that was inconvenient or didn't fit. They only worried about me, they said, divorced and alone and raising a boy by myself, so far from the comforts of home.

When I retired to my cold, bare room with the narrow bed and Indian summer quilt, it was long past midnight. The bed was a recent purchase, the box spring was still in its thick plastic. There was a mirror on the wall, but no dresser. The closet was filled with men's suits and shirts in dry cleaners' plastic and dozens of hangers with dry-cleaned silk saris. Oh, how I missed my bed and all its pillows and comforter, my son, my funky house, the clutter of half-read books, the small bedside television, the open vista across the park to the lighted spires of St. Ignatius Church.

I rehearsed a conversation that had not taken place. Didi, *I'm* not the problem here. My complications are mine, my messes are of my making. I don't blame Daddy and I don't blame Bish and Calcutta, and the nuns might not have equipped me for San Francisco but they're all gone, that world is gone, we're here, we have to stop pretending, we have to stop living in a place that's changed on us while we've been away. I don't want to be a perfectly pre-served bug trapped in amber, Didi. I can't deal with modern India, it's changed too much and too fast, and I don't want to live in a half-India kept on life-support. You think I'm ridiculous, or somehow a disgrace to Indian womankind, a divorcée walking around in my American clothes? It's okay for the Indy Vermas and the girls who were born here and don't know any better, but not for us, the last flowering of Calcutta's golden past? Give me a break!

I may be alone right now, this week, but these past three nights are the first time I've been without a man or the attention of many men, most of it unwanted, in seventeen years! You thought my world ended when I left Bish? You think I'm so unattractive, so uncomplicated, and so unadventurous that I've been sitting at home alone for five years just raising a son? I never told you about Andy, or Pramod or Mahesh or Donald—but could you not have guessed? Why must you presume that my life has been all orange juice and Coca-Cola? Could you not have stretched your sympa-thies just a little to include the possibility that your sister might be capable of creating her own mistakes? Give me a break! It's *your* mistake I can't clean up.

Early the next morning, she registered predictable disapproval of the few saris I'd managed to find in the basement—five years behind the current styles, at least. ("Really, Tara, I thought San Francisco was supposed to be such a fashionable city!") She marched me to the bathroom and under a bank of lights of operating-room intensity, began the ritual, big sister dismantling of my self-confidence: my now-dry skin, ragged fingernails, crow's-feet, eye-bags, and straggly hair. I was a fashion disaster calling for a complete Jackson Heights makeover.

"You're worn out and skinny, Tara, what kind of life are you leading out there? Are you starving yourself? I know, I know, these so-called experts are always going on about too much fat in the diet and girls like you who should have more sense must be listening. I tell you, they should all be locked up, all those skinny so-called experts in white coats, they're killing our girls. There was a case out on Long Island, not a Bengali, thank God, a Gujarati girl starved herself to death—in America, can you believe it! Look at your skin, no shine, no labanya. And eesh! Your hair is a mess! Who cuts it, who styles it, some white homo? Please tell me you're not going bald. I told everyone my chhoto bon was coming, not my auntie! No one will believe you're six years younger. And let me tell you now, no man is going to flirt with such a bag of dried-out bones!"

She still had that stupendous figure, the tight clear skin that would make a Californian ask, who's your surgeon? I could see she touched up her hair, less to cover gray than to soften the black. Nothing had changed, yet I don't know if we'd be taken immediately for sisters these days. Her lips were thin, the lipstick dark, and there was a set to her mouth, a puckering primness like the run-up to a brief, closed-mouth smile, that brought out a line of tiny wrinkles. Her forehead was prominent, perhaps she'd lost a bit of her hairline. That operating-room glare cut both ways.

But how can I do justice to her welcoming comments, her unbidden assessments, the harsh grooming, without making her seem a jealous shrew? Or to the comfort I felt, playing along? She was playing Didi, and I was playing chhoto bon, the youngest sister, bowing my head in submission. We could barely keep from laughing. She let me know she couldn't be seen with me in public ("My reputation, Tara") and couldn't introduce me to New Jersey Bengali society in my present bedraggled condition. She'd have to take me to her hair-and-nails girl, her masseuse and studio-trained makeup man, and her Calcutta-Chinese hair stylist, then unleash me on the sari shops and jewelry stories of Queens, where even movie stars came to shop.

"Didi! You're matchmaking!" She was pulling a brush through my hair, frowning and sucking her teeth. I remembered our mother, brushing our hair every night. Three girls, three hundred strokes, and our hair practically glittered.

"Of course. What are older sisters for? You can't seem to do very well for yourself. If you fixed yourself up and resurrected your flirting skills, there are dozens of catches out there. There are scads of divorced men just waiting, even for girls like you." This was no time for denial or boasting. Besides, she was right. I had no one.

12

On the De Camp bus into Manhattan, on our way to my fashion makeover in Jackson Heights, Didi rehearsed me on the guest list for the first night's party. The ride took forty-five minutes and we needed every second of it to go over the list, their biographies, and the appropriate responses. This was la crème de la crème of Bengali New Jersey society, she assured me. Some were investors in Danny Jagtiani's new cable channel.

The party would be held at Dr. Mrinal and Dr. (Mrs.) Kajol Ghosal's mansion in Basking Ridge, which we were very lucky to get on short notice. He was the major moneybags behind Danny—surely I'd heard of Dr. Mrinal Ghosal, the Bish Chatterjee of the East Coast? Head of technology, resident-genius at AT&T?

"You know me, Didi, always out of it," I pleaded.

"He might even know your ex," she said.

"My lucky day," I said sweetly. If he was as high ranking as

Didi said, I'm sure he did. "Are we letting on, about the ex-factor?"

"We're certainly not putting it in the papers. But you know me, I'm very open and honest with everyone. I just can't pretend things didn't happen. Let the chips fall, that's what I say." I started to laugh, thinking at last we were sharing some new kind of sisterly confidence, but she was only catching her breath. "You must know how to play it by now. I'm told that some men find divorced women extra attractive."

All men, Didi, I wanted to say, *especially* married men. A divorced young Indian woman, released inside a room of married Indian men was a kitten in a dog pound. I could tell you stories, Didi. I remembered their voices. "You divorced ladies have not yet lost your charm. You have only grown more desirable. Divorced ladies must be oversexed, isn't it? For some ladies, one man is not enough. Always looking for adventure, isn't it? Me too, inside marriage is only same everything, same food, same routine, same games in bed, very nice, very well-behaved children doing well in school, very good wife and mother, but no experiments in bed. Not like you, I can tell. I think about you all the time, even in bed. I ask myself where is the masala, eh?"

The divorced Indian lady combines every fantasy about the liberated, wicked Western woman with the safety net of basic submissive familiarity.

In the months after I left Bish, one by one, nearly all of his oldest friends, those boys who had sat in the Stanford student pub with us while I sipped my Coca-Cola, found my new address in Palo Alto. I gratefully opened the door of my new apartment to them, thinking that divorce did not necessarily spell the end of my old social life, and I'd ask about their wives and children—and where, by the way, were they, still in the car?—and within minutes they were breathing hard and fumbling with my clothes.

Your life is already shattered, they said, what more damage can this do? Pramod Sengupta. Mahesh Trivedi, with Meena still in the hospital. Ranjit Shah, at least, had no wife. They'd be doing me a favor. Why shouldn't they take a free shot? I left the peninsula because of them and moved to the city, but it didn't let up.

She consulted her list. From Montclair there'd be Dr. and Dr. (Mrs.) Madhab Roy Chowdhury with their three bespectacled daughters, one already at Harvard, the others to follow. I was not to make the mistake of asking the oldest girl what she was studying. She'd tell me and I'd have to keep smiling and making insincere faces and I'd never break away. The point of these parties was to keep circulating, don't get stuck with anyone. Flirt like crazy, but please don't alienate the wives. "What is she studying?" I asked, "just so I know." Nuclear something, medicine, she believed. On top of that, all three girls used these parties to practice their Bengali, which was ghastly, despite the pride their parents took. Didi did a wicked imitation and I found myself laughing as we passed through the hideous, mall-scarred landsçape. Best not to look out the window. I was missing my San Francisco.

I tell you, Tara, she was saying, these America-born girls have no social graces. Can you imagine if we'd gone on about our schoolwork at a party? I was about to protest that nuclear medicine at Harvard was at least a worthier undertaking than moral science with Mother John Baptist at Loreto House, but Didi was licking her lips over a new confidence. Madhab is just the sort of fellow we would have cut to pieces in Calcutta, all brains, nothing to look at and a family scandal to boot!

She pulled a little closer and dropped her voice, as though repeating the story of a fifty-year-old scandal might cause Bengali-speaking gossipmongers among our fellow commuters to drop their *Times* and cell phones to cock an ear. "Do you remember the story of Madhab's father, Sujit Roy Chowdhury, and the French consul's wife? He was a big newspaperman, *Statesman* or *Times of India*. Maybe it wasn't French, it could have been one of those Communist countries, Poland or Romania or something. It was the juiciest story ever, and of course it ruined his family. The consul tracked them down to a beach hotel in Puri and shot them both dead! Then he claimed diplomatic immunity and was back home the next day. Poor Madhab was all set for a brilliant career in Oxford, and he found himself slinking off to some big American state school instead. I don't know how he found such a lovely woman as Ruma."

I promised to avoid the daughters and not to mention foreign countries in his presence.

There was Dr. Prafulla Nag who'd become a little wild since his parents were killed in an automobile crash for which he was not to blame, and the Sinhas, who were pathetic snobs and to be avoided and the Sen family, who were nice, simple people but dreadful bores. The prospects for an enjoyable evening were sinking fast, and I couldn't imagine why in the world such a boring bunch had all been invited. Where's the masala, eh?

"Didi, just so I can get my bearings. What did this Prafulla Nag do to become so wild?" Drugs, sex, espionage?

"I shouldn't be telling."

I knew she would. "All right. About five years ago, he was convicted of false billing. They called it insurance fraud. He'd been using some of the money to buy and sell cheap real estate." So even Bengalis were into potels, but it hardly raised him to the level of wildness I was hoping for. She must have read my disappointment.

"But he was throwing most of it away in Atlantic City. He was such a big loser they would send a special white limo to pick him up and take him home. They called it the Nagmobile, can you imagine! They say there were women inside and who knows what went on, all the way down the Garden State Parkway no less! It was so embarrassing for everyone. In the divorce papers, his wife claimed he'd gambled away over a million dollars."

"So he's available! How old is he?"

She ignored me with a flutter of her hand. The most intriguing couple for someone like me, she supposed, would be the young Dasgupta brother and sister who lived mysteriously well in a great loft in Hoboken and claimed all sorts of visiting writers and paint- ers as their friends. She'd heard that Arundhati Roy and Salman Rushdie came there, so did Madhur Jaffrey and Ivory and Mer- chant, and what's his name, the old Muslim painter with the crush on the Hindi actress? "Hussein," I answered eagerly, as though I were on a quiz show, as though it mattered or Didi cared, "and Madhuri Dixiit." It felt good nevertheless, exercising what little expertise I still possessed. The Dasgupta sister had once initiated a discussion of a Ray film that Didi had never seen, but thank God Harish had come along and pulled her away.

The pushiest lot all come from Hoboken and Jersey City. She hoped that Mr. and Mrs. Basu of Hackensack would not show, because Mr. Basu always started fights about Calcutta municipal politics with Harish, who knew nothing about it but passionately defended anything Calcutta did. Mr. Basu was one of those tedious Bengalis who court favor with other Indians by insulting Calcutta and Bengalis, agreeing with every stereotype and advancing a few of his own. Calcutta was dirty, corrupt, and impossibly commu- nist. Bengalis like to think their heads are in the clouds, their feet in the gutter, but to Mr. Basu, the exact opposite applied. Harish was the only person she knew who actually cared about Calcutta City honor.

Dr. Gautam Dutta was not to be given the time of day; at least until his pending Medicare fraud cases were settled.

From Ridgewood there would be several retired couples, the Pals, the Naskars, the Dalals, the Chakravortys, and the Hazras, who had set up their own retirement complex by buying all the condos in the same building.

Dr. (Miss) Lata Haldar, who called herself "the busy bachelorette," was bound to be present, because she showed up whether she was invited or not. Could I imagine the cheek of such a woman? She was a professor of literature or some such in one of those poky state colleges, so who knew if her doctorate was real! She was the most insufferable of the obnoxious contingent from Union City. There would be a nice, young, two-engineer family expecting their first child, the Maliks, from Linden, and Mrs. Malik's parents from Irvington. Also from Linden, Mr. Malik's sister, a widow with three sons under ten, if she could get off earlier than usual from her cashier's job in a liquor store owned by a Gujarati from Uganda who was forever propositioning her. Her husband had died of a heart attack at thirty-seven, before getting around to taking out life insurance.

Rutgers always provided a scattering of Bengalis and Bengali-speakers, like the Arun Dalmias—yes, yes, I know you're going to complain that Marwaris are sneaking in, but he's married to a Banerjee girl, can you imagine the shock to *her* family!—and in some ways he's more Bengali than most Bengalis. And having the Dalmia fortune behind you, even if you're the fifth cousin or something, can't hurt, can it? The Desais, Gujaratis raised in Calcutta, both economists with Marxist leanings, and Professor-emeritus and Mrs. Iqbal Ahmad, who were writing a book on Bangladeshi folk songs, and a fiftyish Parsi librarian named Ina Trunkwalla who was married to a Swede or a Finn or a Swedish Finn young enough to be her son.

I was to watch out for Arun Mehra, a Punjabi raised in Calcutta, who was all charm and unbelievable sleaze, not to mention the fact that his young bride, just arrived from India ten years earlier, had been seen crying at her first party and shortly afterward died under mysterious and still unexplained circumstances in their Secaucus condo. Now he was nasty to his fat American second wife in public. He was an immigration lawyer with a fancy condo in Gutenburg and rumors she shouldn't repeat abounded concerning the favors he collected in lieu of fees from desperate clients facing deportation.

I was to be wary of anyone I met from Jersey City. The only good thing about the Jersey City group was that they were high rollers, so they would pop in and pop out. The only person she really looked forward to seeing again was Lola Dhar, who had been a year ahead of her at Loreto College, and now lived with her biochemist husband in Paterson, but they were supposed to have gone to Zurich to spend Thanksgiving with their daughter.

By now, we were in the Lincoln Tunnel. Didi closed her planner.

"They sound like a charming bunch," I said. This time she ignored my meaning. Her commentary on the guest list reminded me of the times Parvati and I would sit in our bedroom, ridiculing just about everyone we met, our classmates, the nuns, and our parents' friends. Sweet, innocent little girls with malice in their hearts. Maybe it was a family trait.

"We always have a great time when we can find an excuse to get together."

Better being the excuse even for a boring party, I thought, than sitting alone at home wondering if Andy would climb out of his Buddhist funk or waiting for a dreaded call from Jack Sidhu. Then I remembered that Sidhu couldn't call me, he didn't have Didi's phone number. It was a little after seven a.m. in California. When we got to a quiet spot inside the Port Authority, I speed-dialed his hotline. At the taped cue, I perked up my voice, "Jack! Hi, it's me, Tara!" Didi watched intently. "I forgot to leave my sister's phone number out here in New Jersey. You remember, I told you about Padma." I repeated the number, despite her frowns. "And you can always reach me on my cell. Love to hear from you. Ciao." I assumed he'd get the point.

"Sooo, it's a Jack, is it? You have a secret admirer, and you never told me! Here I am all worried about you and trying to matchmake—no wonder you were acting so smug and superior. You could have brought him, we're all adults. What is he, a white man?"

I must have hesitated just long enough, pondering if she'd just handed me another perfect moment to pounce, and how many more chances like this she'd give me, without my having to initiate the whole thing from scratch. "He's not what you think," I started, but her Indian radar was up and working. "Don't tell me, Tara— he's Chinese! I have *tons* of Chinese friends. They're taking over the world and I for one am thankful. They're much nicer than Indians, believe me."

We rode four flights of narrow escalators down to the basement of the Port Authority, then pushed through a long and crowded, incredibly filthy connecting tunnel to the lower level of the Times Square station. I was already exhausted. Wrapped in a sari for the first time in years, I was taking twice the number of steps and still falling behind my sister. I was jostled, I heard curses, and I felt hostile eyes assessing me. In a city of foreigners, I was feeling the most alien. A commute like this, twice a day, would press the life out of me. If nothing else came of this trip, at least I would know I belonged in California.

Always pushing, aren't you, Tara? At some time during the day, my SOS to Jack Sidhu would be answered, and I had no idea how I'd react. My little cell phone would go off like a bomb and Jack Sidhu would bring news of my sister's, *this woman's*, son, and she'd be sitting with me, laughing and gossiping and being outrageous, and I would start shaking. We made our way to the lowest level of the Forty-second Street station, to a waiting 7 train, where seats were still plentiful, though filling rapidly.

"So, tell me about him, this Jack of yours." She had fixed her most sparkling smile, her eyes practically devoured me, and I could feel her hand resting coolly on mine.

"I know what I heard. I could hear it in your voice."

"First of all, Jack stands for Jasbir Singh Sidhu, a Sardarji. He's much younger than me, just out of school, really. Stanford," I added, giving in just a little to expectation. I wondered if "Sardarji," our innocently unconscious Hindu name for Sikhs, had become offensive.

"Oh, very good, Tara! Excellent school. And he's in Silicon Valley, I imagine? You seem to do quite well with computer types." Same smile, same sincerity in the voice, eyes a little less confident. "I think Sardarjis are much smarter than we used to give them credit for. Those old Sikh jokes . . . very bad."

"Didi, please listen to what I'm going to say. He's an officer of the San Francisco Police Department. I went to him because I was having a problem."

"Oh, dear, I'm so sorry. I hope he was able to help you with whatever it was. Raising children in this country must be terribly hard." Now, even the sincerity had drained from her voice, and her eyes had shifted down the aisles to the standing passengers, resting briefly on possible Indians. I counted three women in saris and half a dozen South Asian men. There was a time when I could identify faces from any north Indian state (the south being an enduring mystery), let alone related religions and nationalities. Now, my radar was down. I couldn't distinguish Muslims from Hindus anymore. I wasn't even one hundred percent sure of Bengalis. I felt as though I were lost inside a Salman Rushdie novel, a once-firm identity smashed by hammer blows, melted down and reemerging as something wondrous, or grotesque.

Didi was sitting just inches away, a firm identity resisting all change, at least from a distance, on a brief inspection. But under scrutiny, fractured, like cracks under old glaze. Up close, I didn't recognize her. I didn't know who she was. I was following the cracks, fascinated by their complexity, not the simple, shining face. "Puffles and Piffles," Andy once called them, but I never thought that previously unidentified fault lines could refer to my sister, or to me.

A few of the non-Indians were staring at us. The sari I had borrowed from Didi was the last word in Calcutta elegance, six yards of the finest silk and most extraordinary hand-stitched embroidery in a modernist, designer-kantha manner. "Museum quality," she had said, handing it over to me that morning as I had stood in the bedroom, hovering over the stack of insufficiencies I'd brought from California. "From my design," she added. Sure enough, a card declaring it a *Padma Mehta Design, New York* was clipped to its fringes. "Didi!" I must have squealed. "You never told me!" Where was her studio, how had she started? She'd never shown interest, or talent, in design. Modesty was so unlike her, yet she dismissed my questions with a smile and pat of my hand. Its selling price was eight hundred dollars. Several thousand dollars worth of silk saris were hanging on the satin hangers in my bedroom. I would never have guessed.

She did not wear Western clothes, but she'd always had more style and confidence than the rest of us. She could play the New York designer-type. Her sari did more for her than mine did for me; I'd been so many years out of saris and gold accessories that I felt like an American bride trying to please her Indian in-laws. We were ludicrously overdressed, almost garish, for the 7 train to Flushing, but no one in the car seemed to care, not even the other Indian women, whose saris were handwashed cotton. We were a worthy spectacle, nothing more.

"It isn't entirely my problem, Didi. I tried to tell you that on the phone when you cut me off. Sooner or later, we're going to have to talk."

She whirled around. "Don't you ever let up? If you must bring up unpleasantnesses can't you find a better place than a New York subway? Just watch your tongue, this train is full of Bangladeshis and they pick up every word. You say 'police' and their heads jerk around. Then they see me, and believe me, they know who I am and before you know it, this famous person on television is in trouble with the police and it will be all over New York in a Calcutta second. You know how these people are, Tara, they're terrible gossips, they'll have me smuggling gold or falsifying visas or being involved with some cabinet minister. Maybe you're shameless enough out there in California with all your money and your American friends not to care about your reputation, but it's all I have. Now that's my last word on it."

And magically, the smile returned. The eyes grew wide and sympathetic. She gave me a long hug and a kiss on the ear. "Let's just be sisters, again, all right? Like it used to be."

I wanted to say, *But it never was*, Didi. I never knew you like I knew Parvati. You were always a mystery to me, you had that six-year lead on me, and I've been trying to catch up for thirty years.

13

I know Jackson Heights, of course—what dutiful Indian doesn't? I've visited it a few times over the years, usually to buy a house gift for Parvati at the 220-volt appliance stores. And so, the association was always positive; if I was in a sari, walking the streets of Queens, I would soon be sipping gin and lime in Parvati's seafront apartment.

Window-shopping, however, was never a pleasure in Jackson Heights. For the Indian immigrants I know in New York—professional people, friends of Bish—Jackson Heights is tacky, faintly embarrassing. It is the commercial center of Indian life in America (if Indian life in America or anywhere can ever be said to have a center), just as Silicon Valley is its scientific and professional heart, but the shops of Jackson Heights are not slanted to the professional elite. The gold stores of Calcutta and the sari and fabric shops of Bombay are better stocked, more selective, and far more welcoming.

The attraction of Jackson Heights, for me, had always been people pleasures: sidewalks full of Indians, every face is Indian, every shop and storefront features Indian jewelry, Indian clothing, Indian travel, Indian food and spices, Indian sweets and restaurants. The smells and the noises are familiar; Seventy-eighth Street and all the side streets are clogged by double-parked cars and delivery vans. It's the loud, naked swagger of money being made—not quite the hushed music and water fountains of Silicon Valley—but wherever, it's intoxicating.

We're a billion people, but divided into so many thousands or millions of classifications that we have trouble behaving as a monolith. Yet each Indian is so densely packed with family that he or she seems to contain hundreds of competing personalities. Jackson Heights is not a Chinatown or even a Japantown on the San Francisco model. Paint and neon have not transformed a settled old Mediterranean-Queens neighborhood of wood-frame houses into anything recognizably Indian. Indian people shop collectively, but they don't live together in tight little communities. They haven't clustered in Jackson Heights to be nearer to their shops. They travel in from distant suburbs, or like Didi, from neighboring states, every day.

It's still a shock, however, and a kind of inspiration, to see the might of one's community on parade. The swagger is subtle, and perfectly Indian. Poky little storefronts for sweets and spices that look marginal at best are shipping tons of the hot mix out the back door, repackaged in French and Spanish, English, Hindi, Urdu, and any other language, for every Indian specialty store in North America. Every little storefront that looks no more impressive than it might have in India, dim, cluttered, badly painted, indifferently displayed, has an "office" somewhere in the rear where a computer-savvy nephew expands the online client base by factors of several thousand. Travel agents, whose idea of decor is a Scotch-taped Air-India poster on the wall, issue dozens of India-bound tickets every hour, from every airport on the continent.

"Jackson Heights," the concept if not exactly the place, is a rung on the ladder of acceptability that privileged Indians such as myself, who arrived with the right degrees or the right marriage, have been able to bypass. Since there's no "old money" in an immigrant community, most of us start on the same plane. We came with nothing but a degree, or with zeal, and money is the only way to measure success. Announce in an Indian gathering that you have a shop in Jackson Heights, and you are proudly declaring your horde of gold and dollars, but also the shame of degreelessness. If the Jackson Heights success had stayed in India he would still be squatting in a shoulder-wide stall in some provincial town, scooping lentils from a jute sack and weighing them on a handheld scale. What he does here is little different in style or manner. Jackson Heights rewards Indian immigrants for all the skills that three thousand years of caste confinement have imposed; it liberates the class of Indian that India itself kept bottled up.

Jackson Heights is a landscape of potentialities that had been denied in India. Even Bish had experienced a West Coast version of that same enchantment. You need a line of credit? Here it is. You need a license, special visa considerations? See your congressman. No caste or regional or familial strings to pull, no favors to trade. You need a place to funnel in your relatives? Come to America, but if you really want to get rich quick, come to Queens.

Out in California, Bish had gone to a venture capitalist after encountering rejection from a bank. Here are my degrees. Here is my proposal. Here is my target. Bish and Chet raised $50 million in a week. In a way, I had done the same. You're looking for a life outside of the gated community? You're looking for respect, for a life apart from your husband's identity? No problem, sign these papers.

I knew the faces on the streets of Queens and in the shops from the streets of Bombay and Calcutta. Not quite India's underclass, but its hungering classes. They looked like the photos in Jack Sidhu's book of felons. They even looked like the mystery man I knew as Christopher Dey.

And yet, this was the world in which Didi thrived. When we swept into Mei's Calcutta Hair Studio, all three Chinese girls raced to greet her, all speaking perfect Bengali, hoping for the chance to try out the latest designs. In Calcutta, traditionally, tending ladies' hair had been a Chinese monopoly. For Miss Mehta and her family, no reservation necessary, of course. They chopped my lank, California, retro-Beatnik look into something India-modern, short and fluffy, more fitting a woman of my age.

"I tell you, Mei is minting money, hand over fist," Didi said, as we walked down the street past large and busy sari shops and jewelry stores. "We won't be going to any of these," she said, waving at the owners as we passed, "they're all Gujarati. Very friendly chaps, they call me Padma-behn, very good businessmen but absolutely hopeless sense of style. We'll be going to my special gold store, straight out of Calcutta. You remember the Sirkars?" I did indeed; old man Sirkar had handled all our family's gold purchases and gold designs for at least three generations. Possibly, they too hailed from East Bengal. I could imagine ancestral linkages to Dacca or even Mishtigunj. Like everyone I'd ever known growing up, Didi had her own "special" places for gold and saris, people she trusted or over whom she exercised a secret leverage. "He's the son of old-man Sirkar's daughter, so he's not a Sirkar by name, he's a Bose, but Sirkar-honest with best Calcutta craftsmanship, all done on the premises."

My hair, she felt, had gone well. It sent no obvious signals of quiet desperation, nor did it blatantly advertise my availability. I could pass myself off as another busy bachelorette. Didi's hairstyle, still an Indian bun modified to an American beehive, had not changed in twenty-five years. Now, to do the same for my nails, which did send out distressing signals of loneliness and despair. I had simply let myself go to pot out there in California; no wonder I couldn't hook a man. But not to worry, my sister would save me.

Nails Mahal was owned by a Hindi-speaking, Delhi-born Korean widow. A dozen small tables were occupied by Indian women of every age, from traditional old grandmothers in village saris to older teens in jeans and T-shirts. The girls were being worked over, much in the way I was, for a nails-up transformation, prior to starting the marriage negotiation. Nails Mahal was a full-service marriage emporium. A portrait studio was attached. They even did the mehndi, the elaborate, henna decoration of the bridal hands for the formal ceremony itself.

A couple of the giggling younger girls were non-Indian, Greek or Latina, getting their hands painted purely for fun. Impossible to predict what the next crossover style might be. While my nails were buffed, polished, and lacquered, Didi managed to make a full circuit of the shop, sitting at each little stand. "I'm a journalist with India Television," I heard her say to the young American girls. "Can I ask you what exactly attracts you to mehndi?" They giggled some more, muttering "it's cool," and "everyone's getting it done," and Didi gently took their hands, palms up, as though a camera had been rolling. "This is called mehndi," she said in her softest tone. "Do you know the history of mehndi? It's very ancient. We were doing mehndi when Europeans were painting their faces blue. Do you know that all of these lines have a special meaning? Here, let me show you. I think it's fascinating that you girls have discovered a contemporary American use for an ancient Indian tradition."

"Jeez," I heard. "I didn't know I was doing that. Is it okay? I mean, you guys won't get pissed or anything?" Didi patted their hands and moved on.

For other clients, she managed a passable Hindi or Gujarati, certainly better than mine. She kept surprising me. She'd never shown an interest in design, but now she had a label. She had no apparent job, nor did Harish, and they lived parsimoniously, yet she commanded the attention, even the favors, of an entire community. In public, she was calm and gracious, her voice and manner soothing and engaged. In private, nothing outside her immediate interest penetrated, and she seethed with bitterness.

The sari shop and jewelry stores were located on side streets, in houses that looked purely residential except for the bars over the doors and windows. Old Mr. Bose had to unlock his house for us and shout an order to the kitchen for the kettle to be put on. The living room, which contained a sofa and two straightback-dining chairs, was dominated by a giant vault of shiny-brushed steel. Two framed Hindu devotional paintings decorated the walls.

He was small and bald, birdlike, as we used to say of wrinkle-free old men and women who skittered about, without complaints or the apparent burden and misery of their years—old-style, observant Hindus who met all their ritual obligations and practiced morning and evening yoga, and lived on a daily spoonful of yogurt and a slice of fruit. According to Parvati, our father in his mountain retirement was fast becoming one of them. Mr. Bose was dressed in the traditional homespun cotton kurta and dhoti, but spoke in a rotund Calcutta courtliness that I hadn't heard outside of the theater.

He asked to be called Dhiren-da and Didi indicated that he was the father of her dear friend, the wife of Pramod Basu, whom we'd be seeing that night in Basking Ridge. "She has informed me of such," said Dhiren-da. "The gathering I believe is in honor of your dear sister's arrival." He nodded in my direction. "I hope you will permit me to say, my dear Mrs. Chatterjee, your beauty does honor to the Bhattacharjee family, whose warmth and generous spirit I have enjoyed since—if you can indulge me the memory—since I was a very young man. I shall inform my son-in-law that he will have a most delightful evening in the company of such gracious women."

"And will we be favored with Nalini's presence tonight?" Dhiren-da gave a noncommittal shake of the head and small flutter of the hand. "Who can say? My daughter does not fly far from her nest."

If I remembered Didi's instructions correctly, Pramod Basu had been one of many to be avoided, for the constant expression of provocative attitudes toward Calcutta.

"My husband so enjoys his little head-buttings with Pramod," said Didi, turning to me. "Really, Tara, it will be one of the highlights of the evening."

After "the boy," a young man of twenty or so, served our tea and two digestive biscuits, Dhiren-da stood and approached the vault. "We have some new designs you might find attractive," he said, then squatted, and began spinning the dials of his combination lock.

The amount of gold in the form of earrings, nose jewels, bangles, and necklaces heaped in trays inside Mr. Bose's vault could have influenced world values. He slipped out half a dozen jewelry cases, the simple, Old World cardboard boxes with satin linings, sealed by a single brass clasp. Like the dingy shops lining Seventy-eighth Street, there was no way of judging the value of the contents from their exteriors. These were the new designs in haar—necklaces—and earrings, multitiered, like Victorian chandeliers, or miniature golden bird cages stacked one upon the other. Not my style, in all its gaudy excess, not even a style of this century, but the workmanship was inspiring to me, and I reached out to hold

a haar and Dhiren-da placed it in my hand. "My very finest champakali," he said, words I had not heard in fifteen years. "I think it
is the finest I have ever seen."

"It would bow my neck," I laughed.

A way of saying, the price, calculated on an electronic scale
kept under glass like a seismograph, would break my bank.

"Would you like to wear it?" he asked. He leaped to his feet;
spry fingers attached it in no time. He held a mirror. The borrowed
choli under my borrowed sari was generously scooped, almost in-
decently so, given my generous bust. The play of gold against
Indian skin is already a temptation from the gods, particularly
when crafted, intricate designs rest upon the curving, honey-soft
skin of the bosom so rarely exposed. I had no sense of myself, no
sense of the little old man holding the mirror, or of Didi rum-
maging through the trays of gold. Ask me where I was, and the
response, "Jackson Heights" would not have occurred to me. Ask
me who I was, and it might have taken a second or two to remember. I could have been anyone looking into a mirror and being
returned a vision.

Golden birds on golden boughs, I was thinking, *hammered gold and
gold enameling*, remembering the fragments of a poem, recited by
a young Irish nun in long-ago Loreto House. Yeats must be heard
in his accent to set him free, Sister Mary Theresa would say, then
stand before us, that motley crowd of restless girls in their blue
uniforms and braided hair—Hindus, Christians, Muslims, Parsis,
Jews, Sikhs—reciting from memory as tears streamed down her
face, and eventually ours, "Among School Children" and "Easter,
1922," and the Byzantium poems and "The Lake Isle of Innisfree,"
and for a moment I was lost in that memory. Jackson Heights was
Byzantium and ever so briefly, I was one of the lords and ladies of
Byzantium.

"It suits you, madam," said Dhiren-da.

"It's very lovely, but it's not my style. Given the way I live, I prefer simpler things."

"Yes, dear, we know the way you live," Didi cut in. "She means she has no occasion to wear nice things out in California. All the more reason to wear it here."

"Didi!" I hoped she'd get the message. I was not about to spend ten thousand dollars on a necklace-and-earring set that I could wear only once.

"We'll also need a selection of bangles," said Didi, indicating my shamefully naked arms. The bangles came in every degree of thickness, some with stones, and some worked into snakehead designs with emeralds and rubies for the eyes. The thin, plain churis (if anything made of 24-carat gold can ever be called plain) came in sets of four and eight. Back in San Francisco, I probably had enough gold bangles stashed in my bedroom to turn me into some kind of flightless bird, unable to raise my arms. But I'd had things other than ornamentation on my mind when I'd packed to come, urgent messages that I had thought I would be delivering. Now, I wondered if the chance would ever arise.

And so we left Dhiren-da's with half a dozen cases slipped into Didi's purse, bangles for me, earrings and choker for her, my Byzantium set and dangling, jhumka earrings, and even a nose jewel for Didi. Dhiren-da had not tendered a bill, Didi had not signed a paper or presented a credit card, although the total must have exceeded twenty thousand dollars. When I raised the issue of our not having paid, she waved me off. "You liked it, didn't you? It looks good on you, so why not?" And then she laughed, "As if money means anything to you."

"Didi, for God's sake, please! You know absolutely nothing about my situation and you seem to take it for granted that I'm this fabulously rich divorced woman. Well, I'm not."

Bish's money was vested in the company. I might have been

able to insist on its liquidation, and if I had, I probably would be sitting on a few hundred million dollars. But how could I have done such a thing? I'd been there at the beginning, I remembered the excitement of those early months when Chet Yee slept over on our sofa. For a few years, I'd shared that excitement. In my way, I helped foster it. Then Bish and his "team" started walling me off, he wasn't available, and there was no one in Atherton to take me seriously. I had a car and an unlimited credit line on all my charge cards—what more did I want? I had my girlfriends, the other Indian wives, wasn't that enough? He didn't see that my girlfriends were leaving their husbands. Meena Trivedi died. Ah, he comforted himself, they were the wives of underlings; the same thing couldn't happen to the big boss. What I settled for was Rabi's trust fund, my house, and modest support. If I went back to college, he would pay. If I got a job, the support would be reduced. I didn't touch the company, much to my lawyer's despair, but as a result, we were on friendly terms. Rabi still had a father and I got occasional good advice from someone who still looked out for me.

From all I could see, especially if I added the loss of Andy, the complications with Rabi, and whatever threats were still to come from the multiple identities of Christopher Dey, I was living far less securely than Didi.

￼ ￼ ￼

It was noon; time for a little lunch. Didi selected the only restaurant without an Indian name or Indian entrees Magic-Markered on the windows. The waiter who seated us was tall and blond. "Namaste, Padma-ji," she said, folding her hands and bowing slightly, like an Air-India hostess. She rattled off the list of specials, in Hindi. After we'd taken our booth Didi explained, "This is a very famous place, the best restaurant in Jackson Heights." It was another of Danny Jagtiani's little investments that had paid off. Instead of changing the original Italian decor and firing its staff, he'd retrained them in Indian cuisine and service. The result was a bizarre mix of Indian smells, Indian clientele, and old-style Mafia Chianti bottles and red velvet tablecloths. Now that I had achieved rudimentary presentableness, said Didi, the afternoon would be reserved for a meeting with D.J., the man who owned just about every store on the block and more profitable interests we couldn't see.

Nine o'clock in California, I kept thinking; Jack has come to his office. He's listening to my message and wondering, What the hell is up with this woman? And that's when my cell phone went off.

"It must be your Jack," said Didi. "I think cell phones in a restaurant are actually very rude."

I agreed. I caught it on the second ring. "Mrs. Chatterjee? This is Jack. Is it a convenient time to talk?"

"Jack!" I cried. "What a pleasant surprise!"

"I take it you're still not free to talk. I'll be brief. We have at present nothing definite on the status of Christopher Dey. But we do have two people I would like you to identify. If you have a fax number, I can send you their photos."

"That's wonderful, Jack. I'd love to see them."

Didi was watching from behind the menu. "Didi?" I asked sweetly, "do you have D.J.'s fax number? Jack wants to send me something." To my surprise she took out her planner and peeled off the business card of Danny Jagtiani. I read him the numbers.

"Very well, Mrs. Chatterjee. I will send the sheets on a certain Gopal Kishore Sinha and on Abbas Sattar Hai. Both comport with your general description, both are Bangla speakers, and both have recently been seen in the Bay Area."

I thanked him, and tried to ask, indirectly, what they had done. He told me that was not my concern at present. He wanted only a positive identification if I could make one. He went on to ask, if it were not too personal, if I'd had an opportunity to discuss this matter with my sister.

"Many opportunities, Jack, but the answer is no."

Didi jerked to attention. "I'll just go ahead and order for you," she said.

"Mrs. Chatterjee, I don't want to alarm you, but it is becoming extremely important that you clear up all this confusion sooner rather than later. We cannot launch a serious investigation until we know some basic facts about the person we're looking for. Otherwise my hands are tied, and it is most frustrating. The case is growing very complicated, Mrs. Chatterjee. I regret to inform you that we received word overnight that Dr. Ronald Dey was killed in an automobile accident yesterday. We have no word of anything suspicious, but I have e-mailed a friend on the Bombay force to look into it confidentially."

I felt engulfed by a passing wave of sadness.

"You were so distracted, I had to do all the ordering for you. I've ordered puri. I hope you're not still a big rice eater."

"Jack, it's been wonderful hearing from you. I'm really busy here, but I'll try to get everything you've asked for. I'm in Jackson Heights, so if it's not here, it's probably not available anywhere."

"I'll send those pictures right away, Mrs. Chatterjee."

In other words, I might have said—if Didi had not been listening in—*You've found Christopher, haven't you?* "We have at present nothing definite" you said, from which I'd taken some comfort. Foolish woman! You need to compare the visa and the victim photos and you need someone who can make a positive identification and only poor dead Ronald Dey, who thinks his lovely, brilliant boy is safe and being welcomed to his mother's family, could have provided it.

"What was that all about? Tara, you're crying! What did he

say to you? How could he! Oh, if I ever get my hands on him, I'll give him a piece of my mind!" She reached across the table with the moistened napkin to dab my eye. "Just tell me what you want me to do."

"Didi, oh, Didi, if you only knew."

I ordered a glass of red wine. Didi took juice. "You're not going to like what I'm about to say, Didi, but what I need from you is just a bit of honesty. You have a son out there. He's in this country, and maybe he's in a lot of trouble, and he needs you. I've been trying to tell you this in every way I know how, and you keep refusing to listen. And it's only getting worse!" By now I was holding my cell phone and shaking it in her face. "Ron Dey is dead! Does that mean anything to you?"

"I'm very sorry, but what am I supposed to feel? People we knew over there are dying every day. This *filth* is what you wanted D.J.'s number for? Oh, my God, my God," she buried her face ever so briefly in her hands, "what is he going to think?"

"What is *he* going to think? What is *Danny Jagtiani* going to think? Didi, who am I talking to here?" But she was already standing, never mind that our food hadn't come, not even my long-delayed glass of wine. She kept repeating, "Maybe there's still time." As we hurried out past the cashier she said, "My sister just got an emergency call. I'll settle it directly with Danny." They knew her, and wished us a nice day, and the best of luck.

14

The office of Danny Jagtiani was located on the second floor of an ordinary corner house one block off Seventy-eighth Street, behind a window with a Century 21 logo. The ground floor, from what was visible through lace curtains over the glass parlor doors, was still occupied by a large non-Indian family with crosses on the walls and tricycles in the vestibule.

The stairs to the second floor seemed steep only because I was already breathless from the sari-impeded near-dash. As we climbed, the settled world began to change. Clustered around the bottom of the stairwell were rows of real estate photos, mostly of commercial properties in the area for sale or rent. Halfway up, the realty brochures and promotional materials gave way to Bollywood movie posters. Unsavory looking, mustached men with drawn guns confronted muscular police inspectors shielding beautiful women in torn clothing. Good and evil, nobility and brutality, cunning and innocence, masculine muscularity and feminine fragility: I lingered in front of each poster, mesmerized. The posters were so over-the-top they were the stuff of myth.

Didi, anxious about the fax, had hurried ahead of me. She called down to me from the head of the stairs. "Stop, dawdling, Tara! I already told you that Danny's a major movie producer."

I studied the movie posters like paintings in a museum. I made out the legend *Danny Jagtiani and DJ Enterprises USA Present*: above each movie title and the list of stars.

The walls of the second-floor landing were hung with framed newspaper clippings featuring the same fit, smiling man, sometimes in embroidered kurta, sometimes in business suit, sometimes in the Century 21 blazer. The man had to be Danny Jagtiani. The clippings were mostly in different Indian languages from the local ethnic papers, but some were in Greek and Chinese and a couple of languages I couldn't identify. Danny Jagtiani had made it into Bollywood fan magazines as well. He seemed to enjoy being photographed, arms linked with celebrity stars. The captions must have been made up by punsters. *Dough Rising? Bombay Glitz, U.S. Bread . . . Star Producer Arrives from New York to mix money with masala in Indo-U.S. Co-Production . . .* In blown-up photographs from awards ceremonies he had attended, he was either receiving plaques or handing them out, always smiling, always in the company of politicians and entertainers, Indian and American. These blow-ups were on more formal display than the movie posters and confined to wall space inside the glassed-in reception area. Danny Jagtiani was the tallest person in each picture. He looked handsome enough to have been a Bollywood star himself. He was also younger than I had expected. I had the feeling that the climb up the stairs was a fair representation of Danny's rise up the ladder of success, from salesman in yellow jacket to kingmaker in embroidered silk.

We'd arrived in time. The secretary at the front desk had gone to lunch and the fax machine was clear. Three closed doors branched off the converted living room that served as the outer office. Didi knocked cautiously on the farthest door, heard a grunt from inside, and we pushed our way through—two overdressed sisters, one carrying a treasure in gold and the fear of detection, the other, bottled anger and a cell phone.

Danny sprung to his feet, transforming himself in an instant from distracted accountant, head buried in his ledger books, to the very model of charm and ebullience, standing with open arms into which Didi permitted herself to be enfolded. "Padma! How's my star?" he exclaimed with what appeared to be genuine enthusiasm, and then, turning to me, "And you must be the sister I've been hearing so much about! My, my, Padma did not exaggerate one little bit. And, I'm so embarrassed by what happened at the airport. I hope you can forgive me. By the time I heard you were coming, I just didn't have a car and driver to spare!"

"Danny was simply devastated," Didi explained. "I told you how he'd tried to send a backup." No winks, no nods. "By the time *he* got around to calling me, it was too late." The famous *he*, Harish, the unutterable formal name of the husband. This was the first I had heard of Danny's role on the night of my arrival. I smiled, but I wasn't buying. Not anymore. Nothing she could say.

Danny's English, to my ear, was as American as Rabi's. He might have come over as a child, but then, why the continued deep involvement in India? Then again, he was Sindhi and what I knew about Sindhis amounted only to the prejudices of my class and city. Sindhis were certainly more adaptable than Bengalis. They had lost their homes in 1947 and had rebuilt their lives without nostalgia.

Danny seemed to enjoy the glamorous side of his role as real estate mogul and Bollywood backer. Permed hair, I thought; I had never seen Indian hair form itself into such a luxuriant cap of curls.

A toned body, not a hint of the little potbelly that afflicts otherwise lean Indian men long before they reach Danny's age. Fifty? I guessed now that I had seen him in person. Maybe more. Facials for sure, and gleaming teeth. We'd caught him in office-mode, white shirt with sleeves rolled up, but even as he stood making small talk, he was rolling them down and inserting gold cufflinks. He tightened the knot of his tie, and slipped into his blazer. A very presentable, very attractive man.

"I've just been attending to a few last-minute things here, but you must let me take you to lunch." Before Didi could back us out of it, I enthusiastically endorsed the idea. There might still be a glass of wine, somewhere in Queens, with my name on it. He poked his head into the reception area, and finding it empty, shouted out,

"Ramchander, tea for the ladies!"

Danny's office might have served earlier tenants as a child's room; one wall was still covered in a clowns-and-balloons wallpaper. As we sipped our tea, I reflected on the irony of Didi's being dependent on the generosity of a Sindhi, one of the many communities we'd despised growing up—unless she'd planned it all along, as further vengeance against Daddy. Any community whose roots were not in Bengal, preferably in the eastern half of Bengal; anything like the Marwari, Parsi, or Sindhi community, was seen as alien and money-grubbing, worthy of our disrespect, if not outright contempt. No reason needed; that was the joy of being born rich and Brahmin and Bengali in the great city at the center of our culture. God help us.

Perhaps Daddy had had "dealings" with a Sindhi sharpie, but then, according to Daddy, all Sindhis were sharpies, a shade more ruthless than Marwaris, who at least had been making their home in Calcutta for nearly a century while bleeding us dry and shipping their profits back to their ancestral villages in the deserts of Rajasthan. Marwaris, at least, were fiercely observant, vegetarian, ascetic, temple-building Hindus. Sindhis were always a little suspect, a minority Hindu community lost in the vast Muslim sea around Karachi. Even their language was written in Arabic script, like Urdu, and their Hinduism seemed to us negotiable. They'd arrived in Bombay as Partition refugees, more midnight's children, stripped of their wealth, and within five years had outhustled and outschemed the Parsis and Gujaratis who historically dominated Bombay capitalism.

No wonder we hated them. We disapproved of anyone who sullied himself with the exclusive pursuit of money and anyone who lacked culture as we defined it. Anyone who worked harder and became wealthy.

I sipped my tea and listened to the small talk and the preparation for tonight's party. The catering would come from one of Danny's New Jersey restaurants. Didi was to tell Kajol Ghosal to expect the cooks around five o'clock. The guest list was again brought out, this time with Danny's spin and approval. "I see Dr. Nag is back on the A-list, his little episode with our Italian friends all forgotten?" He seemed to like everyone. "*Splendid* chap, Tara will love him and his wife!" and "I *hope* their daughters are coming, so bright and attractive!" and "Oh, she's *so* much fun!" and Didi agreed with every judgment. "I've been trying to prepare Tara for them, but you have a way of making them sound even more amusing!" His regret was that a fund-raiser would be keeping him in Queens. He gave to both political parties; he even forgot which one was picking his pockets tonight. The price of doing business in America, he said, no different than India, just a little less cultivated.

The conversation turned to Mr. Bose and the gold store. "Charming chap, isn't he?" I agreed that he was. Did I know he was a certified hero, that he'd fought the British as a very small boy? Dealing gold was perhaps the least of his accomplishments. He sang Tagore, with the voice of a god. He had taught Bengali literature in university. All five of his children had attained great honors in India and abroad.

"People like Jyotirmoy Bose, like you two, that's why I try to hire Bengalis whenever I can. Bengalis add class to any enterprise." We hung our heads modestly. But Danny was just getting started. Whenever he met a Bengali, he could hear Gilbert and Sullivan playing in the background. Even now, can't you hear it? In the English school he'd attended in Bombay, the priests had said that to truly appreciate Gilbert and Sullivan, you had to see it in Calcutta. Brother Anthony, a Goan, was the first great Bengali-lover he ever met. " 'Bengalis understand the soul,' he always said. We poor Bombay boys, all of us Muslims and Jews and Parsis and Goans and Sindhis, with luck, we might be able to understand the words."

We laughed a little guiltily. All three of us sisters had been enthusiastic choristers through six years of school productions of Gilbert and Sullivan. But when Mummy and Daddy complained that we were always stuck in the back row, Mother Michael Paul pointed out, "Your daughters may look like angels, but they sing like crows." Danny seemed receptive, and I felt it was time, and my duty, to restore some balance to his overappreciative view of Bengal. "Perhaps you'll think a little differently of us if I tell you what happened to me in my only solo in *The Gondoliers*," I began. Didi didn't look too pleased.

"I'm not familiar with *The Gondoliers*," he said in a preemptory tone. It was clear that he was not asking for a summary of the plot. Not unlike Bish in his later years, I thought. I learn what I need to know. This is something I do not need to know.

Out in the reception area, I could hear the secretary's return. Almost magically the outer phones started ringing. A bell had also gone off in Danny's head. I could read it in his eyes. *Enough of this idle chitchat.* Off came the blazer. He sat in front of us in his white shirt, still smiling, but the smile was not one of a raconteur or a romantic. "I wonder if I might see the champak-ali," a soft request that Didi responded to as if he had snapped his fingers. She fished it out of her purse, opened the box, and draped it over his outstretched hand. He stared at the necklace, turning it slowly in the light, as though peering through a jeweler's eyepiece. Slowly, he curled his fist over it, closed his eyes, and mentally weighed it.

"Good weight. Did old Bose say how much?"

Didi answered, "I didn't ask. Tara liked it so much I just told him to wrap it up."

"I'd say eight-five, maybe nine. It's one of his finer pieces. It could go higher, under the right conditions." He opened his fist. I'd never seen so much gold in one hand.

"Might I see it on?" He extended his hand in my direction. Fine gold, 24-carat gold, molds itself to the body and gathers the body's warmth. The necklace huddled and glittered in Danny's hand like something wet and injured. It felt almost hot.

I liked it? It's true, but I hadn't committed to it in any familiar way. Eight or nine thousand dollars worth of gold—I'd never have an occasion to wear it; what a worry it would be in San Francisco, especially in my altered situation. The whole transaction, everything about Didi's job and her relationship with Danny was odd and confusing. The attraction I felt to the necklace had nothing to do with the exquisite piece of jewelry itself, it was toward adolescent memories of visiting the gold stores in Bhowanipur, always ending up at Sirkar's, and the hours spent in front of the jeweler's mirror trying on necklaces and earrings. Never just for the beauty and value of the gold, or even what it did for me, since we were cautioned against vanity for fear the gods would hear and damage us, but for the implication it carried of dowry, and curiosity over the kind of super husband it might attract.

"Very lovely. She will wear it tonight. And please, lower the sari edge just a little, let it be seen against your bosom. You see how it curves in and out," and now I could feel his finger not only on the gold as he cradled the necklace, but the backs of his fingers brushing against my breast. "Only the best craftsmanship allows free play to all the linkages, so it is very important for people to see it properly displayed. Bad quality, and the links don't bend, they go their own way, the necklace juts out, instead of going in, like here—"

We both jumped when my phone went off.

"Oh, really, Tara!" To Danny she explained, "She's my youngest sister but sometimes, I swear, she's more like a daughter. She plays with that thing like a teenager at a shopping mall! There's some boy out in California who just won't leave her alone. It's Jack this and Jack that, till I want to scream! Here, let me turn it off so we can have a quiet little meeting."

She held out her hand. I pulled the telephone closer.

"Mrs. Chatterjee. Can you please have someone turn on the fax machine? I've been trying to transmit for the last hour."

"Of course, Jack. I didn't know the fax machine had been turned off."

"Fax machine is never off!" Danny protested. "How stupid would that be?" He was out the door in a shot, into the reception area, shouting at the secretary. Didi sat grimly in the corner. I supposed that she had managed to turn it off.

"Come, Didi. Let's check what he's sending."

Danny and I hovered over the machine as it began burping out an image. Didi stood outside the office, appearing to read the newspaper clippings. The scolded secretary, a very young, very fair Sindhi girl with henna-rinsed hair, glared at me and then at the machine.

As I watched the slow accumulation of dark lines, all the random dots that began to coalesce, I remembered the PG-13 science-fiction movies that I used to take Rabi to. The slow emergence of an alien from the womb. The paper notched its way onto the tray, extra black for all the hair, extra moist from all the ink. I could tell even before we'd reached the eyes that suspect number one, Gopal Sinha, was not the man. I wanted to pull the paper out, but it still had five more minutes of face and mustache and plaid shirt, and then the intricate printing at the bottom: age, place of birth, offenses, and last known address to go. Gopal Sinha, of Calcutta, was a twenty-three-year-old killer, presumed to have been a gang member and an underworld enforcer, and to have entered through Mexico, likely working in a Mexican or Indian restaurant.

"You keep very lively company," Danny said, as he read the sheet. "How would an upstanding lady such as yourself be knowing Calcutta murderers?" The second sheet started coming through. "Padma never really told me what you do. Is it police work?"

"You mean I'm more interesting than I look?" I was still wearing the champakali, and the whole mismatch struck me as so comic, and so tragic, that only absurdity did it justice.

"It would be very difficult for you to lead a life more interesting than your looks, Tara." I could feel the beginnings of a blush; I had not been approached quite so openly in a good many years. There's something to be said for new hair, new nails, designer saris, and Oscar-quality jewels.

"Perhaps you are writing a book? Bengalis are always scribbling, isn't it?" He was drawing closer than even the fax sharing called for. This isn't right, I thought. Didi had noticed too, she made her way back to the desk. "If you are writing about criminals, I can perhaps offer assistance."

"I'm being stalked, if you must know. It's all very routine and boring."

"There is nothing routine and boring when your stalker is a killer, Tara."

Didi picked up the sheet. "Who is this Gopal Sinha? What is Gopal Sinha to you? Eesh!" She dropped the page. "He's killed people, what are you doing with his picture?"

I knew from the beginning that number two, Abbas Sattar Hai, was my man. Born in Bihar, raised in Calcutta, later joined Dawood gang in Bombay. Wanted for: murder, extortion, kidnapping, arson. He employed a long series of aliases from all regions and all communities.

"Didi, this is the man who has been stalking me." I shifted to Bengali so Danny wouldn't understand. "Take a good look at his face. Take a very long look."

She turned away. "I have no intention of looking at your murderers. Don't expose me to this rubbish!"

Danny was staring intently at the sheet. "I know this guy. I knew him as Abdul Rehman, he even worked a few days in my restaurant till I caught him stealing. This guy's a monster. I got off easy."

"How long ago was that?"

"A year," he thought. Abdul Rehman was one of the aliases. Anthony Thomas. Diego D'Souza. Sunil Ghose. Harilal Guha. Wahid Ali Ahmad. The note at the bottom of his rap sheet noted that he was known to assume the identities of his victims. He is considered ruthless, lacking in conscience, and exceptionally clever, a true chameleon. Adept in many languages including English, Urdu, Bengali, and Hindi.

A third sheet was coming through. Faster and smaller, an INS visa photo. Oh, yes, he looked like us; he had the Bhattacharjee genes, just as Ronald had promised. He looked more like me or Didi than Rabi did. God, Christopher had dimples! A fleshy, Bengali face, a long, thick nose, full lips, an amused smile. I felt a longing to hold them both, my son and my nephew, cousins, and then fear began rising. I had been feeling nothing but anger in the past few weeks: anger at Daddy for having opposed the marriage, anger at Didi for her denial, anger at Parvati for treating it like a joke, anger at Rabi for his secrecy. So much anger that I'd armored myself against legitimate, self-protecting, naked fear.

Andy had felt the danger, Rabi had felt it, Jack had felt it, and I'd been sailing through a minefield like a self-appointed Joan of Arc. Rabi and Bish were roaming around without a sense of caution or a care in the world. My house was empty and just sitting there, dark and inviting. All I had was Jack against this cunning, exceptionally clever chameleon. I folded the sheet and handed it to her. "Keep this, Didi. Memorize this face," I cried out in Bengali. "This may be the closest you'll ever get to your son."

To my surprise, she took it from me. Danny looked on, apparently indifferent. As I watched, it seemed that a mask was descending on her face, or that a mask had been lifted. Every secret line and crevice, every irregularity, every feature that a long, hard life could bloat or pull or flatten, spread for a moment, then stopped. "Handsome lad," she said. To Danny, she added, "Our nephew, coming on his first visit."

The middle door off the reception area, probably the original dining room, was now Didi's "home away from home," the "Namaskar, Probasi" set and studio. The bathroom was now the makeup studio. Darkened today, the set would be a beehive tomorrow. Three interviews with visiting dignitaries were lined up, and Didi herself would be visiting the home of a sixteen-year-old Bengali girl who'd won a national science prize. The permanent set consisted of a curved desk bearing the name of the show and two chairs. The original dining room windows, which had probably looked down on a Queens backyard, were now covered by an enormous color photo of Manhattan-by-night. A television camera, lights, reflectors, and a tangle of cables filled the rest of the room. ("I tell you, Tara, when the lights are on and the crew is here, we have to be lifted into those chairs like astronauts!") The other walls were covered in a glittery, tinfoil-like substance that twisted like crepe paper. It seemed ready for balloons, like a high school gym on prom night.

This sudden madness of my life, I wanted to cry out, where does it end? Two weeks ago, I had been one of you. I would have looked at the walls and pronounced them festive and garish and I would have added, "Danny, you've sure got your finger on the pulse of the community!" This is our gaudy heart and soul, this is why Bombay films wiped Satyajit Ray off the map. And now I could only watch as Danny and my sister rehearsed tomorrow's show, or was it tonight's? Oh, yes, Danny could tell me stories about shady dealings in Jackson Heights, but if she'd been able, Didi could tell me something far worse. I doubted that she would. She had been sucked into something I couldn't begin to understand.

I stepped back into the hall and called Jack with the positive identification of Abbas Sattar Hai. I mentioned that a year ago, under the name of Abdul Rehman, he had been working for a very rich man in Jackson Heights named Danny Jagtiani. And I thanked him for sending the picture of Christopher, and feared that it might be the only contact we would ever have.

"Mrs. Chatterjee—Tara, you once gave me permission—I have to tell you that everything we've learned about this individual is deeply disturbing. You may have noticed from the sheet I sent that he is a known member of the Dawood gang. From my perspective, leaving out the case of Mr. Dey, and even that of Dr. Dey, that is the most disturbing element of all. The Dawood gang controls organized crime in Bombay. They're a full-scale criminal cartel with networks all over Asia and the Middle East. They're headquartered in the Gulf, so they can launder their profits and still be outside Indian jurisdiction. I did my M.A. on the history of the Dawood gang."

"Not lacrosse?"

"Lacrosse got me in. Criminology kept me there."

"My sister in Bombay suspected gangs all along. I laughed at her."

"Look, let's stipulate they're evil and powerful and they're behind just about all the corruption in Bombay, which is saying something. They're into drugs and prostitution, and the movies. They're into home invasions, kidnapping, extortion, arson, and bombing. They've wiped out all the competing gangs and freelancers. Whoever they can't buy, they assassinate."

Now, you want to hear the disturbing part?

"They go where the money is. Drugs are big, movies are big, but the biggest thing in India now is high-tech. Some of these so-called software designers and chip engineers who've recently arrived have very suspicious backgrounds. The gang recruits them in India, so we don't know if they're being planted to steal chips, or codes, or whatever."

I must have muttered something about the joys of globalization. "I'm glad you haven't lost your sense of humor, Tara."

But I had lost it. Fifteen years ago we all sat in a Stanford pub, bright, enthusiastic graduate students and wives of graduate students shoving pieces of paper around the table top, complicated codes, Bish, *can this work?* Literally, we had the world on a string, the string around our fingers. How could it have turned so ugly, so fast? Now I read in the morning paper of Vietnamese gangs in San Jose invading the homes of Vietnamese restaurant owners, killing their children, and I'd always felt so safe, as though forty miles were the other side of the world. Chinese chip-stealing gangs invaded Chinese-owned factories, seizing the owners' children as hostages and killing them no matter what. The ugliness was everywhere. We'd unleashed an international crime wave, sitting there doodling codes on napkins in a Stanford pub. As I held the telephone, I could see Didi and Danny in the studio and hear their laughing.

"The Dawood gang basically draws from guys like Mr. Hai. None of these Chinese or Vietnamese gangs are going to take Indians seriously until they pull off something big, so that's Hai's job. If he follows the same pattern as other foreign-based gangs, the target will be wealthy members of their own community."

"You mean Bish, don't you?"

"Mr. Chatterjee would be an appropriate-sized target, yes. And I'm very sorry to sound alarming, but so is your son. And so are you. Be very careful about your son. I can arrange for surveillance if you want. For them, kidnapping is just another way of doing business. Until we can apprehend Mr. Hai, I would say your husband and your son, and you, Tara, are potential targets."

"If I call him, what should I say? He doesn't know anything about this. In fact, he and Rabi are probably off on some huge trip for Thanksgiving." I had no idea which city or continent Bish and Rabi had decided to vacation in. Tasmania to track the phantom thylacine? Calcutta to check on a sick relative? Rabi had a cell phone but he rarely turned it on.

"Mr. Chatterjee should be informed," said Jack. "He should go over it with his security staff. Give him my number after you've talked with him."

It had never occurred to me that Bish had a "security staff." What a hopeless innocent I was. "Please fax him the picture," I said.

"Tell him to be very suspicious of any new people who show up for work. An unskilled laborer offering to do odd jobs around the house is bad news."

I wondered how much Jack really knew, how much he was

holding back, and how much he was trying to suggest without actually telling. I asked the question I'd been afraid to. "Do you have anything new on Christopher?"

"All I can tell you is that he was admitted to this country at LAX three weeks ago and he went immediately to the Bay Area and was last seen in his hotel two weeks ago. I have to tell you that Mr. Hai was staying in the same hotel under the name of Anthony Thomas. If they had contact, it seems to have been accidental. Nothing conclusive has shown up."

The voice-body-language came through clearly enough. Rabi and I might be the only two people he'd had a chance to kill, but hadn't. I called Rabi, but his phone wasn't on. I called Bish and got the office. Mr. Chatterjee is out. I left my number and just the name Tara, and an urgent request to call.

*   *   *

We went back to Danny's diner for a late lunch. He had a corner booth; the best seat in Jackson Heights, he called it. From his corner, he could watch his money grow. He controlled the cheap sides of the Monopoly board with hotels on every property, all traffic, and a thin profit margin. The waitress brought my wine back, no questions asked. Danny did not drink. He opened up a little more.

"The trouble with business," he started, "is you learn very quickly never to talk about yourself. It sounds weak and confessional, or if you ask, you sound nosy. So you slip into the habit of clamming up around your competitors, and waiting for the other guy to make a mistake. I've spent thirty years in the company of some men and never learned the first thing about them. Personal things can only be used against you, right? It was Padma who got me to think differently."

"You can talk about yourself without being egotistical," she said. "Danny was very uncomfortable in the beginning. If I asked him about Bombay and what his family was like, he'd come right back with 'Why do you want to know?' I'd have to say, 'Because I'm your friend, silly.' He said he was shocked at some of the things I volunteered about myself, and I didn't even give them a second thought."

"To be a fly on those walls, Didi!"

"I envy you girls, the way you can talk so freely about yourselves. It's an art. Literally, it *is* art. It's something Padma had to teach me. I was just this poor kid from Bombay, a Sindhi with dirt in his mouth. Not every Sindhi makes money, just like not every Bengali writes poetry. It was humiliating, being Samir Jagtiani's son, growing up in that city in those years when every Sindhi was minting money."

Didi had taught him very well. He spoke of himself without apparent inhibition. He'd arrived in New York with only one idea in his head, to make piles of money any way he could and find a niche that no one else occupied or push out whoever did. Nothing was beneath him. He delivered papers, pushing little kids off their routes. He had a hot dog cart and fought dirty to keep his corner. He started making kabobs, and when they began outselling the hot dogs, he unloaded his license to a Lebanese and started a kabob stand down the street on Seventy-eighth. He went in with some Sikhs for taxi licenses and sold his share at a huge profit and bought his first building. The agent was an old Jew who'd barely got out of Europe with his life. "Property," he said, and in one afternoon showed him a million dollars just waiting for the right man to put the deal together. That's when Devanand Jagtiani became Danny. He swallowed his pride and went to night school with Colombians and Chinese and got his real estate license and that's when things turned around.

"It's all about timing, isn't it?"

"The right place, Jackson Heights, when it *really* started to take off. But luck? Everything I got, I fought like hell for. Nothing came easy. People look at me now and they think sharp Sindhi guy, smooth talker, very American-sounding, lots of powerful friends, but they don't see how I worked, they don't know the kid I was. I see him every day in the mirror."

The lesson he learned in his first ten years hustling in New York was that buying and selling, even for a healthy profit, leaves you at the end of the day with nothing. You come in, you get out, you take the money and look for the next place to invest it. You don't have to be too smart to make a lot of money if that's your only goal. He never once in his life thought of the higher things, like art or beauty and entertainment.

"If you had told me even ten years ago I'd be making movies and running a television network, you'd have to have been crazy. I would have run away from you."

And that's where Didi came in.

"I suppose it's no secret that your sister was a very popular young woman in New York in those years. You saw her around all the interesting people. It was your sister who changed everything for me."

Didi bowed her head.

"When I was about thirty-five, this stunning new Indian girl started showing up at all the community functions. I used to go to them only to make contacts—I even waited out in the lobby when the music came on. Now I had a new reason to go. I'll confess that I was married. I was supposed to bring my wife over and start a family as soon as I got established. Well, I was getting established, and I still didn't want to bring her over. Things were just starting to get exciting here. And she was a very traditional village girl. She would have been one of those bride-suicides you read about, afraid to go out."

He looked at Padma and thought *that's* the kind of girl he needed. "She was what, nineteen? Nineteen going on thirty-five?" he started laughing and we chimed in with well-timed giggles.

She was kind enough to take him around to parties and introduce him to some of her friends. She'd been in New York maybe six months, and she knew everybody. She knew people at the UN, she knew people in the theater and people on Madison Avenue, and she hung out with a lot of fashionable gay men with antique stores in the Village. She could always come up with tickets to Broadway shows. Someone even joked, "If you get a parking ticket, Padma can fix it." Now that's power. She represented something he'd never seen before. He called it glamour and confidence, and poise.

"You're not to listen to any of this, Tara. What does a Bombay movie producer know about the truth?" she said, with a dimpled smile. "When you were eighteen, could you have done any of the things he says I was doing? Of course not!" I'd never noticed the dimple. "But it makes a good story." In Bengali she added, "I think he's working on that bitch-goddess role I was telling you about!"

"Joan Collins?" said Danny. *Too clever by half*, the nuns would say. So, he understood Bengali. Danny knew everything.

Then, apparently, she just disappeared. He thought she had gone back to India and got married or something. Some people said they had seen her in Hindi movies, but he knew her Hindi was *atrocious!* There were all sorts of rumors, like she'd married a cricket star or some fabulously wealthy guy and was living in the Gulf or Europe. He told people that Padma was a shooting star that burst overhead and then disappeared.

"Isn't he sweet? You see why I'd do anything for him, don't you?"

"About ten years ago, after I'd been puttering around in real estate and starting to get bored, I ran into Padma again. Now she was this very proper married lady in New Jersey. And as soon as I saw her, I started thinking of those first years, and I asked myself, where had the excitement gone, where's the *masala*, eh? She's the inspiration and the energy behind the television network and the movies. There's more to life than running a real estate agency and a couple of restaurants."

I ordered a second glass of wine. God, I thought, bring the bottle.

Danny was finally talking about the blank years in Didi's life. Parvati and I used to get postcards from her, never letters, back in Calcutta. A mad, mad, mad whirl of parties, men, excitement! She always signed off with a "love you!" She met famous actors. Actors with names we knew even in Calcutta. We didn't resent Didi; she was our surrogate in the world, better her than us, because we knew she could carry it off.

"As usual, Danny has everything wrong," said Didi. "I just hope no one asks him for an interview and he starts spouting all that rubbish. The simple truth is there were very few Indian single women in New York twenty-five years ago, especially young women with a basic sense of style rather than Goan nurses or South Indian chemistry students. I'd just come from those months in London, and London was full of these fabulously bright young Indian girls. No one noticed me in London, I had to go to New York. The odds against meeting a man like Danny in London were astronomical."

"Timing is all," I said.

"Maybe I could have a glass of wine? I don't know why we have to pretend we don't have grown-up urges, too."

Danny raised his arm and snapped his fingers.

"I came here with absolutely nothing. Talk about coming to New York with dirt in your mouth! I had less than dirt. Daddy expected me to go back to Calcutta. He said he'd find a suitable

boy for me, but by then I'd already seen some of the world and a
'suitable boy' by Daddy's standards was the last thing in the world
I wanted. Can you imagine me running a house in Ballygunge and
bowing my head to some mother-in-law who found fault with
everything I wore and everything I cooked and everything I said?
Fortunately for me there was a Parsi girl I met in London who had
scads of money and she gave me a loan to buy a ticket to New
York. And do you remember Ronald Dey, from Calcutta?"

"Didi, what are you talking about? I just told you about—"
She was smiling radiantly.

"Wasn't he Poppy's brother?" I asked sweetly.

"Well, Ronny popped up in London to start his medical studies
and *he* even gave me some money. What's that famous line about
depending on the kindness of strangers? He actually offered to
look after me in London, but I told him I wasn't that kind of girl,
so he gave me money to get settled in New York. So when Danny
says I was this 'famous girl about town,' I was really living with
two secretaries in the East Village and paying forty dollars a week
for the privilege of sleeping on a sofa. I was working in the box
offices and the wardrobe department of about six off-Broadway
theaters. Those secretaries were the ones with the invitations, and
they just felt sorry for me. I had the idea that I might be able to
act, but who was interested in an Indian girl in 1976? What plays
were being written for us? In fact, producers used to say it's a pity
there's nothing for me because I could knock them dead, I had the
looks and the spunk."

It never ends. The wine came and it was all I could do to stop
at two.

"Can I ask an innocent question? What exactly are we expected
to do tonight at this party? I thought it was just a small bunch
of intimate friends, then it started expanding and now it's this
huge catered affair for every Indian in northern New Jersey. I

mean, I'm a good sport and I want to help the cause, but it's not what I thought it was going to be. What is this champakali necklace all about? What are these designer saris all about? How come all the guests are high rollers? What am I expected to do?"

"Perhaps your sister has not explained everything clearly," said Danny. "Padma Mehta is a television personality. She is an icon among Bengalis of the tristate area. What she wears and what she recommends are taken as fashion statements in the community. They are high rollers, but their wives don't get out that much, and the men don't like to waste time coming into the city on Sundays. So Padma thought up these parties as a kind of home shopping service for upscale Indians. There's an economic benefit for participating merchants, but the social values far outweigh it. And so, from time to time, we throw these parties so that the community can sample these styles in saris and jewelry that they might be missing by being out of Bengal."

"It's not only Bengalis, Tara," said Didi. "Danny does the same for Gujis and Punjabis and Maharashtrians. There's something going on every night."

"The only people I avoid are Sindhis," he said. "Can you imagine trying to sell things to Sindhis?"

"D.J. knows every Indian who counts in the tristate."

"Except Madrasis. I don't know the south," he admitted. "They're not big partygoers anyway."

When lunch had ended, Danny called for a car to take us back to New Jersey. After all, he joked, he wanted us fresh for the evening. Within minutes, a white limousine with the DJE logo pulled up.

15

We would be alone, in private, for an hour and a half. "Oh, my head is spinning from the wine," she complained. *Oh, no you don't*, I thought. "Didi, what were you doing for those ten years?"

"Ten years?"

Yes, of course, repeat the question. "The ten years Danny lost sight of you." When I thought about it, the ten years I had lost her, too. While I was finishing college, she was "in America," which was shorthand for having a good time, don't ask. Then I was married and the times I saw her would be in midtown Manhattan hotels for a drink if we were feeling like grown-ups, or tea. Then she was married, which involved different shorthand, this one mandating few calls, no visits.

"Padma's 'Ten Lost Years' is it? You should ask Danny what he was doing those ten years. Whatever it was, you can be sure I was working my fingers to the bone."

"Doing what?"

"You should be very thankful to Daddy or to your ex-husband that you've never had to worry where your next meal was coming from or how to keep a roof over your head or clothes on your back. I recommend it to everyone, you might surprise yourself learning what you'll do to survive. Just stop criticizing me for everything I've had to do. You really should examine your selfishness, Tara."

We were still rolling through the cluttered streets and ever-changing ethnicities of Queens. Little India was gone, so was Colombia. We were on the fringes of Korea.

"If I sound critical, I don't mean it personally, Didi. I know that money makes an enormous difference. But right now, all the money in the world isn't buying me even simple security."

In fact, right now I might have traded my life for hers. Her cold, dark house and her basement wraith against my warm, familiar San Francisco where I could meet my death around any corner. Danny's long white limousine was the safest place in the world for me. I hoped for traffic jams around LaGuardia and miles of backup on the Triborough Bridge.

"Do you understand what Jack Sidhu is saying to me? He says that man in the fax, that Abbas Hai, might try to kill or kidnap any of us."

She was staring out the window, unperturbed, maybe unreachable. I wanted to pull her around to face me, shout in her face and shake her.

"And you're involved, Didi. You think I'm violating some secret thing you did twenty-five years ago and threatening to make it public out of what? Jealousy? Malice? What do you think I am?"

"Keep your voice down, goodness, Tara! The driver can hear everything."

"I'd whisper if I could get your attention." I spoke slowly and deliberately. "That killer found Rabi and me and even got into our house—no, he was *welcomed* into our home—because of you, Didi."

"I hardly think so."

"He came looking for you."

"Believe me, I'm sorry for everything you're telling me, and I hope your policeman friend can apprehend him, but to imply that I have dealings with people like that is insulting and totally unacceptable."

That was her complaint? Her reputation? Maybe there was some broken circuitry. Maybe it was more a problem for Bish and Chet Yee: design a *how to get through* program. Or for Rabi, a piece of theater. I remembered the old story, Hindu or Buddhist, about the blind men describing an elephant. It is like a snake, says one, touching its trunk; like a tree, says another, touching its leg, etc. It is an international crime wave, says Jack. A murder, I say. No, no! A conspiracy to smear my reputation, says the New York media star, Padma Mehta.

Rabi and I used to laugh at the plots of the conspiracy movies we rented. A corpse washes up on a beach in Pago Pago and five minutes later secret agents steal the body, and by the end, the murder and theft are tied to a White House cover-up. I was getting a sense of the size and shape of my particular elephant, or something enormously complicated, like Bish's first technical breakthrough. Didi's abandoned baby and all the reasons behind it; the tentacles of the Dawood gang and its poisonous spread, and Bish's money from the signal invention of our time, were all linked and they were all coalescing around me.

I tried to explain one last time. Softly, quietly, sister-to-sister. "Whatever you did, and whatever I did, all of that is knotted together now. I'll never criticize you for falling in love with Ronald or for having a baby or even for walking away. That's your business, and if it means anything to you, I blame Daddy, too. But you keep refusing to see where all of it has led. I'm involved because of what you did."

Suddenly she said, "They weren't secretaries. I didn't know how to explain it to Danny, so I just dropped it."

The girls she was living with in the forty-dollar-a-week East Village share, the girls with all the party invitations. I was about to say, *But Didi, they were the only part of your story that I actually believed.*

"I met a boy in London when I was over there. He had the money—"

"Otherwise known as the 'Parsi girl'?"

"Well, he was a Parsi, one of the Batliwallas, supposedly the most brilliant boy in the London School of Economics. And he was so much fun, Tara, he knew everybody, and I felt like a princess going into restaurants or parties on his arm."

"I'm so glad, Didi, really. And you were far enough away from Daddy to keep it quiet. Or to keep him from storming over there and breaking it up."

"His name was Sohrab. He was supposed to go back to Bombay after his degree, but he had no intention of ever going back to India, and neither did I. He had academic offers from all over the U.K., and then Canada and the U.S. I thought he was going to ask me to marry him, and I was ready to do it. Anything. Padma Batliwalla, can you imagine Daddy's reaction?"

"Did Sohrab know about your . . . mishap?"

"My little 'mishap.' That's a nice word. No one will ever know about my little mishap."

That's where you're so wrong, Didi, the whole world knows it. Somewhere in the Gulf, Mr. Dawood knows about it. Somewhere on the Great Barrier Reef, Bish Chatterjee knows, and Jack Sidhu in San Francisco knows, and Mr. Abbas Sattar Hai knows, and

Andy and Rabi and Parvati and Auro. How many continents is that? And they're all linked by CHATTY, the operating system of billions of tiny cell phones with the ever-widening chips. A romantic might say it began in a Romeo and Juliet moment, an exchange of glances in Poppy Dey's house. But it went back to the decision of Ronald's grandfather to convert to Protestantism and gain favor from the British and lose status with the Hindus. Or even back to Mishtigunj and the decision of a pleader to become more Hindu than his ancestors, more Hindu than the villagers around him.

"So what happened between you and Sohrab Batliwalla?"

"Nothing happened. Absolutely nothing happened. He got his job offer from NYU and came over, and he paid for me to come with him."

"I'd say that's something. You were really discreet, because we didn't hear a thing about it."

"We found a place in the Village and I moved in with him. I thought, if they could see me now, nineteen years old and living in New York, in sin with a Parsi! He absolutely didn't care what I had done in Calcutta or how I had been living in London. He called me his Bengali Sally Bowles, you know, the girl from *Cabaret*? He was so broad-minded, I couldn't believe he was Indian. And on top of that, he had incredible taste in decorating and he was a fabulous Parsi cook, so I learned my way in the kitchen. You know how we were never even allowed in the kitchen back in Ballygunge."

"Oh-oh, I think I know where this is going, Didi."

She was nodding. "It's that obvious, is it? We weren't raised for this century, were we?"

"What did we know about gay men? What did any of us know?"

"We were such silly-billies, weren't we?"

"I hear Gilbert and Sullivan."

Now she was laughing. "He came home one night with a new friend named Darshan and he cooked up a big dhansak and around midnight I started getting sleepy and I was wondering when this poor chap was going home! Oooh, Tara, we were perfect little innocents, even with a . . . mishap. I spent that night and every other night on the sofa. They needed me, of course, and I needed them, so it was perfect. For a while."

"Rabi is gay," I said.

She turned to me with such full-force empathy, her eyes, her voice, her body, and both hands on top of mine that I believed for the first time that she actually could have been the actress she always wanted to be. Acting in the best sense, the ability to pull up something from deep inside her. It would always be about her.

"Good for him. You think it, or he told you?"

"I never saw it coming. In retrospect, of course, it all makes sense. He told me last week."

"What does his father think?"

"I don't know if Bish is ready. They're off together this week, Australia, the office said. I don't know when Rabi's planning to tell him. They can both surprise me."

"Tell him to be careful, dear. Poor Sohrab, he didn't know. He was one of the early ones. They were calling it gay man's disease, so he was afraid the story would get out and he'd lose his job and his insurance. He couldn't tell his parents, of course. You know how Parsis leave their bodies out for the vultures—he wouldn't even do that. I did something worse. I cremated him like a Hindu. It seemed closer to nature than burial."

"I didn't even know the Bengali word for . . . it. Doing it in the same-sex way."

"All in all, I envy them. Does that sound strange? Everywhere I've gone, it's been gay men who've protected me and yes, loved me. Like Sohrab and Darshan, like, oh, God, Tara, like just about every man I've ever met and taken a liking to. And they like me, I don't know what I mean to them, but they make me feel special. Look at what my one minute of so-called 'normal love' has brought me. Do you know what would happen if *he* ever found out? He'd kill me, or maybe kill himself. Danny protects him, gives him little jobs that make him feel useful. It's really very sweet."

It crossed my mind that the "it" she was referring to involved more than Ronald Dey, Danny, or Sohrab, and doing more than fronting for a gay man, and I could imagine, for just a moment, all the things "it" meant, and the fear it generated. I couldn't imagine Harish rising to the heights of a grand passion, but I could picture Didi in just about any fit of surrender. It was the shorthand for self-protection and self-forgiveness.

"It's pretty clear that Danny loves you, Didi."

"Of course he does. He shows it in little ways every day. People already think we're up to something. That's what I've been saying, Tara, don't you listen? Gays are the best. Gays have figured it out. I need Danny and Danny needs me, just like Sohrab did. Toward the end, I could carry him. I could reach under him and carry him to the living room so he could look out the window. I don't care what Danny does in private and whom he does it with. To me, he's everything a man should be."

Danny? I started laughing. "I thought he was coming on to me! I thought it was making you jealous."

"Of course it was making me jealous. You think jealousy is only about sex?" He'd been sending a message the whole time, how hard it is to talk about yourself, the village bride, the taste for glamour, the hair, the body, his identification with the bound- less self-regard of Bengalis, but I hadn't been listening. I was too self-absorbed, my radar down, my cell phone off, the learning curve too steep. Now I turned to her, holding out my arms, "Oh, Didi, Didi, Didi," tears mixing with laughter, "my Sally Bowles."

"Not your Joan Collins?"

,   ,   ,

We rode out to Basking Ridge in the same limo—the cooks, Padma, Harish, and I, and suitcases packed full of Padma's designer saris and cholis.

Harish knew his role, alien presence at a Bengali bash. He called himself "Harish, the hopeful hoverer," edging into conversations he could not understand, hoping someone would supply an American spouse or neighbor with whom he could converse.

Didi fussed with her inventory. Harish prepped me on the Ghosals, from his perspective. He called their mansion "Lucent Mahal" and traced its pedigree from nineteenth-century robber barons to its last American owner, "The Don Next Door," from whom Dr. Ghosal had plucked it at a RICO auction. It came with buzzers and passageways the Ghosals were still discovering.

Harish was gentler in his assessments than Didi had been. Dr. Nag was entertaining, particularly when his inhibitions had been loosened. He was the victim of that well-known Indian disease, SFS Sudden Freedom Syndrome—after his parents' death. Dr. Haldar, the busy bachelorette, was a brilliant and lonely woman who craved acceptance but didn't know how to get it; Mr. Basu was a Calcutta chauvinist with a contrarian streak. In fact, SFS, it occurred to me, might explain the whole lot of us. Harish joked as we pulled into the long, circular driveway, *Tonight, the role of the older husband and monitor of the food and drink supply will be played by Harish Mehta.*

I'd made up my mind to be the good little sister, the pliable Loreto House girl and to help Didi's cause any way I could. I could even say with honesty that I loved my sister, in my way, or hers. I was determined to have a good time.

,   ,   ,

The cooks set up their braziers for lamb and kabobs on the broad back deck. The grounds of the Basking Ridge estate stretched like a fairway to a distant line of Japanese fruit trees, now leafless in the late-November chill. Lucent Mahal was a faux-Tuscan villa whose interior beams and built-ins were stained, sturdy oak and whose tiled kitchen and dining room floors boasted faces and figures copied from the excavation of Pompeii. The front rooms and the his-and-hers studies were decorated in a style that suggested India without actually proclaiming it. Gold Medal Ghosal, as he was known in the community, had won a prize considered to be the stepping stone to the Nobel. He'd had it glass-cased above the fireplace.

He came over as I stood below it, warming myself at the fire. He was a tall man of fifty or so, powerfully built, his hair flecked with gray, wearing a blazer over a cream-colored turtleneck. "Bishwapriya Chatterjee's wife! I am so honored." He gave no sign that he might know differently, and none came from me, being on strict orders not to clarify the ex factor or answer any questions. "We're in related but not identical fields, otherwise he certainly would have captured this prize before me." His Bengali was of the Calcutta bhadra lok, but his English, despite years at the highest level of corporate America, remained where it might have been thirty years earlier. He was no Danny, nor a Bish.

The Ghosals were a multigenerational family of eight, or at least eight outgoing and circulating members. Besides Dr. Mrinal and Dr. (Mrs.) Kajol Ghosal, there were four well-mannered children aged between seven and eighteen, and Mrinal's very presentable parents, who had to be in their late seventies. If the Ghosals followed community practice, there could be a second set of parents, perhaps bedridden or merely quarrelsome, stashed in another wing.

Like her husband, Kajol seemed outsized for a Bengali. My sisters and I are all five foot six, which had placed us among the taller girls in our classes. My height had even posed a difficulty for my father in the selection of a suitable boy, given the need to find someone at least four inches taller. It was a terrible tragedy to reject otherwise stupendous grooms because of the visual mismatch. Dr. (Mrs.) Ghosal was at least five foot ten.

"So, I see she roped you in." She loomed before me with an amused smile, and from her English I knew immediately she'd been a Loreto House girl, at least ten years before Didi. The Loreto accent is as interchangeable as our handwriting. "She's deeply conniving, isn't she?"

"Padma? I'm just along for the ride. She roped you in—you're the ones doing the work."

Maybe because mine was the only unfamiliar face, she offered to take me on a tour of the house. I hadn't expected a pathologist to display quite her flair for the outrageous. She took me by the elbow and steered me down a long, dark corridor.

"Is this where you *really* live?" I asked, and she smiled warmly, "You *know!*" The corridor opened on a large room that smelled like an electronics store. Two young men, servants released from their duties until all the guests had left, sat on the Indian carpets looking up at a Hindi movie playing on a wall-sized screen. Various red and green lights winked from shelves and countertops.

"Our real house starts here, the rest is all public space. *He* has an office out there and we manage to keep it all very tasteful, don't we?" She shifted to Bengali. "The deeper you go back here, the more desi it becomes. We even had to convert an old servant's room back into a traditional Indian kitchen because our servants were afraid of the appliances. Gin and lime, Mrs. Chatterjee?"

"Tara, please. Gin and lime will do quite nicely." I had a sudden vision of Parvati's apartment in Bombay, looking out to the ocean and down on the black rocks of the fisherman's village.

"It's silly isn't it, keeping up the pretense? I make life and death decisions at the hospital every day, but in my own home I have to sneak around, afraid to offend the sensibilities of people I don't care a fig about. Who're we trying to fool?" She gave the order to the servants and they hit the pause button and leaped off to the kitchen to make our drinks. "What is your profession, Tara?"

"What do you see me as, Dr. Ghosal?"

"Kajol, please. Well, first, just between us, we can drop the little fiction about your still being married, can't we? I remember when my husband came home from a conference about five or six years ago, the first thing he told me was that a Loreto House girl had actually left the richest and most important Indian in the country. It absolutely shook him to his boots! And I said to myself, 'Hooray for her.' So, I see you as courageous and a little crazy, if truth be told."

"Leaving your husband's not exactly a profession," I said.

"Some women, even some Bengali women, have done very well with it. I must say, it had an immediately beneficial effect on my marriage. He always measured himself against your husband, even though yours is probably younger. If that could happen to Dr. Chatterjee, think what I might do to him!" She let out a little snort of satisfaction.

We moved on with our drinks into a traditional compound inside the Mafia villa. There was a prayer room, eerie by nightlight, with rows of brass deities and burning sticks of incense. Further on, the children shared two bedrooms, the teenaged daughters in one and the younger sons in the other; nothing Indian about them except the bedspreads and the intense avoidance of gender confusion. Michael Jordan posters and dinosaur charts for the boys; Mel Gibson and some unidentifiable rock stars for the girls. Two computers in each room. The parents' bedroom was a full-scale desi reproduction, dominated by a super king-sized carved wooden bed frame holding a thin slab of rubber mattress, under a slowly whumping ceiling fan. Family portraits lined the walls, some going back to the nineteenth century, judging from the stylized poses. A nearly identical arrangement had kept us three sisters cool and comfortable, and, I suppose, obedient and respectful, growing up.

"Now it gets a little strange," she warned, as we turned a final bend into the faintest light and musty, end-of-corridor air. A series of closed doors ended in a vague shape that looked like a sack of laundry set upon a chair. We passed the servants' quarters, *his* parents' bedroom, and finally, the shape shifted on his haunches, revealing a very old man sleeping on a straight-backed chair outside the final door, his hand still clutching a stout wooden pole. A functioning chowkidar sat like a museum guard sleeping at his post.

"Did Padma tell you about my parents?"

"You know Didi," I said. "Never gossips."

"It's a fairly famous story. My parents were killed in an Indian Airlines crash ten years ago. Apart from that, the rest of the story is so Indian I want to laugh. Those are my *grandparents* sleeping behind that door. They were living with my parents, of course, so we had to bring them over. They were eighty-four then, imagine what they're like now! Most of their servants had died or were too old to travel and they were too set in their ways to adjust to new servants. They wouldn't come over without their old cook and their oldest servant. So, okay, they came and the cook died about six weeks after he arrived. My grandmother said he died of frustration, never mind that he was about eighty. He couldn't find good fish in the market and he didn't recognize the vegetables and he hated the taste of American milk, so he curled up in his bed and died.

"So that left us with old Ram, who'll probably bury us all. He hasn't been outside in seven years, so he probably thinks he's still in Calcutta sitting outside the old house and *they* probably think they're in the old house being protected, so it works out nicely. I doubt that he can even lift that lathi now."

In a moment of profound depression I thought, if this is what truly committed people do to protect their children and grandparents from nonexistent threats, on an estate surrounded by electrified fences, what am I doing to protect myself against named, identifiable forces out to destroy me?

We left Ram to his duties and headed back toward the populated areas. "Wasn't there some poet we had to read in college, Tennyson maybe, or maybe Browning, lines with 'his palsièd grip' in them? I think of those innocent days and those feverish Sundays spent memorizing Tennyson and the sheer terror of disappointing the nuns every time I see old Ram clutching his scepter and every time I go into their bedroom. I swear, if I took you inside, you'd think you'd entered a Calcutta museum. They managed to stuff everything they could carry into trunks and boxes. The smell of moldering paper and old DDT alone nearly knocks you out."

"Where have they gone, the musty smells of yesteryear? I miss them terribly. The memories are so strong my eyes start watering. And those Sunday headaches! I could hear the servants laughing in the kitchen and I'd actually envy them."

"Sometimes I go in there and sit on their bed. It's a pity you're not staying, Tara."

I felt like saying no, the pity is you're not my older sister. Didi was like an off-leash adolescent.

"You remember the DDT pumps, don't you? Old Ram, when he was only Middle-Aged Ram, used to dive under the beds with his DDT gun and pump away at the arshulas and ollas and moshas until the air was purple and all the furniture glistened with that oily spray."

"The poisons we ingested!" I marveled.

"That's all right. We're going the way of the condors anyway," she said. "We're already extinct in our native habitat. Marvelous plumage, though. Wonderful adaptability. A really good captive breeding program is our only hope." She seemed to be smiling. "That's what this party is all about."

"The survival of the species?"

"The apparent survival anyway. We look to be thriving, don't we? Homo Bengalensis, subspecies, Hindu Calcuttan, subbreed, Ballygunge. In your case, Brahmin." I suspected she was more than a two-glass-a-night drinker.

The memory of that sweet, toxic burst of DDT, of servants sweeping up the dead roaches, ants, and mosquitoes, wetting the tile floors with spread-out rags and wringing them out in plastic pails of muddy water, mixed with the memories of fans and heat and bird calls and suddenly my head was throbbing with that Sunday headache of school assignments and ringing with servants' names I'd almost forgotten. The Muslim cook, Bashir, because we liked his food the best and Sunday dinners were his specialty; the Christian cook, David, because he'd learned to make watery soups and treacly desserts at a British cantonment near Chittagong, and the Brahmin cook, Kanai, for Fridays when Bashir was off and Sundays when David was off, and on other nights when older relatives came over. Their caste pieties forbade the taking of food from a non-Brahmin's hand. The maidservants and their children, now grown up with children of their own, still show up, usually at Aunt Bandana's, or any of my other aunts', whenever they hear that I'm visiting Calcutta. How do they know, where do they hear it? The distribution of gifts and money, and their bold demands for better gifts next time, no longer the Hong Kong calculators because now we have Indian calculators that are just as good; now they want a Walkman, or a spice grinder or a rice maker.

All the tender frustrations of dealing with unvarying ritual, the sweet sameness of daily life where anything new or unplanned can only bring disaster, and the guilty irritation of ancient bonds between the bhadra lok and chhoto lok, the master and servant, fills me both with pride and dread, because I have not fulfilled my duties, and I have not passed them on. As far as I've drifted from the path of piety, or even of family, their names suddenly swell by dozens, the hundreds, filling my heart, brain, memory, soul, and if I were to speak at that moment, my words would have come out choked, and I couldn't blame the drinks.

"You asked what I thought your profession might be? I have the sense that you are drifting between two lives. You mustn't let it go on much longer."

"I don't think it can," I said.

When we passed the prayer room, Kajol dipped inside and bowed her head, greeting God. I did the same. In a moment of silence, we repeated the names of God, and the names of God were knotted with the names of servants and the long-dead, and with the odors and tinkling of prayer bells and the Muslim prayers and the nuns' prayers and Christmas carols.

"We have a purut thakur who comes over every evening." She was back to her smiling ways, back even to English. "He reads the Gita to them, and even the kids say they like it."

"You found one in Basking Ridge?"

"He's head of tech support at AT&T. He makes house calls."

"Sounds like a good business for Danny to get into. Priest provider."

"Excellent idea!" The tall, ironic Kajol of Loreto House had reemerged. "Padma would be great at something like that. Strictly upscale, only the finest priests for the most successful people. And why stop with Indians? Yuppies would eat it up! You have your personal trainer and your kids have their math and reading tutors, so why not your personal priest—especially if he can fix your computer at the same time? Padma could design a really short service, in and out in ten minutes, with a designer line of gods and incense on the side. Opportunity's knocking, Tara. Hari! Second drinks please!"

When we rejoined the party, the public spaces were already crowded, Indian and American music was pumping in different rooms, and expensive cars continued to pull up and discharge women in glorious saris and children clutching their school books and Game Boys. A file of well-dressed men enjoying their final cigarettes made their way up the long drive from the shoulder of the highway where they had parked. What a vision, I thought, and what a pity there's no one to record it. Indo-America on parade, the model minority, the most affluent, best educated community in America, and I thought to myself: *Watch out, ladies.* You're just one unannounced visitor away from losing it all.

From across the room, Didi gestured for me to lower my sari edge, which I'd entirely forgotten. After two drinks and flushed with memories, I probably glittered. I bumped into Dr. Nag, whom I'd imagined to be slightly built and vaguely pathetic— linking him in my mind with a shriveled Mr. Nag who'd worked in Daddy's office as a stenographer, and the hapless victim in Didi's stories—only to find him bulky and ebullient with a voluptuous young American in a sari hanging on his arm. "What a fabulous necklace!" he cooed. His date asked, "May I?" and laid her cool fingers between the gold and intimate parts of my body. I willed myself into iciness. I'd not been pawed in public before.

More than half the men invited were physicians. Some of them clustered around me, paying me compliments between talking shop. I learned more than I wanted to about Medicare fraud, patient abuse, and soap opera–style hospital romances. I was just starting to walk away from Dr. Nag's attentions when I overheard one of the doctors say to another as he poured himself whisky, "Did you hear about Ron Dey?"

"Terrible, wasn't it?"

"Never understood why he stayed on in India. He had a chance to emigrate to Canada, but he got as far from Calcutta as Bombay and got stuck."

"Ron Dey?" I barged into the men's conversation, startling them. "What have you heard?"

"How do you . . . oh, I remember now that he had a reputation as being attractive to ladies."

"A car accident."

"Is he badly hurt?" another asked.

"Beyond repair, I'm afraid."

"Killed in a head-on crash near Sion. It's in tomorrow's *Times of India*." Terrible tragedy, they muttered, moving on with their drinks.

I was desperate to hang on to the two men who had read tomorrow's Indian news on the Internet. They had to know the details. Which car was to blame for the fatal collision? What had he been doing in Sion? I remembered the Tennyson poem he had asked me to read. The grotesque sea-monster the Kraken, or was it Goddess Manasha, had risen from the deep.

But terror and tragedy seemed inappropriate emotions in that house, on that night, when every male guest was a successful doctor or engineer, blessed with a lovely wife and brilliant children.

The children *of course* maintained straight-A averages, advanced placement credits, and early admission to the schools of their choice ("Really, given the quality of schools, how could they not?" Kamalini Sinha said to Sarojini Majumdar, a prelude to their own memories of Sunday-night migraines and nausea from studying, and the parental pressure). We are a marvelously tenacious subspecies. But, oh, thinking of the mess I'd made in raising Rabi, the maternal guilt!

Kajol caught my eye, made one condor-like, wing-flapping gesture, and then turned back to conversation with a cluster of relatively tiny women. The groups appeared rigidly segregated as to sex. So this is where those clever but not quite suitable Calcutta boys had all run off to. This is why we'd never seen them, and why I'd been shocked by their height, their loud and unembarrassed self-promotion. They weren't our subspecies, not our breed. Bengalis, thank God, can be as crude as any Marwari or Sindhi.

I could hear poor Harish locked in an argument with the man I presumed to be Mr. Basu: "Calcutta has a subway, what other city in India has one?"

"My dear, Mehta, Calcutta's subway is a joke. Has it relieved the traffic? Has it brought any benefit?"

"It allows men and women to get home earlier and spend more time with their families. You will find greater domestic harmony since the subway was completed. Calcutta couples have more time to go out together to lectures and plays."

What a dear man, I thought, besotted, perhaps demented, but such tender thoughts. Basu retorted, "The subway allows clerks who drink tea all day to get home ten minutes earlier so they can lay one lazy leg upon the other lazy leg and order more tea!" It was a strange inverted world, where Bengalis bullied Punjabis.

And so, with my sari edge down, bosom thrust forward, and new short hair (cut, I now realized, to set off the earrings), and with an icy, walking-mannequin determination to meet and perhaps trouble the sleep of every north Jersey Bengali, I broke into their conversation. For one night at least, I was that odd thing that Didi had been in New York twenty-five years ago, the new unattached woman in town, a regular, made-over Eliza Doolittle.

"I say, do I know you?"

"I know Harish," I said. "And I couldn't help overhearing him demolish your arguments. Well done, Harish."

"Mehta here's a fine chap but he doesn't know . . . us . . . at all." He asked if I spoke Bengali, but when he introduced himself, it was in the clipped British-Indian English favored by men who had been sent to boarding schools before Independence. "Basu here. My word, that's a perfectly gorgeous champakali! Of course, it's all in the wearer, isn't it? I don't believe I've ever seen you at one of these gatherings, and I certainly would never forget you."

"That's very sweet, Mr. Basu. I believe I met your father-in-law this morning at his little shop in Jackson Heights," I said, enjoying his discomfort. "I was looking for your wife."

"My wife is rooted like a tree to hearth and home," he boasted. If it was a song or poem, I missed the allusion. Its meaning was clear, however. *Unlike some.*

In the same register, I continued. "Do you get over to Jackson Heights very often, Mr. Basu?" Those English words blasted through the ambient Bengali like Kajol's secret buzzer system.

I moved on; locking eyes with admiring eyes, dipping my sari edge like Salome's final veil. So many men, so little time. I took another wine and broke into male-only groups, cocking my head just so, letting the lights catch my gold and the slope of my breasts, laughing at jokes that had a quality of being translated from late-night television. Mr. Arun Mehra, the lawyer who reportedly got favors in return for legal fees, was in hot pursuit. His fat American wife had strayed off to the kitchen with Harish. "I saw you at Newark Airport. You were looking stood up. I almost offered you a ride but you seemed so haughty. How long will you be among us?" he begged, and finally, "Are you here with some-one?" I shook my head, swinging my earrings, in that noncom-mittal, teasing, Indian way.

"Do you know what you need, Mr. Mehra?"

"I know very well what I need," he leered.

"You need to buy your wife a special gift after all your naugh-tiness."

"Me—naughty?" he objected. "I am only acting in my official capacity as chairman of your New Jersey welcoming committee. My limousine is at your disposal, day or night. Let me freshen your drink."

Well, I thought, here I stand in Basking Ridge. Just a little slutty, just a little bitchy, my reserves of both running on empty. I looked down on the necklace clinging to the swells and hollows of my pushed-up splendor, barely concealed by Didi's Bombay film star–inspired wisp of a choli, and thought *duh*, Tara, those men didn't have a chance, did they? What better way to get over a breakup, something very few women in this room apart from Didi had ever experienced? I pulled my sari edge a little higher.

"They were out of red. Will white do?" Harish, evidently, had not been doing his job.

"Nicely, thank you." I heard his follow-up, *Now, where were we? I believe you were about to tell me when we can get together* . . . but I wasn't listening. Breakup? Call it by its right name, sweetie. You were dumped. Andy was the first man to leave me, and Andy was not, compared to pursuers I had known, a notable catch. Maybe I really was between two lives, as Kajol had said. Maybe this sad approximation of mass seduction was my last fling.

The two lives don't announce themselves any more clearly than they did that evening. Back in Loreto House, Mother John Paul had trained us to deal with obvious lechers—"Make overly forward men of the wrong type feel like cut worms." Or, I could slip into the back seat of that proffered limo. How easily I could slip into Didi's world.

She waved me over to her wives' cluster. "Didn't I tell you we'd have a fabulous time?" She turned to the other women to explain my desperate situation. "Can you imagine this beautiful little sister of mine staying home night after night?" The women clucked their sympathy. "And I told her, no wonder, Tara, look at those saris you brought! I know, I know, she wears those California things to work, but really, that's no excuse to lose your fashion eye, is it?"

The women agreed. Their husbands expected better of them; what would *he* say? "I told her she could take the saris she brought, pack them right up, and give them to the servants the next time she goes home."

Just then, a scrawny little girl of twelve or so, an unfortunate age in the best of families, flashing braces, thick glasses, and bundled in what could have been a glamorous sari, came by with a tray of fruit juices. Her parents were trying too hard. "I saw you on television," she said to Didi. "You were on 'Namaskar, Probasi.' Mummy's going to buy jhumka earrings just like the ones you were wearing." I remembered myself at her age in a more gracious time and place, gathering compliments and dispensing sweet-lime soda and watercress sandwiches.

Didi focused the full force of her practiced sweetness on the little girl. "You must be Runki Roy Chowdhury. What a beautiful young woman you're becoming!" She was radiant. Little Runki's spontaneous testimonial was enough to neutralize the good advice Didi had given me just that morning: don't get involved with the three tedious Roy Chowdhury daughters, the three granddaughters of Calcutta's scandal of the century. The girls' parents looked as though they would survive amid the alien corn.

"And look! I brought those jhumka earrings with me, just for your mommy, darling." She glanced at me and didn't quite snap her fingers, but I bent over and cocked my head obligingly. "See? This is *my* little sister and she came all the way from California to show them to you." Runki assessed them carefully under her lens-like glasses, then swished away.

And now a word from our sponsor. "Thank God, Didi showed me her fabulous sari collection!" I said. "I don't know what I would have done, arriving in the dead of night with all these parties coming up, and nothing to wear." It sounded to me like a badly designed television ad, two women in a kitchen comparing detergents, but in Bengali it came off as almost sincere.

Didi undraped her sari edge and held it out and let it fall, like a cape. I did the same. The beauty and intricacy of Indian silks are truly a wonder, a bargain at any price, even Danny's. And they removed any guilt over recommending them, whatever my sister's mythical involvement.

"You two are absolute clones!" exclaimed one of the new arrivals, a smallish, fairish, and rather attractive young lady, as we readjusted the folds of our saris. Her hairstyle was similar to mine, but her sari was a defiantly proletarian south Indian cotton. A familiar assessment; we prepared our smiles.

"*Jemon ma, temon meye*," she said, which means, with a nasty twist, like mother, like daughter. I corrected her immediately, *Jemon didi, temon chhoto bon*, a little-sister chip off the oldest-sister block.

"Whatever," she waved her hand. "I'm not doubting the family resemblance," she said. "Stalls in the same market."

She must have been Lata Haldar, the Busy Bachelorette, and what a nasty piece of work she was.

Unfazed, and apparently amused, Didi retorted, "And which of your many admirers, Dr. Haldar, bought you that perfectly lovely south Indian cotton?"

"My friends do not judge me by the price tag on my saris."

"I should hope not," said Didi. I could barely resist a thrust of my own, *What price* do *they judge you by?* At the last instant I realized that such an easy retort applied to us all, and I could feel a depression coming on.

"What's that noise?" asked one of the women. The music was loud, the face-off rather heated and I thought initially that the well-bred woman was trying to defuse the confrontation in the best Loreto House manner—then I realized it was a cell phone. Around our circle, women began reaching into their purses. Men in the nearest ring to us started patting their inner jacket pockets. Since so many of the guests were doctors, cell phones had been going off all evening. Men were pulling pagers out of their pockets, men and women had been drifting in and out of the house and onto the back deck, not just to smoke, as in the old days, but to answer their pages and calls. I felt a proprietary interest since it all derived from squiggles on a paper that Sunday afternoon in Atherton that I'd helped unleash—*scrambling quarterback, short passes in the flat, widen the field, it's the width, not the length!*—with the able assistance of Chet and Bish. Those are my fingerprints, gentlemen.

"Tara, answer your damn phone," Didi commanded.

'   '   '

"How's the reception?" A Bish question.

"Where are you?" A Tara question.

"We just got back to the mainland, if you can call Australia the mainland." It's a Rabi kind of question. "I'm calling from a hot tub in Brisbane."

"Pin drop."

"You're needling me." It was an old joke between us. I was surprised he remembered.

"How's Rabi?"

"Well, he told me his big secret."

"Really?" That hurt. How could Rabi abandon resentment and secrecy, the cornerstones of their relationship, so easily?

"He wants to be a photographer. He even took some underwater photos on the reef. He seems to have a certain proficiency. So, where are you?"

"I'm shivering in a silk sari on a cold deck at a Tupperware party in Basking Ridge, New Jersey, at Mrinal and Kajol Ghosal's house."

"The Ghosals! Get Kajol-di to show you the hidden buzzers. And congratulate Mrinal-da on the prize. The office said you'd called about something urgent."

"It is urgent. And it's very good of you to call."

"Rabi said there have been some changes in your personal life. Tara's mistri has flown the coop?"

"My personal life is not the urgent reason I called." Although, maybe it was. His voice did have that old-time, soothing effect, and I could have jumped just about any man in the room that night. "Ask Rabi about Christopher Dey."

"He's already mentioned something."

"Well, he doesn't know the latest. It's my worst nightmare. Tell him everything I feared is true. Ronald Dey is dead, they say an automobile accident, but I doubt it. The Christopher Dey we met has been identified as Abbas Sattar Hai. He probably murdered the real Christopher sometime in the last couple of weeks, in San Francisco. He's a member of the Dawood gang and there are international warrants against him for murder and arson. For starters."

"Hold on." I could hear bits of my message being transmitted to Rabi, sibilant sounds like "Abbas" and "Sattar" and "arson." I could even hear the hot tub's bubbling waters.

"Okay. Is that it?"

"There is an officer in the SFPD named Jasbir Sidhu who wants to talk to you about security precautions. He can also send you Hai's picture."

"I know Jack, he's a good man. I tried to hire him when he came out of Stanford. He told me I was probably better protected than half the heads of state in the world."

"Well, he thinks that you or me or especially Rabi might be a target. He thinks Indian gangs might try to get a foothold in Silicon Valley and they might try to do it by kidnapping or intimidation."

"It's a small world, isn't it?" That was another of our jokes. Thanks to CHATTY, the world is getting smaller every day. "It's just another virus. I can handle it."

"I'm being serious." To get his attention, I added, "Bish." Ancient Hindu custom had nothing to say about the etiquette between divorced couples.

"Tara." He was just saying my name. "When I hang up, punch in the code I'll give you, and you will always be able to reach me on this phone." Seven numbers and the pound sign. There seemed to be no limit to what Bish's little handheld, broadband miracle could perform. No end to the technical and human networks he commanded.

"We're leaving tomorrow morning for San Francisco and we'll be back some time before we leave. I'll tell Jack to send me the mug shot. You take care, Tara. Keep in touch. Here's Rabi."

"Flash, Rabi to Ma. Australia's cool. Life's not bad."

"Life's dangerous, Rabi. I'll see you on Sunday night."

Back inside, Didi was all smiles, her arms open to embrace me. Apparently, I'd been a stunning success. The price of my success was that I had to take off the earrings and the necklace so that she could repackage them. Madhab Roy Chowdhury was taking the earrings and Arun Mehra had bid on the necklace, both close to the asking price. She'd taken orders on eight saris, making a total of nearly seventeen thousand dollars, with her twenty percent, minus some expenses. Not a bad night's work. She found a dark corner for stripping me of my finery. I felt like Cinderella, and it wasn't even midnight. Thank God she hadn't sold my sari; I was feeling naked enough already. I pulled my sari edge throat high.

Across the living room, Mrinal Ghosal was laughing loudly on his cell phone. When he saw me reenter the room, he merrily waved me over. "Have I got a surprise for you!" I heard him say. He put the phone in my hand and said, "You'll never guess who's just called. Go on, go on."

"As I was saying," came the familiar voice, a little less clearly on Mrinal's phone, "we get in at ten-thirty this morning."

16

"We left tomorrow," said Rabi. "That's pretty cool."

It was noon, Sunday, three days after Thanksgiving. I'd just done the domestic equivalent, leaving from Newark at six a.m. and arriving in San Francisco two clock-hours later in order to be there for him.

For the first time, Rabi, Bish, and I would be in my house together. Bish's plan was to drop off Rabi then return immediately to Atherton. Mine was to delay him. I'd picked up a bottle of champagne for a symbolic christening of the house. Or rechristening, since I'd already done it with Andy. I would not have objected if he wanted to stay.

I hadn't seen Bish up close in nearly three years. He was taller than I remembered and lean in the face, still boyish in appearance with the same mustache he'd worn since college. But, seen in profile, the endearing little potbelly was already forming. His hair was as thick as ever, combed in the style of his student days and plastered with a touch of coconut oil, lending a fragrance not unlike the interior of an Indian-driven taxi. He had also taken to dyeing it. It sat atop his head blacker-than-black, dull and unreflecting. He was Didi's age, forty-two, and desperately in need of a makeover.

We hugged, rather chastely, as colleagues might after a brief separation.

"You're looking very modern," he said, which I took as a reference, perhaps approving, to my new short hair. Even Rabi had noticed the change. Did I mention I was wearing a Padma Mehta designer silk sari?

They'd flown first class, so they weren't hungry. They'd slept on the plane, so they weren't especially tired. They were full of visions and experiences I couldn't share, just as I was, and for the moment we were avoiding the disturbing situation that still connected us. And so, while Rabi went up to his room to unpack and arrange his film, Bish and I settled down with champagne in the floor-through living/cooking space that had been, pre-Andy, a cluttered three small bedrooms, Depression-era kitchen and bath.

The house is fairly typical of the neighborhood, a termite's feast, three stories, clapboard exterior, and a fenced back garden connected by outdoor stairs and decks. Twenty pregentrification years ago, the neighborhood had been as solidly rental as it now is family-owned, as cheap as it now is overpriced. Sixty years before that, during the war, large rooms had been subdivided and rented out to shipyard workers and Navy personnel. Codes and inspections were suspended, and each room sprouted its own water and gas supply. I'd taken over a house with a kitchen and bathroom and three tiny bedrooms on the first and second floors and a "promising" unfinished attic.

Andy had been recommended as a good decks man, but one day I'd asked him to open up one small section of a bulging wall.

What he saw sickened him, he said. The whole house was a time bomb. Retrofitting the back stairs was an ass-backward approach, arranging the deck chairs on the *Titanic*. He found old gas and electric lines, uncapped and frayed, bent and rusted, still drawing intermittent power. He made a list of code violations and stopped after reaching twenty-five. The walls, the floors, the water supply, the gas lines, the electric service, all had to be ripped out and relocated. And so my home was reconsolidated from a gutted shell. It grew like a baby and I felt a kind of maternal tenderness toward it. I watched it grow from demolition to drawings to decoration in a year.

Bish paid all the bills, even though he had no legal obligation. I never knew how to interpret his generosity. For a man of his resources, it could have been the simplest and most efficient way of cutting his losses. He might have been thinking of Rabi's safety, or even of signaling a degree of responsibility for driving me out of the marriage. I'd kept him updated on the progress with photos, and he got firsthand reports from Andy. Now he was touring the house and clucking appreciatively. The third floor, formerly a stiflingly hot, bat-and-squirrel-filled attic with a leaking roof, was now divided into two skylit bedrooms and a spa-style California bathroom.

During our divorce, the lawyers had advised us that mutually assured destruction was built into the California statutes and should not be tampered with. They were appalled, or amused, by our innocence. Bish had not taken the simplest corporate precaution against personal liability. American contingencies like divorce simply had not occurred to him. You married, you had a son, you provided for the family, and if you provided very well, everyone was happy. Or at least unhappily bottled up. As for me, the traditional Hindu marriage ceremony did not include a prenup.

Over champagne, I asked him, "Are you happy?"

"I can't complain." Nor, apparently, could he talk of himself. Happiness, according to Bishwapriya Chatterjee, involved new initiatives, new markets, new applications and CHATTY's second and third generation. The phones were already first generation, new wireless wonders would be smaller and infinitely more powerful. I couldn't imagine the future he already knew. He'd started an assembly plant in Bangalore, a marketing arm in Bombay, and he was in discussions with the World Bank over a start-up in Bangladesh. But his Indian operations were dutiful indulgences, he said, dwarfed by his collaborations in Taiwan and Malaysia. Chet Yee was moving on the Chinese front.

Like the Mughal emperors of old, he maintained a series of palaces around the known world, but unlike them, wherever he settled he bestowed new wealth. One of the few places in the world where he did not have associates, partners, old classmates, relatives, an office, apartment, or factory was Australia. As a consequence he had felt lost and a little useless on his vacation. I suggested that was how one was supposed to feel on a vacation. He didn't ask me about New Jersey.

There it is: all that is blind, and all that is beautiful in the man.

Like me, his family's origins were in East Bengal. I spoke of having made my first visit to Bangladesh the previous year. I wanted to tell him so much more: that it was beautiful, and moving, images of its golden greenery stuck in my mind and the Tree-Bride haunted me still, but all those sentimental words would have sounded as ineffable as "happiness" in Bish's world, and I didn't want to take him out of it. I was enjoying the little visit.

"I knew you'd gone to Bangladesh," he said. He'd been in Bombay a few days after my visit and had talked briefly with Auro on an unrelated matter. My name, and the trip, had come up. If he'd wanted to, Bish could have talked to my brother-in-law with-

out my name ever coming up. I found his roundabout acknow-
ledgment unimaginably charming.

I felt almost apologetic for the small scale of my question, "I
meant, do you have anyone to make you happy?"

"I believe that part of my life is not your concern."

Of course he was right. Five years is a very long time and we'd
both moved on, in our ways. There is very little that Bish does
not know, if he chooses to find out, and I presumed my life was
one of those topics that would linger a few years as a curiosity,
until he'd mastered it. I assumed that he knew the names, at least,
of most of the men in my life. Those old friends who'd come on
to me in the months after the divorce had all lost their jobs, or
had left the Valley. When I moved to San Francisco, in the months
before Andy and the gutting of the house, I'd enrolled at State,
intent on graduate study in English. I was an enthusiastic student,
as newly divorced hatchlings often are, and infinitely better prepared than any of my younger classmates. My professor, I'll call
him Don, had a different idea.

I didn't know he was married, didn't know he had an active
girlfriend and a history of others, and how practiced he was in the
craft of textual seduction. *You must surrender*, he would say, meaning to the poem, but transference to the teacher was not to be
resisted either. His wife showed up one morning at my doorstep,
threatening murder or suicide. Word of my distress might have
drifted down to Atherton. Perhaps I flatter myself. In any event,
Don got an attractive job offer he couldn't refuse, in Texas.

Loneliness had made me a little wanton; wantonness had made
me very lonely. In these five years, I think I have changed beyond
recognition, but Bish had not changed at all. By California standards he was still young, a "Bay Area Bachelor to Die For." By
anyone's standards he was super-successful, but nothing remotely
approximating a midlife crisis had ever touched him. By Bish's

reasoning, preservation was a virtue, hence the dye-job, but transformation a foolish waste, that is, no workouts. He lived and prospered by commonsense precepts that are ingrained in any middle-class Bengali boy, but which graduate business schools have elevated to the five tenets of corporate management.

Whatever he had liked at twenty, and still liked at forty-two, now had tenure in his life. This included foods, recreation, friendships, politics, clothes, and anything falling under the general notion of style. There had been no television in his growing up; there was none now. Any challenge to the tried and true would have to demonstrate—not just promise—an overwhelming logical superiority. He no longer added up grocery slips or restaurant bills.

Change for its own sake must be resisted. Appeals to the emotions are invitations to disaster. His was a formula for the amassing of wealth and protection against its dispersal. He had seen too many of his classmates and fellow immigrants go down, and he'd seen companies based on good ideas founder. He'd avoided every can't-miss come on, and, I had to imagine, he'd probably investigated the online Indian marriage market and determined there was no one out there whose motives, when it came to connecting with the biggest fish out there, Bish Chatterjee, were pure. A non-Indian? Unimaginable.

How can you not love such a man?

"What do you think of this sari?" I asked.

"I have not seen you in a sari for longer than I can remember. This is a particularly nice sari."

I stood up to arrange it a bit more smoothly, but oops, the sari edge slipped just a little. I'm sure he didn't notice. In the television shows that I couldn't help watching, the only couples who seem to get along and truly understand one another are straight and gay roommates—Didi's route—or long-divorced, child-sharing, and living close by—mine, perhaps.

, , ,

Bish does not drink, except a beer on special occasions or with certain foods. A second glass, a concession. The third, a little incapacitating. After champagne, with jet lag, I suggested he should take a nap. Rabi had fallen asleep while sorting his films. While they slept I went out and bought the makings of a Bengali feast. The girl Bish married had never stepped inside a kitchen; the woman she became was a stupendous cook. He loved shrimp in coconut milk, turmeric-rubbed and deep-fried eggplant slices, small, puffy luchi, flaky parathas, and steamed-just-right basmati rice topped with hot ghee. And of course, he had the mother-induced sweet tooth of a typical Bengali son. After such a feast, he might even be convinced not to try the long drive home.

He looked so adorable asleep in my bed, fully dressed atop the duvet. My own certified Bay Area Bachelor to Die For. Of course, he snored, how else would an Indian mother know that her son was untroubled and sleeping soundly? When I crept onto the bed, he didn't stir. I remembered the first innocent morning of our marriage, not the bloody sheets, but the little trick—was it my trick or his?—of raising the dead merely by touching it. But that was sixteen years ago. Just a touch, then I tugged on his belt. He turned on his back and I opened his trousers. Wouldn't you be more comfortable like this? The trousers slid off easily; I did the proper thing and looped them carefully over the back of a chair. Do you remember, I asked, when you showed me something very new and strange and when curiosity drove my hands down here? Oh! I see that you do.

His eyes fluttered open and I read in them a stunned, avid gratitude. I'd never seen this other side of Bish, even in the months of the divorce, or the first night when I'd sprung it on him. If I could read his eyes alone, they said, *What are your intentions? What are you going to do?* The late afternoon, early December light was beginning to fade through the skylights and out the back deck. For the first time in many months, the aroma of Indian cooking filled the house. By the failing light, I pulled the tucked-in sari from the rim of the petticoat, then folded the eighteen feet of silk into a book-sized rectangle the way Indian girls learn to before putting it away. All the many minutes it took, Bish sat jackknifed in the bed reaching out.

Bless the jetlag. Rabi had come down at dinner, rubbing his eyes, taken a few spoonfuls of shrimp malai, then gone back to bed. Not so sleepy, however, that he hadn't grasped the significance of the tableau before him: his parents eating quietly off the bistro table in the corner of the kitchen, wine glasses and a bottle. "Go for it, big guy," he'd said, patting his father on the shoulder.

He came down a few minutes later with his camera and used up a final roll of film on us.

What Bish had been saying, and what he immediately returned to in that single-minded way of his, was the most remarkable confession I'd ever heard, not just from him—a man not given to confession at all—but from any man in my expanded experience. Although his life was cited everywhere as perfection itself, he had failed in his fundamental duty. I braced myself for a complicated economic or technological explanation, but Bish's failure was vastly simpler and more fundamental. He had failed in his dharma, the basic duty of a man in the householder phase of his life, to support and sustain his marriage. He had been brooding over the breakup far longer and more profoundly than I. The legal California no-fault judgment meant nothing to him. How in this world can any action with such profound consequences be called "no-fault"? He was intent on delivering a self-lacerating scrutiny of his failure. He was a man in pain.

"Bish, *please*, it was *my* fault, *my* head was turned. I was so naïve, I had too much time, and not enough to do—" the whole silly mantra. He wouldn't listen. He would not permit collective guilt. Marriage is man's manifest dharma, his test, his duty, the outer sign of his inner strength and harmony.

"My parents are fifty years together. Even our house servants, forty, fifty years. One time, you mentioned the loneliness inside of marriage and I did not understand what you were saying. Two people are together; they have come from the same place; they share the same values, the same language. Practically speaking, they are two halves of one consciousness. They eat the same food; they have a child; they sleep in the same bed, how can they be lonely?"

I was about to answer. Bish! What you eat, what language you speak, where you sleep—in our world they meant everything, but we're not there anymore. Here, dharma and duty, they don't mean a damned thing. Let me tell you about my sister, *sisters three are we, as alike as blossoms on a tree*, you know the verse. We dressed alike, we looked alike, we even had the same birthday. In the ancestral long-ago that might have guaranteed a certain predictability, a lifelong similarity. Look at us, Bish! It's all an illusion.

"But I am becoming a great expert on the loneliness outside of marriage."

I reached for his hand. "Bish," I said, "it doesn't have to be." You are a blind but blameless man. I wanted to know, but couldn't ask, where are you getting all this stuff? Up in San Francisco we get rumors of domestic discord in Silicon Valley. Certain Indian heavy hitters were going the way of their American counterparts, dumping the perfectly decent, upstanding, socially approved women they'd come with, and going back for the high society, movie star, or beauty queen trophy wives.

That would not be Bish's style. He would be forever untouched and unspoiled by wealth, but I wondered if he was expressing the backlash. He sounded like a man who had been reached by the Hindu version of some born-again cult, as though Silicon Valley had become not just a place to make tons of money but a commune full of tech-priests. It was as if the whole nineteenth-century Bengali debate between born-again traditionalists like Jai Krishna Gangooly and Westernized progressives like Keshub Mitter was being restaged and replayed, and my dear ex-husband was caught in the middle.

God created greed to protect us from too much spirituality.

Instead, I said, "Be honest with me. What we did this afternoon, that was good, wasn't it?"

"I worry. I gave in to so many impulses; I lost control. So many years have gone by, and you have been with many more men—"

"Never mind that. What we just did, that was good, wasn't it?"

"Yes," he admitted.

"I mean, it was a good thing, wasn't it? And this food is good, all of your favorites done just the way you like them?"

"It was more than I deserve."

"Listen to yourself, Bish. The words you've been using, 'failure,' 'undeserving,' 'weak,' 'morality,' 'loneliness,' they're not like you."

"I'm not like you. I can't shift my focus. I have tried. I know it would be good to find a new wife. My father is still looking and sending names. I know you and Rabi would not discourage me, but . . . I am a man who has failed at nothing in his life but this one thing with you."

"Darling, Bish, listen to me. You didn't fail," I said. "We both accepted a no-fault judgment, all right?"

I should have dipped into my personal well of hard-won Zen wisdom. In this world, what is failure? Does the raindrop that falls on a landowner's stone courtyard and not on the farmer's field fail? The only failure is the failure to understand failure, etc., and thank you very much.

On his own, he must have decided he'd said too much. "What the hell, eh?" We moved on to the gulab jamuns.

I only wanted Bish to stay with me. Because he knew I wasn't after his money or his status. I might very well have been the only appropriate woman in the world for him. And, because of his rectitude, if only I could bend it or dent it just a little bit, he might have been the only man for me. I think we recognized that. All we had to do was reach across an ever-narrowing gulch. He would know to include me in his world; I would know not to expect from him things he couldn't deliver.

In the middle of the night I sensed something was wrong, but it took me some seconds to remember that I had not gone to bed alone. I was awake and alert, but deserted. When I opened my eyes, I could make out the shape of Bish in his white pajamas standing out on the deck gazing at St. Ignatius Church and the top lights of the Golden Gate Bridge. We were in the last days of the Bay Area fall, that period after the offshore winds from the central valley actually bring us a few days and nights of heat, but before the onset of onshore breezes and low pressure cells that start the winter rainy season. Just hours earlier he'd been sweltering in a subtropical spring and I'd been shivering in the East Coast fall.

I put a wrap over my nakedness and joined him on the deck. He had been smoking, an old habit of his I had broken. In the years I'd been with Andy we'd never stood on the deck at night. There'd always been a cold wind or fog. The upper deck had always been a place to avoid.

"I didn't know I was capable of all that, not at my age," he said, to which I laughed, not at the "all that" of which there had been a considerable amount, but at his professed amazement. I realized that for Bish his "age" was not chronological, but mythic. He was seeing himself as fitting into the ancient, discrete divisions of life. Years of studentship break suddenly into marriage and fatherhood and earning a living, which break again, as in the case of my father, into disengagement with the world. By his age alone, Bish should still have been a householder. But the State of California and my lawyers had aborted that phase much earlier than it should have been. Rabi was still a child; more children might well have followed. Bish might be the reigning genius of Silicon Valley, but he could not reverse the cosmic order and return to marriage and the status of householder at a time in his life when all of that should be drawing to a close. "All of that" meaning what we'd done that afternoon and again that evening and, so far as I was concerned, would do again as soon as I could drag him back inside.

Rabi emerged from his room, fully dressed, as he had been all afternoon and evening, heading perhaps to the bathroom, until he saw us.

"I thought I heard voices, but they sounded like they were coming from the street," he said. We both gestured for him to stay.

"We were barely speaking above a whisper," I said.

"Relationship stuff, I bet."

Bish said, "The answer to your earlier question is that I have no one."

"Tell her about you know who," Rabi prodded.

"You mean I have to learn of your love life through my son?" He was too much the gentleman to turn the tables on me.

"Rabi and I had too many man-to-man talks in Australia. All he's saying is that it looked for a time as if there might be a girl for me, chhoto bon of my cousin's husband. This was two years ago, about the time I went to Bangladesh on that project I mentioned. I stayed in Calcutta an extra week to meet her."

"Sounds very serious. A week in your life is like a year in mine.

And was she the usual? Correct as to caste, slim, fair, and beautiful?"

"I said caste or community no bar. Why should I restrict the possible ideal for the merely suitable?"

"Good for you."

"This girl was not like us, but she was very intelligent and very independent minded. I seem to be attracted to such women."

"How old is she, what does she do?"

"I should not call her a girl. She was a divorced lady, your age, maybe a year or two younger. She wrote books in English. I read two and you know the trouble I have reading made-up stories. I had no trouble reading hers."

"I hope she causes you less trouble than I did."

"She will not be causing any difficulty," he said, then he mentioned her name, which was widely familiar. And then I remembered that she had died in a Bombay street accident. "I have learned that another person is not necessarily the answer to loneliness," he said.

Oh, Bish, if only you'd let me help you. There's nothing to learn, there are no answers. In the world our parents tried to prepare us for, there were answers. "Another person at least can help," I said. He took out another cigarette. I was getting cold but I didn't want to leave him.

"Pop's trying hard to get down with the whole dating thing," said Rabi.

"Getting down," said Bish.

In one second we were laughing, probably the first time all of us had laughed together, and in the next second our lives changed forever.

"There!" said Rabi. "Didn't you hear that? It's that voice again."

We had turned to go back inside and I registered a slight tremble through my bare feet on the deck. Before I could even think, "Earthquake!" there came an explosive roar, the wind and the noise that tornado survivors talk about, a freight train tearing through your bedroom, an airplane taking off, noise of such magnitude that it replaced all thought, all reflexes, with the purest of vision. My life did not flash in front of me. I had stepped outside my life; I had no life. The house appeared in that instant as a living entity struggling for breath; it expanded upward and outward, ejecting its roof, blowing off its shingles. A hideous ball of orange and purple fire rushed up the stairwell, paused a moment in the hall, gathered its force, and filled both bedrooms. How Bish had the presence of mind, I'll never know, but he slammed the deck door trapping the fire a precious second or two until the glass shattered and tongues of flame burst through every new opening, surrounding us as though we had been condemned to the stake, licking the clothes off our backs, taking our hair and eyebrows, but almost immediately, the fireball retreated. The front half of the house sloughed to the street, sucking the fireball in its wake.

All of this must have occurred in a timeless void. The next instant, the doors and windows blew inward, and the whole house took its final deep breath, and consciousness came back to me as well. The decks and the outside stairs between them were still intact, just as Andy had guaranteed they would be after the Really Big One, but wouldn't be for long. Flames from the ground floor were already out the windows and curling up the dry shingles on the back of the house. Rabi reached the backyard first, but even the dry garden grass was spurting into flame from sparks and burning shingles. We could hear him, "Ma! Pop!" because now the lower deck was on fire, hotter and more sustained than the actual explosion, and we would have to run through it. I hesitated, seeing flames where I would have to put my bare feet, and then Bish picked me up as though I were just a stick. I could hear his prayers, the names of God, and my lips joined in, silently. I buried my face in Bish's soft flesh, but there is nothing in this world to silence the scream of flesh meeting fire, the smell of dying human flesh. Drop me Bish, it's all my fault, I don't deserve to live. I could only think, Tara you fool, you cooked a meal and forgot to turn off the gas. It's been so long since you've entertained a proper guest, and now you've lost everything. You deserve to lose everything, but not the only people you've ever loved.

I saw clearly the man in white tails and tie, holding the single red rose. Yama.

His feet were also bare. His feet and legs were spotted with black, the soles of his feet were pink where flesh had been lifted off or black where the flesh had been seared, with channels of blood running from them. Everything below his knees bubbled with blisters. Rabi was crying, uncontrollably, hysterically sobbing in a way I'd never seen. I was shaking, wailing, naked. We couldn't hear the sirens over the noise of destruction, but lights were on in all the neighboring houses and I could hear our back-facing neighbor already chopping through the wood fence that separated our gardens.

Bish was on the phone, my God; he'd kept it in a Velcro sling around his waist, and in a calm voice, in Hindi, was apologizing for the late hour. The person, I realized, he was apologizing to had to be Jack Sidhu's wife.

"I believe Tara's house has been attacked by very powerful explosives. We are miraculously alive in backyard, but also prisoners of same. Arrange immediate evacuation to hospital. I am . . . I am afraid . . . somewhat incapacitated . . . from burns . . . Tara and Rabi appear safe."

And with that he dropped the phone, fell back, and let out a moan, not a scream, a moan that started low, but mounted higher and louder than the fires and winds and sirens. I could hear the neighbors, their cries of "My God!" and "Get blankets!" Bish, mercifully, had lost consciousness.

17

The ATF determined that my house (and, effectively, those on both sides as well as lesser damage caused to windows and parked cars in a two-block area) had been bombed by persons unknown using a signature device previously known only on the Indian subcontinent. Their agent was on the air two days after the "event." On the cable news shows it was nonstop coverage of "the San Francisco Bombing," right up there with a school shooting or a government scandal.

It hadn't required the hit-or-miss delivery system of a rental truck or stolen car, or the easily traced purchase of tons of fertilizer and theft of blasting caps or any other crude bomb-making ingredients read off the Internet. This was sophisticated killer-hardware with a dedicated purpose—to destroy its designated target, not engender mass hysteria or random injury in a crowded public area. Its concussive power alone had cleared the neighborhood of nesting birds. It had probably been housed inside an innocent piece of home electronics, a gutted computer monitor, even a VCR. The timer could have been self-contained or been remotely triggered using something as simple as a reconfigured cell phone.

"Which is ironic, given the apparent target," the officer went on, "or perhaps that was part of the message."

A suspect was immediately hauled in and paraded before the international media. He happened to fit one kind of profile, not the exotic international terrorist, but something more familiar and equally exploitable. Another of America's underclass, a high school dropout and part-time laborer with old drug arrests, a paunchy, red-bearded ex-biker and "hippie laborer" with proven demolitions capability, operating under the convenient and "very San Francisco" cover of innocent-appearing Buddhism and highly lucrative earthquake retrofitting. (Cut to "breaking news" footage of a dented van with provocative slogans being towed to the forensics lab.)

Wait, America, there's more!

This story keeps getting more and more interesting, there's something here for everyone.

Buddhists from all over the world were interviewed. American scholars, robed monks, and Hollywood celebrities all came on the air to discuss the sheer complexity of Buddhism, its harsh discipline, and its corrupted West Coast version. More to the point, this ex-biker (cut to file footage, Andy leading a pack of "Bikers for Brotherhood") was suspected of being the insanely jealous live-in lover of the owner of that house, the exotically beautiful Tara Chatterjee, divorced wife of the seriously injured "Icon of Silicon Valley," Bishwapriya Chatterjee. (Cut to browless, lashless, stubble-headed, cut-faced Indian lady in hospital lobby dashing to the elevators. Make that "once-glamorous.")

"Speculation grows today": that under the innocent cover of a retrofitter beat the heart of a violent and insanely jealous sexual predator, using his privileged access to the rich and unwitting, often divorced women with sizeable fortunes. What set him off could well have been the attempted reconciliation of the Chatterjees.

All of this in the first forty-eight hours of the "news cycle."

Apparently, the Chatterjee divorce, now six years old, contained "anomalies." It was Mr. Chatterjee who was with his ex-wife that night, not the hippie laborer. (Cut to a sullen Andy refusing to cooperate with a single question, but looking straight at me and crying, "Why are you doing this?" Cut to Bishwapriya Chatterjee at the White House, receiving a presidential medal.)

And that became the headline for the next cycle: Why had I thrown him out? (But he left me, I pleaded, he is deeply religious and sincerely peaceful; all of my protests to no avail.) Was it drugs? He didn't look like a Buddhist, so they stuck with "erstwhile biker" and "flower child gone to pot." C'mon, Tara, give us a break. I'd become "Tara," an overnight one-named lady, the stubbled hair became "fire-chic," my "look" for the media (but don't try this at home). Tabloid headline: *Tara's great retrofitter!* Honey, are you actually living off a generous divorce settlement from one man while playing around with another? And still keeping the first one on the leash? That's so cool! That's so trashy! Can you talk about your connection to terrorists and international criminals? Were they using you to blackmail Bishwapriya Chatterjee? CHATTY's stock value plunged thirty percent on the rumors: $8 billion was lost on a day when Bish was still fighting for his life in an oxygen tent on a sterile ward. As if one little bomb could upset the world's economy!

In the paper Tuesday morning, the morning of screaming headlines and pictures of Bish, Andy and myself, and the remains of my house, there was another story on the back page. The body of an unidentified Asian male, perhaps that of an East Indian tourist who had been reported missing, had washed up in the delta. Police were investigating possible links to suspected Indian gang activity. No evidence linking the apparent murder-robbery to events surrounding the recent bombing of the house of the ex-wife of Mr. Bishwapriya Chatterjee had yet turned up.

We used to laugh at those movies, Rabi and I, at the chain of absurd coincidences, the hysterical links of improbability, the rapacious media and the plodding, unimaginative investigators.

On Thursday morning, a spokesman for the investigation, Sergeant Jasbir Singh Sidhu of the SFPD, announced Andy's release (with apologies for the intrusion and unwarranted suspicions heaped upon him), and the identity of the body found in the delta. It was Mr. Christopher Dey, Indian national, of Bhopal, Madhya Pradesh, India. A new picture was then distributed to join Bish and me on the front page now that Andy had been eliminated: Mr. Abbas Sattar Hai. Sergeant Sidhu was not at liberty to discuss any aspect of this ongoing investigation or to speculate, as some in the press have, on linkages to other stories currently in the news.

He did take up one question, however. Sensationalized press coverage to date, based on the absence of hard facts and the crude exploitation of victims' lives, had created a speculative frenzy antithetical to good police work. The focus of the SFPD remains on locating Mr. Hai. Answers will emerge in the trial.

You see your every action called to question and summarily judged, you see yourself portrayed as Tara, a scheming bitch, a user of men and a destroyer of lives and property, and in short, as the poet said, you are afraid. Calls came to the school, my only known outside contact, from television talk shows, from publishers, from publicists out to market me or spin doctors offering to counterspin. The Indian press was on it, the London tabloids. The only calls I initiated were to Didi and Parvati, and to both I raised the issue of Christopher Dey, the link to all the stories, the smaller story inside the story that the press had not yet linked. Didi laughed, I'm glad you finally have something bigger to deal with than your silly little fantasy about me and Ronald Dey. *Ronald Dey is dead, Didi.* Is it true you are getting back with Bish? She thought the news of our reconciliation was very exciting. Just don't blow it again, she advised, but I'm afraid you will. Didi was right. I had been the target, not her.

Parvati, too, wanted to know. All of India, apparently, wanted to know.

And then, I broke down. Isn't anyone listening? Wanted to know what for God's sake? Are we getting back together?—he could die! Will CHATTY collapse and take the world's high-tech markets down with it? Who would profit from such a collapse? Am I a whore and sleazebag? Can any good come of all this pain and dishonesty?

"I have the answers," she said. "They're very clear."

"Nothing is clear."

"You need to get out of that place. Come home."

"Home?" Her voice was calm and confident, ringing with clarity. I don't know where my response came from, but it too seemed entirely natural. "I need to see Mummy and Daddy."

"She's not well, the Parkinson's. It might be the right time. We'll send Cousin Montu packing off to the YMCA or someplace. You and Rabi can have your old rooms back."

⋅　⋅　⋅

Between the early Monday morning bombing and the beginning of Rabi's Christmas vacation, I stayed with Bish all day, every day. The burn and trauma center at the UCSF medical center was a ten-minute walk up Parnassus from where my house used to be. Rabi and I took rooms in a residential hotel a few blocks away that provided a stove, plates, silver and skillets, and thankfully, no other conveniences, including telephone and television.

Bish would walk again, we had the assurance of the chief surgeon, who happened to be Indian. When, and in what manner, he suggested, was up to Bish. He would walk but not stride, not play tennis, not take up golf. Nerve endings had been lost. There would have to be reconstructive surgery, then plastic surgery. After the wheelchair there would be canes, and after that, with luck and much therapy, a shuffling gait.

All that Bish said of that night was, "It is a sign." Walking like an old man? That too was a sign. A confirmation from the gods of cosmic order that a segment of his life, his walking phase, was over. Its final act had been the saving of my life.

His voice was now high and strained, not uncommon after burn damage, said the nurses; there had been scarring of his vocal cords. Short sentences left him breathless; some smoke inhalation, lung damage, they said. Until the passages healed, he'd be kept in a rich mix of oxygen and a sterile environment.

"Walking is the symbol of all movement," he said, panting to catch his breath. I held my hand up just to stop him, that I understood, nothing more was necessary. I gathered there would be no more globe hopping. He spoke of "fire-binders," men from villages in central India who could walk over coals with no apparent ill effect. The world offered many new challenges, did it not? There is much discipline and self-control still to master. He would continue his journeys, but not leave his chair.

He was not allowed newspapers—too unsanitary—and he'd never watched television. If a brilliant man can ever be unaware of his surroundings, innocent of the world's judgment upon him, it might have been Bish at that moment. And so, I fed him the whole long story of Didi and Dey and Mr. Hai, my role, Andy's role, Rabi's role, and the news that Christopher's body had been found.

"I can imagine the effect on stock prices. It must be devastating." He could have been discussing a cyclone in Bangladesh or an earthquake in Turkey. Distressing, but somehow, divinely ordained. I could hear the echo of a corollary: Let it go. Once, I held the world in my hand. I opened my hand, a grain of sand fell out.

Ordinary lives enclose an extraordinary kernel, do they not? I said. Some force, whether biological or cosmic, more powerful than individual will or the bias of caste and neighborhood, incarnates us in the physical form it deems desirable.

Buried deep in the consciousness of every Hindu is a core belief. Bish had it and in him it was rising to the surface. My father had embraced it like cool water on a summer day. Even Loreto girls with their superficial Westernization and Catholic influence can tell the same story, and draw the same strength from it. It is strength, I've come to believe, although it can sound cruel, indifferent, fatalistic. We measure passing time on two clocks that coexist: one that ticks in God Brahma's eye and one that hums on our wrists. Time moves in cycles when it belongs to gods, in straight lines when it belongs to mortals. In Brahma's eye-clock four eons add up to one complete cycle. The cycles repeat themselves and will keep doing so until Time itself is no more. Eon succeeds eon with the swiftness of a single godly blink. The eon of dissension precedes the dissolution of the cosmos. But why fear dissolution when you know for certain that Brahma-time moves in cycles? After wrecking there will come the needed rebuilding. After misery and meanness, an eon of bliss, purity, and perfection.

After ten days or so, the threat of infection was deemed averted. He had refused all pain medication, trusting to discipline and fearing any interference with the clarity of the mind. He must embrace his pain to understand it. The nurses allowed me to help change his dressings. I could push him now on outings to the solarium. We could talk only at close range, as though every word we exchanged was something of a confidence.

On a rainy December afternoon I confided to him a vision I'd had, a vision of discipline and self-knowledge and of misfortune turned to new energy. It was small, I warned, but hear me out. The scale of his achievement made it difficult for a wife to set her own sights.

"I worry for Rabi, not for you," he said. "You will go on."

I said to him, I am now thirty-six years old, your age when we divorced, your age when you made CHATTY the operating system for the world. I'm not capable of anything so grand—who is? But there is one thing in this world that I might be capable of, and that thing has been speaking to me and it is growing increasingly impatient that I have not yet responded. Bish, I have stories to tell.

"I'm sure you do." He must have thought, Lord, please, not another storytelling lady, in English no less. When will I ever escape them?

"Not those stories."

In the two weeks that Rabi and I had been in the hotel without a telephone or a television set, I'd been writing at night on a rented typewriter, and the story that had begun to emerge was of the Tree-Bride and of the class of Calcutta girls born a century later, both of them witness to dying traditions. Tara Lata Gangooly had turned the tragedy of her husband's death and a lifetime's virginity into a model of selfless saintliness. My story was different, perhaps even an inversion. But I'd been having hot Calcutta flashes, moments of intense recollection, smells so strong I sneezed. Just the memory of my mother bent over the fish stall selecting the freshest and firmest by smell and the iridescence of scales and eyes, had set me crying. If I didn't write their stories I'd explode; there'd be no one to mark their passing.

"What is the value of a passing moment?" he asked. "What is the value of groups marked for extinction?"

"Their beauty," I answered without hesitation.

Part Three

18

*T*his luxurious, spacious, orderly, safe Bombay apartment. These little sessions with my sister over gin and lime, waiting for Auro's nightly return, his bathing rituals and change from business suit to kurta and pajama. The long unwinding from a stressful day that cannot be discussed, only in some way reenacted, with Auro not the victim of others' imperious behavior, but its instigator. Cook and servant wait in the kitchen for the order to reheat the curries, begin the rice, and lay the table. It is a life that preserves as much of the old ways as sanity permits. On a good day, meaning a day when Auro's new Belgian bosses—thanks to globalization and a new collaborative agreement—have been out of town, Auro comes home smiling and we have a happy evening. Most days, their boots are on his neck. He comes home surly, biting back at every question, and Parvati quietly spreads her hands out flat, tamping down the air itself.

"The Tree-Bride, Tara? Really, I haven't thought of that poor thing in eons." We'd spent the first day shopping for a wig to cover the slow-growing chopped stubble; otherwise people who know nothing of our divorce will assume my widowhood. Think what *that* will do to the markets! Before Auro and his mood swings can poison the evening, we've started a bit early with the ritual drinks. The wig is hot but the style is very Bollywood; I forget the name of the star and the movie it's modeled from. Rabi has taken his new camera out to the streets. He bought it yesterday at Frankfurt Airport to replace the unreplaceable. Doing his Cartier-Bresson number, he says.

"What do you remember?" I press.

"If I ever thought about her, I guess it's her patience. She's like one of those Victorian heroines, exemplary in virtue but locked in an attic waiting for deliverance. The pure and blameless being held accountable for death and dishonor. It has all the ingredients, Tara."

What Parvati and I know of the Tree-Bride comes from family stories. My maternal grandmother told them to teach us daughters the power of even minor village deities. She was Jai Krishna's granddaughter through the son of his ninth wife. I confess to hoping for something epic, not just Victorian, in all that effort and disappointment, but to Parvati I'm just indulging my melodramatic self. She's even forgotten the tales of Manasha's army of serpents striking anyone anywhere, from the boy-bridegroom of Mishtigunj, to even the King of America and the Queen of Europe. The richest and most guarded are the most vulnerable, don't you remember?

I have no idea how old Didima was when she came to us from Uncle Subodh's and Auntie Bandana's flat across town. Uncle Subodh was Mummy's brother. We were four, seven, and ten. Didima stayed with us for two months twice a year. She was a tiny woman who walked around bent double. It must have been from bone loss, but I assumed she'd been born that way. That's how we thought. In a world of permanent forms, bent old ladies had been bent little girls. I knew, therefore, that my sisters and I had been spared such a fate. Her skin had the opaque sheen of waxed paper. We tried our best not to giggle when her breasts, which were long, skinny, and deeply creased, swung wildly free of her sari whenever she tried to hurry. They made loud, slapping noises against her waist and midriff.

"I remember those flapping things! What did we learn to call them later—'withered dugs,' right? Didi told me Didima'd been a legendary beauty back in Dhaka or wherever, and of course I didn't believe her. I mean, if that were the case, then life simply was not going to be worth living. That was just Didi, always looking at film magazines and wondering if she would measure up."

The slapping sound of breasts as she chased ghosts and demons out of the house, ghost-plagued room by demon-haunted room, using a brass cobra-shaped, five-flame oil lamp and a smoking bouquet of incense sticks. How exotic can you get? "A ghost" was her explanation for all disorder. Something is missing? Ghosts moved it in the night. Something fell? Pushed by ghosts, and what have *you* done or not done to get them so angry? Generally, ghosts were lazy; they hung around like useless servants and unemployed grandsons, attending to ghostly business and interfering with us only when we failed to show them the proper respect.

She did her driving-out at twilight because that's when they congregated, getting ready for the night. She encouraged Parvati and me to follow her with auspicious noisemakers like conch shells. We could only get sputtery, belchy noises out of the conch shell, so we hopped and skipped behind our grandmother, Parvati ringing a brass bell and I clapping brass cymbals together.

"The legendary musical ability of the Bhattacharjee sisters! That's where it comes from!" we're both laughing. "We had ghost-scaring voices. Can we help it if nuns couldn't appreciate us?"

"We could sue for all the horrors of Gilbert and Sullivan."

" 'Mr. Bhattacharjee, your daughters look like angels but they sing like crows!' I was devastated, my life was ruined, my self-esteem, poof, out the window."

Where do the ghosts go? I would ask. Parvati had all the answers in those days. She told me they settle for the night in the deodar trees on the street, silly-billy.

"Where *do* the ghosts go, Parvati?" I asked again. Back on Rivoli Street, I used to ring a bell and carry a lit candle through the rooms on both floors. Threats can take many forms, I thought, although it seemed to offend Andy's austere Buddhist sensibility.

"Allow me my last little Hinduism," I'd joke.

"Ghosts? I've been too busy to think of ghosts. If they're smart they'll give Bombay a very wide berth. Even a ghost could get run over here." Bombay traffic had kept Bish a bachelor. Bombay traffic was responsible for everything. Ron Dey, decent, tormented Ron Dey had been backed into an alleyway by person or persons unknown, the papers now proclaimed. It had been a car jacking or a murder. What a dangerous city it had become. Its tentacles reached all the way to Rivoli Street.

Auro came home in a foul mood, and everything changed.

⁄   ⁄   ⁄

Whenever I visit Parvati, I try to cultivate what Rabi calls "that Indian vision thing," meaning the distant focus, the trained exclusion of the upfront and personal. In her high-rise apartment, that meant staring out to sea and never looking down. I have never been fascinated, as Rabi was, by the mini-township clustered on

the black rocks where the fishermen—or whatever they were—
had pitched their tents, and so I almost missed it. A tall young
visitor with an expensive German camera had just arrived to take
their pictures. "My God," I breathed, because if Parvati knew,
there would be no controlling the response. He'd told me he was
going for a walk. He promised to be careful, maybe he'd find
something to shoot.

Dangerous men were clustered around him. Little boys and
girls had made a game of it, tagging him, then running back to
safety, as though he were a bull in the ring. He was down on one
knee, snapping away. If the men turned on him there would be
no saving him, no way of intervening. One thrust of a knife and
the equivalent of a year's wages are guaranteed. They're Muslim,
Rabi, doesn't that mean anything, even now? Forget the murderous ways of Mr. Hai, think of their prohibitions against images.
No way to open a window and shout a warning, no way a voice
can carry fifteen floors over the slap-slap of tiny waves. He'd defied
me, he'd ignored warning signs, and he'd never developed the
innate suspicion of a true-bred Bengali. If Parvati or Auro got up
from their chairs at that moment and saw it, they would rouse the
building's chowkidars to action and we'd ignite a full-scale Hindu-
Muslim riot.

I tried to act casual. Parvati and Auro were masters of that
Indian vision thing. What will happen has already happened, we
just don't know it yet.

"Where's Rabi?" Auro asked. "He probably doesn't realize how
quickly it can get dark. I don't want him walking dark streets
with an expensive camera."

"That's very wise advice," I said.

Their cherished sons, Dinesh and Bhupesh, in Ivy League boot
camp, a boarding school in Dehra Dun, had never been allowed
out alone at night in Bombay. Always the driver followed them,

and a guard. "He said he wanted to walk over the bridge. I told him to stay in public."

"Foolish, foolish."

"*And* to be careful," Parvati reminded. "I don't know which is worse these days, a dark empty place or a street full of people."

"Stupid woman. If you honestly don't know that, then you have no business living in Bombay."

"I seem to have no business anywhere, do I?"

✎   ✎   ✎

My grandmother, Didima, was the first girl in her family to be sent to school, which in her case was Bethune High School in Calcutta. Though she was married off the week after she'd sat for her matriculation examination, she considered herself a modern woman. In her telling of the Tree-Bride's story, she played down the actual ceremony. She dwelled on Jai Krishna's proud standing-up to his Anglicized colleagues in the High Court of Dhaka and on his scornful dismissal of crude schemes for collecting his daughter's dowry. None of this Brahmo nonsense of sacrificing dowry for education. Our heroic relative had stood up for family honor.

She lingered longest on Tara Lata's learning to read and to write; how her reading of nationalist newspapers like *Jugantar* and novels like Bankim Chandra's *Ananda Math* inspired her to shelter fugitive freedom-fighters. And so, always the dutiful daughter at six or seven, I'd started reading the Bengali classics. This was before English entered our lives. It didn't matter that Didima's early childhood had been spent in Dhaka and not in the isolated village of Mishtigunj. She was a natural storyteller, she could evoke the smell of rain and swamp and sweat and the panic and head wounds crusted with blood and putrefaction, and the adrenaline rush of revolution mixed with the perfume of sweetened betel nut.

We lived the Tree-Bride's courage. We were child-soldiers in Mother India's army. We knew from our history books the consequences of being caught by the Raj police. Mummy chipped in with her wartime memories of cheering the Japanese planes and of a Calcutta swarming with refugees from the fall of Burma.

Proud Bengalis, we hated Mahatma Gandhi, that worm of a Gujarati. We thrilled to the martial cadence of our homegrown hero, our Netaji, our leader, the martyred Subhas Bose. His Indian National Army would march with the Japanese to plunge a dagger into the retreating back of the British Raj. No Gandhi, no Partition, no loss of our beautiful, green and golden East Bengal. The blood of our martyrs would be avenged. Women in our family, however distant and legendary the connection, had been beaten by colonial police. The Tree-Bride, although we were never told at the time and perhaps no one knew until I'd gone to Mishtigunj and seen the marker, had been killed. Neighbors and their servants (never members of our immediate family, for obvious reasons) had been killed "or worse." Their children publicly flogged, adolescent boys hanged or deported to harsh jails on islands ruled by headhunters.

The Tree-Bride, the aged virgin who did not leave her father's house until the British dragged her off to jail, the least-known martyr to Indian freedom, is the quiet center of every story. Each generation of women in my family has discovered in her something new. Even in far-flung California, the Tree-Bride speaks again. I've come back to India this time for something more than rest and shopping and these gin-and-lime filled evenings with my mirror-self. I'm like a pilgrim following the course of the Ganges all the way to its source.

As silently as he left, Rabi reenters. Auro is furious, for now it is fully dark. "For snap-snap only you are giving us heart attack!" he shouts. *Don't tell, don't tell,* I pray.

"Snap-snap only, Auro-mesho. Every square inch there's something unbelievable going on," he says.

"And most of it bad," Auro finishes.

At least, in Auro's mind, Rabi has given up painting for something commercial and technical. Painting is for perverts. Look at that old Muslim with the young film star! Case made, case closed. What of the *Mona Lisa*? Rabi had parried. You had this old pervert, this gay, sorry, this homo, as you call them, painting a pretty young woman. What's with that? Maybe she was a famous lady of the night, eh? Who knows? Who cares?

Auro had been reduced to grumbling that night. Rabi had turned then to his play, making it sound like a rollicking farce. "When you said two Indian sisters, I thought oh-oh," said Parvati. Rabi just smiled.

He's slowly learning how this family works. I couldn't be prouder. He didn't flinch over Auro's "homo" talk, didn't rise to the challenge, asking only once, and very sweetly, what he thought a homo was. Could a person, man or woman, be a homo without looking like a member of the opposite sex? Of course not, Auro shot back.

"Okay, just checking," he smiled, and I saw a flicker of understanding pass over Parvati's face, a moment's pondering of the incomprehensible.

⸱　⸱　⸱

A stranger's light, limp body curled into a crescent on a wrinkled sheet, a wife comforting her husband. *His mind is imprisoned in a stone fortress*; that's all I knew of Parkinson's from the brief visit I'd made with Bish's mother, still in my bridal sari, to one of his distant relatives. It's never too early for a wife to learn her eventual duties, to adopt the proper resignation. Our horoscopes had predicted that I'd be gone long before him. Perhaps Bish should have been sent on that particular mission.

Parvati had pretended to let drop the news of Mummy's illness casually, but I understood what she'd meant by "we all have our troubles" in her letter. Auro is troubled, she has troubles, Bombay is a headache, but Mummy is dying. Parvati was worried sick that Rishikesh, which might be perfect for hippies and ashrams and rip-off holy men, didn't have the doctors we did in Bombay and San Francisco. We both knew that there was no cure for it. L-dopa didn't work forever.

Two months ago, I had offered Mummy and Daddy a place with me and access to the finest doctors in the world. Now, it was Bish in the finest hospital and me without a roof. I could as easily be the one begging a room in Bombay or Rishikesh.

I picture Mummy as always getting in or out of the backseat of her car, a fifteen-year-old Ambassador with dented fenders and bad springs. She was a busybody who, in the early seventies, was persuaded by Mother Teresa to focus her hyperintensity on volunteer work. Mummy hadn't been keen on Mother Teresa, when the nun was known to Calcuttans for prowling on the holy grounds of the Kali Temple in Kalighat and helping the dying die, as she claimed, with dignity. Mummy, like most of her friends, cynically suspected that it was an ingenious ploy for converting people who were too weak to resist.

She changed her mind when Mother Teresa set up her leprosarium on land donated by a Hindu and asked her, and other Hindu women, all of whom had graduated from Loreto House school, to help the lepers with money, time, and prayers. Mother Teresa once belonged to the Loreto order. Ironic, on one level, when you think of what she and the school have come to symbolize. On the worldly level, God guides the giving of the wealthy as He does the hearts of the helpless.

Mummy soon discovered a talent for organizing fund-raisers and for delivering inspirational speeches on behalf of the needy. I loved the confident way, at leprosy-medicine packaging lunches in our house, that she would wait for the desserts to be cleared, then tap her water glass with her teaspoon, push her chair back and bounce to her feet, then launch into an emotional speech about privilege and duty.

I couldn't bear to let her turn into a stone statue. I was living, or had lived until very recently, near the heart of all West Coast research, the UCSF medical center. There were Nobel Prize winners in my neighborhood. It was up to me more than Parvati to fly Mummy and Daddy over to San Francisco and find her the best Parkinson's specialist. I'd written right away to Rishikesh, since Daddy had removed the phone line. I'd tried to reason that a phone is merely prudent, not distracting. In the third stage of man, he said, the less distraction the better.

Mummy's response had come back in a quick two weeks. She wrote one sentence in English and two sentences in Bengali. Her penmanship was almost as neat, rounded, and evenly paced as it had been when I was living in Atherton and we wrote each other twice a week. The English sentence was simple: Tara dear, you and your sisters have proved that a daughter is as good as a son. The Bengali sentences, I recognized as part of a prayer chanted during Kali Puja. *Om kali kali kalike papaharini / dharmathamokshade devi narayani namo-stute.*

I folded the single sheet small enough to fit into my billfold. She didn't intend to visit me in San Francisco. She wasn't going to scurry from specialist to specialist. Her husband would not leave the mountains, and she would not leave *him*. Goddess Kali, the Destroyer of Time, the Dissipater of Darkness, the Scourge of Sinfulness, I too beg you to free me from earthly terrors and longings.

19

*M*ummy, Daddy, and I are drinking tea—our first pot of many for the day—on the roof terrace, watching the cold December dawn lighten the buffalo-gray hill directly behind the house. Rabi is on the terrace too, standing by the waist-high wall of the parapet, his back to the sky and forested slope, skimming a paperback collection of English poems written over a hundred years ago by Swami Vivekananda, a Bengali saint. The house is actually beyond the town limits of Rishikesh and its clusters of ashrams, tourist lodges, and pilgrims' hostels that keep thickening on both banks of the Ganges between the fancy new Ramjhula bridge and the old ropey Lakshmanjuhula, and, depending on your footwear and your physical fitness, a twenty- to forty-minute walk north on the road to Tehri. Daddy had the house built within a year after marrying me off to Bish, but he'd bought the plot years before.

I must have been eight or nine at the time when on an impulse he chose Mussorie instead of Darjeeling for our annual two-week summer vacation. Mussorie was out of state. Mummy was upset about that. What if Padma, who was always madly in love, actually fell for some fast Delhi boy or any other non-Bengali staying at the same hotel? In Darj, July after July we stayed in the same suite of the Mt. Everest Hotel, strolled the same easy trails, rented docile horses from the same groom for a slow ride around the mall, nibbled on pastries at the same cafe and bargained for bone and turquoise necklaces at the same Tibetan stalls. Daddy was a man of habit. We found that comforting. Each of us sisters knew how we were expected to behave in Darj. My sisters especially knew how to flirt with the boarding-school boys in blazers from St. Paul's and St. Joseph's, and I was their avid apprentice. "What's come over your Daddy?" Mummy lamented over and over again, but not to Daddy's face.

As it turned out, Daddy had been doing his slow-mo version of an early morning "constitutional" on Camel's Back Road in Mussorie with Hari the houseboy and Shakespeare, our golden cocker puppy in tow, when his path was barred by a shoeless, orange-robed swami who'd materialized out of a fog bank.

"One moment, he was not there," Daddy told us later, "next moment he was there. Very strange." The swami said that earlier that morning he had been famished and exhausted, trekking in the snow-shrouded mountains above holy Gangotri. He said that he then clearly remembered standing face to face with Daddy on Camel's Back Road. And suddenly he was. Either the swami spoke to Daddy in Bengali or through telepathy. Both men agreed that their encounter must have been ordained. They walked on for a while. Then the swami communicated again. He was going on to Rishikesh and wanted Daddy to accompany him.

Not so strange, I think now. I have a telephone in my purse that can summon Bish instantaneously from any place in the world. *You will do the traveling for me*, he said.

Daddy brought the swami back to the hotel and ordered us to pack our bags. We were all going to Rishikesh. The swami didn't speak in front of women. He sat cross-legged in an armchair with a saggy seat smelling of mold and chain-drank cups of tea. Hari corroborated Daddy's story about the swami having stepped out of thick fog. We hired a taxi to drive us to Rishikesh. The swami indicated, according to Daddy, that he wanted to be let out by the Lakshmanjhula bridge. He meant to hike up to the top of a hill where there was a tiny, neglected temple. Goddess Shakti was waiting for him inside the temple, she was calling him, couldn't Daddy hear the demanding voice of the goddess?

That morning, Daddy had also heard the voice of the goddess. She was saying to him, "It is time, Motilal Bhattacharjee, to prepare for the beginning of the third phase of your life." He understood from the swami that his worldly mission was a success and now it was time to begin preparing his spirit.

The last we saw of him, the swami was skipping with the energy and springiness of a youngster across the bridge. That very day Daddy found a wooded plot for sale on the east bank of the Ganges, though he didn't start construction on this house until after my wedding. After I became pregnant, he sold the tea estate, then the big house in Calcutta, and let go of the cooks and all the servants except for Kanai, who by then was too old to work for another family. The three of them moved into a small residential hotel in Rishikesh so that Daddy could supervise the construction, which mostly meant making sure the builder wasn't skimping on the quality and quantity of cement.

The house took nine months to be finished just right. It has four rooms, two baths, and a kitchen, all on one floor, a flat roof with a spectacular view of the hills, an easy-to-care-for garden of potted flowers in front and a wide brick patio in back. Kanai and Daddy take care of the gardening, whose major purpose is to provide fresh flowers at various hours for the full range of Hindu devotion. At most times of the day, Daddy is in direct communication with God.

It vexes Mummy that she has had to give up cooking. Her muscles do what they want to, or nothing at all. Her feet and hands don't pay any attention to her head. She makes light of having fallen several times in the last month. I've seen, but not asked about the bruises. The fresh ones are purplish blue, the older ones yellow brown. We keep our panic politely to ourselves. For now, the cooking and the light cleaning are done by a young Garhwali mother who comes twice a day with her toddler and infant sons, whom Daddy loves to spoil. Is not Lord Krishna most often portrayed as a mischievous, butter-stealing little baby? For the heavy cleaning, the young cook arranged for a man distantly related to the niece-in-law of her neighbor to come in once a day. The cook and her five young brothers have assumed the responsibility of shopping not just for food, but incidentals such as headache balms, antacids, hair oil, razors, shaving cream, moisturizer, and toothpaste.

In the careful old days, it would have been unthinkable to entrust so much of one's life to strangers, and hill people at that. This frail little man once stood between two Bengali lovers because one professed the Christian faith. Now their house is full of men, women, and children oddly dressed, practicing forms of Hinduism we barely comprehend and speaking a language outside our competence. Whenever they need to go into town, which is usually once or twice a month to see their doctor, to send money orders to needy relatives, and to buy stamps and aerogrammes to write us, Mummy sends Kanai to the nearest tea stall to send word through bus drivers to taxi drivers that the old Bengalis need a ride. Tea stalls are where the pilgrims' buses stop regularly on their way to or from the holy temples high above the town.

"Hey, listen to this!" Rabi breaks into recitation mode.

Daddy is thrilled that Rabi is so engrossed by the saint's lectures, sayings, and religious verses. "You see," Daddy beams at me, "God doesn't care if you eat beef." He tugs a length of his sacred thread out from under his shirt and wool vest. "To find God, our Rabindra doesn't need to wear a sacred thread."

Bish shouldn't worry about Rabi's SAT potential. With the voice he has, Rabi could make a living doing voice-overs in TV commercials.

> *Have thou no home, what home can hold thee,*
> *friend? The sky thy roof, the grass thy bed, and food*
> *what chance may bring, well cooked or ill, judge not.*
> *No food or drink can taint that noble Self which*
> *knows itself. Like rolling river free, Thou ever be,*
> *Sannyasin bold! Say* OM TAT SAT OM.

Mummy fakes horror. "Get that book from him. We don't need another Sannyasin in the family. Daddy's doing enough praying and giving up life's good things for all of us. Home is where you belong, Rabindra. Tara, don't let him get bad ideas in the head."

I remembered how Mummy would never allow a picture of Buddha in the house, even though she believed, like everyone in our family and every Hindu on our block, that all religions led to the same destination: salvation. She did not at all approve of Buddha's having prematurely thrown away a good home, a loving family, and a promising future. There was something too eagerly renunciatory about Buddhists that she couldn't understand. Be-

cause they'd broken off from Hinduism, the similarities only con-
trasted our differences.

Tolerance came from the teachings of Ramakrishna; another of
those spiritually tormented nineteenth-century Bengali Brahmins.
He'd had his first taste of spiritual ecstasy at the age of seven. All
religions were true, he preached. If you want to reach the roof,
does it matter whether you get there by marble staircase or bamboo
ladder? Or just by slithering up a bamboo pole?

Mummy was very fond of that particular saying. Parvati and I
used to try and visualize Mummy slithering up a pole all the way
to heaven with the agility of a coconut picker, moving like a
whisper up the tall naked trunks.

"Pay no attention to the women," Daddy said. "After tea, we'll
go through the books on my shelf of the bookcase." He shouted
down to Kanai, who was having his tea in the kitchen. "Dust the
books! Take them out of the bookcase and dust them individu-
ally!"

Mummy countered that order. "Kanai, the tea's ice cold!" she
called. "Put the kettle on again." She tried to lift the felt tea cozy
off the teapot, but couldn't manage. She asked me to confirm how
cold the pot had become. "What can a poor tea cozy do these days?
The weather is changing. It's a global phenomenon." If she wanted
to believe in global cooling, based on a teapot on a frosty morning,
it seemed no less absurd than what I had come to view as normal.

And I remembered the bookcase with its four shelves and glass-
paneled double doors. It was a showy place to stash books that we
rarely read, like the many heavy volumes of *The Book of Knowledge*,
or the English dictionary bearing on the flyleaf the names of
his father, grandfather, great-grandfather, back eight generations,
which my paternal grandfather had penned for posterity. *The Collected Shakespeare*, four volumes of Palgrave's *The Golden Treasury*,
and gilt-lettered, morocco leather–bound, pocket-size works by

Carlyle, Burke, Dumas, Kingsley, George Eliot, Scott, Stevenson, Blackmoor, Dickens, Ballantyne, and Austen.

The books that Mummy loved and read over and over she piled on cloth-covered tin trunks and every available horizontal surface like chair seats, doily-decorated dresser tops, and under the beds. I can see those books, even smell them, each book with a different fragrance: Elizabeth Gouge, Marie Corelli, Howard Fast, Turgenev, Gorki, Mrs. Wood, Mazo de la Roche, Daphne du Maurier, Bankim Chandra, Sarat Chandra, Rabindranath Tagore, and Bibhuti Bhusan. Those books are the X-ray pictures of a class, a time, and a consciousness. Daddy wasn't a bookish type, but on Sunday evenings after taking us to the movies, he would settle back with P. G. Wodehouse, Erle Stanley Gardner, and Agatha Christie. To relax, he would drink beer from a stein he'd bought in East Berlin while on a failed tea-promotion trip arranged through the Russian consulate.

"I'll go down and put the kettle on," I said, though I could hear Kanai filling it downstairs. My nostalgia seemed to have a mind of its own, just like Mr. Parkinson's disease. I wanted to— I needed to—check what books my parents felt they could not live without, even as they had begun their partial renunciation of the material world.

The bookcase was in the thakur-ghar, God's room. All their favorite Bengali novels had made the trip, the literary apotheosis of my class and city. *Lorna Doone, Jane Eyre, Wuthering Heights, Pride and Prejudice, The Old Curiosity Shop, Ivanhoe, The Mill on the Floss, Uncle Tom's Cabin*, and *East Lynne*. *East Lynne* had to be the novel Mummy liked best. Its binding had fallen apart, so she'd had to tie the covers with strips torn from old saris.

The books that were new for me were by or about the Hindu saints: Ramakrishna, Swami Vivekananda, Yogananda, Anandamayi Ma. There were two copies of Christopher Isherwood's

Ramakrishna and His Disciples. One was thumbed through, where Daddy had inked brief comments on the margins of several pages. On the frontispiece of the newer copy, I recognized the handwriting. "To Dr. Motilal Bhattacharjee, my esteemed father-in-law. I, too, am groping . . . Your loving son-in-law, Bishwapriya Chatterjee."

Bish is a mystery to me.

✶   ✶   ✶

I offer to take the tray with the new pot of steaming tea up to the roof, but Kanai won't allow it. I follow him up the flight of cement stairs. His arthritic knees give him a rocking gait. Still, Kanai seems the fittest of the three. The pleasure that Mummy and Daddy take in the view of the hills from the roof will soon have to be renounced.

Back up on the roof, I ask if a motorized seat, attached to the handrail might not be a good idea.

Daddy shrugs. Undoubtedly a good idea, the shrug is saying— but not for me.

"Remember what you told us when we were little? All religions are true and their goal is simply to reach the roof? How are you going to get yourselves to this roof five years from now?"

"I have myself only three more years." He shrugs again.

"Why not put in a lift?" Rabi asks. Very good, I thought, you're trying hard. "Pop's got this really cool elev . . . lift in his house, very *Cage aux Folles.* I think he bought it from a Paris hotel that went out of business."

Mummy laughs. "No, no. Daddy is convinced he has only *two* more years. His age at the time of death is predicted in his horoscope."

Rabi whistles. "Cool. The things you guys talk about. You just don't find that in America."

"Pay no attention to Mummy," Daddy snaps. "Horoscopes are calculated by people and therefore may be fallible. My knowledge of when Yama will come derives from a more reliable source."

"Death," I explain. "Yama, the Grim Reaper." Otherwise, the distinguished-looking man in a tuxedo waiting patiently for the light, in Castro.

It seems that the swami who had appeared out of the fog and mist in Mussorie decades ago had reappeared in Rishikesh just last year. "It was just before dawn, and I was picking flowers to offer to Goddess Kali as I do every day, and I was thinking how disappointed she will be. Not one aparajito blossom! Goddess Kali has a special fondness for my bluest of blue aparajito—I've seen her eyes light up in a smile—but that day the creeper had no blooms, no blooms at all. I knew I had to offer her something living and I plucked as many hibiscus as I could and handfuls of marigolds, but I was feeling despondent. The day had not even started, and already I had failed the goddess."

In that light, in those mountains, in view of the holy and not yet polluted Ganges, the story made perfectly good sense. Even Rabi was taking mental notes.

"And suddenly, the same swami was standing in front of me, smiling and holding out three aparajito flowers of the deepest blue. He looked younger than he had the first time. I took the blossoms from him and as they passed from his hand to mine I understood he was telling me that in three years my mission on this earth would be fulfilled. I nodded to him. He walked out of the garden and kept walking down the road."

"Cool." You know who.

"Yes, precisely. Essentially very cool," Daddy agreed.

"He says three years, his horoscope says two years, but swami-ji's three years was already one year ago. So which one of us is the silly old woman, eh?" Mummy challenged. "I don't need to look at the hills to think of God." She is trying to assure me that she is resigned to Parkinson's and to her widowhood, whichever claims her first. Neither of us has mentioned her illness. She has passed beyond tremors. If anything, her body seems to be stiffening into stone. "I don't need to make the pilgrimage up there to the Char Dham temples. All places are holy. You can talk to God from the bathroom and he will listen to you."

The one big reason that she'd let Daddy talk her into moving from Calcutta to Rishikesh, I knew, was that ever since she'd been a little girl she remembered her mother wanting to make a pilgrimage to the four Char Dham temples for which Rishikesh was a convenient base. By the time she got there, her body wouldn't permit it.

My maternal grandmother, grand-niece of the Tree-Bride, the link between our lives, had been a student in Bethune English School for Girls when a famous traveler-photographer whose name Mummy couldn't remember had come through and exhibited her pictures of mountains, glasslike glaciers, wildflowers bright as macaws' plumage, deep valleys with boulder-strewn riverbeds. The city-child had been seduced by Nature. It didn't matter that she was witnessing God's splendor thirdhand. The initial wonder that had made her shiver with excitement in a darkened classroom she managed to pass on to her children, especially to Mummy.

Mummy is just warming up. "You don't have to go outside yourself to find God," she says. "You must first of all value yourself. Vivekananda has written a person who doesn't believe in herself or himself cannot believe in God." She asked Rabi to find the saying in the book he'd been reading from. Vivekananda was a disciple of Ramakrishna. He didn't fall into trances. He didn't experience religious ecstasy firsthand, as did his guru. He was a handsome, urbane, skeptical, Westernized young Bengali who fell in love with Ramakrishna's unorthodox acceptance of all religions.

Rabi made a further observation, after reading more letters and poems. "These guys are so gay, I can't believe it. Doesn't anyone ever talk about it?"

"Yes, you have understood it all, Rabindra. We all embrace the goddess gaily. Gay is the secret word."

*   *   *

Later that day, I blurt out to my parents how close Rabi, Bish, and I had come to our own deaths. I shed my wig; Mummy recoiled, as though I'd lived through death. *But none of this would have happened*, I want to say, if you hadn't opposed the marriage, if you had let her act. And before I could say it, I realized the futility of questioning fate, or blind random chance, or character. If Didi had married, would she have stayed married in Calcutta? I could not imagine it. Would she have made a loving mother? If she had acted, would she have risen to diva status? Something else, equally calamitous would have happened on the same date, at the same minute. Perhaps an earthquake, a plane crash, an automobile accident. Who are we to question God?

These horoscopes cut both ways, don't they? According to my charts, I'm supposed to die at sixty-eight, downright youthful in California terms; Bish at eighty, if I remember. So was it the astrologer in Calcutta who saved our lives last month—should we have confronted the fire with the full knowledge that it was not our time—or was it the fallibility that Bish's bravery and quick-thinking had exposed? Whose voice was it, really, that Rabi had heard that caused him to leave his front room?

Daddy is mildly sympathetic to Bish's suffering, and my loss. He has no curiosity as to why my house, of all houses, had been targeted for destruction. The man I described, Abbas Hai, seems a true agent sent to waken mortals, doesn't he? A form of Goddess Manasha, perhaps, the ever-opportunistic snake goddess who can slither into any space, over or under any barrier. My father has made connections on the cosmic level, the rest of it didn't really matter.

I don't know if my parents know, or remember, or even care about my divorce. Bish had been with me, as he should be. He saved my life at great suffering to himself, as is the husband's duty. And now he is in a rehab center learning to walk, which fulfills some larger destiny. Sometimes, *bishey bish khai*, the only antidote for poison is poison. Meaning, I guess, the harsh poison of the bomb is not, in the eye of God, any more tragic than the poisonous maya of attachment to making money. Bish's nickname is a cosmic pun waiting for a punch line.

"God pulls our strings, we dance the dance," Daddy says. "Feel the tug from God, do not cut the string. Dear Bishwapriya doesn't fool himself into thinking he's totally independent."

"What's that supposed to mean?" Apart, that is, from *don't think I don't know*.

Mummy does the explaining. "You've moved away from us in your heart. But your husband has not."

Next thing I know, Daddy has launched into a long, strange story about Manasha, an insecure and therefore demanding goddess. It was Manasha in her familiar cobra form that had killed the Tree-Bride's boy husband-to-be. It was Manasha, whose father was either Shiva or Kashyapa, one of the seven original sages, and whose mother was Kadru, a mortal who had prayed to either Shiva or Kashyapa for a thousand offspring in the shape of serpents. Daughter of God or holy sage, but not accepted as half-goddess or half-sage, she used her identity as queen of snakes to call our self-protective little lives into question by injecting them with venom and demanding reverence through the infliction of unexpected pain.

Bishey bish khai.

. , .

After Kanai had cleaned the books, we went down for a final inspection. Here they were, the collected inspiration of Tara Bhattacharjee, comfort food for the soul, to which has been added in
recent years, and in recent days, urgent dictates from the unthinkable and unimaginable. Rabi found the trunk of old magazines
and newspapers and many of my Loreto House essays, which he
reverently read, chuckling at a few howlers.

Then, "What's this?" He came to me holding a small book,
obviously old, in Bengali. In free translation it read, *My Happy
Days on the Dhaka High Court*, by Sir Keshub Mitter. Daddy had
bought it in one of the Park Street auction houses, maybe thirty
years ago. He'd never read it, and the name of the author, though
obviously a prominent man in his time, had not survived. Chapter
Three was entitled, "The Man Who Married His Daughter to a
Tree." Chapter Four, "The Corruption and Coming Collapse of
Hinduism in the Modern World." Chapter Five, "The Blight of
Child-Marriage and the Sin of Polygamy: A Hindu Perspective."
Chapter Six, "The Myth of the 'Brown Sahib.' "

"But don't you want to take some of your essays back? The
Eve's Weekly with you on the cover? 'Beauty and Brains' do you
remember that?"

"Here's another one, Ma. You'll like this." He might have been
joking. Or perhaps God had directed his fingers. I translated the
title: *With the Freedom Fighters of East Bengal*. The names, a rich
assortment of Hindus and Muslims, were unfamiliar to me until
I read, "The Betrayal and Death of Tara-Ma, Tara Lata Gangooly
of Mishtigunj."

If the gods were pulling strings, they'd just given me a tug of
encouragement. "These books are more than enough," I said.
Maybe the years of blackness had begun to lift.

20

People in Mishtigunj, now a crowded river port, still describe what is left of the Tree-Bride's home as a rajbari, a palace-house. My son and I stroll through its ruins. Trees thrust their roots, thick as battering rams, against its foundations. Leafy branches push through cracks in the freestanding walls. Packs of stray dogs lounge in roofless rooms with marble floors. Birds nest in the decorative hollows of plaster columns. Carp fatten in the stagnant green water of a bathing pond. Snakes nest in the cool dark of the family's Kali temple. Near the broken steps of the ghat leading down to where the bajra carrying the body of the Tree-Bride's betrothed had docked over a hundred and twenty years ago, a village deity shows up at the same hour every day in the shape of a crocodile to accept devotees' offerings of flowers and fruits.

But Mishtigunj is a place of magic where the hour and date on my wristwatch melt into the hours of the Tree-Bride's last day in her home. The year is 1943 by the wartime English calendar. My parents are just toddlers in the great city. The month is December by the English reckoning, the weather cool enough for wool vests and shawls. It is a day very much like today, which it matches on the calendar, some sixty years later, and a day very similar to that of her forest marriage.

Men have been sneaking into the house in twos and threes since before dawn. The Tree-Bride, now sixty-eight, with a strong face that might once have been pretty but too assertive—she has her father's eyebrows, for what does she know of prettiness and for whom should she have plucked that thick bar of a single brow?—and iron-gray hair shorn weekly by a man's barber, sits behind her late father's desk in a room of the rajbari's "outer chambers," where he had given legal counsel to nationalists and peasant debtors.

The desk is littered with placards. QUIT INDIA. JAI HIND. JAI MA KALI, JAI BHARAT MATA. SHAME! BRITISH DEVIL, GO HOME. BANDEMATARAM! INDIA FOR INDIANS. Some of the placards are blood-splattered. In the hall outside this room and in the inner courtyard, rows of the wounded are being tended by housewives, schoolgirls, and widows. Skulls broken by policemen's lathis; stomachs ripped by soldiers' bullets. For any deep wound, under these conditions, no help is held out, but for prayers and divine intervention. A boy of twelve has had half his face shot off. The amateur nurses dip the ends of their saris in potable water and squeeze drops into thirsty mouths. They staunch blood with old saris and rub kitchen-brewed herbal pastes and poultices on the opened wounds. There are two surgeons in town, one Hindu, one Muslim, but both happen to be in the British jail, awaiting exile to the Andaman Islands.

The Tree-Bride is writing quickly on lined sheets of an exercise book:

MISHTIGUNJ

Killed by bullets	9
Wounded by bullets	35
Rape and assault on women	65
Assaulted by lathi-charge	359
Homes looted by police	100
Homes burglarized by miscreants	70
Houses burned by soldiers	20
Arrested	617

Details of atrocities perpetrated on women:

Kanonbala Devi (pregnant); raped repeatedly by 4 policemen

Sonamoni Devi (widow); raped once before daughters-in-law

Shefali Dutta (virgin); molested before being taken into detention

Chhaya Devi (mother of six-week-old infant); beaten, raped twice

Radha Devi (new bride); stripped naked, beaten, raped repeatedly

Charulata Devi (pregnant); kicked in the stomach by five policemen

Manoda Devi; skull broken by lathi for waving Congress flag

Giribala Devi; shot in both legs for giving water to fallen fighters

The results will be dispatched to a sympathetic English journalist. It will be on the wire and tucked somewhere in the world's papers behind the war news, in three days' time. A one-legged man, dressed in homespun cotton, brings her new information. Tree trunks and branches have been positioned across paths likely to be used by reinforcements. Telephone and telegraph wires have been severed, and some telegraph poles cut down to stumps. Students from Dacca Medical College and volunteer nurses have been organized to attend to the fallen, buckets for water and medical supplies hidden in culverts on the roadside.

The police surround the rajbari as the Tree-Bride finishes her evening prayers. The police will not halt her evening routine. She picks up the five-wick oil lamp in one hand and a marble incense-holder in the other and walks through rooms filled with the hurt and the dying. From bed pallets on marble floors, bandaged hands reach out to touch her bare feet. Hoarse whispers of "Mother!" and "Bandemataram!" float toward her. Static-filled radio, impeccable accent: Authorities wish to complete their sweep before Christmas week and mean to have the entire East Bengal insurrection quelled by the new year . . . Ministry sources deny any shortfall in grain deliveries. Congress Party officials who predict famine, particularly Mr. Subhas Bose, are provocateurs seeking to spread discord among the people and pave the way for a Japanese invasion of eastern India . . .

And for whom is that sympathetic journalist really working?

A magistrate in the gymkhana grumbles to a constable, One holds one's fire when a woman is involved, of course, but this woman does not look like a woman and she certainly does not behave as a woman. I've been in these parts twenty years, I know the Bengali mind, if I say so myself. There's something not quite on the up and up with that creature. It's said she's not ventured beyond the walls of her compound in over sixty years. Most extraordinary thing.

Yet she is behind this insurrection, sir, I am certain.

I don't doubt it. It would take some sort of supernatural force to get these babus off their backsides and up in arms. I'll be the one who's bloody glad to quit India. They got that right. Bloody hell.

Perhaps the time has come to show her the outer world, sir, don't you agree?

Their voices drift through time, they penetrate the thickest stone fortress. I open myself to them. *Bishey bish khai*, only poison delivers us from poison.

The winter night of East Bengal falls quickly. The mosquitoes are fierce. Rabi and I walk along the paved road from the Tree-Bride's house to the last of the permanent structures. The road gives way to crushed stone, rising above ponds on either side. This is called a shanko, I say, a word I have not used in my life and only now suddenly remember. Many words are flooding in and the trail ahead, as far as I can see, is lighted by kerosene and naphtha lamps held by the children of fruit and vegetable vendors sitting on the carts.

"Rabi!" I say. "Remember this. It's a miracle."

DISCUSSION QUESTIONS FOR YOUR READING GROUP

1. Who are the *Desirable Daughters* in this story? What does the title mean? Why are the first few pages in italics?

2. In India, what kind of family are the Bhattacharjees? How are they perceived in America? How are arranged marriages portrayed in *Desirable Daughters*?

3. Examine what Tara means when she says she is "exploring the making of a consciousness . . . No. Yours" (page 5). Consider the implications of being "thrown into the middle of a modern enigma. My enigma, and yours" (page 26). What does she mean by "a modern enigma"? Discuss how these ideas play out in the book and what the author is telling us.

4. Briefly discuss the lifestyles and choices of the three sisters. How different or similar are they?

5. Is Tara secure and self-confident, or searching for her place in the world, or both? Aside from her son and life in California, what drives Tara? Tara is often self-conscious—for example, on page 79, she is convinced she stands out in her community. If you can, share whether or not you have ever felt this way.

6. What is Tara's response to the revelation about possibly having a nephew (pages 45–49)? How does she describe her disbelief? What insights do you gain here about Tara and her upbringing? How would you respond to such news?

7. Look at page 96 and scan the letter from Parvati. What information does she reveal about herself? What does she add to the emerging mystery of Chris Dey? Why is Tara so dismissive of her sister Parvati's take on the situation? What, if any, are the ramifications of an illegitimate child for a family like the Bhattacharjees?

8. What kind of person is Bish? What about Andy? Consider the philosophical and/or spiritual emphases of the men in Tara's life—Zen (master carpenter Andy) and Hindi (Bish and Daddy). If you are familiar with them, compare these ancient religions. How are they manifested in this modern-day story?

9. Why is Tara so focused on—even consumed with—her ex-husband's opinions?

10. Examine the Tennyson poem on pages 132–133. What does it mean—on its own and in the story?

11. Share your response to Bish's assessment that American children are soft (page 154). What kinds of pressures is Rabi feeling? What do you think about his coming out to his mother via a letter read out loud by his counselor?

12. Can you explain why Didi, who as a child eschewed her family and culture, leads a traditional Bengali life in New Jersey? Look at the description and word choices on page 203; how does the author provide a fleshed-out portrait of Didi?

13. Is Tara being a reliable narrator on pages 184–185, beginning with, "I rehearsed a conversation . . ."? Is Didi the one with the problem, or is Tara? Share who you think is better adjusted, and why.

14. What is the significance of Tara's almost out-of-body experience at the jeweler's (page 205)? Looking at the paragraph that begins "Would you like to wear it?," discuss how several of the book's central themes are reframed here.

15. On page 33, look at the paragraph beginning "Bengali culture . . ." How does the narrator describe an essential dilemma of cultures? Can you relate? What does it mean to say, "even a damaged consciousness, even loneliness, become privileged commodities" (page 34)? Examine this statement on page 6: "The communities suffer, as Freud puts it, the narcissism of small difference." With that in mind, share your thoughts about the Indian communities in the book and more familiar ones in America.

16. Houses and shelter and keys are prominently featured throughout *Desirable Daughters*. What is the significance of the Gosals and their huge home in Basking Ridge? What is symbolic about Tara's home being destroyed? Talk about Mummy and Daddy's very different homes in two markedly different locales. With their choices, what are they saying about their lives—and essentially their souls?

17. What do you learn about Tara through the ancient story of Tara Lata Gangooly? How does it relate to Tara and her family?

18. Look at the end of Part 2 (page 280); how does Tara's life compare to Tara Lata Gangooly's? How do you respond to the last three lines: "What is the value . . . hesitation"? Consider the last paragraph on page 289, "The Tree-Bride . . . source." Discuss what it means. What is Tara's "mirror-self"? Why is she like "a pilgrim"?

19. Share your response to Daddy's interpretation of the fire (pages 303–304). What does the story of Manasha, the snake goddess, have to do with Tara?

20. Why does Tara say to Rabi, "Remember this. It's a miracle" (page 310)?